D0594181

3/97

KEEPLOCK

A NOVEL OF CRIME

DAVID CRAY

OTTO PENZLER BOOKS

NEW YORK

East Central Regional Library
244 South Birch
Cambridge, Minnesota 55008

#31655829
ETCH
89695

OTTO PENZLER BOOKS

OTTO PENZLER BOOKS
129 West 56th Street
New York, NY 10019
(Editorial Offices only)

Simon & Schuster Inc.
Rockefeller Center
1230 Avenue of the Americas
New York, NY 10020

This book is a work of fiction. Names, characters, places, and incidents are either products of the author's imagination or are used fictitiously. Any resemblance to actual events or locales or persons, living or dead, is entirely coincidental.

Copyright © 1995 by Stephen Solomita
All rights reserved,
including the right of reproduction
in whole or in part in any form.

Manufactured in the United States of America

1 3 5 7 9 10 8 6 4 2

Library of Congress Cataloging-in-Publication Data

Cray, David.
Keeplock: a novel of crime/David Cray.
p.   cm.
I. Title.
PS3553.R315K44   1995
813'.54—dc20   94-42113
CIP

ISBN 1-883402-97-2

ACKNOWLEDGMENT

Because I always do a fair amount of research before beginning work on a manuscript, I have, over the course of time, built up an impressive (to me, anyway) list of law enforcement contacts. But the defense lawyers, prosecutors, and cops who helped me in the past were unable to provide me with the kind of detail necessary to write a novel centered on the lives, in prison and out, of criminal offenders.

For a time, I was at a loss. I went into several homeless shelters, looking for ex-offenders who spent time in the Clinton Correctional Facility (often referred to as Dannemora), then considered the toughest prison in New York State. Although my efforts were not entirely unsuccessful, my progress, needless to say, was slow indeed, and I was on the verge of abandoning the project when I wandered into the Fortune Society on West 19th Street. The Fortune Society is dedicated to salvaging ex-convicts, accepting any offender, no matter how hardened by prison life, who walks through the door. The question, of course, from my narrow (and admittedly selfish) point of view, was whether they'd accept *me*.

I've had to contact any number of city agencies over the years (the NYPD, naturally, but also the Transit Authority, Fire Department, Department of Corrections, Human Resources Administration, Division of Housing and Community Renewal, etc.), usually with frustrating results. Obstacles were inevitably put in my way, so many and so uniformly that I began to view overcoming them as a ritual test of my worthiness to be a novelist in the first place.

This was not the case at the Fortune Society. I came through the door a complete stranger and found people who actually listened to what I had to say, who, in fact, welcomed me. Now it's time for pay-back.

The simple truth is that I could not have written this book without the help of the Fortune Society.

Thank you Joanne; thank you Alan; thank you Bryan.

KEEPLOCK

ONE

Even though I've got the required tattoo—the one that says DEATH BEFORE DISHONOR—and I've been in and out of the required institutions since I was nine years old, the simple truth is that I've lost my nerve and I can't go back. The tattoo was applied with India ink and the sharpened tine of a dining hall fork. I was in the baby jail on Rikers Island at the time, trying so hard to impress the few white boys in my housing area, that I believed my own advertising.

That's the trick, of course. If you mean to survive in the Institution without giving up your soul, you have to believe that you're ready to kill at any moment. The myth goes like this—if the other cons think I'm willing to kill (or die) for what's mine, they'll leave me alone. If they think I'm soft, they'll suck out the last drop of my blood. All prisoners subscribe to this myth, even the ones who give up that last drop. Even the snitches.

It makes perfect sense, when you think about it. With no money, no friends on the outside, no one coming to visit, now or ever, what else have we got except the belief that there's some value in never taking a backward step?

I was in my cell. Eight days before I was scheduled to go out on parole. The cell block was in a lockdown because a Rican he-she named Angel had shanked his husband, Pito, with a filed-down plastic toothbrush. It wasn't much of a cut and rumor had it the two would make up as soon as the hacks let Angel out of the box. Meanwhile, it was every con in his cell while the Squad went through the usual bullshit shakedown. As if they didn't know we'd dumped our weapons and our contraband as soon as Pito began to yell.

The Squad came onto the block about ten minutes after the stabbing. They wore black padded vests and black helmets with plastic face shields—a platoon of Darth Vaders accountable only to the warden. In the minds of the corrections officers, fear of the Squad was all that stood between them and the convicts.

But on this particular day the Squad seemed as bored as we were. Angel and Pito had been removed by the time they came pounding onto the block and the cons had gone back into their cells without being ordered. Still, the Squad went by the book. They called us out, one at a time, for questioning, while the corrections officer in charge of our block tossed the cells, scattering our possessions.

"I didn't see nothin', boss. I was in my cell when it happened." No expression of concern on my face, though I could end up in the infirmary for a cocky smile imagined by a paranoid C.O.

A deputy warden named Maason wrote down every word I said, nodding as he went along. Everybody knew that Pito loved to kick his sissy's ass. The stabbing was Angel's way of telling Pito where the line was—part of a prison ritual so boring it made time into God. Angel wasn't trying to kill Pito. If Pito died, Angel would have to find someone just like him. That or become a prison whore, which in the age of AIDS means certain death.

The dep grunted and sent me back to my home—a one-man cell on the only block in the Cortlandt Correctional Facility that wasn't given over to housing areas twice the size of basketball courts. It took me five years to get that cell. I put myself on a waiting list when I came through the gates and paid ten cartons of Kools to the posse who controlled the block when my turn came up. Of course, I could have bought a cell at any time, but the going price for new fish was a thousand dollars cash. Which is why my neighbors were wise guys or big-time Colombian dealers like Pito or embezzlers with enough brains not to show fear.

The Squad left after the dep finished his investigation, but the lockdown would continue through the night. Baloney sandwiches in the cell, no gym, no yard. In a Max A institution like Cortlandt, withdrawal of privileges was a routine punishment, even for those who hadn't participated in the infraction.

In the army, when you take a break, the sergeant says, "Smoke 'em if you got 'em," meaning cigarettes. In the joint, when you're stuck in your cell, the rule goes like this: if you got it, then smoke it, shoot it, eat it, or stick it up your ass in the form of a suppository.

"Hey, Frangello?" It was Joe Terrentini, my neighbor. "Do yiz got anything?"

"Speed," I said. "I got two reds."

"Could I buy one from yiz?"

Half an hour later, time became bearable. Cells like mine had many advantages over the crowded dormitory blocks, the most obvious being safety. I was stoned past the point of boredom, crazily rapping with Joe Terrentini about Angel's declaration of independence. Terrentini hated homosexuals. He'd been in the garbage business until the Organized Crime Task Force nailed him for hauling bodies off to the dump.

"The fuckin' faggot got his fuckin' just deserts. He got just what the fuck he deserved." Terrentini had a strong tendency to repeat himself even when he was straight. Zipping along on speed, he would have talked to his toilet if I hadn't been there.

I asked him who he meant—Angel, who was in the hole, or Pito, who was being sewn up in the hospital.

"Both them fags are fags, right?"

I couldn't see his face, just his short, hairy forearms and folded hands extending through the bars of his cell. Terrentini was a slow man. He believed in every aspect of the American Dream except the one that says you can't bury people in garbage dumps.

"Pito says that when he gets out of prison, he'll never look at another man, but he's gotta have sex and he doesn't wanna hump his hand. He says what he does with Angel doesn't make him a homosexual."

Every butch con makes the same declaration, including wolves who call themselves gay in order to be placed on E3, the homosexual housing area.

"He fucks boys, Frangello," Terrentini said flatly. "He's a fuckin' fag."

Terrentini only spoke to me when he was speeding—the rest of the time he felt he was above me. I was a common criminal, he once told me, and he was a businessman. Whereas I hadn't seen my wife or kids in years, he had a family, went to Mass every Sunday, and was connected to the mob by blood.

"Ya know what is ya problem, Frangello?" he asked. "Yiz don't have values." His finger flicked toward a porter moving down the cat-walk. "Ya just like that fuckin' yam with the bucket. Can youze see what I'm sayin'? That nigger's been here thirty-five years. He's gonna die here. Ya let that moulie out tomorra, he'd be poundin' on the gate to get back in. That's you in thirty years, cuz. Because yiz don't have values."

The trusty was even with Terrentini's cell before I realized that something was wrong. Then the alarms went off hard enough to wake the dead. The porter wasn't cleaning. He was pushing a bucket on wheels along the catwalk's outer railing and he didn't have a mop.

"Can youze see this fuckin' nigger is so stoned, he can't hardly stand up?" Terrentini said calmly. He'd been paying the hardest crew in Cortlandt to watch his back from day one and he probably thought he was untouchable. "That's you. All ya fuckin' life waitin' for the next fix. This wouldn't be the case if yiz had proper values."

The porter bent down, picked up the bucket, then stumbled toward Terrentini's cell. The biting odor of turpentine filled the air as he slammed the bucket against the bars.

"Whatta yiz doon?"

The porter flipped open the top of a Zippo lighter and spun the wheel against the flint.

"Whatta yiz doon?"

Terrentini's cell exploded. The porter stumbled away, one trouser leg on fire. There weren't any screams at first, but I could hear the fat beneath Terrentini's skin as it bubbled and cracked. Then he began to run from wall to wall, crashing into the steel. I watched his reflection in the smoked glass window on the other side of the catwalk. I watched until the C.O.'s came, then I turned back to my own business.

In their haste, the C.O.'s had forgotten to throw the switch that opened Terrentini's cell door and one of them ran back to the control room while the other tried to spray Terrentini with an extinguisher that wouldn't work. When the cell door opened and Terrentini, still in flames, ran out, the C.O. jumped backwards. He had no intention of getting himself burned in order to save a convict. Then the second C.O. appeared with a charged foam extinguisher and put out the fire. Terrentini screamed when the foam hit him. A long, high sound that didn't waver. It went on and on and on, then shut off forever.

The porter, a lifer named Bo Williams, was caught immediately. He'd fallen down trying to smother the flames on his trouser cuff and couldn't get back up. Four hours later, when he came off the prison hooch and the pharmaceutical quaaludes, he turned snitch.

A friendly C.O. named Bugavic brought me the news after the ten o'clock count. He told me that I'd been the target. Bo Williams had been sent to kill me by a con named Franklyn Peshawar. Peshawar had threatened the old man, even as he pushed the hooch and the pills down Williams's throat. Old men are legitimate prey in the joint and Peshawar had made Williams fear him more than he feared the administration.

It was a good plan. As an administrative porter, Williams had access to the block. He had what the lawyers like to call "opportunity." But Williams had been drinking prison hooch for several decades and most of his circuits had popped long ago. Further numbed by Peshawar's drugs, he'd made a simple mistake and burned the wrong man.

About an hour later, I asked Bugavic for protective custody. He got permission within minutes. The administration was only too happy to discover that I wasn't planning revenge. Feuds are a headache to administrators under pressure to keep incidents of violence down. The politicians don't care what happens to prisoners, but the reporters do.

The fear began to control me as soon as the C.O. locked me into a protective custody cell. I felt it stirring like a sudden return to a childhood when I was always frightened. In order to fight, I forced myself to consider Peshawar's motives. Examining problems was one of the ways I overcame fear. After all, facing enemies instead of running away is what DEATH BEFORE DISHONOR is all about.

About two months before Terrentini was burned, Franklyn Peshawar had come up to me in the dining hall and pointed at my pork chop. To my knowledge, it was the only time I'd ever been near him.

"Yo, boy, I want that meat."

"The only meat I see around here is you, asshole."

A C.O. drifted toward us and Peshawar took off without the chop.

For cons like me, who couldn't afford protection, challenges were part of everyday prison life. I wasn't particularly aggressive, but I had my tattoo and I didn't think much of the incident. Most likely, Peshawar was trying to impress one of the all-black posses that dealt in contraband, maybe the one that ruled his Housing Area. Since I'd gotten in the last word, I didn't have to worry about losing face. In fact, my response had drawn laughter from the cons sitting at my table. I watched my back for a couple of weeks and then forgot about it altogether. Peshawar had remembered.

Protective custody is nothing more than voluntary keeplock. You stay in your cell for twenty-three hours on most days. A C.O. accompanies you whenever you leave the block, because now that you've informed the administration of your personal danger, the state can be sued if somebody fucks you up. Not that you're ever completely safe. There is no safety in the Institution. Readiness for combat is the first test of the instinct for survival.

But protective custody is also the hardest way to do time outside of being someone's punk. If I hadn't been due for parole, I would never have requested it. I would have sought out Peshawar with the intention of eliminating him before he eliminated me. It's also very likely that if I wasn't scheduled to go out, I wouldn't have lost my nerve. The need to survive would have controlled my actions, as it always had.

Unfortunately, once your courage goes, it's hard to get it back and I lost my nerve forever during that week in P.C. I began to think about Terrentini, about what I was doing inside myself while he burned. I'd watched him calmly, but the expression on a convict's face never reveals what he's actually thinking. In truth, the only emotion I'm sure I felt was relief. Somehow, fate had skipped over me, stopping one cell down the line to snuff Joe Terrentini.

Knowing I was the target should have heightened that feeling of escape. Instead, it scared the shit out of me. In a week, the incident would be forgotten. Peshawar and Williams would be transferred to an Albany jail where a judge would eventually add twenty-five years to their life sentences. Instead of looking for revenge, I'd be in some halfway house in New York City. True, Peshawar's murder method had been spectacular. But in the Institution, where disputes are commonly settled by tossing homemade lye in your enemy's face, Terrentini's memory would be obliterated by the next stabbing. Or the next mini-riot. Or as soon as one of the dealers got hold of some decent shit.

Little by little, no matter how tough you are, the Institution destroys you. The cons, trapped in their own bravado, try to live by the credo that "what doesn't kill me, makes me stronger." The idea is total bullshit. Everything kills you—the violence of the other cons, the C.O.'s with their small humiliations, a parole board that decides your fate without knowing who you are, the endless division of time into small, contained segments.

Eventually, I came to understand that my life had been dishonorable from the beginning. I'd been dishonored by the world because of my birth and I'd bought the label. I felt courage dissolving. Despite all the fights. Despite the idiot belief that living by the rule of fang and claw made me superior to the judges and the C.O.'s and the society that provided my definitions.

I was dead and I was afraid to die. I surrendered all hope of protecting myself with psychological courage. Other prisoners gave me curious looks, sensing the change. I fought to maintain my regular expression, but I was convinced that I couldn't survive in the Institution, that my life depended on getting out. I found conspiracy on the face of every convict passing my cell. I watched hands, expecting a knife. I refused to answer simple questions. I saw my death in every greeting.

I was so scared, I could easily have killed someone by mistake. A prisoner carrying a toothbrush or a pencil. With my record, any attack on another con would result in my finishing my time inside. At the least. The rest of my sentence, five years of a fifteen year bit, would nail my coffin shut forever. DEATH BEFORE DISHONOR was the only truth I had and it vanished the minute I realized that I had no honor to defend.

TWO

Eight days after the death of Joe Terrentini, I pulled on a pair of gray trousers, a blue shirt and a blue jacket, white socks and black shoes. All courtesy of the state. Most prisoners have clothes sent up to them by relatives, but I had burnt my bridges to the world long before. Still, despite the poor fit and cheap quality, it was the first time I'd been out of a prison uniform in ten years. It should have felt good, but it didn't. It frightened me.

After seven bits, I feared getting out of prison as much as I feared going in. Another chance at failure. Another chance to confirm the psychologist who'd labeled me a sociopath when I was eleven years old, a label that stayed with me for twenty-four years. I knew how to deal with prison, but the world was another matter. The skills that enable a prisoner to survive in a Max A prison don't apply to the world.

I was the only prisoner to be released on that May 4th. That was because, technically, I wasn't given parole. The board had turned me down three times. I think they would have liked to keep me inside for the entire fifteen years of my sentence, but in New York prisoners who behave themselves must be granted conditional release after serving two thirds of their time. (This, of course, does not apply to inmates serving life sentences. What, after all, is two thirds of a life?)

A short, fat screw named Pierre Braque came to get me about ten o'-clock in the morning. Having nothing to pack, I'd been dressed and ready since five-thirty, listening to the radio for any news of New York City, which was where I was going. The Cortlandt Correctional Facility is located in the town of Danville, twenty miles from the Canadian border. It was forty-one degrees in Danville and fifty-five in Manhattan.

Braque and two other C.O.'s led me through the tunnels that connect H Block to Administration. Technically, I was entitled to protection until I left the Institution, and that's what they were going to give me. We passed other prisoners in the tunnel and a few of them greeted me, offering good luck. I tried to smile back, but I kept my eyes on their hands.

I didn't relax until I was in the office of Deputy Warden Jack Camille. His greeting, "Hello, scumbag," twisted my fear into anger—that barely suppressed rage felt, justifiably or not, by every prisoner. There are only two industries in the town of Danville: lumber and prison. Jobs in Cortlandt are handed down from father to son, and most of the C.O.'s are related. Their own code of honor requires them to humiliate the prisoners at every turn. The prisoners' code of honor requires them to hate the C.O.'s. It all works wonderfully until the day you come out.

Camille had a special reason for hating me. Five years before, when he was an ordinary C.O. with a special reputation for provoking prisoners into responses that justified violence, I'd made him look bad. Not that it was my fault.

Prisoners coming into the mess hall at Cortlandt divide into two serving lines. One line is entirely black and the other is white and Puerto Rican. It was like that when I got to Cortlandt and it hadn't changed in ten years.

For some reason the white serving line on this particular evening was much longer than the black line. The evening meal is voluntary and many cons choose to stay out in the yard. Apparently, more blacks had taken this option than whites and Puerto Ricans. It could easily have been the other way, with the black line running out the door while the white line was empty, and I wasn't paying much attention until Camille, who had mess hall duty, said, "Get over in the other line. Even it up."

At first, I didn't realize that he was talking to me. Then he called me by name and number, his voice dripping sarcasm. "Frangello, 83A4255, get your ass over to the other line."

I'd never had a beef with Camille, though I was aware of his rep. Why did he choose me? I didn't know and never would. But I had to react. To accept his disrespect, to step into that black line, would have meant an extreme loss of face. Blacks, whites, and Ricans, with rare exceptions, don't mix in prison. If there had been a third serving line in the dining area, either the whites or the Puerto Ricans would have been on it.

"You mean me, boss?" I asked.

He walked up close to me. His square red face was twisted with rage. "I told you to get in the other fucking line. What's the matter, you too good to eat with the niggers?"

There are no blacks living in the town of Danville. No Puerto Ricans, either. Eighty percent of the population is made up of French Canadians who wandered south a hundred years ago. The younger screws are afraid of the inmates, most of whom come from the big, bad city. They cover their fear with macho bullshit.

"Can't go over there, sir." I said, trying to sound subservient and firm at the same time, which is a good trick. "That's not my line, sir."

I accepted the fact that Camille would write a ticket and I'd be hit with a two-week keeplock, but I'd been confined to my cell before and the punishment didn't particularly frighten me.

Then he shoved me. "Get in the other line, you piece of shit."

Goodbye freedom, I thought, *here comes the box*. The box and the beating that goes with it.

I shoved him back. There was nothing else I could do. Not with a hundred cons watching me. But instead of clubs and fists, Sergeant Paul Cartier, one of the oldest guards in the Institution and Jack Camille's uncle, stepped between us.

"You're in trouble, Frangello," he said to me as he led his nephew away.

Then I noticed that the cons on both lines were stirring. There aren't many freedoms for prisoners, but those we have, including racism, are jealously guarded. Cartier hadn't stepped in to protect me. He was trying to prevent what the administration likes to call a "disturbance." As the ranking C.O., he was responsible for the dining area, and he wasn't about to let an asshole like Jack Camille start a riot.

I got my two weeks' keeplock. Two weeks in my cell doing a thousand push-ups a day, reading magazines, drinking prison hooch smuggled in by my crew. No big deal, like I said. After I came out, Camille and a few of his buddies tried to put the heat on me, cursing me and ordering me about. Only now I was allowed the privilege of not reacting. Once the heat was official, once I was a target, obedience was honorable. It doesn't make a lot of sense, but, then again, it's not the world, either. After a few weeks, the C.O.'s grew bored and moved on to some other amusement.

Camille shuffled through my folder, shaking his head. He had deep blue, redneck eyes and blond hair cut to within an inch of his scalp. In the summer he rolled his shirtsleeves up far enough to show the black swastika tattooed on his shoulder. "Hey, Frangello," Camille finally said, "you buying a round-trip bus ticket? Says here you ain't been out of jail more than three straight years since you were sixteen."

I didn't answer. This was my day to return to the world.

He shook his head slowly. "I know I live in a fucked-up society when I have to release a piece of shit like you. Damn, I feel like a traitor to my country signing these papers."

"I'm not coming back."

I knew it was a mistake as soon as I said it. Camille laughed until snot ran out of his nose. Then he wiped his face on the back of his sleeve and lit a cigarette. "What I'd like to do is put out this butt in the middle of your face. Make a mark so the world can see you coming. Like a sign: SCUM WARNING. Whatta you think about that, 83A4255?"

We were alone in Camille's office. No witnesses. And I knew that a prisoner would have to commit a major, major offense to be remanded on the day of his release. My answer was cold and calculated. At that moment, I hated Camille more than the life I'd led for thirty-eight years.

"Why don't you cut the bullshit, Camille, and sign the fucking papers?"

"What did you say?"

"What I said is that you're a chickenshit faggot and the only place you've got the balls to put that cigarette is in your cunt mouth." His face reddened, matching the ordinary color of his neck. "You'll be back, Frangello. You ain't been straight for ten minutes in your whole miserable life. I already sent out a letter to your parole officer. You're a piece of shit and you're gonna get violated the first time you spit on the sidewalk." He paused, managed a wet smirk. "Personally, I can't wait to welcome you home."

THREE

There's no way to describe what it feels like to step out into the open air after a long incarceration. Unless, of course, you've done it seven or eight times.

The Cortlandt Correctional Facility sits in the center of the town of Danville (pop. 1433), New York. Forty-foot walls, complete with gun towers, line one side of Main Street. A mix of shops and homes and a single cheap hotel lines the other. I stood with my back to the walls and swept the street with my eyes. It was just like stepping onto the flats in Cortlandt where hundreds of prisoners milled about, many of them strapped and ready. *All* of them willing to kill.

I missed nothing, but even ten feet away, you wouldn't have picked up the movement of my eyes. The trick, inside, is to see everything without revealing the intense fear that necessitates the search for enemies. It's not a trick that's easily unlearned.

The few citizens on the street seemed mild enough. They undoubtedly made me for a released convict, but that's the way it goes. As my eyes swept the rooftops, I walked across the street and strolled into the 7–11, where I bought a pack of cigarettes, a Snickers, and a can of Coke. Then I went back outside to wait for the bus. I had no illusions about freedom. With $97.85 and no job, my life would be anything but free. What I *did* have was a list of the phone numbers of convicts from my crew who'd been released before me. If I wanted quick money instead of poverty, an apartment instead of a homeless shelter, all I had to do was dial a number and tap the old cons' network. That's what jail's all about. That's what the cons talk about on the courts. The crimes they've committed and the ones they intend to commit.

The good citizens of Danville walked on the outer edge of the sidewalk, as far from me as they could get. I was aware of their distaste, just as I was aware of everything happening on the street, but I couldn't summon up any indignation. The myth of paying your debt and returning to the community was just that, a myth.

An experienced con, faced with a long bit, plans the time so it doesn't stretch out into blank emptiness. I knew I was going away long before I heard my sentence and I decided to get myself an education. I'd graduated from grammar school and gotten my high school diploma in jail. Why not go all the way? The parole board didn't figure to smile down on me, but a sincere effort at rehabilitation couldn't hurt. I had to do at least a third of my fifteen-year sentence before I could be considered for parole, and I hoped to be cut loose after seven or eight years.

I spent the first three years working double shifts in the tailor shop, which was the main industry at Cortlandt. The tailor shop manufactured uniforms for state prisoners, American flags for municipal offices, and nightgowns for women in New York State hospitals. I already knew how to operate a sewing machine and I worked hard enough to please the C.O.'s, who rewarded me with extra work hours.

After I'd accumulated enough money in my prison account to keep me in cigarettes and coffee, I got myself transferred to the State University satellite school, which operated inside the walls, and graduated four years later. Not that I had any illusions about using my degree after I got out. I didn't expect the business world to be any more impressed with my rehabilitation than the parole board. The largest part of any employment application (and I've filled out hundreds of them) is set aside for the applicant's working history. What could I put down? Car theft? Burglary? Armed robbery? What would I write under "place of employment"? Spofford Youth House? Rikers Island? The Cortlandt Correctional Facility?

Work and school had gotten me through a ten-year bit. I never had a major beef (until Franklyn Peshawar) in Cortlandt, because I knew how to do time. I was an experienced con. It was the only experience I had to offer.

The bus rolled into Cortlandt, a shiny chrome Adirondack Trailways. It pulled up in front of the 7–11 and the driver, a short, fat man in a gray uniform and peaked cap, stepped out to welcome the only passenger.

"Luggage, sir?" he huffed.

Sir? Was he kidding? The man had to know what I was. I held out my empty hands and muttered, "No luggage," warning myself not to overreact. This was the world, not prison. I handed him my ticket.

"One second."

The asshole actually put his hand on my chest. I felt my own hand slowly drifting toward my belt buckle. I'd been carrying a weapon for ten years and, most of the time, kept it just below my belt. "This is the world," I said.

"What?"

"Do we have a problem?"

"You can't smoke on the bus."

I looked at the burning Marlboro in my hand. "Why not?"

"It's been the law for two years. Where you been?" He shook his head, then looked into my eyes for the first time. "Hey, the goddamn bus is empty. Sit in the back and smoke if you wanna. But if someone gets on and complains, I'll have to ask you to put it out. Hell, I smoke, myself. I know how it is."

"You ever been in the box?" I asked.

"What?"

"Can't smoke in the box." I ground out the cigarette and stepped onto the bus.

We took Route 7 west to the Interstate, then turned south. I stared out the window, feeling like an aborigine in a movie theater. Not that the view was all that strange. Whiteface Mountain, which is visible from high up on the courts, was still snowcapped. I'd spent the last ten years measuring the seasons by watching the snowcap grow and shrink.

I sat in the back of the bus and I didn't smoke. It seems stupid, but I saw it as a test. The bus driver didn't offer to let me smoke because he was nice guy. He offered because I scared the shit out of him. I know all about fear. Fear runs the Cortlandt Correctional Institution. Fear of the C.O.'s, fear of other prisoners, fear of the box, fear of the psych ward. Respect, itself, is gained by inspiring fear in other inmates.

The myth, among citizens, is that if you stand up for yourself in prison, the other convicts will leave you alone. But the price is much higher than that. I never saw a fistfight in Cortlandt. Men were stabbed every day. Or cornered and beaten with pipes. Or even burned in their cells. The simple fact is that dignity is preserved by a willingness to kill. Nothing less is acceptable, and the worst mistake a prisoner can make is to have another prisoner at his mercy and let him go. Mercy equals soft and soft equals prey.

Everybody carries a weapon. Or has one stashed where he can get to it in a hurry. I carried a shank with a thin wooden handle just underneath my belt buckle. It fit neatly through a loop sewn into my pants an inch below the top button. When the C.O.'s pat you down, they go over your legs thoroughly, grab your balls and your ass, but for some reason they don't reach around in front. I was searched hundreds of times. If the C.O.'s had found the weapon, it would have meant the box and a beating. Weapons scare the shit out of C.O.'s, but the blacks have a saying. "Better the man should catch me *with* it, than the boys should catch me *without* it."

"Say, mister." It was the driver calling me from the front of the bus. We'd been traveling for about two hours. "C'mon up here. We got a problem."

I walked up and sat across from him, trying to keep my voice friendly. Trying to be a citizen of the world. "How we doin'?"

"See this here?" He pointed to a glowing red light on the dashboard. "We're overheatin'. I'm gonna pull into Bolton's Landing and order up another bus. That's the next stop, anyway."

"Bolton's Landing? Where is that? How long will it take?" I was expected in a parole office on West 40th Street in Manhattan. That afternoon. To miss the appointment for any reason would be a technical violation of the conditions of parole. I was also supposed to pick up a housing assignment when I reported and if the office was closed, I'd be spending the weekend on the street. The street is not the best place for me.

"Well, the company claims it can get a replacement bus anywhere within two hours, only it usually takes three or four. But don't worry, mister, we'll get you where you're goin'. Bolton's Landing is near Lake George. It's mostly a tourist town and we're still off-season."

"There's no way you can push it to Albany? I gotta make a connection in Albany."

He looked over at me and shook his head. "Now, mister, if this was my bus, I'd give it a shot. But I can't be burnin' no engines up. The company'd fire me in a minute. See this here?" He pointed to a clipboard attached to the visor with a rubber band. "This here is a log. I already wrote down the exact time when the light went on. If I tried for Albany, I'd be in trouble, even if I made it."

"All right, I get the picture."

He was smiling, now that he was sure I wouldn't become violent.

"Wanna get back to the big city, right? Hey, I understand. You're probly goin' home."

I was going back where I came from, though I wouldn't call it home.

FOUR

There was a time when a prisoner coming out after a long bit emerged to a totally unfamiliar world. That was before television came to the Institution. Not that there's a TV in every cell. Or even in every block. That's just media bullshit. But there were sets in the mess hall, the gym, and the yard. They were usually tuned either to the most violent movie or the most violent cartoon, except at six o'clock, when choices were limited to the news or the news.

Which is why I wasn't terribly surprised by the Port Authority Bus Terminal in Manhattan. There's no cable TV in Cortlandt, and the two snowy stations we got originated in Plattsburgh, New York. The local newscasters loved to spell out the differences between evil New York City and virtuous Plattsburgh. One of them went so far as to run a series on "New Calcutta," spending the better part of a segment on conditions at the Port Authority.

The era of homelessness was just beginning when I went inside. Now I was stepping around the assembled multitudes. There's some kind of a law against sleeping in the terminal, but it hadn't had much effect on the assorted mutts, crazies, and confused elderly who wandered through the building. The good citizens danced little circles around men and women talking to the empty air. Or dodged determined panhandlers. A beggar approached me as I walked through the concourse. He shoved a jingling coffee container in my face, started his spiel, then looked into my eyes.

"Hey, bro, how you livin'?"

"Get the fuck outta my face."

"Yes, sir. Yes, sir." He bowed deeply as he backed away.

Out on the street, the dealers, two or three to a block, whispered, "Crack? Blow? Smoke?" At the time, I thought it was just another case of being recognized for what I was. Now I realize there's so much dope in Times Square that the dealers, mostly kids, offer it to anyone who doesn't look like a cop. That's why they'll spend most of their lives in jail.

But I was in a hurry. It was almost seven and I had a hot date with a parole officer. Fortunately, New York State has a parole office on West 40th Street, half a block away from the terminal. (And smack in the middle of Dope Heaven.) I was thinking of what kind of bullshit I'd have to spout to keep my P.O. satisfied, and I was more than happy to find the office open and staffed. The receptionist, a career civil servant, examined my papers closely, then motioned me to a seat.

"Who am I gettin'?"

He looked up at me through watery eyes, considering the question.

"I didn't know it was a secret," I said.

His skin was so white, I could see the veins on his cheeks and forehead. "Please take a seat and wait for your name to be called."

I wasn't feeling particularly hostile, but I *was* free. Wasn't I?

"Working overtime get to you, does it?" I asked.

He glanced down at my paperwork, then back at me. "Mr. Frangello, if you don't get your ass in a chair by the time I count to ten, I'm going to ring for security."

I started to say something, but thought better of it. "And, considering your background, Mr. Frangello," he continued, "I don't think security would be overjoyed at having to deal with you on the first day of your *conditional* release."

He couldn't have weighed more than a hundred and thirty pounds, but he wasn't taking any crap from the likes of me. I had a brief fantasy involving the speed with which my right fist could reach his left cheekbone and how many times he'd bounce before he hit the wall behind him. Then I sat down.

"Welcome back, Pete."

I recognized the voice before I looked up. Simon Cooper. "How you livin', Simon?"

"Same old shit, Pete." He hadn't changed much in ten years. He was still black, still bald, still fat, and still as powerful as a prize bull. His handshake nearly broke my fingers.

If I was a little more paranoid, I might have understood his assignment to my case as part of a conspiracy, but I knew that cases were given out randomly to any P.O. without a full caseload. Besides, Simon Cooper was one of a rare breed. Sending parolees back to jail didn't interest him very much. Nor did rehabilitation, in the ordinary sense. He was into crime prevention, and he'd give you a lot of room if he thought you needed it. I ought to know, because he'd been my P.O. the last time I came out.

Cooper had given me plenty of room and I'd fucked him at every turn. They didn't make you pee in the bottle in 1979, but any experienced P.O. can recognize a nodding junkie. Not that I'd been an addict, but I'd reported stoned on more than one occasion. And that's when I reported at all. Cooper had babied me through, running me down when I failed to report, easing me into a treatment slot when my habit began to get out of hand. I'd rewarded him by getting myself busted for a felony two months after I came off parole.

I followed him back to a room covered with gray, metal desks and took the required seat by Simon's desk. It was Friday night and the room was deserted, which meant that he'd waited for me. Most of the functionaries I've met in the course of an Institutional life have been scumbags. They begin with the belief that all orphans are criminals and work hard to fulfill their own prophecies. As a white orphan, I'd been adopted before I left the maternity ward, but my parents, Warren and Bonnie Walsh, had returned me to the state when I was nine. They'd claimed I was uncontrollable, which may or may not have been true. I can't remember any more, but I know they never mentioned the fact that they'd managed to conceive three kids of their own in those nine years. And had no further use for me.

Not that I'm making excuses. Or even looking for an explanation. I gave that up long ago. It's just that I've met a few good people along the way. Civil servants who were in it for more than the check and the pension. I inevitably reacted to them as if they were fathers, wanting desperately to please them. And failing miserably.

Simon Cooper was one of the good ones. He had a fat, benevolent face, a walrus mustache, and huge brown eyes that softened a hardened core. He wouldn't take any lip from the toughest ex-con, but he would plead your case to the board, even if you'd been violated for committing another crime. Assuming, of course, that he felt you were worth the effort.

"You been away a long time, Pete." His voice was neutral, but his eyes seemed to reproach me. "Ten years."

"Shit happens, Simon." I was sorry that I'd hurt him, but, of course, I wasn't about to show it.

"You know what it says here, Pete?" He held up my file. "It says 'career criminal.' It says 'sociopath.' It says 'high-risk offender.' "

"I don't remember it ever saying anything else. That's why the board turned me down three times."

"It also says I should put my foot on your head and keep it there for the next five years. It says, 'Intense Supervision.' "

"I wouldn't blame you, Simon. You gotta do what you gotta do."

"I'm glad to hear that. I've been thinking about you ever since I got the assignment and I've decided to follow the recommendations of the board. Things have changed in New York since you went inside. Caseloads are way up and I don't have time to supervise anymore. None of us do. Now it's all mechanical: check the urine, check the pay stubs, check the residence. Violate for any fuck-up. The media's all over us. 'Soft on criminals' is what they call us. 'Bleeding hearts.' They don't know a fucking thing about what we do, but every reporter's an expert."

"Reality doesn't sell papers, Simon. We both know that." I was hoping for a smile, but I didn't get it.

"You could always talk a good line. That's probably why I let you play me for a fool."

"It's not gonna be like the last time. I can't go back inside."

He held up my folder again. "Says here that you got yourself a college degree."

"I had a lotta time, Simon, and not much to do with it."

"You figure to use that degree to get a job?"

"Maybe a few years down the road. I don't think my résumé would interest IBM right now."

"Yeah, well that's realistic. In the meantime you're gonna flip hamburgers or push a broom. I'll give you a referral after you settle in."

"Where am I going?"

He ignored the question. "You report on time, Pete. Miss an appointment and you're violated. You pee in the bottle on every visit. Come up dirty and you're violated. You maintain a residence. You get a job and show up for it. Quit your job or change your residence without my permission, you're violated."

"Look, Simon, something happened to me inside. Or almost happened to me." I went on to tell him about Terrentini and, to his credit, he heard me out.

"The first thing, Pete, is that you're going into a shelter. What they call a Tier II facility. It's run by a private agency—The Ludlum Foundation. You like that? The Ludlum Foundation? They'll explain the setup when you get there, but I guarantee it's a lot better than a six-hundred-bed shelter. You'll still be associating with other criminals, because we've been assigning ex-offenders to The Ludlum Foundation for the last year. The facility is right in the middle of Hell's Kitchen, which is one of the biggest dope and coke neighborhoods in the city. That's another problem for you. I expect you did drugs in Cortlandt."

"Not all the time. I couldn't afford it. And I stayed clean while I was in the school program. Stayed away from every kind of trouble."

"You said, 'Shit happens,' a little while ago. Now you're telling me that shit didn't happen to happen while you were going to school?"

I didn't have a ready answer to that. I'd managed to avoid a beef during the school year, but caught my share of keeplocks in the summer, when school was out. "Could be somebody was watching out for me. Could be I was just lucky."

"Well, you better hope that lucky star is still shining up in heaven, because I'm gonna be on your ass until you prove yourself. This ain't no courtroom, Pete. You're guilty until you prove yourself innocent."

I'd been living with that reality for a long time, but since I was mostly guilty, I had nothing to complain about. "We're goin' in circles, Simon."

He drummed on the desk with sausage-thick fingers. "You in a hurry, Pete? You got an appointment?"

"Maybe I 'matured out.' Isn't that how the penologists like to put it? Maybe I've had enough. Life is worthless in Cortlandt. Wait a second, let me take that back. Life does have a value in Cortlandt. It's worth a pack of cigarettes. That's the fee for a young kid looking to make a rep. An experienced killer will do it for a carton." I waited for a response, but he continued to stare at me. "I know I fucked you last time, Simon. I walked into your office a criminal and I used your goodwill to advance my career. But I *can't* do the time anymore."

"Are you afraid, Pete?"

I bristled inside. A prisoner never challenges another prisoner's courage unless he's looking for a fight. It's the ultimate disrespect.

"I'm not afraid of dying. It's more than that."

His face softened and he sat back in his chair. "You have any idea how 'high risk' you are? No family support. No job. No home. Institutional from age nine. Long-term drug abuser. You're gonna have to fly upwind in a hurricane."

"That's been my whole life, Simon. That's what it's all about."

"All right. Enough with the lecture. Here's the referral slip. The address is 707 West 39th. You come back here on Monday at nine o'clock and I'll try to line you up with a job. As long as you're not particular."

"I'm not. I need something to fill up the days."

"You might wanna think about Narcotics Anonymous. Or something like it."

"I'm not crazy about the twelve steps. Too much like religion for junkies."

"Just think it over. It's easier if you have help."

"I'll think about it."

He got to his feet and stretched. "It's been a long day. Shit, it's been a long week. I'm goin' home."

"Sorry I kept you late, Simon. The bus broke down near Albany."

"I know. I called Trailways and checked." He smiled and shrugged. "That's the way it's gonna be, Pete. You still have my home number?"

"It's been ten years."

"Ten years?" He shook his head. "Take my card and put it in your wallet. Carry it all the time. You have a problem, which you *will*, call me first. *Before* you do something stupid."

FIVE

The Ludlum Foundation was so far west it was almost in the Hudson River. I walked to it through a neighborhood that hadn't changed very much in ten years. The garment district was still a collection of low-rise manufacturing lofts, still deserted after eight o'clock. I'd been in any number of these lofts at night, though I was neither customer nor worker.

The funny part was that most of the time I'd been there with the help of bosses who wanted their inventories to disappear. Clothing manufacturers sink lots of money, usually borrowed, into new lines, speculating on the future tastes of American women. When those lines turn out to be unpopular, the only option is insurance. The clothing wasn't worth much, but our piece of the insurance check made the jobs profitable.

I got my first surprise at Eleventh Avenue. Not the whores, who'd been working the southern end of the deuce for a hundred years and were out in force on a Friday night. What stopped me in my tracks was a huge black-glass building that seemed to fly off in all directions. I stood on the corner of 39th and Eleventh, staring at it, wondering what held it up.

"Hi, sugar. You new in town?"

The whore was tall, black, and muscular. Too tall and too muscular to be a woman. She was dressed in a pair of red pantyhose that almost hid the bulge in her crotch, and a red brassiere that almost covered her implants.

"What's that?" I pointed to the glass building.

"That's the Javits Convention Center. They built it about five years ago. Where you been?"

"I been upstate."

"All this time?"

"Yeah. All this time."

"Then you must be ready to rock and roll, Sugar. Come upstairs with me and I'll take you 'round the world. Broaden your horizons."

She put her hand on my arm and I slapped it away out of instinct. "First thing is you don't touch me without my permission. Second thing is I spent the last ten fucking years avoiding whores like you."

She was rubbing her arm as I walked off. "You gotta lighten up, sugar," she called after me. "Smoke a few rocks and you'll feel better. I can get it for you."

The Ludlum Foundation was housed in a four-story building that used to be called the Paradise Hotel. I know, because after a successful job we used to grab a few whores and party all night at the Paradise. Snort and fuck until the sun came up or the coke ran out. The Foundation must have taken the hotel over, converting it into some kind of halfway house.

The change, on the outside, wasn't all that impressive. Same sooty red brick, same sooty windows, same broken steps leading up to a narrow wooden door. I stood across the street for a few minutes, fending off the whores and sucking on a cigarette. The whores I'd gone to the Paradise with had been one thing, but these women (and men) looked ravaged. Even the young ones. The bodies were still okay, especially half-naked under a streetlight, but the faces were drawn, the eyes bulging and red with lack of sleep.

It was time to go inside and get settled, but I stayed where I was, lighting another cigarette, wishing for a family, a home. Macho is the standard fallback for prisoners swept by loneliness, but I had no one to kick or punch. Simon had called The Ludlum Foundation a "Tier II Facility," but I couldn't see it as any more than a homeless shelter. Coming out of jail is hard under the best conditions. Living in a shelter, no matter what they call it, in the middle of whore and drug heaven, pounds home the reality of being a loser. I'd spent ten years protecting my honor and, with it, my ego. But, in reality, I was just another homeless asshole, dependent on the state for a mattress and a half-cooked meal.

There was a phone booth on the corner. As if someone had dragged me (as if a Cortlandt C.O., backed by the Squad and their steel batons, had ordered me), I jammed a quarter into the slot and punched out a number I'd sworn never to call. A woman answered on the second ring.

"Hello."

Her breathless voice seemed faintly familiar. Close enough for me to hope. To take a deep breath and hold it.

"Ginny?"

"Pardon me?"

I let my breath go, called myself a schmuck. "Is Ginny there?"

"You must have the wrong number. There's nobody here named Ginny. Sorry."

And why should there be? Why, if I hadn't once heard from Ginny Michkin in ten years, should I expect here to be out here waiting for me to finally call? The apartment we'd shared must have enclosed as many painful memories as my prison cell. The only difference was that she'd been able to move out.

"Is this 555-8473?" I felt like a fool even as I asked the question.

"Yes, it is, but there's no Ginny living here."

"Sorry."

I hung up the phone, ground out my cigarette butt, and walked across the street, up the steps, and into The Ludlum Foundation. The guard at the security desk, a black man, was dressed in designer jeans and a leather vest over a New York Mets t-shirt. His hair was shaved on the sides and rose six inches to form a flat shelf on top. He was obviously one of the residents.

"Hey," he said, "check this shit out. We got ourselves a slice of white bread for a change. What happened, white bread, they run out of niggers where you come from?"

He was well over six feet tall and thickly muscled, but even though I was barely five foot eight, I felt no fear whatever. Size has no importance unless you plan to fight with your hands. I didn't plan to fight at all.

A short Spanish guy wearing a white t-shirt with a Puerto Rican flag on the front laughed uproariously. He was sitting off to one side of the desk, reading a comic book. Apparently, I was more amusing than Archie Andrews, because he put it down and leaned back to enjoy the game.

There's no sense in showing your hand before the cards are dealt. I was willing to play the fool if playing the fool would get me through. I put my referral slip on the desk and calmly watched the guard slap it onto the floor.

"Don't throw that shit in my face, motherfucker," he shouted. "When I want your shit, I'll ask for it." He turned to his buddy. "White bread come in here and think he gon' run all over us. Jus' like he been doin' for four hundred years."

"Now, Calvin, don't lose your temper." The voice came from the hallway behind us. The middle-aged white man who followed it into the small foyer wore carefully pressed slacks and a white shirt under a tweed jacket. He had straw-colored hair and a thick, neatly trimmed beard. "Welcome, brother, welcome," he said to me. "I'm Arthur McDonald, Director of The Ludlum Foundation. Don't let Calvin put you off. He has a warm heart beneath that rough exterior. Don't you, Calvin?"

"Hot motherfucker," Calvin replied, setting off his buddy again.

"That's enough."

Arthur McDonald's voice sharpened and Calvin straightened in the chair. He stared up at me, grinning, but I refused to meet his eyes. I'd been through this in every foster home, every jail.

"I'm Peter Frangello," I said, handing him my referral slip.

"Yes, yes. I spoke to Simon Cooper this afternoon. Come into the office. We'll do the paperwork and get you squared away."

"See ya later, white bread."

I followed Arthur McDonald past a series of small offices to the back of the building. His own office was enormous, twenty feet deep and running the width of the building. I don't know much about furniture, but the blond desk and matching cabinets, the signed photographs on the walls, and the thick cream carpeting hadn't come out of a Goodwill thrift shop. Old McDonald was doing all right.

"We have some rules, here." Everything about him, including his voice, was mild. "We sleep in teams, four to a room. Each team is responsible for one aspect of caring for the Foundation. For instance, your team has the garbage detail. You collect it from the bedrooms, the offices, and the kitchen. Then you bag it and get it out front in time for Tuesday and Thursday pickup. Teaching responsibility is one of the ways we prepare the homeless for independence. I hope that's not a problem for you."

"No problem at all." I'd worked for thirty-five cents an hour in Cortlandt. Now I'd work for nothing.

"Good, good. The rest of it's simple enough. No drugs. No fighting. Be inside by ten o'clock, midnight on the weekends. Meals are served at seven, one, and six, but you don't have to eat here if you don't want to. How does that sound?"

"Still no problem. Mr. Cooper's got a job lined up for me, so I don't expect to be here too long."

"That's very interesting, Peter. May I call you Peter? We're not very formal here."

"One big happy family?"

He smiled and leaned back in his leather chair. "I'm not surprised to find you cynical, Peter. I know how hard it is to come out of jail and be homeless."

"How?"

"Pardon?"

"How do you know? How do you know how hard it is?"

"We've had our share of ex-offenders. In fact, most of our residents have been incarcerated at one time or another." He paused, looking up to the ceiling for inspiration. "May I ask you how long you were incarcerated? May I ask what prison you were in?"

"I can't see how it's your business." I was willing to follow the rules, but my life belonged to me.

"It isn't, it isn't." He waved his hands in protest. "Peter, I'm trying to reach out to you. This isn't a city shelter. It's a small community and we share problems. We try to help each other on the road back to independence."

"If I was looking for therapy, I would have asked the board to place me in an RT."

"You're quite right, of course. Quite right. We're not licensed to provide residential treatment, but there's no law that says we can't give each other support."

"Look, Mr. McDonald . . ."

"Oh no, no. We use first names here. Call me Artie."

"Yeah, well the thing is, Artie, I've only been in the world for a few hours and I need a little time to get adjusted. It's all kinda strange to me. Maybe in a few days I'll be ready to talk, but for now, I gotta have some room."

"Perfectly understandable," he said, not repeating himself for once.

"You room is number eight, one flight up. Here's a lock and a key for the cabinet by your bed. Oh, by the way, we have a full-time social worker. Ms. Boronson is her name. She can help you with welfare and medicaid, if you need it.""

"I'm planning to get a job, Artie." I was already standing.

"I understand, I understand." He shook his head. "But sometimes things don't work out. You should know that if you do find work or if you're collecting benefits, you're expected to pay a small amount, ten percent, toward your maintenance here. That teaches responsibility. Now, I think you're ready to meet your roomies."

He held out a soft, wet hand and I shook it, then wiped my palm on my pants as I left the room. Number eight was right at the top of the stairs, and the two men sitting by the window, pulling at a pint of apricot brandy, turned as I came into the room. They were nearly identical twins, despite the fact that one was black and one was white. Aging juiceheads living in a shelter, sucking out the last drops of life. One of them held a small pair of binoculars.

"Hey, bro," the black man said, "come over here. The Flasher's out tonight."

I walked over to the window and looked outside. A single prostitute stood under the light across the street. She was pretty far from the main stroll and maybe she figured she had to go to extremes to attract attention. Or maybe she was just stoned and having a good time. But whatever her motivation, she flipped up her mini whenever a car drove past. It didn't seem to matter who was driving, man or woman. I watched for a few minutes, then walked over to the only unmade bed and laid down.

"What's the matter with you, boy?" the black man said. "The bitch is fine."

"Maybe he don't like pussy," his twin responded. "Maybe he likes somethin' else."

I might not be very tall, but I'd spent a good part of the last ten years in the weight box with my crew, slowly building myself up to a hundred and eighty prison-hard pounds. The two alkies looked to be in their sixties.

"We're not gonna have a problem here," I said without getting up. I was holding the look (the one that says, "If you disrespect me one more time, I'm gonna kill you before you take another breath") in reserve. I didn't think I'd need it and I was right.

"He's jus' funnin'. Don't pay him no mind. They calls me Monty 'cause I used to flip the cards on the street. My bro's name is Harry. He's a little drunk."

"*Me?*" Harry asked indignantly. "Man, I bet five dollars you can't walk 'cross the goddamn room."

Monty laughed happily. "You probly right. I know I ain't gonna try. Ah'm stayin' right here and check out this pussy."

The two of them returned to the show across the street and I leaned back on the bed, trying to sort out my thoughts. I'd been looking forward to my first weekend in the world, but I couldn't get Calvin out of my mind. Calvin and how I was going to deal with him. Maybe that's why I wasn't surprised when he came into the room ten minutes later.

I wasn't surprised by Calvin's companion, either. He was a short, thick black man with a four-inch scar on his forehead. He fixed me with his best, baddest prison glare, staring at me like I was a cockroach he was about to crush.

"Time for the *real* interview," Calvin announced. He turned to Monty and Harry without waiting for a response. "Take a walk, boys. I'm doin' bidness here."

"But Calvin," Monty whined, "we watchin' the Flasher."

"If ya like the pussy so much," Calvin suggested, "why don't y'all jus' go outside and fuck her?"

Monty and Harry looked at each other in amazement. "Let's go downstairs," Harry said. "We could watch her from the front room."

Calvin waited for them to stagger out the door, then walked across the room and sat on my bed. He took out a pack of Salems, lit one, and offered me the pack.

"No, thanks," I said, without sitting up, "I got my own."

He put the cigarettes back into his pocket, then lit up. "This here is Rakim. He jus' come outta *Sing-Sing*. His P.O. says he's hostile. Wha'chu think?"

Sing-Sing is a medium-security institution, a nothing prison compared to the nightmare of Cortlandt. Rakim didn't frighten me, though he continued to throw me his "vicious killer" look. Nevertheless, I was careful not to show any disrespect. Either one of them, or both, might be strapped, and I really wasn't looking forward to being shanked on my first night in the world.

"He seems okay to me," I said.

"*Okay*? What you mean by that?"

"I don't mean anything by it."

Calvin fixed me with *his* baddest bad look. "How you like Artie?" he finally asked.

I shrugged. "I guess he's tryin'."

"The onliest thing Artie's tryin'," Calvin said, "is to fatten his bank. Man don't like to come out the office. He got himself a few assholes that he rehabilitatin', so the government money keep flowin' in, but he don't give two shits 'bout what happens out here. Fact is, y'all don't have to worry 'bout makin' Artie happy, 'cause ah'm the man runnin' The Ludlum Foundation. Y'understand what ah'm, sayin', white bread?"

"I understand."

"What detail you get? What's your job?"

"Garbage. I'm supposed to pick it up and bag it for the sanitation." I allowed a touch of fear to creep into my voice. Knowing it was exactly what Calvin wanted to hear. He glanced at Rakim and grinned. Rakim grinned back, though his eyes never left my face.

"Now, Rakim," Calvin said, turning back to me, "he got himself a kitchen assignment. He washin' dishes. Rakim hate washin' dishes 'cause washin' dishes give the boy dishpan hands. Tomorrow night, after the evenin' meal, you gon' come back to the kitchen and wash his dishes for him. Ain't no maybe about it, white bread. Y'understand what ah'm sayin'? You ain't wanna wash no dishes, y'all better pack yo shit and get yo ass in the wind."

His message delivered, Calvin got up and left the room. Rakim trailed behind, strutting for all he was worth. Twenty minutes later, I fell asleep. That's how scared I was.

SIX

I've been having the dream every few months for nearly thirty years. What the psychologist (who begged for dreams the way panhandlers beg for quarters) found most interesting is that the dream recurs over and over in the course of a single night. I wake, shake it off, drift back to sleep, and dream it again.

I'm nine years old and newly removed to a group home on Church Avenue in Brooklyn. I'm Pete Frangello, now. No more Petey. My adopted parents don't want me and I don't want them. Petey is dead as far as I'm concerned.

Sunlight, filtered by thin white curtains, streams through the windows. A light breeze stirs the curtains, throwing faint shadows across the room. Starched white sheets reflect the brilliant sunlight while the black floors and walls absorb it. Jesus hangs from a metal crucifix on the front wall, his head slumped against his shoulder.

The door opens and an older boy, maybe fifteen or sixteen, slides into the room, a finger pressed to his lips. "Shhhh," he whispers. "I'm supposed to be sick." He crosses the room and sits at the foot of my bed. "My name's Jack Parker. What's yours?"

"Pete Frangello."

His hair is long enough to cover his ears and swept back along the side of his head. A single curl, a wave, hangs down over his forehead. He has pimples on the right side of his face and the bare beginnings of a mustache on his upper lip.

"You got parents, Pete?"

"I had adopted parents. They don't want me, but I don't care about them. I'm finished with them."

He takes out a cigarette and offers it to me. I shake my head and he lights it himself. "My mother is a drunk," he announces. "She loves me, but she's too fucked up to care for me. I don't have no father. Do you know who your real mother and father are?"

"I don't even know if I have a real mother and father."

Jack nods his head slowly. "That's the way it is with a lot of the kids in here. I asked Sister Margaret to find out who my father is. Maybe my father would give me a place to live. But she wouldn't do it." He takes out a candy bar, a Snickers, and offers it to me.

Suddenly I'm in the shower room. There's so much steam that I can't see the kid next to me, but I can hear kids laughing and shouting.

I soap my hair and lean into the shower. When I pull back the kids have disappeared and the only sound is the splatter of water on the concrete floor. A figure appears, pushing the steam ahead of him. It's Jack Parker and another boy named Ramsey.

"Say, Pete," he says, "you remember that Snickers I gave you? Well I want it back. You took it and now you have to give it back to me. Matter of fact, I want that same Snickers I gave you."

"How can I do that?"

"You took it. Now you gotta give it back. You don't take nothin' in a place like this. This ain't a place where people give you somethin' for nothin'."

"I'll buy you a Snickers this afternoon," I say, though I have no money.

"I want the one I gave you. If you can't give me the one I gave you, then you have to pay me back the way I say."

They fuck me, the two of them taking turns. There's nothing I can do and I offer no resistance, but they beat me anyway. When they finish, I fall to the floor. The floor is gray and the steam is gray. The blood on my legs offers the only color in a black-and-white frame.

I woke up for the last time at six o'clock. After ten years of bells and counts, it takes more than a day of freedom to change prison routine. The dream was fresh in my mind and for the ten thousandth time I wondered if that was the way it happened. I can't remember anymore, but it seems to me that adolescents were kept apart from the younger kids.

It really doesn't matter, anyway. Rape is so common in group homes and adolescent jails that the only important thing is your reaction to it. I'd snuck into the kitchen four times and was caught and punished four times before I was able to steal a knife. By then, Jack Parker and his buddy had been transferred to private foster homes (a reward for proper Institutional behavior?) and the opportunity for revenge was gone. But I'd held on to the knife, stashing it during the day and keeping it under my pillow at night.

A couple of weeks later, two boys my own age explained the facts of life. They knew what had happened to me—everyone knew, except the nuns who ran the home—but they could see that I wasn't a punk. They were part of a gang composed of the few white kids in the Institution and they had to protect themselves like any other minority. They never mentioned the fact that both of my assailants were white.

"Survival, Pete," one of the boys had insisted. "*Survival*. Anybody fucks with one of us, they fuck with all of us."

Don't Trust Anyone is a prison cliché. You can have allies, but not friends. Today's bro is tomorrow's witness for the prosecution. Survival is what it's about. The ethic is transparently stupid, but at nine years old . . . The problem is you don't find out how stupid it is until you're too old to believe in anything else.

My two juicer roommates were snoring away. A third man, who must have come in after I fell asleep, also slept soundly. I dressed quickly and went downstairs.

Calvin was still at his post. His eyes were wide open and he ground his teeth continually, his jaw moving in little circles. He was coked out of his mind.

"Where you goin', white bread?" he asked.

I didn't turn around, didn't want to show him anything of what I was feeling. "I can't sleep. I'm going for a walk."

"A walk? It ain't but six-thirty in the gottdamn mornin'."

"I can't sleep," I repeated.

"Yeah, well maybe y'all could do me a favor. Pick up a package for me."

He wanted me to transport drugs. In Cortlandt, prisoners unwilling to kill in order to survive, homosexual or heterosexual, are often used as mules by prisoner-dealers. The dealers themselves rarely touch the drugs or the money. Rape isn't very common in adult male prisons, though it's rampant in adolescent facilities. Heterosexual prisoners characterized as soft are usually "maytagged." They wash underwear and socks, surrender cigarettes and commissary, transport drugs and other contraband. The proper translation of the word "maytagged" is "enslaved."

"I'm not coming back until tonight."

He sniffed loudly, then sniffed again. "You gon' be back for dinner, right? If you ain't back for dinner, don't be back at all. You got a 'pointment with a sink."

I left without answering and walked straight across 39th Street to Seventh Avenue, then turned uptown. It was early spring and still chilly, but I was too fascinated with the cars and the fashions in the windows to pay much attention to the weather. The garment center with its unionized workers had been deserted, but even at seven o'clock on a Saturday morning, secretaries and executives emerged from subways and cabs to work in the glass skyscrapers. The homeless were everywhere, sleeping in the doorways or the plazas, pushing overloaded shopping carts, or dragging plastic garbage bags stuffed with their possessions.

I stood in front of the Marriott Marquis for a long time, staring up at the enormous hotel. It hadn't existed when I went away and I wondered why had they'd put it so close to the 42nd Street sleaze. The Deuce is famous for porno, drugs, and violence. I tried to imagine an Iowa corn farmer checking in for the vacation of a lifetime, then stepping out to get his head busted by a desperate junkie.

The Marriott's elevators, visible through the glass facade, looked like space capsules as they moved up and down, carrying early risers to breakfast. I was hungry, too, but I wouldn't be dining at the Marriott Marquis. I found a small deli and had the counterman grill me a bacon and egg sandwich, added a cup of coffee and a cheese danish, then made my way uptown to the fountain outside the Time-Life building on Sixth Avenue.

Watching the women hurry into their offices was like watching a movie. It'd been ten years since I'd seen women moving freely through the world. I undressed them with my eyes as they hurried past, noted the curve of breast, buttock, and hip, yet my feelings weren't particularly sexual. It was too exotic for a physical reaction. Besides, I had no illusions about my own situation. From their point of view, I was just another homeless asshole. Another potential menace to be evaluated and avoided.

And, of course, I had Calvin to consider. I wasn't about to become his slave. I've played any number of roles in my life, but slave wasn't one of them. Still, it was obvious that although I could evaluate Calvin the way office workers evaluated me, I couldn't avoid him. I couldn't just walk away and take my chances on the streets. Simon Cooper had threatened to violate me if I changed my residence without his permission, and I had no doubt that he'd do it.

I suppose I could have called Simon at home, but even if he gave me permission to leave the Foundation, where would I go? I had to have an address or Simon would violate me to protect his own butt. There was no way he could justify letting a documented sociopath like Peter Frangello sleep in the street. He might let me move to another shelter, but the shelter trail from the Foundation went straight downhill. The next stop would be a massive city shelter with as much violence as a prison, but without the supervision.

The simple truth was that I'd have to deal with Calvin. I was locked in to the Foundation and there was no way to go around him. The question I kept asking myself was why Calvin couldn't see who I was. If a panhandler in the bus terminal could look into my eyes and turn away, why did Calvin take me for a punk? A prisoner's cell is his only real possession. To step into another man's cell without permission is the ultimate disrespect. Calvin had set himself down on my bed as if he owned it.

There were only two possibilities and they were obvious enough. The first was that Calvin was a stupid punk who thought he could do whatever he wanted to a collection of helpless, homeless men. But Calvin, himself, was living in a shelter, so how bad could he be? Maybe he and his Sing-Sing muscle had been assigned to the Foundation by P.O.'s of their own, but really dangerous ex-cons don't go to shelters. If they don't have families, they go back into the shooting galleries and the crack dens and worry about their P.O.'s later.

The other possibility was that Calvin had some hidden resource that I didn't know about. He was probably connected to one of the dealers outside the Foundation. Maybe his connection would supply him with muscle if he got into a beef. And maybe his connection wouldn't. There weren't more than forty beds in the entire Foundation. How much action could that represent to the millionaires who control the street corners in Hell's Kitchen, especially if Calvin's beef had nothing to do with drugs or territory?

The cabs swarmed over Sixth Avenue, timing the lights as they made their way uptown. The buses plodded along, leaving small black clouds behind them when they pulled away from the curb. The fountain spit columns of water into the air. The sound of the water falling back onto the reflecting pool reminded me of the shower in my dream.

My problem, I realized, was not whether Calvin was a punk or well connected. There was only one way to deal with Calvin, no matter what he was. My problem was that I didn't want to go back to prison. I wanted to do the right thing, but the right thing wasn't there to do. I was locked in, without any real choices, and the knowledge brought my anger to the surface. There was, of course, only one possible outlet for that anger.

I got up and began to walk. I went straight uptown into Central Park, then wandered aimlessly along the pathways until I found myself at Fifth Avenue and 79th Street, next to the Metropolitan Museum of Art. Fifth Avenue, with Central Park on one side and massive stone apartment buildings on the other, is the richest street in Manhattan. There had been times in my life when I'd walked down Fifth Avenue, daydreaming myself into the life enjoyed by the people stepping past fawning doormen. Now I ignored them altogether. It wasn't my world and it never would be.

I wandered east to Third Avenue, then turned downtown until I located a Woolworth's. It was a little after eight and the store didn't open until nine. I ordered breakfast in a small coffee shop, but I couldn't eat. My whole being was focused on Calvin and what I was going to do to him. At nine, when the manager unlocked the door, I wandered through the aisles of the five-and-dime until I found what I wanted, a denim tote bag with a drawstring top. The girl behind the register took my money without comment, then returned to her chewing gum.

I walked across the street to a D'Agostino supermarket and bought four large cans of stewed tomatoes. I put the cans in the bottom of the tote bag, then picked up a couple of newspapers on the corner, carefully stuffing them into the bag until the cans were trapped at the bottom. Finally, I hailed a cab and told the driver to drop me at 39th and Tenth, a block from The Ludlum Foundation.

The adrenaline pumping through my veins kept telling me to hurry, but I deliberately slowed down, saving it for Calvin. The weapon I'd constructed was perfectly legal, at least until I used it. Up at Cortlandt, the administration gives prisoners a small canvas bag to carry commissary back and forth from the cells to the courts. A few cans of tomatoes transforms a swag bag into a weapon. It's not much use against a shank because it takes too much time to put the bag in motion, but a shank isn't always available to newly arrived convicts, while the potential for violence exists from day one.

I found Calvin on the third floor. He was in the shower, all alone. The symmetry was delicious. I stepped into the mist and swung the bag in a vicious arc, taking him in the lower ribs. He never saw it coming, and by the time he looked up from the floor, he was in too much pain to do anything but moan. Not everyone can beat a helpless man into the hospital. It takes special skills, the kind you develop in the course of an Institutional life.

I worked on Calvin until my shoulders ached, until he begged for mercy, until he stopped begging. Then I went looking for Sing-Sing. I found him in the dining room, sitting at a small table by himself. He tried to muster up his bad-ass prison stare, but the sight of me, dripping wet, raised just enough doubt to show in his eyes.

"Your boss needs you upstairs, Sing-Sing," I hissed. "When you get up there, you take a good look at him, because that's gonna be you if you disrespect me again. *Ever* again. I don't want no part of whatever bullshit scam you're running, but I *will* kill you. I'll walk away from your corpse like you were a cockroach under my shoe."

He started to get up, but I grabbed his wrist and pinned it to the table, leaning forward until our faces were inches apart. "You hear what I'm tellin' you, asshole?" I gave him a chance to answer, but he didn't take it. Instead, he tried to yank his wrist away, but he didn't come close to succeeding. "You think I spent ten years in Cortlandt just to run away from a piece of shit like you? You're in over your head, Sing-Sing. Do you hear what I'm saying?"

When I said the word Cortlandt, a glimmer of understanding finally showed in his eyes. Cortlandt is the ultimate threat wielded by administrations in the various minimum- and medium-security institutions. You fuck up one too many times and you get an administrative transfer to a prison where you can be controlled. Cortlandt is the end of the line.

"You hear me, Sing-Sing?" I repeated.

"I hear you," he said finally. "How come you didn't say nothin' 'bout Cortlandt last night?"

"That's not the way it works, Sing-Sing. People who *talk* their way out of trouble are soft, and soft don't take you out of the shit. Calvin disrespected me and he paid the price. From where I'm sitting, the only thing *you* owe me is respect."

"What about Calvin?"

"Go upstairs and find out for yourself."

SEVEN

I left the shelter as soon as Sing-Sing was out of sight, walking south a few blocks before giving the canned tomatoes to a knot of homeless men gathered around a fifty-five gallon drum filled with burning planks. The tote went into the sewer and the newspapers into a corner trash can. There was no sense in returning to the Foundation before the excitement died down, so I hiked over to Macy's and bought myself a pair of jeans, a knit shirt, and three pair of underpants. The prices amazed me. When I went inside, you could still buy a pair of jeans for under twenty dollars. The first pair I picked off the shelf in Macy's had a French name on the back pocket and a sixty-dollar price tag. Even the Wranglers I eventually bought cost me twenty-eight bucks. By the time I added the knit shirt and the underwear, my bankroll was reduced to thirty dollars and forty-seven cents. But at least I'd have something to put on while I washed my state clothes in the sink.

I walked down to Washington Square and passed the afternoon with the folk musicians and singers. The chess hustlers still gathered in the southwestern corner of the park, just as they had ten years before, and the drug dealers still whispered "coke and smoke" as I strolled past. It was a beautiful day, warm and sunny, without a hint of the summer heat to follow. I felt my freedom for the first time. In a few days, I'd have a job. A shitty job, true, but still a job and a steady income that might, one day in the future, buy me a room of my own in a building run by an ordinary thieving landlord instead of a grant-hungry director with an MSW.

I headed back uptown at five o'clock. I was hungry and I wanted to get to the Foundation in time for a meal. Calvin would be gone and I wouldn't have any trouble with Sing-Sing. Sing-Sing would be too busy finding a substitute dishwasher to bother with me. Of course, there was the always the possibility that some of Calvin's buddies would be waiting, but I simply wasn't afraid.

Still, I wasn't surprised to find Arthur McDonald waiting in the foyer, a worried look on his face. I wasn't surprised when he asked me to join him in his office, either. By this time, everyone in the Foundation must have known who and what had happened to Calvin. That was the whole point of the exercise. What shocked me were the detectives lounging in McDonald's office. One of them was short and fat. His face was all jowls and cheeks, his eyes little dots. The other cop was taller and muscular. His cheeks were dotted with acne scars and he wore a gray sport jacket over a tightly buttoned charcoal vest. He would be the bad cop.

They rose as I entered the room, evaluating my potential for violence, bracing me with hard cop stares. Then they handcuffed me, read me my rights, and told McDonald to take a walk.

"You got anything to say?"

I'd first begun to hate after I was attacked in the group home when I was nine. Before that, I'd had a full quota of anger and resentment, but I was (I think I was, anyway) still reachable. After Jack Parker and Ramsey, my anger hardened until hatred became the focus of what little self-esteem I possessed. I began by hating my adopted parents, then my real parents, then the group home and the people who ran it, then cops and politicians, then ordinary citizens. I was an outlaw in the literal sense of being outside the law and I was proud of it. Watch out, world, Pete Frangello's gonna get even.

"Fuck you."

As soon as Simon found out that I'd been arrested, he'd violate me, which meant I wouldn't be eligible for bail or a hearing before the parole board until the assault charge was resolved. I was amazed that Calvin had given my name to the cops, and I couldn't imagine him testifying in court, but even if I beat the new charge, the board could decide to send me back to prison. There are no standards of proof at parole board hearings, no rules of evidence, and while you can bring a lawyer to the hearing, the board may resent his presence enough to remand you for that reason alone.

The tall cop reached over and slapped me in the face. It was his way of opening a conversation. The fat one grabbed his hand before he could do it again. I'd been right about the good cop–bad cop routine, but that was small consolation to my face.

"Take it easy, Rico," the fat one growled. "You wanna go before the review board?" Rico backed off and his partner returned to me. "I'm Detective Condon and this is Detective Rico. We're arresting you for Assault in the First Degree."

"Yeah," Rico said, coming back at me. "One fuckin' day out of the joint and he commits an assault. Somebody oughta give this asshole an IQ test. Find out if he's a fuckin' nigger."

"Okay, so you made a mistake," Condon said, ignoring his partner. "Shit happens, right? You wanna talk about it?"

"Fuck you."

This time Rico hit me hard enough to knock me out of the chair. I ate the pain, ate it and turned it into hatred. *What Doesn't Kill Me, Makes Me Stronger.* Handcuffed and as helpless as a nine-year-old trapped in a shower, I fought back with the only weapon I possessed. Later, when I was dragged over to a holding pen at Central Booking, the other side, the depression and the failure, would overwhelm me.

Condon continued to play his part in the charade. He got up and pushed his partner out of the room. Rico cursed me as he fell back. "Piece of shit. Piece of shit." There was a window in the office door and I watched Rico's lips move after Condon shut the door.

"My partner's a head case," Condon announced, helping me to my feet. "The Department shoulda given him a desk job ten years ago." He righted my chair, sat me in it, then plunked his fat ass into the chair next to mine. "Tough break, Pete. I mean about only being out *one* day and gettin' into shit like this. I *know* you had to do what you did, 'cause I know Calvin. Calvin's been workin' with us for a long time."

"Calvin's a snitch?" I was so surprised that I spoke without thinking. The rule of thumb for experienced criminals like myself is never give the cops a statement. The detectives try to make you believe that you can talk your way out of jail, but it never happens like that. What happens is your lawyer reads your statement and advises you to plead guilty.

" 'Confidential informant' is the way we like to put it."

He gave me a chance to respond, but I pulled back into myself again. This conversation should have been happening back at the precinct. What did they want from me? There was no good reason to speculate, because they'd tell me when they were ready.

"Jeez, I gotta pee bad." He shook his head in disgust, setting his jowls in motion. His cheeks were red and lined with small blue veins. "I eat too much, smoke too much, drink too much. My whole fuckin' body's fallin' apart and I'm only forty-three. You believe that?"

He waddled out of the office and Rico, as expected, came back inside. With my hands cuffed behind my back, I had to lean forward in the chair, making my face an easy target. Rico put his skinny ass where his partner's fat ass had been and shook his head. His face was all angles. Sharp nose and cheekbones, thin slash for a mouth, pointy jaw and glittering black eyes. He looked like a terminal speed freak. Even his ears had little points on top.

"How does it feel, asshole?" he asked. "One day on the outside. One fuckin' day. You probly didn't even get laid. Or maybe you didn't wanna get laid. Maybe you got laid so many times in the joint you don't even remember what a pussy tastes like." He lit a cigarette and blew the smoke in my face—a Grade A asshole with a badge and a gun—then reached over and casually slapped me. "I don't like that look on your face. That look is sayin', 'Fuck you.' I don't like that." He slapped me again. "Ya know what else I don't like? Calvin was settin' up half the goddamn street dealers in Hell's Kitchen and now he's in the fuckin' hospital. I'm losin' twenty collars because a piece of shit like you can't control himself for one fuckin' day. I oughta throw you out the window."

Condon rushed back into the room, right on cue. "Hey, hey, hey, hey. I told you to stay outta here." He grabbed Rico and dragged him away from me, pushing him out the door. "Damn psycho. I musta asked for a new partner twenty times. Might as well have spit in the wind for all the good it did me. But about Calvin . . . "

"Who's Calvin?" I asked.

"You sayin' you don't know who Calvin is? How come you asked me if he was a snitch if you don't know who he is?"

"Who's Calvin?" I repeated.

"Calvin's the guy you had words with when you first came into the shelter." Condon was patient, like any other smart detective. Patient and persistent. First he would convince me that I was buried, then hit me with what he really wanted. "I mean we got the story from McDonald. Calvin was working the security desk when you arrived and he disrespected you. Plus, your two roommates told us that Calvin came up to your room last night and had a talk with you. I hope you're not gonna deny *that*?"

"If you're talkin' about the black dude, he never told me his name. He ran me down a list of the shelter rules and left. You don't believe me, ask the guy who came in with him."

Condon's disappointed look told me that Sing-Sing wasn't cooperating. "You shouldn't have done what you did to Calvin. It hurt us."

"What'd I do to Calvin?"

He glanced at the door and Rico came back into the room. It was time for the bad cop again. Rico yanked me out of the chair and drew back his fist.

"You're wasting your time," I said, my face and voice as calm as I could make them. "In Cortlandt they beat you with ax handles. There's nothing you can do with your fists that'll scare me. And if you wanna pull out your gun and shoot, go ahead. At this point I really don't give a shit."

Rico hit me in the chest to show me how tough he was, then dropped me back into the chair. The two cops looked at each other for a moment. Finally Condon shook his head and turned back to me. "Look, Pete, the point is that you're in a lot of trouble. You found Calvin in the shower and you beat him into the hospital. We got witnesses who say you were soaking wet when you walked back through the shelter. Maybe you were smart enough to get rid of the weapon, and maybe it's true that Calvin's got a sheet so long that a jury would give you a medal for putting him in the hospital. But even if you beat the charge, you're gonna go back up to Cortlandt and finish your time. We already spoke to your P.O. He says he went to a lot of trouble to find you a job and get you into this shelter. He says he's not gonna protect you under any circumstances. We persuaded him not to violate you for the time being, but if you don't cooperate with us a little bit . . ."

"Forget that shit," Rico snapped. "Whatta you *askin'* this piece of shit to cooperate for?"

"Take it easy, Rico. You're gonna get your pressure up."

"Fuck my pressure." He put his face a few inches from mine. I could taste his breath. "You understand payback, asshole? You took somethin' from me and if you don't pay it back, I'm gonna put your ass in the joint for the next five years. Even a criminal asshole like you could figure out what I'm sayin'. You owe me and you gotta fork up the ante, one way or the other."

"I'll tell ya what, Rico," I said, forcing a smile, "you bring Calvin in here and I'll pray over his broken body."

Rico flew into a rage, a genuine rage this time. He knocked me out of the chair and began to kick me in the back. I tried to curl into a ball, knowing full well that I'd be pissing blood in the morning, but McDonald's desk was in the way. I was pinned against it and Rico was taking his time, carefully avoiding my head and face. He didn't stop until I cried out.

"Cuff his ankles." It was Condon's voice. He waited until I was shackled before he spoke again. "You're a tough guy, Frangello. I admit it, okay? Tough guy. So what I'm gonna do is lay it out and give you some time to think about it. When you were up in Cortlandt, you were part of Eddie Conte's crew. Don't bother to deny it. I been on the phone with a deputy warden named Jack Camille all afternoon. Camille don't like you, Frangello. He says he can't wait to see you again. He also says you were assigned to Eddie Conte's court up on the hill. Matter of fact, you were assigned to that court for more than five years. A little birdie told us that Conte's plannin' somethin' big, a little birdie Eddie tried to recruit. The birdie don't know what Conte's big score is, but Conte was talkin' seven figures. Me and Rico, we're businessmen, we're willin' to trade twenty street dealers for one big collar. You don't wanna trade, you go back to Jack Camille. It's up to you."

They left without another word. I struggled to my feet and managed to hobble over to a couch by the wall. I'd done a lot of shitty things in my life, but I'd never been a rat. Rats sit at the very bottom of the prison hierarchy, below the shorteyes and the rapos. That is, the *known* rats are at the bottom. Half the prisoners, if the truth be told, have given up a name or a date at one time or another. But this was different. Rico and Condon wanted me to set up Eddie Conte.

Eddie and I had watched each other's backs for six years, until he made parole five months before I came out. Eddie loved prison hooch and, by prison standards, I was a master brewer. On Saturdays, when nobody was working, our crew would gather on the courts after the morning count, cook up a spaghetti dinner, then eat, drink, and bullshit until dark. We usually kept away from the hustlers and the dealers in Cortlandt. Like most of the cons, we just wanted to do our time and get out. Eddie loved to talk about the big score he was going to make when the parole board finally cut him loose.

"What I done wrong, cuz," he'd say, "was takin' on a lotta small jobs for the wise guys. I wanted to get in with the mob so bad, I would'a cleaned the fuckin' toilets. Ya keep doin' jobs, sooner or later you gotta get popped. You hear what I'm sayin', cuz? That ain't the way to go. I'm gonna set up one big fuckin' score, then walk away."

I had Eddie Conte's phone number in my pocket. He'd been luckier than most because his old lady had waited for him and he'd had someplace to go. It was a joke, really. If I had a home, I wouldn't be trussed up on old McDonald's couch. Meanwhile, my next address was going to be the House of Detention for Men on Rikers Island.

They have a special jail in H.D.M. for parole violators. It's not a happy place. There are no jobs and no activities. Everyone's done hard time, and most of them are about to do hard time again. They scream, cry, curse. The air is filled with anger and the cells are filled with roaches. Prisoners only leave their cells for an hour a day, but they still make shanks and stab each other with monotonous regularity. Despite the shakedowns and the strip searches.

Terrentini floated up to me. "Ya problem is that yiz don't have values." I heard the whoosh of erupting flame again. Smelled the turpentine. Five more years in hell. I couldn't do the time, and I couldn't be a rat, either. Fortunately, I had another option and it was real fucking simple. I could pretend to go along with Condon. Feed him bullshit until the job was done, then let the money take me as far away from New York as I could get.

Condon and Rico came back fifteen minutes later. By that time my resolve had hardened. I'd been entertaining a ridiculous fantasy. I thought I could stay out of jail by avoiding crime.

"You make up your mind, asshole?" Rico asked.

"I got a couple of questions first."

Condon smiled and nodded to his partner. Rico backed away and took a seat off to one side of the room. They knew they had me. "What kinda questions?"

"Suppose Eddie's got his crew together. Suppose he already pulled off whatever he's gonna do. Suppose he moved away and I can't reach him. Do I have to testify if you bust him? Do you want me to wear a wire? Do-"

"Awright, I get the picture." Condon lit a cigarette and put it between my lips. "Look, Pete, the situation is real simple. You took somethin' from us and you gotta give us somethin' back. That somethin' is the where and when and how of Conte's move. If you can't get to him, you're goin' upstate. On the other hand, you *don't* have to wear a wire and you *don't* have to testify. There was a cop killed about twelve years ago, cop named Bower. The killer was never caught, but we got reason to think your pal was involved. In the old days, Conte would've just disappeared, but now we do it different. Now we'll settle for puttin' Conte back in the joint. He's forty-five and he still owes seven years to the state. If we add on a few felonies and he's sentenced as a multiple offender, he'll come out in a box. You know how to get in touch with him?"

"I got his phone number in my wallet."

"You wanna call him?"

"Yeah."

"Take the cuffs off, Rico."

Condon sat back in his chair and watched his partner fumble with the keys. I resisted the urge to rub my wrists and ankles, going to my wallet instead. Rico snatched the list out of my hand and examined it closely. I don't know what he thought he was looking at, because the names and numbers were coded, but he handed it back to me a few seconds later.

"Rico's gonna stay here with you," Condon announced, "and I'm goin' into the social worker's office. Listen on the extension. I don't think I gotta tell you what to say."

"You don't." Two minutes later I was punching out the phone number. Eddie answered on the third ring.

"Yeh?"

"Eddie?"

"Yeh."

"It's Pete. Pete Frangello."

His tone changed immediately. "Cuz, you're out. Son of a bitch. Where ya stayin'?"

"In a shelter, Eddie. Over in Hell's Kitchen."

"Not for long, cuz. Not for long. I got big fuckin' plans, cuz, and you are the last piece of the puzzle. I mean if you ain't decided to go straight." He laughed at the utter stupidity of the idea.

"Straight's not part of my agenda. Never was."

"Agenda. That's funny. Ya learned to talk real good in that school. Too bad you're a fuckin' criminal."

"Yeah? Well, whatta ya gonna do?"

"You're gonna do what you do best. But, look, talkin' on the phone ain't the smart thing to do. We gotta have a face-to-face. When could we meet?"

"It has to be soon, Eddie. The board ordered Intense Supervision. I gotta be back here by ten."

"No problem, cuz. There's a restaurant on Ninth Avenue and 27th Street. Mario's. You still like spaghetti?"

"With pepperonis," I answered. Pepperoni was the only meat we could buy in the Cortlandt commissary.

Eddie laughed appreciatively. "No pepperonis in Mario's sauce. But the shrimps are fantastic. I'll see ya in an hour, right?"

"One hour, Eddie."

Condon waddled back into the room a minute later, obviously pleased with the conversation. "You did good, Pete. Real good. Here, take this." He offered his card and I accepted it. There were two phone numbers on it. "I want you to call me every night at ten-thirty. Use the second number, *not* the precinct number. You could do it from a pay phone, but you might wanna tell Conte you have to be back here by ten o'clock. Tell him your P.O. won't cut you any slack. I already squared it with McDonald so you can use his office to make the call. And I'm gonna have a conversation with your parole office, so if you *gotta* snort a little coke, you're not gonna get busted for dirty urine. Basically, you don't gotta worry about makin' your P.O. happy. You're workin' for *us*."

EIGHT

It's not much of a walk from the Paradise Hotel to Mario's Restaurant on 27th Street. Unless you've just had your ass kicked by a sadistic cop. I wasn't angry anymore. It was all in the line of duty for both of us, just a piece of the dance known as "cops and robbers." Most of the bruises wouldn't hurt until the next day, but I did have this very sharp pain on the right side of my lower ribs. Being as I didn't want to limp into my appointment with Eddie Conte, I practiced a natural gait as I made my way down Ninth Avenue.

"Dope-n-coke. Dope-n-coke." The dealer stood back in the shuttered doorway of a freight elevator, offering his wares the way an aggressive panhandler offers his cup. I was tempted for a minute. A little dope to ease the pain; a few lines of coke to make me alert. I couldn't tell you why it mattered, but I walked on by. Maybe it was the part I was going to have to play with Eddie. I'd already told him I was subject to Intense Supervision, and if I walked into the restaurant stoned, there was always the chance that he'd notice. Or maybe I was still holding on to my fantasies.

Eddie Conte had been the undisputed leader of our crew in Cortlandt. He had a sharp Roman nose and he kept it tuned to the prison rumor mill, avoiding trouble when he could, making alliances when he couldn't. "Fix it before it breaks, cuz," he'd instructed. "Sniff it out and fix it up."

I recalled an incident in 1987 when a white prisoner named Andy Grant got into a beef with a Black Muslim. A few other Muslims had joined in to protect their brother and Andy caught a shank in the process. The entire white population took it personally, and the next day the yard was packed with armed men, blacks on one side, whites and Puerto Ricans on the other.

The administration showed good sense for a change. They could've waited for the show to start, then opened up from the guard towers, but instead they defused the situation. They chose one black con and one white con to talk things over. The black prisoner was the Muslim Imam, Tariq Muhammad. The white prisoner was Eddie Conte.

The further I walked, the more determined I became. I didn't want any part of Eddie Conte and whatever he was planning to do to the world, but I wasn't a rat. If I sold Eddie out, I wouldn't be any better than a nurse stealing dope from a dying prisoner.

Not that I was in a good spot. Not only couldn't I turn Eddie down, even if his plan was idiotic, even if it was guaranteed to send both of us back to Cortlandt, I was going to have to invent some kind of bullshit for the two cops. Two sets of lies to keep straight, two sets of professional paranoids to fool. A decent performance would buy me time, which was all I could hope for.

Mario's was packed and the short, fat man who approached me was already shaking his bald head as he took in my prison haircut.

"Do you have a reservation, sir?"

"I'm supposed to meet someone here."

His expression changed instantly, a quick professional smile erasing the frown. "Are you Mr. Conte's guest?"

"That's me." I ignored the Mr. Conte bullshit. The fat proprietor was probably one of Eddie's gombahs. Eddie had spent his whole life doing time for the mob. He didn't have to go to a stranger for an Italian dinner.

"Please. Come." He led me through the crowded dining room, weaving between tables with the freaky grace of a dancing bear. A door in the back, just off the kitchen, led into a small private room. Two women sat by themselves at a table in the far corner. Eddie's table was in the center of the room. He was pulling on a Heineken.

"Hey, Mario, I see you didn't have no trouble findin' my cuz." Eddie had a small, thin mouth. Set underneath that nose, it had a tendency to disappear altogether, but this time his grin was so broad that I could count his teeth.

"Naw, Eddie. He's as good-lookin' as ya said he was."

I blushed. I couldn't help it. My pretty-boy face had gotten me into more beefs than everything else put together, especially when I was young. Eventually I'd accumulated enough scars and made enough friends to be left alone, but the adolescent joints, Rikers and Spofford, had been rough. I'd also learned to use my looks to good advantage, practicing my innocent choir boy smile until I could melt a rich old lady's heart at fifty paces.

I raised a clenched fist. "One day, Eddie. Pow! Zoom!" It was an ongoing joke between us. Eddie Conte was five inches taller than me and dead game in a fight.

"Right," he answered, "one *day*. Only now it's night, so ya gotta wait. Mario, see if you could get my friend a bowl of minestrone. You drinkin' tanight, cuz?"

"Sure. Coca-Cola."

"And a large Coke, Mario. With a cherry." He turned back to me. "What's doin', cuz. Still adjustin'?"

"Not anymore." He nodded his appreciation. "Too bad about the conditions." He meant the conditions of my parole. "What's it like in the shelter?"

"Actually, it's not too bad. It's in the old Paradise Hotel near the river." I went on to describe Calvin's reception and my response, omitting any reference to the cops.

"Sounds like the joint, cuz."

"Just like the joint," I agreed.

"Here." He stretched across the table and put a small roll of bills in my lap. "Five hundred. For comin' down to talk."

"You don't have to pay me to talk, Eddie. You're disrespecting me here." I started to pass the money back, but he pushed my hand away, then leaned forward and tapped his nose.

"Take it from one friend to another. For what I got planned, cuz, this five hundred ain't toilet paper."

I put the money in my pocket, mostly because I needed it.

"Good. Now I got somebody I want to introduce." He turned to the two women. "Big Momma, could you come over here a minute?"

The woman who rose from the chair furthest away from me was well over six feet tall. Dressed in a light blue sweater and a black skirt that came to the tops of her knees, she projected a demure femininity despite her size.

"Hi, Pete," she said, sitting next to me. Her eyes were sky-blue and lively. "I heard a lot about you. My name's Louise."

"And this here," Eddie announced, "is the woman who waited for me. This here is my wife, Annie."

The woman who sat on his lap and planted a kiss on the top of his rapidly balding head was short and wiry. In her thirties and homely to begin with, she nevertheless held on to Eddie as if she owned him. Grinning an idiot's grin, he nipped at her arm like a playful puppy.

As for me, I was jealous. Eddie Conte was a younger, poorer Joe Terrentini. He had values. Ties to the community. For him, crime was a freely chosen career. For me, it was a sentence. Nevertheless, I managed my sweetest smile, said hello to Louise and Annie, then reminded Eddie that I was supposed to be back in the shelter by ten.

"I know," Louise announced. "Eddie told us about your problem, but we wanted to come down and say hello anyway. Maybe we'll see each other again."

"I already got my fingers crossed," I flashed her my sweetest smile.

Louise returned the smile as she got up and turned to leave. Annie jumped off Eddie's lap and leaned over me as she passed. "Watch this fuckin' guy," she warned, jabbing a thumb in Eddie's direction. "He's dangerous."

Eddie's smile vanished before the door closed. He started to speak, then stopped as Mario reappeared with the soup and my Coke. Eddie looked annoyed for a moment, then asked me what else I wanted to eat.

"The soup'll do, Eddie. I don't have a lot of time."

"Bring us a couple of cold antipastos, Mario. And a garlic bread. Also, bring me another beer." He turned back to me. "Maybe we'll pick a little while we're talkin'. Pickin' helps relax me."

"I could see that, Eddie." I nodded at his waistline. He'd put on a few pounds in the six months he'd been out.

He looked down at the small roll hanging over his belt. Touched it as if surprised to find it there. After Mario left, he started talking. "Yeah, cuz, I'm livin' good. And I like it. You know what's hard about this life? First ya go in the joint, then ya come out. You go in; you come out. Alla time like a fuckin' yo-yo. It don't make sense. I wanna do somethin' that'll settle the shit once and for all. Either way."

The warmth drained from his eyes. They grew sharp and cold, as life defying as ten years of Adirondack winters. I could do the same trick, of course, go from jovial boyishness to cold killer in the blink of an eye. I used to practice the move in the mirror while I was shaving.

Eddie wasn't using it to threaten me, only to drive home the importance of his message.

"Guys like you and me," he continued, "got no chance in the world. It's already over as far as we're concerned. Pete, it was over before we got started. We never had a chance."

I nodded wisely, just as if it wasn't total bullshit. Just as if it wasn't the ultimate disrespect. I *know* that I'm responsible. I'm not a child or a dog. Prisoners love to blame it on the past, on hard lives and bad breaks. But what about all those kids I'd met in the course of an institutional life who'd survived the foster care system? Who'd gone out to live normal lives (relatively normal lives, anyway) in the world? I'd chosen defiance, and even if I was locked into the cops and robbers game, it was my game and nobody forced me to play it. On the other hand, blaming the past is an important part of official prison mythology and ex-cons don't challenge that mythology. Nobody burns the flag on a battlefield.

"You know what I had to face in Cortlandt, cuz? I had to face the fact that all my life I been a complete asshole. The wise guys ain't gonna let me inside where the money is. They was usin' me like a baseball team uses a player off the bench. Put me at short, put me on first, let me pinch hit when there's nobody else left. I'm shovin' that garbage behind me, cuz. What'd I come out, six months ago? I done four jobs for the boys, but only so's I could get the money to set up the job I wanna do." He leaned across the table again, his voice dropping to a prison whisper. "I'm gonna do an armored car. One time, one car, and I'm outta the life forever. You, too, cuz. You, too."

The door opened and Mario walked in with the two antipastos and the garlic bread. Eddie didn't move, even after Mario left. He held me with his eyes and waited for a response.

"You got an inside man, Eddie?" I asked. My voice was calm, but my heart was pounding.

"Nobody."

"Then how will you know what's in the truck? How do you know you won't hijack ten thousand pounds of quarters?"

Armored cars are the favored fantasy of hijackers. After all, they sometimes transport millions of dollars in old, untraceable bills. But they also sometimes carry coins and non-negotiable securities. Or brand-new, consecutively numbered bills, which is the problem with payrolls. Sometimes they're empty because they're on their way to make a pickup. Sometimes they're empty because they've just dropped off a payroll. Schedules are deliberately juggled so that following individual trucks to determine their routes is useless.

The traditional solution, from the hijacker's point of view, is to corrupt someone inside. But the cops are well aware of this and inevitably begin their investigation by asking all employees to take a lie detector test. The inside man is rarely a professional criminal. Faced with ten years in prison, he (or she) jumps at the chance to testify in return for a light sentence.

"Cuz," Eddie said, finally sitting back, "you should just take my word for it. I mean it ain't like I'm an amatcher. This part of it I got covered."

"You're asking me to come in blind, Eddie."

He shook his head. "You don't understand. The job is stone-cold done. I'm only lookin' for one more piece and that's you."

"I don't wanna disrespect you, Eddie, but when you do a job on the street, you gotta take a risk. Even if it's only that the cops'll stumble across you while the job's in progress. You can't control everything."

He shoveled a forkful of the antipasto into his mouth. The hard look was gone now. Eddie's grin was smug and proud, as if he was about to show me pictures of his kids.

"I got an ace in the hole," he said.

"Which you don't trust me enough to talk about, right?"

He looked hurt. "Lemme tell ya somethin', cuz. You ain't the first guy I spoke to about this job. But you're the first one I even told about the armored car. Tell me right now that you want in, I'll pass over every fuckin' detail. But if you decide to stay out, it's better ya shouldn't know."

"What about my end of it? What do you want from me, Eddie?"

"I need you for the job, natrally. And I need you for one other thing. Remember Tony Morasso?"

"He's a fuckin' bug." I lost my composure for the first time. Tony Morasso was a certified psychotic. He never learned the hard, cold stare because he couldn't control the fury that kept him in and out of the psych ward and the box for fifteen years. He was mean and unpredictable, a combination that spelled danger for anyone who came into contact with him. I remembered an incident when Tony went off on another con with a piece of pipe. I remembered his tongue hanging outside his mouth and his eyes rolling in their sockets.

"I need him, cuz. I gotta convince the guard *inside* the car that if he don't open the door, the guys *outside* are gonna die a very unpleasant death. I don't know anybody could do better convincin' than Tony Morasso."

"That's real good, Eddie, but who's gonna convince Tony?"

"Who's gonna convince Tony about what?"

"About getting up in the morning. About eating dinner. About not going off and shooting the guard before the door's opened. About not going off and shooting us. About not freaking out in any one of ten thousand ways. This is a guy, Eddie, who attacked a kitchen worker because the worker put too many peas on his plate. You remember that one?"

"Yeah, I remember."

"So who's gonna control him?"

"You."

NINE

Eddie liked to talk, and once he got going, he was hard to stop. "The big score, cuz. This is it." He repeated the message again and again, scattering it throughout his pitch like a farmer tossing seeds onto a plowed field. "One time and we're done with it forever." But the amount of money he was talking about, three or four hundred thousand per man, wasn't near a life settlement. I'd accumulated that kind of money once or twice in the course of my career. A bad coke habit can eat it up in a couple of years. Just about the time it takes the coke to eat through your nose.

I didn't mention this to Eddie, of course. No, what I did was listen politely, then get depressed as I walked up Ninth Avenue. I'd been at this point time and time again, plotting the perfect job whose only perfection was the speed with which it led to a jail cell. Toward the end of the conversation I'd managed to wrangle one promise out of Eddie Conte. If I decided I wanted to come in, he'd explain the missing details, and if I didn't like the deal, I could still throw in my cards and walk away.

Eddie had no problem explaining the details of my personal role. He wanted to play the leader, the calm, efficient general, always in control of himself and the situation. Unfortunately, Tony Morasso wasn't responding to calm, rational direction. In the best prison tradition, he was asserting dominance over his co-conspirators by threatening them with violence. They were still about two weeks away from doing the job and Eddie was pretty sure that either Tony would go off and hurt one of the boys or that one of the boys would take Mr. Morasso out without benefit of a warning.

"These guys ain't punks, cuz. They're puttin' up with Morasso's shit because the job is good, but how much could they take?"

I was supposed to control Tony, to shepherd him through the job, then kill him when we made the split. "Sooner or later", Eddie'd explained, "this fucker is gonna get popped for goin' off. I don't trust him not to rat us. I also don't trust him not to shoot off his mouth in some bar. He's a weak link, cuz."

As if we were so tough that murder was no more than a business decision.

The city was alive and breathing all around me as I walked back to the Foundation. The whores stood on every corner, whispering their promises. The junkies eyed me through cloudy eyes. Prey or predator? I could see the question flick through their minds. I had fifty dollars in my pocket. The rest was tucked into my underwear behind my balls. It doesn't matter how tough you are. A hundred-pound junkie with terminal AIDS is as big as an elephant if he's holding a gun. Fifty was enough to keep the muggers happy if they decided to move on me.

On the corner of Ninth and 29th I stopped to watch a pimp in an ankle-length fur coat and jet-black shades slap one of his whores around. "Bitch! Bitch! Bitch!" The one word, repeated over and over again, the sum total of all the information he wanted to communicate.

I imagined him on one of the galleries in Cortlandt, pissing his pants as the Squad came to get him. The Squad never walks onto a gallery, even if there's no immediate danger. They run, their boots pounding on the concrete floors. They run to your cell, drag you out, and haul you off to the privacy of the tunnels below the cell blocks. "Piece of shit! Piece of shit! Piece of shit!" Swinging their clubs. Communicating a single message.

As if on cue, two ragged junkies left the shadows of a doorway, threw the pimp up against the side of his Lincoln, and produced badges. Five minutes later two squad cars pulled up, lights flashing. The Lincoln was searched, the pimp arrested, and the whore bundled off to Midtown South where she would probably refuse to sign a complaint.

On impulse, I decided to call Simon Cooper. There are phones on every corner in midtown Manhattan and I only had to walk three blocks to find one that worked. The young man standing next to it, a beeper on his hip and a half dozen gold chains on his neck, shook his head.

"This phone is in use," he announced, not even bothering to take the receiver off the hook. Not even bothering to look at me. The rest of his crew were sitting in a car across the street, watching with blank eyes. When I went into Cortlandt, the kids were still using shanks and Saturday night specials. Now they carried 9mm automatics and M16s. Up on the courts, we used to talk about the new breed. The word on the street was that they were savage beyond anything we had known. They were crude and merciless and rich.

I walked on by and was rewarded for my temperance with a working phone on the next corner. Simon answered on the third ring.

"Simon?"

"Yeah."

"It's Pete Frangello."

"Oh, shit." It was a few minutes after ten and the last thing Simon Cooper wanted to hear was my voice.

"You said I should call you."

"I said you should call me *first*. The only kind of medicine I practice is *preventive* medicine."

"It's hard to talk about this over the phone, Simon. What I'm looking for is a way out. They want me to be a rat and I don't think I can do it."

He took a few seconds to consider it, then sighed into the mouthpiece. "I'm baby-sitting," he said. "My mother-in-law's sick, as usual, and my wife's in Washington. I can't get out of here tonight."

"All right, Simon, maybe I'll see you in the office on Monday."

"Wait a fucking second." He was obviously pissed off. What had he done to deserve me? "Man, my wife'll kill me if she finds out about this. Can you get down to 14th Street? I'm in Stuyvesant Town."

"I don't wanna bother you in your home . . . "

"You didn't mind bothering me to go meet you somewhere. Get your ass over here and let's see if we can work this out."

He gave me the address, then hung up. I grabbed a cab and was standing outside the complex ten minutes later. Stuyvesant Town is a huge, middle-class housing development near the East River. With its own parks and tree-lined paths, it has the feel of an oasis in a desert. A heavy contingent of rent-a-cops keeps it that way. The entrance to Simon's building was across from a deserted children's playground. The wind had picked up a little and one of the swings was creaking softly as it swayed back and forth.

Simon answered the door with a toddler in his arms and a young boy clinging to his leg. He stepped back to let me inside. "The baby's almost asleep. I'm gonna put her in her bed and see if she'll stay there. Find a chair in the living room. I'll be right back."

There was a baseball game on the TV in the living room. I sat down and glanced at it curiously.

"Are you a Mets fan?" the boy asked.

I hadn't seen a baseball game in ten years, didn't know the names of the players or how the team was doing. "Sure," I said agreeably. "What's your name?"

"Junior. Who's your favorite player?"

"All of them."

"Yeah, but which *one*."

"Ya know, kid, your father never lets anyone off the hook, either."

I don't know what he made of that, but he settled back to watch the game. "They're playing the Dodgers. That's why it's starting so late."

I glanced around the room. It was cluttered and messy. Family photos crowded one wall, two framed prints hung side by side on the other. A bowl of popcorn sat on the coffee table in front of the couch. Junior was stuffing his mouth as he watched the game, washing the popcorn down with orange juice. It was a scene out of a sitcom. The middle-class family pursuing its middle-class life. After ten years in prison I found it both exotic and depressing.

"Wake up, Pete." Simon's voice cut through my thoughts. "Junior, you go in my bedroom. Watch the game in there while I talk to Pete."

"Can I take the popcorn with me, Pop?"

Simon nodded wearily. "Just don't spill it, Junior. You spill popcorn on my bed, you're gonna clean it up. I've got enough to do here without pulling out the vacuum cleaner."

He watched his son retreat into the bedroom, then turned back to me. "The kids miss their mom. They get worried when she leaves. Don't wanna go to sleep."

"You blame 'em?"

"I kinda wish they'd trust me a little more. I spend a lot of time with my kids."

"Well, I trust you, Simon. That why I came here."

"You didn't trust me enough to give me a phone call before you went and beat somebody into the hospital. One day after you got out of prison."

"I thought about it for a long time, but I didn't see how you could help me. I thought I could take care of it myself."

"You thought wrong."

I ran it down to him in detail, describing my reception at The Ludlum Foundation, my interview later in the evening, my response the next day, and my conversation with Condon and Rico.

"You should have called me before you did anything."

"And what would you have done? Send me over to another shelter? Don't tell me you would have found me an apartment, because we both know that's bullshit. I had to make myself a place in the Foundation, just like in Cortlandt. How could I know that Calvin was a snitch, that he'd go out an file a fucking complaint? Shit happens, Simon. That's all there is to it."

"I could've put you in a residential treatment program," he said. His voice was filled with contempt.

"An RT? I'm not doing any drugs, Simon. I'm clean."

"So what? At least you would've been safe. You wouldn't have had to near kill someone over who's gonna wash the dishes."

The name, Residential Treatment Program, means exactly what it says. You live in a building with a hundred assorted drug addicts and participate in various work/therapy programs for six months to two years. Some of the programs allow you to leave the residence for a few hours a day. And some of them are as secure as a prison.

"What you're saying is that I should go to jail to avoid going to jail. After ten years in Cortlandt, what you call residential treatment doesn't look so good to me. You wanna see something funny, Simon? Wanna have a good laugh?" I took out my wallet and removed the list of phone numbers I'd been carrying since I left Cortlandt. "Those are the numbers of some of the boys who came out before me. I could've called any one of those numbers and set myself up with an apartment and a job. A lot of jobs, as a matter of fact. There's one guy on that list who offered me a thousand dollars a week to ride shotgun on his coke buys. Plus he'd sell to me wholesale and whatever I made on the side would be mine to keep. He kept telling me I'd be rich in a year. I didn't wanna do that. I wanted out of that life, so I went along with your program. *You* sent me to The Ludlum Foundation."

He sat there for a moment before heaving his bulk out of the chair. "You want a drink, Pete?"

"No, I don't want a drink. I want a way out of this."

He took his time, filling a jigger with scotch, pouring it into a glass, adding ice and a little bit of water. "There's only one answer and it's obvious," he said as he settled down in the chair.

"Don't keep me in suspense."

"Sit it out in Rikers. No jury will convict you for what you did to Calvin. I pulled his sheet and he's got a dozen arrests, mostly for assault and robbery. If he testifies, even a Legal Aid lawyer'll pull him apart. What's he gonna claim, an unprovoked attack? You told me that Calvin was doing heavy cocaine. Talk about unreliable. Pete, when Calvin gets out of the hospital, he'll go right back into the street. No prosecutor's gonna put a strung-out coke junkie on the witness stand. Condon and Rico are bluffing you. What you have to do is call their bluff. Go back to Rikers and sit it out."

"How long would I have to sit there, Simon?" We both knew the answer. "It takes at least six weeks to get a hearing on a parole violation, and the process won't even get started until the assault charge is resolved. There's no bail for a parole violator. No way out before the hearing."

I leaned forward. "What it is," I said, "is that I can't go back inside."

"I don't buy that. It doesn't make sense. The way you handled Calvin proves you're not afraid. You've been doing prison all your life. Six weeks is nothing."

I shrugged my shoulders. "I can't figure it out either. At first I thought I was afraid of the violence, but that's not really it. The only thing I'm sure of is that I can't live that life anymore."

"You know I can't help you with Condon and Rico." He spoke softly, admitting his own impotence. "They called me this afternoon, told me they had an arrest warrant and I should be prepared to violate you. They didn't care about your background, didn't care if you went to jail for child abuse or tax evasion, but when I told them you were in Cortlandt, they got real interested. Then they called back a couple of hours later and told me you decided to cooperate. I think–"

"Don't violate me, Simon." The abrupt change of subject brought him up short. "If you don't violate me, if you talk to the court, I have a shot at a low bail. That's why I came over here. To ask you not to violate me if I turn Condon and Rico down. It's my only chance."

He shifted in the chair, crossed his legs, then uncrossed them. "If I didn't violate you, my supervisor would. It's an automatic when there's an arrest. Even if you made bail before my supervisor found out, Condon and Rico would re-arrest you. I don't know if you plan on running, but if you do, you'd be better off making your move before you get arrested."

"Daddddddyyyyy. Dadddddyyyyyyy."

"That's my little girl," Simon said, as if it was some kind of a mystery. "I'll be there in a minute, honey." He shook his head. "I shouldn't have waited so long to get married and have kids. This shit is too crazy for a man my age."

"Anytime you wanna trade lives, Simon, you just let me know."

It was nearly eleven by the time I got back to The Ludlum Foundation, an hour past the curfew. Sing-Sing was alone at the security desk in the lobby. He smiled as I walked into the building.

"You late, man."

"Is that a problem?"

"Not with me. You wanna do a few lines?" He held up a small vial filled with white powder. "It's bad shit, bro. First cut."

"Look here, man. What I want is to be left alone. You understand what I'm telling you?"

He threw up his hands. "Chill, man. I know you got your own thing happenin'. And I got my thing. We jus' two lonely bidnessmen happen to be stayin' at the same hotel."

I walked up the stairs to find four men in my room. Three of them were roommates, but the fourth was a stranger. He was sitting on my bed, pulling on a quart bottle of Thunderbird. I went off on him without even thinking about it.

"Where the fuck do you think you're sitting?" I slapped the bottle out of his hand and ripped him off the bed.

"I didn't mean nothin', man."

His eyes were filled with terror, but his breath stunk of cheap wine. I sent him flying after the bottle.

"He didn't mean nothin'," Monty said.

"Listen, you alkie bastard, nobody sits on my bed without my permission. And nobody touches my shit." I took out a twenty and laid it on the small table next to my bed. "You see this money? This twenty disappears and I'm comin' to *you* to get it back."

"Oh, shit, don't leave it there, Pete. You leave it there, somebody's gonna take it. Nobody'll sit on your bed. I promise. Never again."

I picked up the twenty and put it back in my pocket. "This bed is mine for as long as I'm staying here. It's my property, my home. You don't enter my home or use my property without permission. I don't wanna hear any bullshit about how you got drunk and forgot. Now it's late and I'm gonna go to sleep. Take the bottle and find someplace else to fry your livers."

They filed out of the room, glad to be rid of me. I closed the door behind them and washed my face in the sink. There was no good reason for me to go off on four hapless juicers. The point could have been made without violence. But I was frustrated and angry and perfectly willing to play by prison rules. If Sing-Sing had challenged me in the lobby, I would have taken it out on him.

TEN

I woke at six, as usual. The sun wouldn't be up for an hour, but enough light filtered in from the street to let me get up and dressed without falling over my roommates. All three were snoring, honking away like cabs in a traffic jam. I washed my face and brushed my teeth without any fear they'd wake up. Lost in their alkie dreams, they would have slept soundly in the gutter if that's where the last drink had taken them.

Clean and dressed, I left them to their stupor and went in search of an empty room. Despite an assortment of aches and pains, I wanted to work out, to feel my body stretch until I had to fight the pain to continue. The Ludlum Foundation was still a foreign place to me. There was probably a day room, maybe even an exercise room, but I didn't know where they were. I went down to the front desk on the first floor and found Sing-Sing manning his post. He looked up at me through bleary eyes.

"No disrespect, but you better get some sleep," I said. "You look like you're goin' down for the last time."

"You right, my man. Ah'm jus' waitin' on someone. Bidness, y'understand what I'm sayin'? Then I'll fall out."

Unless he put a little taste of his business up his nose. "Say, Rakim, you know where there's an empty room I could use?"

"Just the day room. That good for you?"

"Perfect. Where is it?"

"On the third floor. Arnie don't want the boys hangin' out where visitors can see 'em. Look for the door with the bulletin board next to it. The one that advertise all the wonderful programs we got."

I started to turn away, but he called me back. "Sometime it stinks pretty bad in that day room. Before the porters clean it up. Boys like to drink in there and most times they don't make it to the toilet when they got to puke. Specially on Sattiday night. The boys gets lonely on Sattiday night and they drink heavy."

"Where should I go, Rakim?" I knew what he wanted. He wanted me to be friendly. I'd humiliated him and friendship was a way to salvage his ego. There's no logic to it, but it works. I'd been on the other end often enough to know.

"You could use Artie's office. He don't come in on Sundays."

"Thanks, Rakim. You're okay."

"I got to unlock it." He hauled himself out of the chair. "Anybody ask what bidness you got in there, y'all tell 'em to see *me*."

He led me back through the building, unlocked the door, and left without ever asking me why I wanted the room. It was his way of showing me respect, of telling me that we could peacefully co-exist. My acceptance of this small favor implied that he could ask a small favor of me, should he ever need one. It didn't make us brothers, or even co-conspirators, but I wouldn't have to watch my back.

I went down on my face and began to do push-ups—ten sets of thirty. The last set took almost as long as the other nine put together, and by the time I was finished, my arms felt like they were dead. I let them hang for minute, shaking it out, then lay down on my back, hooked my legs underneath Artie's desk, and began my sit-ups. Sit-ups are incredibly boring and counting them only makes the boredom worse. Instead of counting, I make it a matter of honor to keep going until I can't do any more, until my gut begins to throb with pain and my body is covered with sweat.

I took a rest after the sit-ups, five minutes to let my body cool off, then began to shadow box. Before I tore up my right knee in a basketball game ten years ago, I used to run every day to build endurance. Now, even shadow boxing can set it to throbbing, but I've found a trick to help me keep going. I imagine an opponent, usually a hack, at the end of my jabs and hooks. Today, I chose a more immediate adversary. I put Tony Morasso's face out there.

Tony Morasso didn't begin his sentence in Cortlandt. He had to fight and claw his way to the end of the line. His father was an officer in the Teamsters and he got Tony a twenty-two-dollar-an-hour job driving a cement mixer after Tony quit high school. Twenty-two dollars an hour, plus time and a half over thirty-five hours, plus double time on Saturdays and triple time on Sundays.

Tony thought it was paradise. He married an Italian girl from a good family, had three kids in five years, bought himself a TransAm and a house on Staten Island. I know all this because he bragged about it on the courts. Most prisoners are tight-mouthed about their past, especially the crime that put them in the Institution. Not Tony Morasso. He was always willing to talk about the good life and "the niggers and Jews who took my life away from me."

"One day," he told me, "I get to this site on East 78th Street and there's no fuckin' place to park the mixer. The scaffolding is out on one side of the goddamn street and there's a car parked on the other side. Right away I'm thinkin', 'What am I supposed ta do, ride around the fuckin' block like an animal?'

"I leave the mixer in the street and go over to look for the job foreman who's nowhere around. There's five mixers waitin' in line and nobody to pour the concrete. That's how they run these fuckin' sites.

"You could see how I ain't in such a good mood, but there's nothin' I can do. You get too loud with the wrong guy, you end up under the concrete. So I give up and go back and find this cabdriver walkin' around the mixer like he fuckin' owns it. He sees me and right away starts gibberin'.

" 'You must to please move. I have passenger in cab. You cannot block street.' "

"A fuckin' foreign nigger, like from India or some shit. Mouthin' off to me like he was an American.

" 'Back the cab down the street,' I tell him, which is the logical thing ta do, right? But not this asshole. He keeps on with his bullshit. 'You must move truck. You must move truck.' I mean why don't they fuckin' learn to speak English if they wanna come here? It gave me a headache just listenin' to him.

"Meanwhile I tried to do the right thing. I tried to walk away, but the asshole grabbed my arm and I had ta teach him a lesson about American manners. It wasn't much of a beatin', because he didn't fight back and my heart wasn't in it, but he got a pretty deep cut on top of his head when he fell back into the mixer.

"Then the pigs come and like they take *his* side. I mean the whole thing woulda been nothin' if the pigs was white, but, my luck, I get a nigger and a spic. Right away, they start writin' shit down in their little notebooks and I know I'm in fuckin' trouble. 'But officer,' I tell 'em, real polite, 'it was self-defense. He attacked me and I had to do somethin', didn't I?' Which is true, because he put his hands on me. How could I let a fuckin' nigger put his hands on me and not do somethin' about it?

" 'You are under arrest,' the nigger pig says. 'You have the right to remain silent . . . '

" 'Are you fuckin' crazy?' I says.

" 'Don't give us no trouble. Just get in the car.'

"I'm standin' next to the mixer with the door open while this bull-shit is happenin'. Like anybody who's got any fuckin' sense, I had a little somethin' stashed under the seat for emergencies. In my case it was a sawed-off pool cue which I whipped out and landed on the pig's head before he even thought about goin' for his .38. Like one second the nigger's standin' there with the cuffs in his hand and the next second he's lyin' in the street with his head split open. I'm so mad that I'm ready to off the spic, too, but he gets his gun out before I can make a move on him, so we end up facin' off. He ain't gonna shoot me as long as I don't jump and I'm not gonna jump while he's got the fuckin' piece in his hand. Then about a dozen cops pull up and somebody sprays some shit in my face. You wouldn't believe the fuckin' beatin' they gave me when they got me back in the precinct."

Unfortunately for Tony, the sentencing judge was also black, and despite Tony's clean record, gave him eighteen months to think about his attitude. Tony was slated to do his time in a minimum-security institution, but he had problems adjusting to the fact that whites are a minority in the prison system. At that time, all state prisoners were shipped up to H Block in Cortlandt where they were sorted out and sent to various institutions, depending on the length of their sentences and the nature of their crimes. Tony began his incarceration by shanking a black prisoner who tried to take his commissary and by assaulting the two C.O.'s who stepped in to pull him off his victim. The C.O.'s don't really care about prisoners stabbing other prisoners unless the stabbing takes place right in front of them. They shipped Tony to the Albany County Jail to await trial for these new crimes. In the course of that incarceration, he descended into madness.

Experienced cons like myself, who've spent most of their lives in institutions of one kind or another, know that hard time gets harder if you try to fight your way through it. You have to establish yourself, but once you've settled in, it's best to keep as low a profile as possible. Tony had no experience whatever and he reacted to the indignities of prison life by attacking anyone who frightened him. Eventually, a judge (white and Jewish, this time) added eight years to his eighteen months and he was shipped back up to statewide reception in H Block.

By this time Tony had earned himself a reputation. Most of the other prisoners, no matter what their color, shunned him and the fury that surrounded him like a halo. But the system didn't see what was obvious to the prisoners. They sent him off to a medium-security institution where he continued to fight anyone who excited his paranoia. Gradually, they moved him up the ladder—Attica, Comstock, Greenhaven, then Cortlandt, the end of the line.

Most likely, if Eddie Conte hadn't stepped in, Morasso would have spent most of his eight years in the box. Eddie decided that we needed more muscle in our crew and he personally recruited Tony. I was against it at the time.

"Look, Eddie," I told him, "this guy is a loaded gun that pulls its own trigger. If he goes off, we're liable to end up in a war. Who needs that?"

We were on the courts. Morasso was sitting by himself, pulling at a jam jar filled with hooch and eyeing us with suspicion. Eddie took me off to the side and explained the facts of life as he saw them.

"First of all, cuz, this asshole's got *family* on the outside. He gets a money order every month which he don't even know how to spend. That's good for us. Plus, I been thinkin' we're too fuckin' laid back. Sure, Tony's a bug, but we could deal with that. As long as we keep him under control, we could point him wherever we want."

What I wanted was to be left alone, and being part of Eddie's crew was a major step toward achieving that goal. The courts where I hung out belonged to Eddie. I could have walked away, but I didn't see how isolation would improve my situation.

"So tell me how you're gonna control him, Eddie."

"Cuz, it ain't that hard to figure out. I'm gonna keep him stoned until I wanna use him. Plus, I'm gonna educate him about keepin' his big mouth shut."

The drugs and the hooch helped, but the education failed miserably. Morasso still managed to fight his way into the box every couple of months. We'd always lived in peace with the black and Puerto Rican crews—mainly because we weren't competing with them—but Morasso's attitude got us into one beef after another. It finally built up to the point where I lost control of my temper and kicked the crap out of him. It happened out on the courts after he told a Muslim that Jesus liked to fuck Muhammad in the ass. That Muhammad spent his time in heaven bent over and begging for more.

There were over a hundred Black Muslims in Cortlandt at the time and they wanted satisfaction. I gave it to them, though I wasn't thinking about them when I went off on Tony Morasso. I was so mad, I wasn't thinking about much of anything. Eddie tried to get between us, but I tossed him away like he was a sack of potatoes. If I'd had a real weapon instead of a piece of firewood, I think I would have killed Tony Morasso. But I didn't and the best I could do was bust his head open before the boys pulled me off.

Eddie was pissed, but like any other convict, he had to accept the reality of the situation. Eddie needed me (or, so he said) for my brains as much as he needed Morasso for his ferocity. My cause wasn't hurt by the fact that Morasso's beating had worked out well for the whole crew. The Muslims were accepting it as a kind of blood payment for his big mouth. As for me, my only problem was that Tony would probably try to kill me when they took off the casts. Even when Eddie returned from a bedside visit with a promise of no retaliation, I continued to prepare for war.

But Eddie was right on the money this time. Not only didn't Morasso want to kill me, he was actually afraid of me. I understood that fear lay at the bottom of Tony Morasso's violence, but Tony had always expressed his fear by trying to exterminate the supposed source. Now he kept as far away from me as possible, even though he renewed his war on the rest of the prison population. When we were together on the courts, he couldn't even look me in the eye. I could have taken advantage of the situation, but I never tried. I was heavy into school at the time and glad to be left alone.

The truth hit me as I stepped into the shower, the same shower where I'd confronted old Calvin. Eddie Conte had begun planning this job before he left Cortlandt. While the rest of us were cutting up pepperoni for the spaghetti sauce, he was putting the pieces together. Tony Morasso had been one of those pieces, and it was no coincidence that he and Eddie left Cortlandt within a week of each other. I was a piece, too. That's why Eddie had spent hours trying to convince me to call him as soon as I got out. Eddie needed someone to control Morasso and I was the man with the track record.

All my fantasies of a straight life went the way of the water when I turned the shower off. Right down the drain. It just wasn't happening and that was that. I was back to being a criminal and the role felt as comfortable as an old pair of jeans. For the first time, I really felt like I'd gotten out of prison. Even though my head kept telling me that I was turning onto a dead-end street, I was rocked with emotion. Free at last. Free at last. Taking the easy way out. Made even easier by the simple truth that it was the only way out.

ELEVEN

I knew that feeling (that illusion) of freedom would gradually die out, as it always had in the past, but I intended to enjoy it while it lasted. No cuffs, no shackles, no bars, no buzzers, no C.O.'s with their clubs and their attitudes. Only my fear of a new, straight life had kept me from enjoying it up till now, and fear, as we all know, is dishonorable.

I took a taxi up the West Side to Lincoln Center, near Central Park, and found an open coffee shop. It was going to be a beautiful day, warm and clear, especially for April. Central Park (at least the way I remembered it) would be packed—the jugglers and the hustlers would be out, the joggers and the bicycles. Magicians and street singers would perform behind upturned hats while the pockets of affluent, applauding New Yorkers were picked by their less fortunate brethren.

I ordered pancakes and scrambled eggs, home fries with bacon on the side, orange juice and coffee. It wasn't the jazz brunch at Fat Tuesday's, but at least the eggs were fresh instead of powdered. And I didn't have to shuffle along behind the prisoner in front of me, wondering which one of the cooks had spit into the orange juice.

The waitress who took care of me was cute, thirtyish, and exhausted. I flashed her my best smile, willing her to ignore the scars, and shook my head sympathetically. "Long night? Hope you had a good time."

"Yeah? Good time?" she squawked. "I been on since eleven last night. Fucking Greek bastard didn't show up to relieve me and I won't get outta here till four. The next time I see that cocksucker, I'm gonna do Lorena Bobbitt on his dick. What kinda syrup you want on them pancakes?"

It was still early when I walked into the park. The New York I remembered didn't wake up before noon on Sundays and it was barely ten o'clock when I strolled past the big statue at Columbus Circle and headed north along the road that circles the park. There were a few runners out, wearing their smartest outfits, the men bare chested despite the morning chill. The women were encased in shiny tights made from a fabric I'd never seen before and which I later found out was called Spandex. It looked like rubber.

Up near 72nd Street, I saw single-blade roller skates for the first time. Someone had set up a row of small traffic cones and the skaters were running them like a slalom, crisscrossing their skates as they went. The youngest, a girl, looked to be about ten. She flew through the course like the tiny pro she was. The oldest, on the other hand, a middle-aged man with feathery white hair, locked his skates and went over, skidding twenty feet on elbow and knee pads. The other skaters held back their smiles and helped him to his feet.

"Don't worry, pops. You'll get it next time."

Pops didn't look too enthusiastic about "next time," but when a young lady in green and blue tights sat down next to him, his demeanor brightened considerably.

"Did you cut yourself, honey?"

Honey? Now where can I get me a pair of roller skates?

In spring, a young man's fancy turns to thoughts of . . . Especially if the young man's fancy has been honed on ten years of springtimes passed in the company of convicts. The rumor in the joint was that good girls weren't promiscuous anymore. Women ready to jump into bed with the most attractive male body available were as likely to be HIV positive as not.

Maybe that's why my best Tom Cruise smile got me nowhere. I did manage to have a brief conversation with one woman, a blonde wearing blue shorts, a white halter, and no wedding ring. She had her son with her, a rambunctious three-year-old who zipped from place to place while she followed dutifully behind. When the kid ran over to the water fountain, I scooped him up and held his lips to the stream of water.

"Looks like a handful," I said to his mom.

She smiled and tossed her head, sending her blond hair flying. "According to the books, they're supposed to become more cooperative by the time they're three and a half. Joey has a one-word vocabulary."

The kid looked up at me and shouted, "No!" at the top of his lungs, then shrieked with laughter.

"I see what you mean."

Joey, by way of an encore, spit a stream of water onto my shirt. Instead of squeezing his little chest until his tongue popped, I set him down.

"I told you not to spit water on people." She gave him a gentle shake, too gentle to discourage him, then turned to me. "Did he get you wet?"

"No big deal." I peeled out of the shirt, exposing the calculated result of all those calisthenics. "I could use a little sun. It's been a long winter."

When she ran her eyes over my chest and belly, hope, as they say, sprang eternal.

"It *has* been a long winter, hasn't it?"

The boyfriend came strolling along the path just as I was about to ask her name. When he saw the two of us together, he picked up the pace.

"Jo-Ann," he called, still twenty feet away.

"Hi, Marty," she trilled, enjoying the drama for a moment before dismissing me. "Well, I gotta go."

Marty threw me the darkest look in his white-collar repertoire, then walked off with his property. I stood and watched for a moment, feeling utterly stupid in my bare skin. For no good reason, I began to think about Eddie Conte. If Eddie had recruited Tony Morasso while they were both inside, if he'd spent hours trying to convince me to call him when I came out, who else had he talked to?

I stopped at a hot dog stand and bought a couple of dirty-water dogs and an orange soda.

"How much?" I asked.

The vendor looked at me like I was crazy. "Three dollar twenty-five," he announced, pointing at the sign on his wagon.

I took my lunch to the top of one of the boulders that dot the park and settled down to enjoy my meal. Halfway through the first hot dog, two Spanish kids showed up, lugging the obligatory boom box. They looked at me, claiming the boulder for their own, and I looked back at them. Nobody said anything for a minute, then they turned and strutted down the path. I finished my hot dogs and my soda as a matter of principle, but I wasn't stupid enough to wait around until they came back with the rest of their crew.

Up at the bandshell on the east side of the park, a salsa band shot waves of frenetic Latin jazz at a large, receptive audience. I stopped to watch the young Spanish girls dance and eventually fell into a dreamless sleep.

When I woke up, it was late afternoon and the park was beginning to empty. I wandered back to the West Side, found a movie theater on Broadway, and spent the next few hours watching a movie called *True Lies*. Luxuriating in the mindless violence and the equally mindless sex, I shoveled Goobers into my mouth while bodies flew to pieces on the screen. They show films in Cortlandt, usually in the mess hall. Prisoners file in and file out. They sit on hard benches and watch their backs as carefully as they watch the screen. A long way from the upholstered seat where I sat and the empty spaces around me. On the other hand, Cortlandt movies are free and this one had cost me seven bucks.

I went from the movie theater to a Mexican restaurant on Columbus Avenue. The Upper West Side of Manhattan was just making the turn from heroin heaven to upscale pretentious when I went into Cortlandt. It'd been dotted with small dark bars, welfare hotels, and greasy diners. Now both sides were lined with expensive restaurants and young white faces.

It was ten o'clock by the time I finished dinner and headed back to The Ludlum Foundation. Time to face the music. It was a coin toss as to whether Rico and Condon would be waiting for me inside the shelter or out on the street. I should have called them after I spoke to Eddie—that's what they expected—but I wanted to establish a little distance, a little independence. There was every reason to believe that I'd need it sometime in the future.

I let the cab drop me at 39th and Seventh and walked the rest of the way. No sense letting the boys know I had money. No sense letting them know *anything* they didn't have to know.

"Frangello! Get ova here!"

I found them across the street from the shelter, sitting in a black Plymouth sedan that screamed COP at every mutt on the street.

"Whatta ya say, Rico? I was just gonna call you."

"Get in the fuckin' car."

"What's the matter? You lonely?"

Despite my attitude, I was shaking inside. I was still sore from yesterday's beating, and the morning's workout wasn't helping the situation.

Nevertheless, I had my part to play in the grand drama. I got into the car and Rico shoved in after me, pushing me against the far door.

"You askin' for a beatin'?" he demanded. "You askin' for it?"

"Ease off, Rico," Condon said wearily.

"This guy only understands one thing," Rico insisted. "He's a smart-ass and if we don't shut his mouth right now, he's gonna fuck us in the end."

Rico was smarter than he looked.

"I think there's something you should know," I said quietly.

"Now he's gonna make another smart remark."

I looked down at my hands for a minute, then let my eyes jump into his. "I'm not goin' down without a fight. You put your hands on me again and I'll tear your skinny ass to pieces. You wanna shoot me, go ahead, because that's the only way you'll stop me. You understand that, you guinea bastard?"

Anybody can run his mouth, and cops are used to calling bad bluffs. A lot of cons think cops are yellow, but the truth is that in a violent situation the cops do just what the cons would do—they try to bring overwhelming force to bear on their enemies.

Rico stared at me for a moment, trying to gauge my resolve. I stared back at him, a relaxed smile on my lips. Letting him know that I *did* mean it. I was drawing a line and telling Rico and Condon that if they crossed it, all bets were off. If they chose to stay on their side, I'd have that independence I mentioned.

"Cool out, both of you." Condon to the rescue.

"You tellin' me I should let this mutt get away with that?" Rico was so mad his acne scars glowed red. They made little semicircles along the edge of his jaw.

"Get away with what? You been puttin' the muscle on him since he walked up the street. We told him he had to call us at ten-thirty every night. It's ten-twenty. Maybe he shoulda called us earlier instead of fuckin' around all day, but we didn't *tell* him to call so we'll just have to chalk it up to experience. Meanwhile, let's not cop any attitudes. We're all doin' our jobs here."

At least I'd convinced *someone*. Condon didn't give two shits about me, but he knew that if he gave in to his cop macho, he'd blow his big bust. It took Rico a little longer to figure it out, but I guess he finally got it too, because he dropped his hands to his lap and turned away from me.

"Your meeting with Conte go all right?" Condon asked.

"Yeah, it went fine." I'd accomplished what I wanted to do. There was no profit to be made by antagonizing Rico any further. "Eddie's gonna do a bank and he wants me to go along. He's gonna go into the home of the branch manager and hold the slob's wife and kids until after the job's done. Two of us stay with the family, the other three arrive in the morning with the manager before the bank opens. We clean the vault, then lock up the manager and the tellers. Once we're out of the bank, we let the family go. Then the wife calls the cops and the cops open the vault. Nobody gets hurt."

"Unless somebody resists," Rico growled.

"Look, Rico, it wasn't my idea. You're the ones sending me in there. Besides, you're gonna take care of business before the shit goes down. Which means there's nothing to worry about, right?"

"What's the name of the bank?" Condon, representing the practical half of the dynamic duo, cut to the heart of the matter.

"I don't know."

"When's it goin' off?"

"Not for a few weeks. I don't know the exact date."

"Who else is involved?"

"I don't know that either."

"What's the name of the bank manager?"

"I don't know."

Rico couldn't stand it anymore. "You tellin' me you went in a job without knowin' what's it about?"

"I didn't go in on the job. I told Eddie I'd think about it and he told me that I'd learn the details after I made up my mind."

A moment of silence while the boys digested the information. "You want out?" Condon asked. Rico was already going for the cuffs.

"I jailed with Eddie for eight years. He's paranoid. The more eager I come off, the less he'll trust me. If I'm gonna work with you and your partner, I'm gonna need room to maneuver. I'm much more likely to get that room if I don't suck up to him like a puppy at its mother's tit."

It made perfect sense. It was just what I'd done with *them*.

"When're ya gonna make up your mind?"

"Today's Sunday. I told Eddie Wednesday, but I'm gonna call him tomorrow night and set up a meeting. I'm gonna tell him that if the job's right, I want a piece of it. That way he'll have to give me the details on the spot."

They stared at each other for a minute, not liking what they heard.

"Look," I said, "the deal's not goin' off for a few weeks, so what's the rush?"

"I want you to call me every night," Condon said. "You understand? Every fucking night. If you move outta this shelter without tellin' me first, I'll put a warrant out the next day."

"We should take him down and book him," Rico insisted. "We shoulda done it yesterday. Let him spend a night in Central Booking."

"Wednesday." Condon's tone left no doubt about who the senior partner was. "You got until Wednesday. After that, you don't come up with something besides bullshit, you're goin' over to Rikers. Now get the fuck outta here."

"Jeez," I said, opening the door, "I thought you were the *good* cop."

"You could be a smart mouth all you want, Frangello, but the fact is that we *own* your ass."

I stepped out of the car and gently closed the door. Rico, unable to contain himself, slid over and called to me through the window.

"Why don't ya tell us what ya plan to do until Wednesday?" he asked.

"What I plan to do," I said, "is enjoy my freedom."

TWELVE

Despite what I told Rico and Condon, I spent the next day working. I had to invent a kidnap/bank robbery convincing enough to fool two veteran New York cops. Cops are dumb, but they're not stupid. Just like the robbers, they don't believe in trust. They assume that everyone lies to them, sometimes for no reason at all. Which is why I took the subway down to Battery Park and the ferry out to Staten Island on Monday morning.

I needed a large bank with a branch manager (or a small bank with a vice president) who lived in a private home, not an apartment. It's much harder to get into an apartment than a private home, and the whole trick in a kidnap/bank robbery is to get inside without being seen by a nosy neighbor. The Borough of Staten Island, though technically part of New York City, has always been considered foreign territory, the place where civil servants go to die. Except for a small section near the ferry, the island is covered with single-family homes.

It could have gone badly. Lacking a driver's license, I had no access to a rental car, which limited the number of banks I could visit. Still, I plodded along, riding the buses down Hylan Boulevard, stopping each time I saw a bank. My plan was simple enough. I'd go up to a teller and exchange a twenty for two rolls of quarters while I noted the name of a branch manager or a vice president. At the next bank, I'd change the quarters back into a twenty.

By two o'clock, an hour before the banks closed for the day, I had a list of ten names. Time to make a decision. I found a Staten Island telephone book in a small coffee shop on Guyon Avenue and began to run through the names on my list. The first four either lived somewhere else, had unlisted numbers, or names so common I found multiple listings. But the fifth came up roses. There was only one Daniel Jashyn in the phone book. His address—1915 Buttonwood Road—was a few miles from where I stood. Two hours later, when he arrived at his Todt Hill home, I was waiting. I watched him greet his wife and daughter, noted the high fence surrounding his home, the sliding glass doors on his patio.

The setup was perfect. As vice president of the tiny Grant City Savings Bank, Daniel Jashyn would know exactly when the vaults opened, exactly what they contained. His relatively isolated home would be easy to penetrate, while his young daughter—she couldn't have been more than ten years old—would make the perfect hostage.

An hour later I was standing on the corner of Broadway and State Street in lower Manhattan, watching a river of human beings pour out of the office buildings and into the subways. It was raining pretty hard and I had my new umbrella up. Apparently the office workers, seduced by the perfect weekend, had forgotten to take their rain gear. They were trying to run, but there were so many of them, they jammed up at the subway entrances. By the time they got down in the hole, they were soaked to the skin.

I found a phone and called Eddie. I told him I was ready to go and we agreed to meet at Mario's.

"I'm glad you decided to come in with us, cuz," he announced. "Because I need ya."

"We shake hands after I hear the details. If it doesn't sound right, you can forget about me. I just finished ten years in Cortlandt and I'm not jumpin' over any cliffs."

"After I lay it out, you won't have no doubts. You'll be countin' money in your dreams."

There was no sense in pursuing it. "Look," I said, "I can get up to Mario's in about a half hour. I'm downtown. Is a half hour too soon for you?"

He must have wondered what I was doing downtown in the rain, but he didn't disrespect me by asking questions. "I'm out in Queens, cuz. I don't know if I can make it that fast. What I'll do is call Mario and tell him you're comin'. If you get there first, have a beer on me."

"No problem, Eddie. I'll see you when later. And, by the way, give my regards to John Parker."

It caught him off-guard. "You was always a smart guy, cuz. You was always the smartest."

Too smart. He didn't say it, but his tone made it clear. Maybe annoying him wouldn't pay off in the short run, but I had to establish the same independence with Eddie that I was trying to establish with Condon and Rico. There would come a time when I'd need room to maneuver and I wouldn't get it if I began by playing the part of the obedient soldier.

"I'll see you in a little while, Eddie."

I didn't destroy my mood by trying to find a cab in the rain. That pass was too difficult, even for a high roller like me. I went down in the subway with the rest of the schmucks, breathing in the anger of the soaked commuters along with the stink of wet wool. Fifteen minutes later I got off at Penn Station.

Eddie must have put some punch into his phone call, because Mario greeted me like I was his brother come back from the war. He pumped my hand, stared into my eyes, led me through a mostly empty restaurant to a completely empty private room. This time there was only one table.

"Can I get you a drink?"

I ordered a Heineken, drank it while I thought about John Parker. I didn't dwell on the fact that it was the first drug I'd put into my system since that night with Terrentini. I didn't want to think about Terrentini at all.

Making John Parker for one of Conte's crew was proof that I was dealing with my problems in a constructive manner. Parker was not a criminal. He was a poor schmuck of a computer scientist who'd caught his wife in bed with another man and responded by hitting the man twenty or thirty times with a table lamp. His wife, or so he told me, had been next in line, but she'd deserted her lover and run naked down the road, screaming at the top of her lungs.

The gung-ho assistant district attorney assigned to the case had wanted to go for murder by depraved indifference, but the D.A. was afraid the jury would come back with a medal instead of a conviction. Mild-mannered John Parker looked too much like a victim. He was tall and skinny, with a bobbing Adam's apple and a permanent hang-dog expression. You looked at him and you wanted to mug him. The District Attorney told his A.D.A. to find a plea that Parker and his lawyer would accept, and all had eventually settled on second-degree manslaughter with a five-year max.

The sentencing judge took one look at pitiful John Parker and directed the Department of Corrections to place him in protective custody, which at that time meant H Block in Cortlandt. Parker didn't care for the company in H Block. His fellow inmates were mostly snitches and homosexuals with a few high-profile killers like David Berkowitz thrown in for seasoning. After a few months, Parker formally requested a transfer to population, but the administration, instead of shipping him out to a medium-security institution (which is where he would have gone if he'd never been put into protective custody in the first place), walked him across the yard to B Block.

John Parker would not have survived if it hadn't been for Eddie Conte. Parker entered B Block dead broke, wearing that same "hurt me" expression on his face. It was only a matter of time (and not *much* time) until someone discovered that he couldn't fight back and transformed him into a permanent victim.

Eddie not only protected John Parker, he took Parker up to the courts and made him part of our crew, which meant that we were obliged to protect him, too. Eddie also toughened Parker up, patiently explaining the realities of survival in the institution. He introduced Parker to the weight box, taught him how to make and carry a shank, recited the prisoner's code: Death Before Dishonor, What Doesn't Kill Me Makes Me Stronger, Don't Trust Anyone.

The softer virtues, the *feminine* virtues, are almost unknown in the Institution. Pity? Compassion? Mercy? These are signs of weakness and weakness is a crime punishable by shankings and beatings and extortion and rape. So why did Eddie Conte save John Parker?

I don't remember spending much time thinking about it. Unlike Tony Morasso, Parker was no threat to our crew. As he toughened, he began to show a talent for jailing. He had an infinite supply of jokes and an equally infinite hatred for the Institution. He willingly participated in whatever scam we happened to be running and he refused to back down when challenged. He became, all in all, a model prisoner.

I took a basic computer course while I was getting my degree in Cortlandt and John Parker had helped me with the homework. He loved computers. If they'd given him a computer while he was in protective custody, he would have done the whole five years without leaving his cell. That was why Eddie had recruited him in the first place. What I had taken for a moment of weakness had been cold calculation.

As I already said, Eddie's big job, like all armored car robberies, had one gigantic flaw. He had to know where the car would be and what it would carry. The penalty for heisting an armored car, especially considering Eddie's prior record, would be severe, twenty or thirty years, even if the car turned out to be empty. But Eddie had assured me that he'd already solved that problem and his air of confidence had left no room for doubt. He was much too sharp to have settled for some half-assed scheme.

Eddie Conte was going to get his information from the horse's mouth. He was going to use John Parker to break into the company computer. I didn't know how Parker would do it, because Parker had always insisted that without inside knowledge, it's virtually impossible to get access to computer information, despite the prevailing myth that any fifteen-year-old with an IBM can steal all the secrets in the Pentagon. But he *would* do it. Eddie was nobody's fool, and if he hadn't believed that Parker would come through, he would have tossed him back to the wolves.

THIRTEEN

Eddie must have lost his resentment somewhere on the Long Island Expressway. He greeted me with a smile, shaking his head affectionately.

"Ya some piece of work, cuz. Some piece of work. How'd you figure it out?"

I searched his face carefully, looking for any trace of anger, but his eyes were twinkling. He seemed as happy as a pedophile in an orphanage.

"I always wondered about Tony Morasso," I explained. "Why would you bring an M.O. onto the courts? That wasn't your style, Eddie. You were always low profile, a smart con. For a while, after Morasso showed up, I lost confidence in you altogether."

"But you stayed. Why? Seein' as how you didn't trust me?"

"Because they were *my* courts, too. I wasn't gonna let you chase me off."

"Don't get hot, cuz." He put his hands out in mock defense. "You always had a short fuse."

He was laughing now and like good leaders everywhere, his mood was infectious. I dropped the question of who owned the courts and began to recite my lessons.

"When you told me that Tony Morasso was in on this job and what you needed him for, it all came clear. While the rest of us were putting away mugs of prison rotgut, you were putting this heist together. You were one step ahead of us. As usual."

He leaned forward and took a modest bow. "What'd I always say? There's easy time and hard time. You wanna do easy time, you gotta plan things out."

I nodded agreement. "So, the question I asked myself, last night before I went to sleep, was why did you bring John Parker onto the courts? He had nothing to offer. Were you doing the Mother Teresa bit? That wasn't like you, but at least Parker wouldn't start any wars, so I forgot about it. Now Parker makes sense. He found an untraceable way to get the information you need to do this job. The cops'll investigate every company employee, looking for the leak. It'll be months before they figure it out, if they *ever* figure it out."

After a polite knock, Mario appeared in the doorway with a plate of stuffed mushrooms and a bottle of red wine. He filled two glasses, dropped a couple of plates in front of us, then backed out.

"Mario treats you like you're the Godfather."

Eddie shrugged it away. "I helped him out with a shylock once and natrally he's grateful. So what else did you figure out?"

"I don't think there's anything else to figure. Two guards outside the truck and one inside . . . the three of us should be able to handle it."

He shoveled a forkful of mushroom into his mouth and chewed it slowly and thoroughly, washing it down with half a glass of wine. "You told me you wouldn't come in until ya heard the details, but it seems like you know the details already." A trace of annoyance slipped back into his speech, but I didn't respond and he kept going. "So tell me what ya think, cuz. We gonna make it?"

"If you know where the truck'll be and what's inside it, the only way it goes bad is if the cops happen to show up while we're doin' the job. But you still haven't told me where and when."

"The when is April 30. The where I couldn't tell you because the schedules for that week haven't been made up yet."

"Why April 30?"

"I take it you ain't partial to religion." He was teasing me.

"C'mon, Eddie. Don't string it out."

"No room for style, cuz? I'm tryin' to put a little drama into my pitch. I mean, seein' as how you figured everything out already, you gotta let me play with the few surprises I got left."

He was rebuking me. It was gentle, but unmistakably there. Just as I had placed limits on my own personal level of submission, he was reminding me that he was the boss.

"You got a pretty good temper, yourself," I said, smiling. "I'm not trying to take your play away, but if you want someone who can't think for himself, you should find another boy. There's fifty guys out there who'd spread their cheeks for a score like this."

He mulled it over for a moment. "No, that ain't what I want. I gotta have one guy who's smart enough to keep his head if we run into problems. Morasso's already causin' trouble. You're gonna have to be a fuckin' psychiatrist to keep him in line until we finish this."

"What kind of trouble, Eddie?" As if I couldn't guess.

He put down the fork and shook his head. "He's makin' Parker for soft. Thinks he can break Parker's balls and get away with it. The problem is that Parker's not gonna take it much longer and he's not stupid enough to fight Tony with his hands. You could figure the rest out for yourself."

"Tony's a complete asshole. You knew that when you brought him in."

"What could I say, cuz? Maybe if I could do it over again, I'd do it different."

It was an amazing thing to admit, but I wasn't sure whether his confidence in me was genuine or just part of the hustle. Maybe he was catching flies with honey. Eddie, though he didn't say it, couldn't very well dump Morasso at this stage of the game. He'd have to kill Tony and that would lead to the kind of complications that blow jobs apart.

"I take it you got the two of 'em holed up in some apartment," I said. "Nice and cozy."

"You figure correct. I was afraid to let Tony out of my sight, but I couldn't put him under my thumb unless I made it the rule for *everybody*. Which is what I did. We're all stayin' together until the job is done."

"Except me, Eddie." I repeated it in case he missed the central message. "Except me."

"No exceptions." He forked half a mushroom into his mouth.

"I already explained my situation. If I'm not back in that shelter every night, my P.O.'s gonna put out a warrant. What if Tony blows before the job comes off? What if Parker has a heart attack and can't push the keys on his computer? What if you get hit by a truck? What if *any* fucking thing goes wrong? You could always walk away and start over, but my ass would be up in Cortlandt."

"You got a point," he admitted. "Lemme think about it. Where the fuck is Mario with the dinner?"

"Forget the goddamn dinner."

He looked hurt. "I been eatin' Annie's cookin' for the last month. With Tony Morasso for company. Gimme a break, already."

As if on cue, Mario knocked softly, then led a waiter into the room.

He served us personally, sighing over the platter of meat and the bowls of rigatoni. I had less than no interest in the food. Maybe I have an Italian name, but the only culture I absorbed in my youth was criminal culture.

Eddie cut a piece of meat and swirled it in the sauce while Mario waited like a child with a good report card. "Outta sight, cuz," Eddie said. "As usual."

"Thank you. Thank you." Mario left in triumph, taking the waiter with him.

"You think you could handle Tony?" Eddie spoke as soon as the door closed. His voice was sharp, his interest plain. He needed me badly and he'd make whatever compromises were necessary to bring the job off.

"Not forever, Eddie. But we're only talkin' about a couple of weeks. I've been thinking about how to control Tony since you mentioned his name. The way I see it, I can make Tony understand that if he wants to fuck with Parker, he has to take me out first. That way I become the target. Don't forget, Tony's *already* afraid of me. Like I said, we're only talkin' about a couple of weeks. If you think about it from that angle, it doesn't hurt us if I go back to the shelter every night. The fact that I'm getting a special deal will make him hate me all the more. It'll eat him up. And it'll take his mind off Parker."

"And you don't mind whackin' him when the job's done?"

I'd never killed anyone and had no desire to kill anyone. And the simple fact that I might be able to kill in a moment of anger didn't mean I could perform an execution. But that's not something you can admit in the Institution. The myth is that every con is a merciless killer with all the conscience of a cat digesting a canary.

"Well, don't worry about it, cuz," Eddie continued before I could respond with the obligatory display of prison macho. "I decided to hit the cocksucker myself. And I'm gonna make sure he's lookin' at me when I do him. I want him to see the shit coming."

I burst out laughing and, after a moment, Eddie laughed with me. "Morasso must be giving you a very hard time," I said. I didn't add *and you're afraid of him, too*, but I filed the information away for later use. "By the way, I have a little room at the shelter. They're using residents on the security desk. I could be a little late gettin' back without causing problems. Might even be able to spend a night out, somewhere down the line."

He nodded and went back to the food, shoveling it into his mouth and smacking his lips in appreciation. "We're stayin' in Queens, cuz. Got an apartment in Woodside. My old lady's stayin' with us."

That admission was the last piece of the puzzle. The thought of Tony Morasso alone with his wife must have been driving Eddie crazy.

"So how come April 30?" I asked.

"The Pope's comin'."

"You gettin blessed, Eddie? You gonna buy a fuckin' rosary?"

He took a yellow piece of newspaper from his shirt pocket and passed it to me with the solemnity of a priest distributing communion. It contained an article someone had cut out of the newspaper several years ago. The article was undated, but the paper was yellow with age. It was about the security measures taken to protect the Pope on what I assumed was a prior visit to New York. According to the article, the Pope's security had required the use of 15,500 cops, more than half the force.

"What'd you tell me a minute ago?" Eddie asked. "Didn't ya say our only problem was if the cops happen to come on us while we're doin' the job? You was right, cuz, but that don't mean we couldn't reduce the odds."

I handed the newspaper back to him. "Nice touch, Eddie. Very nice. It's like taking advantage of the terrain in a war. You don't have to do anything. It's already there."

"True. We don't gotta do shit to make the Pope work for us. He's comin' and we're gonna take advantage. But there's still a *chance* we'll get caught in the act. Even a small chance is still a chance."

He leaned forward, staring at me through cold eyes. It was time for the kicker he'd been holding in reserve. "This is my *last* job, cuz. One way or the other. And I don't wanna have to consult a gypsy before I do it. I got somethin' I want ya to hear. Listen close." He took a small tape recorder out of his jacket pocket and flipped it on. A series of sharp beeps sounded, followed by a voice.

> *All available units. Ten-thirteen in progress. Officer down.*
> *Shots fired. Eleven Forty-three Union Turnpike in front of*
> *the Burger King. All units, k.*

"That's the dispatcher," Eddie said. "The rest of it's the cops responding."

Fifteen Charlie, going.
Fifteen Bravo, going.
C-POP, going.
Crime One, going.
Crime Two, going.
Fifteen Sergeant, going.
Fifteen George, going.
Second Sergeant, going.

The tape became a blur of overlapping voices. Not that it mattered. I stopped listening as soon as I got the point of the exercise. Eddie continued to stare at me and I had a sudden flash that if I pulled out now, there was the distinct possibility that my life would end sometime in the next two weeks.

"You ain't talkin', cuz." Eddie rewound the tape without taking his eyes off me.

"You've a got a way with surprises, Eddie. I'll give you that. Never know what you're gonna do next."

"I know what you're thinkin'. I'm readin' ya mind. You're thinkin' about how much time you could do for killin' a cop. You're thinkin' how you'd be lucky to get out in forty years. Me, I'm forty-one. That would make me eighty-one before they opened the gate. But I got three felonies on my record, cuz. Three. If I go down for this job, I'll do twenty without the cop. That'd make me a sixty-one-year-old con with lifetime parole. No job, no education, no money. I'd rather stay in prison."

He paused, waiting for a response, but I just shrugged my shoulders. "The point is not to get caught," he continued. "I got new i.d.'s for all of us. The best, cuz. Passport, social security card, driver's license. Yours'll be made as soon as you say you're comin' in with us. After the job is done, we're gone. The cop I got in mind is guardin' a witness on the other side of the precinct from where we're doin the job."

"Wait a second, Eddie. You told me you didn't know where the job was going down."

He wasn't happy to be interrupted, but he couldn't very well dispute my right to ask the question. He took a deep breath and let his eyes drift away from me.

"I got a target, but it's only *probable*." He leaned forward, jabbed his fork in my direction. "For the last month there's been a truck that makes pickups at department stores. They do Alexander's, A & S and Macy's on Queens Boulevard, then three Waldbaum's supermarkets, then Stern's in Bayside. I haven't been sittin' on my ass, waitin' for April 30. That's not my way of doin' things. I study, cuz. I study all the fuckin' time. Like you used to put your face in those books when you was gettin' your school? That's the way I been with those schedules."

"I believe you, Eddie. There's no other way to do it, if you wanna do it right. But why the cop? What's the point of doin' the cop?"

"You worried about a pig, cuz?"

Of course, I *couldn't* be worried about a "pig." I might be worried about the consequences, but not about the human being wearing the uniform. "It's too much, Eddie. You wanna control everything and you can't do it. Maybe the armored car'll break down before it gets to us. Maybe we should have a tow truck ready, just in case."

"It ain't that simple. This Stern's I got in mind is set in a little valley. The loading docks are behind the store, and the only customers who go back there are pickin' up shit too big to come through the front doors. There's a steep hill back there, too. *Very* steep. That fuckin' dock is completely hidden from the street unless you walk right to the edge of the hill, which is I what I been doin' every Saturday for the last month.

"The first time I was there, I thought the setup was a gift from fuckin' God. The truck pulls up, the guards come out and go inside the store. They don't even have their weapons drawn. Twenty minutes later, they come out with two canvas bags and their .357s in their hands. They walk back to the truck and signal the guard inside, who opens the door and takes the bags.

"What could be better? We'll know the schedule exactly. Twenty minutes before they pull up, we walk back to the loading dock like ordinary customers and persuade the two assholes workin' the platform to wait in the closet while we're doin' the job. Then we take the two guards *before* they go into the store, when they're walkin' around with their dicks in their hands."

"Back up a second, Eddie. You know for a fact there's only two workers on the loading docks?"

"Two workers, cuz. Except when they take a delivery. When the big trailers drive up, they pull a few boys out of the stockroom to unload. But they don't get deliveries on Saturday afternoon, *capisch?*"

I looked down at my plate, found it as clean as it had been when Mario laid it in front of me. "There's a problem somewhere," I finally said. "It's like getting hustled. When it sounds too good to be true, it usually is."

"Smart, cuz. Very smart. The bullshit here is that two out of the four times I been there, a fuckin' cruiser came by while the truck was pickin' up the money. Bayside's a low-crime neighborhood and I guess the pigs ain't got much else to do. Well I'm gonna give 'em somethin' real intrestin' to occupy their time."

"Why not go somewhere else? Find another target?"

"Couple of reasons. First, it ain't that easy to get into a computer. I thought all Parker had to do was press a few buttons and we'd know what kind of toilet paper they used to wipe their assholes, but it turned out to be a bitch, so we're stuck with this company. Now I been through *all* the schedules and this route gives the most bucks with the least risk. In fact, what I think is that, if we take the pigs outta the picture, we don't run no risk at all. There's a school up on a hill two blocks from where that cop is sittin'. You got a clear view from the roof. I been up there and I know. Figure it like this, cuz. Half the fuckin' cops are out protectin' the Pope and the rest of 'em are pickin' up the pieces of a dead pig. We're lookin' at three quarters of a million bucks. Maybe more. We're talkin' about two days' receipts from Macy's, A & S, Alexander's. We're talkin' about a *minimum* of three supermarkets. We're talkin' about gettin' rich and gettin' the fuck out."

I wanted to ask him why he had to kill the cop. Why couldn't he fire a few shots through the cop's rear window? Or blow out the tires? But I could see that his mind was set and I knew I couldn't refuse. I could accept the deal and then take off the minute I was alone, but I couldn't turn it down outright.

"It works," I admitted.

"Ya fuckin' right it works. Every inch of it."

"But I gotta say I hope you're not thinkin' of me to pull the trigger on the cop, because I couldn't hit an elephant with a shotgun if I was six feet away." This was a complete lie, but there was no way for Eddie to know it. Actually, I was a pretty fair shot with a handgun.

"Your primary job is to handle Morasso. I got someone else for the pig. An old friend of yours. Avi Stern."

"Avi Stern? It's startin' to sound like a high school reunion." Avi

and I had done a number of jobs together before I went up to Cort-
landt, then met again inside. He was the quietest man I'd ever known.
Quiet and steady. There'd been any number of jokes about the "silent
Jew," but none had drawn more than a cold smile from Avi Stern.

"You know that Avi grew up in Israel, right?"

"Sure."

"Did ya know he was in a special unit?"

"No, he never talked about it."

"The fucker never talks about anything, cuz. Except last night when
he told me if I didn't do something about Morasso, I was gonna wake
up with Tony's body in my bathtub."

"He means it, Eddie."

"This I already figured out. Anyway, Stern was in some kind of
antiterrorist unit in Israel. It had a Jew name that sounds like you got
dog food stuck in your throat and you're tryin' to cough it up. I could-
n't say that word if my life depended on it, but one of things they
taught him was how to kill from a distance."

"Sounds like they taught him to *be* a terrorist. How'd you find out
about this? How'd you get Avi to talk about his past?"

"Ya know how Avi didn't do drugs, didn't drink? Well, one day I
conned him into takin' some speed. That was the hard part, gettin'
him to drop that dexie. But it got him talkin', cuz. I got his whole life
story. He was so pissed off, he didn't come back to the courts for a
month."

"But he did come back."

"What was he gonna do, cuz, spend the rest of his bit walkin' the
flats with the losers? He *had* to come back."

"When you're right, you're right." I forked a chunk of meat into my
mouth and chewed slowly. "Any more surprises, Eddie?"

He laughed. "Nah, that's it. The rest is all details. We got a big
garage in the Bronx where we're gonna make the split. The van we're
usin' came from Westchester. We took it out of a garage with the keys
still in it. The plates came off another van in Jersey. We didn't buy
nothin' in our own names. The apartment, the phones, the electric—
everything was done with a phony i.d. that's goin' right in the sewer
after we make our move. Also, we didn't buy no guns on the street.
We picked 'em up in Pennsylvania, where you could buy an arsenal
with a driver's license."

I nodded my agreement. Eddie's profession was crime and he was good at his job. "When do you want me to come over, Eddie?" It was Morasso time.

He looked at his watch. "It's eight-thirty. What time you gotta be back at the shelter?"

"Ten-thirty." I didn't tell him that my deadline involved a phone call to Condon and Rico.

"There ain't enough time to get out to Queens and back tonight. Come tomorrow morning. See if you could fuck up Tony's breakfast for him."

FOURTEEN

He went on and on, piling up the details. Tony Morasso and John Parker would stay out of sight in the van while Eddie and I secured the loading dock. Morasso would then come out, but Parker would remain inside to play with his electronic toys. The guard locked in the armored car would try to radio the base before opening the door, but Parker had pulled the radio's frequency from the company computer and we would jam the guard's transmission by broadcasting a wave of static.

Another myth is that guards locked in the backs of armored cars are supposed to hold tight in the face of a hijacking. In reality, they're instructed to give up the loot before allowing their co-workers to be shot to death. Tony Morasso would make sure the guard in the truck understood that "shot to death" was imminent. There would no attempt to stall.

There are two highways within spitting distance of the department store, and one leads directly to the Throgs Neck Bridge and the garage where we'd empty the canvas bags, split the loot, and deal Tony Morasso the kind of justice he deserved. Morasso's body would be left in the garage, but the money would be transferred to the trunk of a car. The van, fitted with still another set of plates, would be abandoned on a Bronx street, miles away.

I listened carefully while Eddie laid it out, nodding occasionally, asking questions. My eyes remained hard and skeptical, my posture casual. Telling him that I wasn't about to accept any bullshit, but the potential for violence, even death, didn't trouble me at all.

Business being business, why should it? Human beings are potential problems and problems have to be dealt with in a forthright, businesslike manner. Let's see . . . we need a van, a computer, false identification, and several murders. No problem, bro.

I recalled a half-remembered Biblical quotation, a holdover from some forgotten Sunday school class: *Whatever the work of thy hands finds to do, do it with all thy might.* Eddie Conte was a prime example of that philosophy and I was not. Eddie Conte's stay in Cortlandt had been used to good and proper ends. My stay had been characterized by a ludicrous attempt at education and independence. The books hadn't come easy, not after thirty plus years of hating every authority figure who stood between me and anything I desired. Now, sitting across from Eddie, my goals seemed as childish as those of a school-yard shortstop dreaming about the major leagues.

It was nine-thirty when I finally shook Eddie's hand and said goodbye. I threaded my way past the whores and the pimps, the dealers and the junkies, the knuckleheads and the johns. I knew what was coming. I was going to dream and I didn't want to dream. I didn't want to go to sleep at all.

Sing-Sing was at his post. I got him to open McDonald's office and began to work out as soon he closed the door behind him. My body was doubly sore, from my workout of the prior morning and my workout with Rico. The pain would be a blessing. It would keep me awake. Or so I thought.

I'm dressed to the nines. Black, double-breasted Ungaro silk jacket with shoulder pads like gargoyles on a cathedral wall. Scarlet linen shirt (fitted, of course) with the top buttons open to expose a dark blue t-shirt that hugs my sculptured body like a second skin. Balloon-legged trousers that flop around my calves and ankles as I strut into a downtown jewelry store.

No adrenaline. I've perfected my craft, my art. I don't have to pump myself up with bullshit justifications. The worm behind the display case rushes out to greet me, gesturing to the rows of diamonds, rubies, emeralds, and sapphires. His eyes glitter in anticipation.

"What may I show you, sir?"

He has every reason to welcome me. A week ago, after handling every watch in the store, I bought a two-thousand-dollar Rolex with a forged credit card.

I can see the wheels turning in the worm's greedy mind. Am I back to make a really big purchase? One of the designer pieces? One of the antiques? An intricately filigreed brooch, its huge emerald surrounded by perfectly cut rubies?

"You wanna live, pops?"

I'm moving from one display case to another, examining each piece as I go along. The worm follows behind me, begging.

"Please, please, please."

I like big, heavy guns, Colt .45s straight from WW II. I watch the one I'm holding glide through the air, describing a graceful arc before slamming into the worm's face. The worm's mouth opens, but I don't hear his scream. I see it come out of his mouth. I see his scream and I hear the blood running along the side of his face.

"Wanna shut up, pops?"

I'm holding a watch up to the light, a Patek Philippe worth about ten thousand dollars. Something's wrong with it. The diamonds set into the face are slightly out of balance.

The worm is right behind me, still begging for his property, ignoring the blood and the pain. I stare at him for a moment, lost in admiration. At least he's got his priorities straight. A good surgeon will sew up his face without leaving a scar. His property is about to vanish forever.

"This a fuckin' knock-off, pops?"

"Please, please, please."

"It's a knock-off, right? It's phony. Patek Philippe? It looks more like Taiwan Tommy."

"Please, please, please."

What a waste. The worm doesn't hear me. He can't hear anything. I give him another tap and his skin splits open. Now he's cut on both sides of his face. Maybe they'll give him two surgeons when he gets to the hospital.

"I asked you a fuckin' question."

I push the watch into his face and he manages to focus long enough to hear what I'm saying.

"I'm talkin' about this fuckin' watch. It's a knock-off, right?"

The worm looks horrified, then offended. His bloody features assume a sullen distaste.

"I do not handle counterfeit merchandise."

I can't believe how much crap there is in this high-class jewelry store. This is where the big boys shop. The bankers, the builders. David Rockefeller comes here every Christmas to pick up a little something for the grandchildren. There's a picture of him on the wall behind the cash register. He's shaking hands with the worm.

Everything I touch seems to be shit. Cubic zirconia diamonds set into gold-plated rings. Paste rubies on base-metal chains. Emeralds the color of dishwater. I toss the garbage at the worm, bouncing the pieces off the top of his head.

Do worms say "please"? Maybe they make a sound that sounds like "please." You'd have to put your head very close to a worm's mouth to hear it make any sound at all. I've never put my ear close to a worm's mouth. How do I know they can't make a sound that sounds like "please"?

There's no way for me to express my disappointment. I expected to net at least a hundred big ones, but I'll be lucky to pry ten grand out of my fence. I sift through a small pile of loot at the bottom of a large canvas bag. It's just not fair. I once spent sixty days in Rikers for shoplifting a twenty-dollar scarf. The worm sells phony watches for a thousand and up, but he goes home to Scarsdale every night.

"How do you get away with it? Huh, worm?"

Where the fuck is he? I look around the shop and find him crawling toward a door in the back.

"It's not enough you rip me off, you fuck? Now you're gonna try to escape, too?"

"Please, please, please."

"Can you wiggle? Worms wiggle."

"Please, please."

"I want you to wiggle."

There's nothing like the roar of a .45 automatic. It fills the store with black light. For a moment I can't see anything. Then a small red dot at the very center of the blackness begins to expand. It doesn't seem to be liquid, but I know it must be.

It must be the worm's thieving life running out of his body.

I woke up on the floor of McDonald's office and heard the echo of the expected denial.

"That's not the way it happened." I was right and I was wrong. It hadn't happened that way, but over the years my dreams have come to be more powerful than reality. There was no designer suit, no Patek Philippe watches, no hope of a big score. I'd been sitting in the same chair in the same room of the same apartment for three days. Doing line after line of first-cut cocaine. My companion, Armando Ortiz, had been matching me, line for line. The two of us stunk of a continual sweat brought on as much by the coke as the unbearable New York summer. My jeans clung to my legs, and my hair was pasted to my skull, but, of course, I wasn't terribly concerned with my appearance. Not as long as a pile of white powder remained on top of the mirror.

But the coke was running out, as it always does, and there was no money to buy more. I was gearing myself up to face the hard-edged comedown. It would be hours before I fell asleep, hours of terror alternating with dark depression. I would wish myself dead a dozen times, close my eyes only to open them minutes later, wide awake and terrified.

My companion had other ideas.

"Petey, we got to go out an' do a job. We in a good thing, man. I know a bodega on Avenue C which is wide open."

I glared at him contemptuously. "Just what I need, Mando. A fuckin' twenty-dollar score. Twenty bucks, a can of red beans, and a bag of rice."

Mando dipped into the dwindling pile of cocaine. I waited until he finished, then matched him.

"Petey, man, this bodega is a place where people go to buy weed. The old man is takin' in hundreds of dollars every night. He don't go to no bank with his money. The whole thing gonna take fifteen minutes. I know these two sisters. Soon they will be *putas*, but for now they are schoolgirls who like to play with the snow. They will do *anything* for us."

I knew it was stupid. I had less than no interest in Armando's coke whores, was deeply in love with a woman who had no idea where I was or what I was doing. Who loved *me* enough to believe my lies, to pick me up whenever I fell, and I fell as often as an infant learning to walk. Each time I put a line of coke up my nose, I betrayed her. And each time I betrayed her, I consoled myself with a line of coke.

"You know how much time you could do for an armed robbery?" I asked. "You want to take that risk for a few hours of cocaine?"

It was Armando's turn to show contempt. "Fuck the pigs. Fuck their *maricón* jails. You got to take what you want in this life. Hombres like us? How long we gonna live? You got to enjoy your life while you got it. How come you packin' that pistola if you wantin' to be safe?"

I didn't have an answer that would meet the macho code I was expected to personify. The Llama .380 tucked into my waistband was proof positive that I aspired to the heights implied by the word "macho." If I wasn't a tough guy, ready to go at a moment's notice, why was the gun laying against my clammy skin?

Maybe I could have gotten away with declaring myself to be a *professional*, not a two-bit stickup artist with a dirty gun and a bad attitude. Mando Ortiz was a street junkie who lived a crime-to-coke existence with an occasional bag of heroin to season the stew. I'd been doing lofts and hijackings, carefully planned jobs that took weeks to set up. Mando's apartment might be as good a place as any to do cocaine, but Armando was the last person I'd take along on a job. Like Tony Morasso, he was violent and unpredictable.

"You got to be a *man*," he insisted. "You mus' to take wha' you want. The old fuck is jus' sittin' there, countin' his bags of weed. We goin' to cover our faces. Nobody gonna know what we done."

"Drop it, Mando."

He jerked in his seat, but held his tongue, which was okay by me. I thought the issue was dead, but an hour later, as the coke dwindled down to the last lines, I was the one to resurrect it.

"If this bodega's so easy, how come you don't take it yourself?"

Mando grinned happily. "There's a kid there. Like maybe fifteen. He got a little pistola in his jeans an' he thinks he's *muy hombre*. They won' say nothin' when we go in there, because they know me."

If they knew him, they'd come after him, but that had nothing to do with me.

"All right, Mando, but if I see it's wrong, I'm walkin' away."

"No pro'lem, Pete."

The bodega was exactly as advertised, from its sagging yellow awning to the bags of rice and the shelves of Goya beans. The old man was fat and tired, his pants belted so far below his hanging belly, they barely covered his butt. The kid was pimple-faced and bone-thin. He nodded to Mando as we walked inside the store, then turned white when Mando put the barrel of a .357 in his face. I put my own piece on the old man, who raised his hands and began to speak in rapid-fire Spanish.

Mando took the kid's piece, a cheap .22, and pushed him behind the register.

"What's the old man saying?" I asked.

Mando ignored me, answering the old man in Spanish. They went on for a minute, then Armando raised the .357 over his head and brought it down on the old man's head.

"What the fuck are you doing?" I yelled. "Let that shit go."

He turned on me, the .357 hanging in the air between us. "I ain' leavin' without the bread, man." The sweat was pouring off his face. His eyes were so wide they threatened to jump out of the sockets.

"We'll *find* it, all right?" The last thing I wanted to do was spend half an hour searching that store, but I couldn't think of another way to slow Armando down.

"Why we got to look when this *canto maricón* could tell us in a minute?"

The old man, blood streaming down his face, turned to me. "Please, please, please. I don' have no money."

I knew he was telling the truth, knew it with absolute certainty. Armando Ortiz had taken me for a ride on the psycho express. Not that I had anything to complain about. I'd been a willing passenger.

"Check the register." I kept my voice deliberately hard, trying to gain some control over the situation. When Mando hesitated, I let my automatic drift over toward him. His eyes grew even wider. "Check the register," I repeated.

He muttered, "Nobody don' keep no shit in no cash register," but he did it, moving around to the back of the counter and pounding on the buttons until it opened. "Ten fuckin' dollars, Pete. Wha' we gonna do with ten fuckin' dollars?"

He turned back to the old man and screamed at him in Spanish. I stepped behind the counter and began to paw through the paper bags, the twine, the account books. Mando stopped screaming and watched me closely. I found an ancient sawed-off shotgun behind a case of dog food, broke it, and tossed the shells across the room. An open carton of canned tomatoes caught my eye. I pawed through it, discovering an empty can packed with singles and fives.

"You got it, man?" Mando whispered.

"Yeah, I got it." I counted out the money. "Eighty-five dollars. That's your big fuckin' score, Mando. Eighty-five dollars. You want me to count the pennies, too?"

Without waiting for an answer, I bent down and continued to search. At the very end of the counter, across the room from where Armando held the old man and the kid, I found a box of register receipts and a woman's ring with a small red stone. I remember thinking that the ring might be gold, but was too thin to be worth much. The stone wasn't much larger than a chip, but the setting, a bird's nest of thin gold wire with a tiny red egg in the center, had been carefully done. I admired it for a fraction of a second before slipping it into my pocket.

"Let's go," I announced, standing up. "We been here too long as it is."

Mando answered me by jabbing the barrel of his .357 into the old man's mouth. The kid, his courage restored, jumped to his feet and said something in Spanish. Mando grinned, turned slightly, and shot him in the chest.

FIFTEEN

The dream began during my first year in Cortlandt. Once a week, in the beginning, then more and more often until I couldn't close my eyes without seeing this ludicrous figure, shoulders padded out to eternity, strutting through the glass doors of a nonexistent jewelry store. At first I dismissed the dream as a joke. Telling myself: "That's not the way it happened, the kid *didn't* die."

The dream ignored my objection, pounding home the same message, night after night. In the end, it broke me down. I suppose, if I'd been outside the Institution, I could have avoided it. Walked the streets. Watched television. Boozed or drugged myself into dreamless oblivion. But the lights go out at ten o'clock in Cortlandt and all you have is a cassette player and a pair of earphones. They weren't enough.

There are black holes in outer space. I first read about them in an old *Reader's Digest* years before I went to Cortlandt. They were millions of miles across and contained millions of stars, yet they appeared to be empty spaces in a sky filled with light. It was as if a careless artist had forgotten to finish his painting. The explanation, at least in theory, was simple enough: there was so much gravity in a black hole, not even light could escape. Once there, suns and planets, meteors and comets, were trapped forever. Each day, I woke up more tired than when I'd gone to sleep. I stopped going out to the courts or the weight boxes. Marching down to breakfast, eating the watery powdered eggs, and drinking the watery orange juice exhausted me. By the time I reached my job in the tailor shop, I was ready to go back to sleep.

There's a bonus system in the tailor shop—exceed your quota and the man rewards you with an extra two dollars a day. Since I had no one on the outside to send me the occasional money order, I was what the C.O.'s liked to call a motivated worker. I put in as many extra hours as I could because I was planning to go to school and I wanted to put aside enough money to keep me in cigarettes and coffee until I got my degree.

After the dream began, I started to slow down. Each day I completed fewer uniforms, fewer flags. I was losing money, but I didn't care. I studied the dream like it was a puzzle I had to solve, but I couldn't get past the literal images. Then I tried to edit the dream, to resurrect it while I was awake and make the necessary changes. To, for instance, transform the jewelry store into a bodega, to put the gun in Armando's hand, to make Armando pull the trigger.

After a month of fighting and losing, I refused to leave my cell. One morning, after the count, I went back to my bunk and laid down with my face to the wall. The C.O.'s ignored me. If I was after a voluntary keeplock, it was okay with them. I wasn't the first prisoner to avoid a beef by staying in his cell.

Four days later, when my friends told Sergeant Petti that I wasn't eating, he decided to come down and talk to me. Petti had a reputation as a con's C.O. If you had a beef with one of the other screws or a problem with the administration, he would try to square it for you.

"Pete," he said, "you wanna tell me what's the matter?"

I ignored him as I'd been ignoring everything else. The astronomers had been wrong about the black holes. They aren't filled with trapped starlight. Not even close. They're just as empty as they appear, devoid of sight or sound or smell or taste. And gravity isn't a factor, either. How do you find your way out of what isn't there in the first place?

"C'mon, Pete, you can't stay like this."

He reached over and put his hand on my shoulder. I suppose I should have warned him not to get too close, not to risk falling in, but I was a million miles away and I didn't give a shit.

"For Christ's sake, Pete, if you don't get it together, they're gonna take you to the annex and let the psychs work you over."

The Cortlandt Psychological Annex was more feared than the box or the Squad. Rumor had it that every kind of torture was practiced within its brick walls, that patients were laced into straitjackets and beaten with ax handles, that shock therapy was routine. Half the prisoners who went into the annex never came back into population. They were transferred out to Mattewan, the state hospital for the criminally insane.

The cons who did return to population usually refused to discuss their treatment. And their bros didn't ask. You could beat the honorable convict down, but you couldn't *break* him down. The honorable convict was not dishonored by rape or assault (or by raping or assaulting). He was dishonored by losing control of his violence or, in my case, by abandoning violence altogether.

I should have been afraid of the annex. Petti wasn't making an idle threat. The administration, though it didn't give two shits for my life, couldn't afford to let me starve in my cell. Helpless prisoners wasting away in eight-by-five cells are the stuff from which riots are made. If I didn't respond, the C.O.'s would force me to eat. They'd put me in a straitjacket and push a tube down my throat.

But I barely heard Petti speaking. The words came into the hole and disappeared immediately. If I tried to grab them and draw them close enough to have meaning, if I opened myself enough to receive Petti's words, other things would flood in behind them. Things like regret and despair. Much better to play the three monkeys and float safely in the darkness.

"Hey, Avi, come over here," Petti said.

I heard footsteps coming across the gallery, then Avi's voice. "Yeah?"

"I'm gonna give Frangello a five-day keeplock. I'm gonna say it's a punishment for not comin' out of his cell. That means you got five days to get him together. After that, he goes to the annex."

Time passed. People came up to my cell and spoke to me through the bars. Sometimes the voices were familiar, but often they came from so far away that by the time the words reached me, they'd been reduced to mere sounds. Then the C.O.'s showed up.

"Get outta that bunk, you piece of shit."

When I didn't respond, they pulled me to my feet. I felt the jab of a club in my ribs. It should have hurt, but I didn't feel the pain because I wasn't really in the body they were hitting. Still, I managed to stumble along the gallery and down the stairs to the tunnels. There were other C.O.'s manning their posts and a few cons being escorted from one block to another. I didn't look at them and, as far as I could tell, they didn't look at me, either.

We arrived at the annex without ever going up into the daylight. I was ordered to strip down, then shoved naked into a cell. A C.O. was stationed outside to prevent me from killing myself. There was no mattress on the bunk, because a mattress cover can be stripped down to make a rope. That's why they'd taken my clothing. They were afraid I'd hang myself with my underwear.

It was cold inside the cell. I knew it because I could feel my body shivering, especially when I lay down on the bare metal bunk and faced the wall.

Time passed. An hour, a day, a week, a month, forever—I really couldn't say. Time was as irrelevant as everything else. At some point the C.O. on the other side of the bars began to take an interest in my therapy. In his own way he tried to talk me down.

"Ya know somethin', Frangello?" he said, already laughing at his own joke. "You got a pretty ass. And the way you're hangin' it out there, I could go for a piece myself. Just bring it over to the bars. I'll use hair oil so it won't hardly hurt at all."

I felt something smack into my leg, felt it through the cold and the indifference. Suicide watches are long and boring. The C.O. was keeping his interest up by shooting paper clips at me with a rubber band. On the few occasions when I got up to drink or use the toilet, I found myself stepping on them.

"Hey, Frangello, you want a cigarette? Come and suck me off. I'll give you a pack of Marlboros."

Ping, ping, ping.

After a number of tries, he managed to hit me in the crack of my ass. "Bull's-eye," he shouted. "Right on the money. And it is money, right Frangello? Your ass is money, right?"

At some point a second C.O. joined the guard outside my cell.

"He movin'?" From the tone of his voice, I knew he was either a sergeant or a deputy warden.

"He gets up to piss. That's about it."

"I thought you were such a tough guy," the second one said to me. "I pulled your package and it says you been committin' felonies since you were ten years old. Now, all of a sudden, you're curled up like some faggot. You turn sweet, Frangello? Maybe you're sweet and you don't wanna face it."

"See what I mean," the first one said. "He don't move no matter what you say. Watch this."

He shot off a paper clip and got himself another bull's-eye. Both C.O.'s found this hilarious.

"I still think he's fakin' it," the second one said. "The piece of shit's after the drugs the pinko fuckin' shrinks give out like candy. If we didn't make it hard, every convict in Cortlandt would be on a psych ward. Takin' the shrinks' dope and goin' back to bed. Hey, Frangello, how come you're up here, anyway? You look like a white man. How come you're up here with all the niggers? You like niggers? You a nigger lover? Your sister fuck niggers?"

The door of the cell slid open. I knew what was coming and my body curled into a ball without my willing it. The blows continued to fall, thudding into my flesh, until someone began to scream. It couldn't have been me, because I was too busy trying to figure out if they were using ax handles, which were forbidden, or standard issue batons. But the C.O.'s didn't really care who was screaming. They were satisfied with the scream itself.

"Get your shit together, Frangello," the second one called out as the cell door slid shut. "If you don't, I'll be back."

I know that he kept his word, though I couldn't say how many times he returned. In the end, it was Haldol and not C.O. therapy that brought me out. Haldol transformed me from a nearly comatose zombie into a sitting, shaking, drooling zombie. A zombie who, when he closed his eyes, didn't dream of jewelry stores and .45 automatics. Who didn't dream at all. Eventually the psychs had me brought onto a regular ward. The aides, all convicts, kept urging me to fight back, I heard them and, at some level or other, understood that if I managed to escape the Haldol, I wouldn't fall back into the dream.

I stopped taking the Haldol, hiding it under my tongue and spitting it into the toilet. The aides knew what was happening and they encouraged me. Gradually, I returned to some sort of normalcy. I began to eat and talk. The dream receded, but never disappeared altogether. Occasionally, when I least expected it, I'd wake up sweating. Telling myself: "It didn't happen that way. It didn't happen that way." Saying it over and over until I was ready to get up and face the realities of prison.

You can't make the past over. You can't undo what's been done. That doesn't mean you don't have to deal with the past. Convicts accomplish this task in any number of ways, from the bug who claims to be acting under God's orders, to the amateur social scientist who can offer a hundred reasons why he commits mayhem whenever society lets him out of a cell, to the true sociopath who takes what he wants just because he wants it.

"Hey, I told him not to move. He shouldn't have moved."

"The world been hurtin' me all my damn life. Ain't nothin' wrong with puttin' a little hurt on the world."

"I saw the bitch standing there and I wanted to fuck her, so I fucked her. How was I supposed to know she was a cop?"

You never hear anything resembling remorse. Not among convicts, anyway. Remorse is a ritual. When the time for sentencing finally arrives, whether you've copped a plea or been convicted at trial, you're allowed to make a statement. Some choose to remain silent, but many take the opportunity to state their deep sorrow for any pain they've caused their victims. The speech isn't for the judge's benefit. The judge has already made a decision based on reports sent over by the Probation Department. The remorse expressed by the prisoner before the bar of justice is for the ears of some parole board in the distant future. It will be repeated to the parole board each time the convict is up for consideration. Without an admission of guilt and an expression of deep sorrow, it's almost impossible to get parole. Your remorse doesn't have to be sincere, but it has to be stated. In the end, it becomes just another prison humiliation.

SIXTEEN

It was six-thirty in the morning. I was on the phone, waiting for Simon Cooper, when Old McDonald came into his office. He took one look at my face, spun on his heel, and left the room.

"Yeah?" Simon didn't seem too happy either.

"What's the matter, your corn flakes gettin' soggy?"

"Who is this?"

"Pete Frangello."

"Shit."

"Don't kill me, Simon. I'm only the messenger." I gave him a second to respond, but he kept his mouth shut.

"I gotta speak to you as soon as possible."

"It can't wait until I get to the office?"

"It can if you leave soon. The thing is, I *have* to be out in Queens at nine o'clock. If I'm not there by nine, I can't go at all."

"Damn," he whispered. Then: "I'll meet you at the office in half an hour."

"I'll bring the corn flakes."

"Fuck you, Pete. This better be good."

Thirty minutes later I was sitting across from him in his office, going over my story. I didn't mention the dream or what had happened to me in Cortlandt, but they were the only things I left out. When I finished, he sat back in his chair and shook his head.

"The problem, Pete, is how do I know you're telling me the truth? You've scammed me so many times, it's hard for me to believe anything you say."

I didn't answer. Just stared across at him. He was massive, his neck bigger than my thigh, his face as blank and empty as my own. "My problem," I said finally, "is that I don't know what to do. I can feel the urge to just take off. You understand what I'm saying? I wanna get on the next bus and keep going. I wanna get to Los Angeles, jump in the ocean and start swimming west."

"You don't need me for that," Simon observed, lighting his pipe. "You can do that without my help."

I ignored him. "If I go back into Rikers and take my chances with the board, Eddie's gonna find someone else and do the job anyway. What kind of cops do you think they put in a patrol car to guard a witness's house? You figure they take experienced veterans? You think they use sergeants or lieutenants? Kids do that work, Simon. And I keep seeing a twenty-year-old rookie with half his head blown off. I can't deal with it."

I hadn't mentioned the dream, so I couldn't tell him that I knew the dream would come back if I let it happen. He wouldn't have understood, anyway. If you haven't spent a couple of weeks not caring whether you live or die, there's no way you *can* understand. Maybe that's why the psychiatrists deal with that reality by drugging it into oblivion.

"What Eddie Conte does or doesn't do is a problem for the cops," he said. "*Your* only move is to walk away. Which, as you say, means going to Rikers for a few months. Of course, the fact that you've been bullshitting Condon and Rico makes the deal a little more complicated. If you tell them what Conte's *really* up to and then refuse to help, they're gonna do everything they can to bury you. They're gonna go to the D.A.'s people and they're gonna go to the parole board. I make it 70–30 you end up in Cortlandt. On the other hand, you could always let the cop die. What's a pig's life mean to you, anyway?"

He was pissed, no question about it.

"I thought you didn't believe me."

My wise-guy attitude wasn't helping. I knew it, but I really didn't have another way to deal with parole officers. Or any other agent of law enforcement. It's what they expect and what the honorable convict delivers.

"The way I see it, you don't have a lot of choices." He didn't bother answering my question. "That's *if* you really want to save that cop. If you want to save the cop, you have to go back to Condon and Rico and tell them you lied. You have to tell them what's really happening and you have to go through with it. You have to become a rat."

"You enjoying this, Simon?"

"Very much."

"At least you're honest."

"Which puts me one up on *you*." He wasn't giving an inch. "Now, maybe you wanna tell me what you're doing here? Tell me exactly what magic trick you expect me to perform?"

"You blaming me, Simon? If you were in my place, what would you have done?"

"I *couldn't* be in your place, because I wouldn't have dealt with Calvin by damn near killing him. I'd have found another way."

"You can't change the past. It's not stored in some computer's memory. It doesn't erase."

"But it *does* crash." He broke a smile and I followed him into it. "So what'd you come here for?"

"If I told you I needed to talk to someone and I don't have anyone else, would you believe me? Nobody, Simon. Not a fucking soul."

He thought about it for a moment. "Yeah, I'd believe it."

"And if I told you I had a second reason, would you believe that, too?"

"And a third and a fourth and a fifth."

"I thought *I* was the wise guy."

"Why don't you just give it to me?" His voice was gentle now. "What do you want me to do?"

"I want somebody else to know what's happening. There are gonna be a lot of guns behind that department store. Guns that shoot real bullets that kill people. If something goes wrong, Condon and Rico will let me fry."

"You told me that last time I spoke to you, but I get the point. Remember what you said about the past? That it can't be erased? I'm thinking about all the times you came in here and lied. The past being what it is, how could you blame me? Like, for instance, if you can't defend yourself by telling the truth, what good does it do for me to know it?"

"You work with the prosecutors all the time. You can tell them what's going on. If they think you'll testify for me, they won't go to trial."

"What if I refuse?"

"You can't refuse. No more than you could handle Calvin the way I did. You've got a conscience, Simon. And you believe in really stupid things like justice. Once you know, you won't turn your back."

* * *

It was eight o'clock when I left Simon's office. Winter was taking a last shot at New York and the commuters were hustling along, driven by a sharp wind. Instead of going directly to the subway, I walked back to Tenth Avenue until I found a dealer who needed money bad enough to freeze his butt at eight in the morning. I bought ten bags of dope from him, a bundle, and stuffed it into my jacket.

The ride out to Woodhaven, in Queens, involved two subways and a bus. I'd probably be a little late, but I stopped in a candy store and bought a package of rubber bands and a small box of paper clips. I didn't have to worry about how I'd pass the time, because there was only one thing to think about at that point—Tony Morasso. The space between controlling Tony and having to kill him or hurt him so bad that he wouldn't be able to do the job was no larger than a crack in the sidewalk.

I was going away from the morning rush to work, and the E Train I took in the Port Authority was only half full, while the G I switched to in Long Island City was nearly empty. A couple of stops into Queens, a tall kid in a black leather jacket got on the train. His blond hair hung down to his shoulders and he had it tied with a red bandana. He sat down, put his feet up on the seat, and lit a cigarette.

I took out a paper clip, bent it very carefully, fitted it to a rubber band, and let fly. I missed my target, the cigarette hanging from his mouth, but I caught him on the tip of his nose. His first reaction was confusion. He brought a finger up to his nose, then looked down at the paper clip resting on his knee, then across at me.

The shrinks say that depression is just a cover for deep-seated anger. That rage is the real basis for suicide. I sat back in my seat and folded my arms across my chest, putting all of that deep-seated rage into my eyes, then blew the anger through the space between us. He looked back at me, trying to figure out what had happened and what he had to do about it. I helped him along by slowly stretching my lips into a broad smile.

"Get the fuck out of here," I said quietly. "Get out." I was making him for a punk, but if he happened to have a piece tucked into the waistband of those greasy jeans, I'd be in a lot of trouble. It's called "walking the line," which is what I was going to have to do with Tony Morasso.

"Why are you doing this? I ain't botherin' you."

"Get the fuck out." I started to fit another paper clip into my trusty rubber band when he jumped off the seat and almost ran into the next car. I think he was crying.

The rest of the trip went smoothly enough. I took a bus up Wood-haven Boulevard to Sixty-ninth Avenue, then walked the four blocks to the two-family home where Eddie had stashed his gang of would-be murderers. It was the perfect spot. The blocks surrounding Wood-haven Boulevard, white working class for the most part, form a narrow tongue that separates the black slums of Brooklyn from the black slums of South Jamaica. Most of the families are either German or Italian and have been living there for generations. They're far more afraid of the darkies to the east and west than of the mob within their midst. Over the years, they've learned to mind their own business and keep their mouths shut.

I stopped in front of the address Eddie had given me, a two-family home surrounded by a narrow strip of lawn, and suddenly realized that I didn't know which floor he was living on. Eddie had told me that he'd used a phony name when he'd rented the place, but he had-n't told me what name he'd used. So much for the master criminal. I suppose I could have gone up and pushed a bell at random, but what would I say if some little old lady answered?

My dilemma was solved when Eddie's wife, Annie, opened the front door and waved me forward.

"Jeez," she said as I went by, "am I glad to see you. Eddie's upstairs keeping Tony busy until you come, but you're here and now we can have breakfast."

The words flew out of her mouth. For a minute, I thought she was on speed or coke, but her eyes were clear and it didn't seem likely that Tony would let drugs into the house with the job so close.

"You're renting the whole house," I said.

"Of course. It wouldn't pay to have nosy neighbors, would it? I'm doin' the breakfast. That's my job, because I ain't crazy about guns. I take care of the house, do the shopping and cleaning and like that."

Eddie's use of his wife as a domestic servant might seem out of date, but in the old days, Italian criminals kept their families away from the action. I followed Annie back through the lower apartment into the kitchen. She was short and wiry, full of life and spunky to a fault. I realized both that I liked her and that I was going to send her husband to jail for the rest of his life.

Annie didn't waste any time. As soon as we were in the kitchen, she went to the stove and lit the burners under two huge frying pans. "Jeez, that Tony's a crazy one. Avi's gonna kill him, I just know it. Avi ain't a bad guy, for a Jew, but ya never know what he's thinkin'. I mean I always heard Jews liked to talk and stuff, but he never says nothin'."

"What about Parker? How's he doing?"

"John's a real doll. He's showin' me how to use a computer, keeps tellin' me about how I can get a good job, but what do I need a job for? We're gonna be rich, right?"

She was shoving Wonder Bread into a toaster, buttering the pieces as they popped out, turning the bacon in a third frying pan, cracking eggs into a bowl. "Sometimes my husband can be a real dope. I mean bringing an asshole like Tony Morasso here. God, what a mess. Eddie says you can keep Tony under control and I *sure* hope he's right. You must have a magic wand or something, 'cause Eddie's been trying like crazy and he can't get Morasso to lay off Avi and John. I mean, how are you gonna do it?"

"I'm gonna ask him real nice."

She reached across the table and hit the back of my hand with a wooden spoon. The gesture was affectionate. "Eddie told me you were a wise guy. I said maybe you could handle Tony, but who was gonna handle you?"

"What'd he say to that?"

"Eddie said you were a professional, even if you were too independent. He said Avi used to be in the Jewish army and Parker used to work in a big corporation. They were part of a team and you were always independent, but you wouldn't screw up the job."

I heard the sound of footsteps on stairs and turned to face the doorway. Eddie came in first, followed by Parker, Stern, and Morasso. Avi and John smiled. Eddie must have told them I was coming on board. Tony, on the other hand, stopped in his tracks when he saw me.

"What the fuck? What the fuck? What the fuck?" His eyes were rolling in his head.

"I see that freedom hasn't improved your vocabulary."

"What the fuck? What the fuck? What the fuck is this shit?"

"But it's nice to know that you're trying."

SEVENTEEN

I glanced over at John Parker and Avi Stern. Parker wore a look of joyous anticipation, like an altar boy in a Norman Rockwell painting. Avi's heavy-boned face was impassive, as always. I could understand why Eddie had picked Avi to shoot the cop. Jews are supposed to be great politicians and lawyers, but Avi had no middle ground. When he went off, he tried to kill. I considered him the most dangerous man I'd ever met and I was proud to be able to perform for him. I wasn't so sure how I felt about ratting him out.

"Pete's comin' in with us," Eddie said matter-of-factly. "He's the last one. Now we're ready."

Tony Morasso's confusion turned to fury. He raised shaking fists to his chest and turned on Eddie. "Nobody asked *me*," he shouted. "How come nobody didn't ask *me*?"

"Because you're a bug, Tony," I said, "and bugs don't make decisions."

"Why do you let him talk to me like that?" Tony spoke without looking at me. Small drops of spit flew off his tongue, spattering Eddie, who stared into Tony's eyes without flinching.

"Pete's comin' in with us, cuz," Eddie said calmly. "I didn't ask you because I didn't feel like it. What the fuck have you got to do with it, anyway? I'm runnin' the show, here. Which is what I told ya when ya signed up. Now, I expect you to get along with Pete. Just like I expect everyone else to get along with *you*. I got too much to worry about to be a fuckin' baby-sitter. If you got a problem, work it out with Pete. You understand what I'm sayin'?"

There was no profit in allowing Tony Morasso to pick his time and place. I wrapped a paper clip around a taut rubber band and let fly.

Ping.

The clip bounced off his forehead and landed on the floor. Just like the asshole in the subway, Tony stared down at the clip in disbelief.

"You fuckin' bastard."

Ping.

This one hit him in the neck and fell to his shoulder. He brushed it off like it was a cockroach, then spun on his heel to face me. His eyes were rolling wildly.

"You better cut that shit out. We ain't in the joint now."

His voice was so sharp it sawed its way into my brain. I started to flinch, then thought better of it. "I'm your baby-sitter, Tony," I said. "And I wanna tell ya somethin' out front—if you're a bad boy, I'm gonna punish you. On the other hand, if you're good, I'm gonna give you a cookie."

He stamped his foot so hard the glasses rattled in the cupboard.

Ping.

"I want out. I want out. I ain't doin' this job with him in it."

Dead silence. Every eye was fixed on Tony, including Annie's. I could see the truth wash over him, penetrating his rage. There was no walking out. He was trapped.

Ping.

He rushed at me, his small blocky hands curled in front of him like claws. I have to admit that his contorted face and his high-pitched squeal were frightening. In most situations they would have given him an advantage, freezing his opponent for a split second. But I'd dealt with bugs before and I knew that self-control, if you can accomplish it without surrendering to the fear, gives you a big edge. I stepped to one side and kicked hard at his right leg. He went down head first and I jumped on his back, grabbed his hair, and slammed his face into the linoleum. I didn't wait for him to acknowledge the pain. He was too far gone for that. I cupped my right hand and crashed it into his ear.

His eardrum must have been vibrating like a harp string. It should have hurt enough to catch his attention, but when I got off his back, he tried to get up. Fortunately, he was too dizzy to do anything but wobble forward. With all the time in the world, I curled my right hand into a fist, rotated my shoulder back and smashed him in the ribs. This time he stayed on the floor.

I walked over to the kitchen table and sat down. "Somebody say something about breakfast?"

"Comin' right up," Annie announced. Her face was flushed with excitement. If this little drama had gone down in a bar, I would have rolled out with Annie hanging on my arm.

Avi and John were already sitting at the table. Eddie came over and joined us, leaving Tony Morasso to consider the dynamics of the situation.

"I fucked up the eggs," Annie announced, ripping the pan off the stove. "Anybody like burnt eggs?" She answered her own question by dumping the mess in the garbage and starting over.

"I can't tell you how glad I am to have someone to talk to," Parker announced. "I've been trying to show these guys how I got into the computer. It's like teaching physics to an amoeba."

"Later, John," I said. "Let's do it later."

I was watching Tony carefully. He had struggled to his feet again, then staggered over to Annie. For a minute I thought he was going to attack her, she being the weakest person in the room, but when he turned back to me, he had a knife in his hand.

The room went silent. Except for the click of a revolver being cocked. Fortunately, the revolver was in Eddie's hand.

"Put the knife down, Tony, or I'll blow your fuckin' heart through the back of your chest. Put it *down*."

"You said no guns before we do the job." Tony was on the edge of tears. "How come you got a gun?"

"Put the knife down, Tony. Or I'll kill you."

Eddie's voice was rock hard. His eyes showed all the emotion of a preying mantis contemplating a butterfly. Tony put the knife back on the counter.

"See, it's not hard to be a good boy," I said. Tony tossed me a hate-filled look. "Remember what I told you? About if you were a good boy, I'd give you a cookie? Here's the cookie."

I held up the tiny envelopes of heroin, pinching them gently between my thumb and forefinger. He blinked several times, trying to process the information, then greed replaced the rage in his eyes.

When shrinks use the phrase "drug of choice," they know what they're talking about. Some addicts are natural dope fiends, others prefer coke, and still others are content to drink themselves into oblivion. I don't know if the shrinks have devised a test to predict which individual will turn to which drug, but over the years I've noticed that the psychos almost always prefer heroin.

Tony Morasso was the most natural dope addict I'd ever seen. He'd never used heroin before he'd come to Cortlandt, because he hadn't had the opportunity. Once inside, however, he'd taken to it like a duck to water. Not that he'd become an addict. Drugs of any kind are too expensive in the Institution. Unless you're dealing yourself, it's almost impossible to accumulate enough money to become addicted. But each month, as soon as his money order arrived, he'd convert it to cartons of cigarettes and trade the cigarettes for heroin. With Eddie, of course.

Eddie and I had devised a scam to get a small amount of dope into the Institution. We'd intended to use it ourselves, doling it out over the weeks between deliveries. I was working as an administrative porter at the time and one of my jobs was to sweep the visitors' reception area, a large room where visitors were processed and searched before meeting their loved ones. Annie made the seven-hour bus ride to Cortlandt once a month, being sure to arrive on a weekend morning when the reception area was most likely to be crowded. She'd stand on line for a while, then stroll over to the water fountain, take a drink, light a cigarette, and throw the pack into a little wastebasket next to the fountain. Fifteen minutes later, I'd come by with a large black trash bag. In the course of emptying the wastebasket, I'd casually palm the cigarette pack. All prisoners receiving visitors are strip-searched, before and after they enter the visiting area. Administrative porters, on the other hand, receive only an occasional frisk, and no frisk was going to uncover the dope because Annie delivered it in a balloon and I shoved it up my ass at the first opportunity.

Eddie and I had occasionally shared the dope with a few of the cons on the courts, but we never told anybody where it came from or how much we had. There were too many snitches and, of course, the rule in prison is DTA—Don't Trust Anyone. When Morasso's turn came around, the tension dropped off him like a turd from a pigeon's ass. You could almost see it splatter on the ground. After that first time, Tony had begged Eddie to give him more. He might have gotten it himself—it was more than available—but his relationship with the black and Spanish crews who controlled most of contraband was so bad that he was afraid to approach them. Eddie and I, understanding his plight, were happy to sell him a piece of Annie's dope. At double the going rate, of course. When your motto is Death Before Dishonor, can you do less?

"No drugs, cuz." Eddie finally broke the silence. "No drugs till after the job is done. That's the rule."

"It's not drugs, Eddie," I said, "it's medicine. Tony's a sick man, he needs his medication."

I glanced at my companions. John Parker's head was bouncing up and down. Even Mr. Stern had broken a smile. Eddie looked serious, almost grim. Maybe he was doubting the wisdom of recruiting me, as he'd doubted the wisdom of recruiting Tony Morasso.

"I think this is wise to give it to him," Avi said. He'd never come close to losing his Israeli accent, though he claimed to have learned English when he was seven years old. "It is to be medicine as Pete is saying."

"You think so, cuz?" Eddie asked the question seriously. Avi spoke so rarely that his words automatically carried weight.

"Yes, this I think." Avi looked directly at Tony. "Give him or kill him. I do not care which."

Tony didn't react to Avi's threat. He wanted release from the fury that dominated his life, to be able to sit peacefully in front of the television set and watch cartoons without having to jump out of his chair every few minutes.

"Give it to him," Eddie said, finally. "Give him the shit."

I tossed the envelopes at Tony. He caught several, but the rest fluttered to the linoleum floor. Tony fell to his knees and began scooping them up. He looked like a dog sniffing for table scraps.

"Do you have works? You got a point?"

He was asking for a syringe. I shook my head. "Just put it up your nose, Tony. It'll work all right."

We ate breakfast while Tony puked in the bathroom, forking eggs, bacon, and sausage into our mouths to the sound of his retching. Heroin is a poison. If you take enough, you die. If you take a little less, you throw your guts up and love it.

When Tony reappeared, he had less than no interest in breakfast. He went upstairs without bothering to say goodbye.

"I don't like it," Eddie said. "It ain't the way I figured it."

"I'd like to know what you did figure," Annie said. She stood by the stove with her hands on her hips, all five feet of her. "I'd like to know why you brought Tony Morasso into this in the first place.

The guy is a lunatic. Did ya think you were gonna get Little Miss Muppet?"

If anyone else had challenged him, Eddie would have jumped down his throat, but the soft spot he had for his old lady became even more obvious when he answered her meekly.

"We been all over this, Annie. We need him."

"We need him like we need cancer."

John Parker gave me an elbow in the ribs. "I think I've heard this song before," he said to me. "Come upstairs and take a look at my equipment."

"Are you propositioning me?"

"I mean my computer equipment."

Even Eddie managed a grin. "You could do worse, cuz," he said to me. "John ain't bad lookin'. Put him in skirt, he could work the cell blocks."

The truth was that I really didn't give a damn about John Parker's computer genius, but there was no way I could get out of it. We were all partners, now. I looked John over carefully. From his pepper and salt crew cut to his even features and firm mouth, he still came across as an eager junior executive about to make a presentation to the board of directors.

"Okay, but try not to make it too technical. One goddamned course doesn't make me a computer genius."

"You know something, Pete," Parker said, standing up and moving toward the stairway, "the beauty is that it isn't really technical. It's military. It's about finding a weakness and exploiting it."

EIGHTEEN

Morasso was in the living room of the upstairs apartment. He was sitting in a recliner, watching Popeye kick the crap out of his archenemy, Bluto. As we passed, he turned toward us. His eyes were empty.

"Pete," he said. "I didn't mean nothin' before. I was like fuckin' shocked when I seen ya face. Nobody told me you was comin'."

What Tony wanted was more dope and he knew I was the only conceivable source. That's why he was apologizing for getting his ass kicked.

"We had a lot of trouble between us when we were inside," I said, "but now we have to put it behind us. The job comes first, right?" I watched his head bob eagerly. "The thing that's good for you is that I gotta go back where I'm livin' every night. If I don't show up, this motherfucker of a P.O.'s gonna violate me. Now it just happens that my official place of residence is in the middle of a heavy dope neighborhood. As long as you don't fuck up and get Eddie pissed off, I'll take care of you."

He grinned happily, then leaned over and threw up into a wastebasket. I shook my head in disgust. This was everything I wanted to avoid when I left Cortlandt. I could feel the anger starting to rise. If I let it go, it would own me.

Parker led me into the master bedroom. Aside from a small bed in the corner, it was filled with equipment. I recognized the computer, of course, but the rest of it meant no more to me than a pile of scrap metal.

"Something, isn't it?" Parker asked. "One thing, Eddie didn't cheap out." He turned on the computer and waited for it to load. "No disrespect, Pete, but I gotta ask you to turn around. I don't want you to see the access code. The others, Eddie and Avi, they wouldn't know what to do with it, but you have enough knowledge to put it together. Especially with what I'm going to tell you about it."

I turned without comment. Parker was playing it smart, smarter than I gave him credit for. If he was the only one who could access the computer, Eddie would have to make sure he stayed in one piece. That was another reason why Eddie had been so happy to hear from me.

"Okay, turn around and take a seat. This is going to be a long story."

"Gee, and I was plannin' to attend the opera."

"Don't be a wise guy."

"That's what *she* said."

He answered by turning to the computer and pounding out a series of instructions punctuated by the inevitable beeps and boops. The cursor danced under his fingers for a moment, then the computer shouted, "Shut up and sit down, please!"

"Damn," I said, taking the requested seat, "that thing talks like a human."

Parker smacked the keyboard for a moment and the computer spoke again: "And no talking!"

"A voice synthesizer," Parker announced. "Nothing but the best. That's what I told Eddie. Does it matter if I picked up a few toys so I wouldn't get bored? Morasso has his dope. Avi plays with his guns. Eddie struts around like a tin dictator. I've got my computer. It's all working out for the best."

"Including murder, John?" I kept my voice calm.

His mouth tightened and he looked away. "I had a problem with that, but I worked it out. Look, Pete, suppose a soda company asked me to write a program that would allow them to schedule deliveries. Suppose the company was located in Chicago and wanted to deliver as far away as Los Angeles. Would it make sense for me to write a program that only gets the soda bottles to Phoenix?"

What he could do was write programs for a company that didn't commit murders. I didn't mention that, of course. What I said was, "Ya know, Eddie says it doesn't matter for him and me. With our records, we'll do twenty-five years whether we kill the cop or not. But you? You're not in that position."

"Come on, Pete. I was busted for a homicide. I pled to manslaughter and I'm on lifetime parole. If I get popped for a million-dollar armed robbery, I won't see daylight until I'm sixty-five. At the earliest."

Maybe I had some small fantasy of using Parker and Avi to convince Eddie to forget the cop, but I gave it up on the spot. "John, my boy," I said, "when you're right, you're right. Now, weren't you about to show me something?"

"Not so fast, son. Let me begin at the beginning. I want you to get the whole picture."

"This I already figured out."

He ignored me. "You remember how we talked about breaking into a computer? When we were stoned on the courts? You remember what I told you?"

"You said it was almost impossible if the company took reasonable precautions."

"Right. You remember what those precautions were?"

"As a matter of fact, I don't. I lost interest when you told me it was impossible."

"Allow me to refresh your memory. The first precaution is the use of multiple access codes. Note that I don't use the term 'passwords.' Access codes are random numbers, usually five digits. Let me show you a real example."

He slid his chair over to the computer and typed: C:MODEM. The computer searched its memory, beeping away merrily, then displayed: ENTER NUMBER HERE. Parker typed in a phone number and the modem began to work. Finally, a single sentence appeared on the screen: ENTER ACCESS CODE.

"Note that the system has *not* identified itself." He entered a series of numbers and the modem stopped flashing. "The system hung up on us. That's what it's designed to do. If you don't enter something within thirty seconds, or if you enter the wrong code, the system automatically disconnects. Now let's assume that you *know* the phone number of the system you want to penetrate and you *know* the number of digits in the access code. You could write—hell, you could *buy*—a program that would keep calling back and entering codes until it found the right one, but it would take several years to do it. Meanwhile, most sophisticated systems, like the one owned by Chapman Security, trace calls back after a given number of disconnects."

It was the first time I'd heard the name of the armored car company. Chapman was one of the biggest. Not as big as Wells Fargo or Brinks, but still a national company.

"Chapman? Eddie doesn't aim low."

"Actually, Eddie didn't aim at all. You have to start with a company large enough to need phone access to their system. For most of the little guys, the computer is no more than a large filing cabinet. With an operation like Chapman's, you have salesmen on the road, executives working out of their homes on weekends. Chapman has thousands of trucks and they rotate their schedules. A computer can write a new schedule in a couple of minutes. *Without* having eight trucks show up at the same place at the same time. It would take a hundred man-hours to do it manually."

He leaned back in his seat and lit a cigarette. "The computer's second line of defense is a callback system. When you enter the right access code, the computer hangs up, then calls you back, using a number you've left in its memory. This way, even if you've learned the access code, you'd have to use it from a phone known to the computer."

"So it's impossible," I said.

"That's what I told Eddie when he first brought it up. I told him, 'Forget about it. Put it out of your mind. There's no magic formula that can pluck an access code out of thin air.' "

"Did he accept that?"

"Yeah. What could he do? For Eddie, it was just another trial balloon. But after he spoke to me, I began to think about it. You spend a lot of time alone when you're in prison."

"Gee, I think I read that somewhere."

"The question you should be asking is how systems are *ever* penetrated."

"How are systems ever penetrated?"

Parker ignored the sarcasm, taking a moment to lean back and stretch. I shook my head in wonder. He was so absorbed in the pleasure of telling his story that he looked like a twelve-year-old boy bragging about a Little League home run. Fifteen years ago, he'd come home to find his best friend pumping his wife. If he'd come home thirty minutes later, if he'd been delayed in traffic, he'd still be sitting in an office somewhere, the very essence of the respectable, slightly befuddled computer scientist.

"In the old days," he said, "when passwords were still common, there were always a few schmucks who used words like 'open sesame' or 'bravo' or their kid's first name. Now I admire hackers because I used to be one, but with thousands of computer freaks pounding away in their bedrooms, there were bound to be a few who liked to play near the edge. Some of them wrote programs that tried the most common passwords first. If that didn't work, the program started at one end of the dictionary and worked through. Remember, the systems they were trying to penetrate didn't trace calls back. Some of them would let you enter five or ten passwords before hanging up. That approach became impossible when the industry switched to multiple-digit access codes."

"But computer break-ins still happen, right? I read about them every once and a while."

"They occur because the few hackers who like to commit felonies get the access code from a third party. Usually by looking over some asshole's shoulder when he enters it."

"You know a worker from Chapman Security with a low shoulder?" I lit another cigarette. It was my turn to stretch it out. Parker's story had grabbed hold of me despite my earlier indifference. It was the *big score* come to life, the collective dream of every caged human being.

"I'm just trying to let you understand my frame of mind after Eddie spoke to me. Of course I didn't know anyone at Chapman Security, and even if I did, that person would be very unlikely to lower his shoulder for an ex-convict. I suppose I could have gotten Eddie to kidnap some executive and force him to give up the code, but that wouldn't necessarily help us. Modern systems use multiple codes. You punch in one number to enter the system as a whole, but you need other codes to access sensitive information. The only way to be sure you have all the codes is to grab one of the top executives, preferably the director of computer operations. Unfortunately, if you beat the codes out of your director, you can't very well let him go back to the computer and change them. Maybe Eddie wouldn't mind killing him (and maybe I wouldn't mind, either), but the sudden disappearance of the director of computer operations would be certain to arouse suspicion. On top of that, you'd have to use the director's personal phone, which is clearly impossible if you're thinking long term. How many times can you break into someone's home? You could always change the callback number in the computer's memory, but if you did that, the director wouldn't be able to access the company computer."

"There's gotta be a punch line here," I interrupted. "I don't mind long stories, but this one's a fucking novel."

He grinned happily, then continued in the same breezy tone. "The point of vulnerability isn't in the computer itself, it's in the system that links the computer to the executive sitting in his den. It's in the phone system. It came to me one day when I was in the shower—"

"While you were bending over, looking for the soap?"

He ignored that one. "Visualize the phone system as a long wire stretching between the central computer in Chapman Security head-quarters and the home of the director of computer operations. If you tap into the line, you get everything going back and forth, including the access codes. I grabbed Eddie that afternoon and told him that if he could find someone who knew enough electronics to install a phone tap, I could probably do the rest. Three days later he brought Avi to my cell."

"Avi?" I was so used to thinking of Avi as a kind of homicidal wooden Indian that I was shocked to hear that he had other poten-tials. Apparently Eddie had looked a little deeper.

"Avi was a trained Israeli soldier. He served in a unit that specialized in collecting information on terrorists. They taught him to bug tele-phones, to plant listening devices, to jam broadcasts. Didn't you know Avi before he went inside? I thought you were friends."

"I guess I didn't know him well enough to ask him the right ques-tions."

"Well, between Avi and myself, the deal went down smoothly enough, even though Eddie's a maniac for detail and made us work it out ten times before he was satisfied. First, Eddie and Avi went up to the Bronx and relieved a New York Telephone repairman of his uni-form and identification. That's when Morasso and I got into it."

"You had trouble with Tony?" I hadn't been far off the mark. Eddie had needed me badly. It was a fact I could and would use to my own advantage.

"Pete, I wanted to kill him in the worst way. I had a knife alongside the cushion where I was sitting, but I knew that if I used it, I'd blow the job. I tried to calm him down, to tease him into a better mood, but he wouldn't let me off the hook. He was sitting next to me, running his hand up the back of my neck, telling me I was sweet as sugar. It wasn't a proposition, just another excuse to humiliate me. I went after him with my hands, but he was too strong. He probably would have killed me if Annie hadn't brained him with a frying pan."

"I don't understand why Eddie doesn't get rid of him," I said. "His part isn't that important. It just isn't."

Parker shrugged, his eyebrows lifting over his gray eyes. "Everybody's got a flaw somewhere. I've worked with enough senior vice presidents to know. Eddie's stubborn. He has to be the top dog and he won't admit it when he makes a mistake. This fight happened *before* we got into the computer. We could have cut Morasso loose without killing him, because he didn't know anything about where or when the job was going down. But Eddie refused outright. He promised to find a way to control Morasso and left it at that. Your solution, the dope thing, is perfect. I didn't think of it myself, but I'll bet it occurred to Eddie. The only thing was Eddie had already decided that drugs were forbidden, and he was too stubborn to change his mind."

"That's why I brought it without asking." I was filing Parker's insight away for later use. Up in Cortlandt, Eddie had always been quick to compromise. Now that he was top dog, another part of his personality had emerged. "Let's get back to the computer. This is starting to become a two-semester course."

"I went over to the library on Fifth Avenue and got the annual reports for several companies, including Chapman Security. Annual reports are super-slick glorifications of whoever happens to be running the company. Chapman's included a piece on their new computer and the man who'd designed it, Dominick Spinelli. According to the report, Spinelli lived and worked in New York City.

"It took us a week, but we finally tracked him to a high-rise condo on East End Avenue. Then Avi used the telephone company uniform and the i.d. to get down to the switchboard in the basement. There were two lines—they're called subscriber loops—running from the punch-down connectors in the basement up to Spinelli's apartment. Avi put a bug with a transmitter on each of them. Like I expected, one turned out to be for the computer and the other for his regular phone.

"Now the thing is that the transmitter on a small listening device doesn't have much range, so we couldn't sit in a nice warm apartment and eavesdrop on Spinelli's communications. Avi and I had to put all our equipment—the receiver, the modem, the computer, and the telephone—into the back of a van and sit in front of Spinelli's building for almost a week before we got the details. The damned van had an exhaust leak. If we kept it running so we could have heat, the stink made us want to vomit. On the other hand, this was early March, so if we shut the engine down, we froze our asses.

"Avi's from Israel, where they don't have any winter, and he doesn't care for the cold, but we kept at it until we got the access codes we needed. Then, still working from the van, I got into the program that controls who gets access to what part of the system and simply added an executive, complete with telephone number and personal access codes." He reached out and tapped the computer. "Now everything comes and goes from right here, and once we have the final schedule, our fictitious executive will disappear forever."

"Does that mean we can't be traced?" It was too good to be true.

"Chapman or the cops could go over every phone call originating from the computer. Eventually they'd come up with our phone number. But it would take months, and the phone we're using to communicate with Chapman's computer actually belongs to a man who lives across the street. We took it right off the telephone pole in front of the building."

"Avi again?"

"Right. The guy across the street lives alone and he works. That means we have all day to use his phone. Personally, I don't think the cops'll ever figure it out. The tap we put on Spinelli's phone has already been removed, and the extra line from the telephone pole will come down as soon as we get the final schedule. But what's more important is that between the Pope's visit and the diversion with the cop, the chance that we'll get caught in the act is so small it's almost nonexistent."

"Are you trying to say it's the perfect crime?"

To my surprise he took the question seriously. "I survived in prison," he said quietly. "I didn't think I would, but I did. That doesn't mean I want to go back. If I thought there was any way this job could go wrong, I'd walk away from it. Now, maybe you see something I don't see. If you do, I'd appreciate your telling me what it is."

I could have told him but I just shook my head. I didn't have the heart to burst his murderous bubble.

NINETEEN

I stayed with Parker throughout the morning. We played computer games. John had more than a hundred of them stored in the computer's memory and he was phenomenally skilled, blasting aliens with no more conscience than if they'd been cops sitting in front of a house in Bayside. As a young teenager, I'd spent my time away from the Institution in Times Square arcades. I'd disdained the newly arrived computer games, like Space Invaders, in favor of the traditional pinball machine. Still, the games in Parker's computer got my competitive motor running and I spent the better part of three hours chopping away at monsters who responded to my violence by returning in ever greater numbers.

By the time Annie stuck her head in the door, I'd been stuck on the fifth level of a game called "The Saurian Labyrinth" for half an hour.

"Eddie wants to talk to you for a minute," she said. "If what ya doin' ain't too important." She nodded at the game in progress. My hero, unattended, was being stabbed to death. He was screaming in agony as a dozen helmeted lizards drove their swords into the top of his head.

"John," I said, "I'm gettin' a little tired of being killed every five minutes. I'll see ya later."

I started to get up, but Parker restrained me. "I can't tell you," he said, "how glad I am to see you, Pete." He hesitated for a moment, clearly embarrassed. "You're a good guy. For a convict, of course."

"You're a sweetheart, too, John." What else could I say? Friendship is acceptable in the Institution. As long as you don't dishonor yourself by talking about it.

"I mean it, Pete. We needed somebody to bring us together. Morasso's a lunatic. Avi never leaves his room. Eddie sits in his office like a king. We needed someone who can talk with everyone."

I left before he could say anything else. Annie led me down to the first floor, then turned to face me.

"The way you handled Tony," she said. "It was great. You took him down like he was nothin'."

Her dark brown eyes—whether she knew it or not—glittered with lust. Looking at her, I could understand why she was in love with Eddie. All it would take was the tip of my finger tracing a line from her ear to the soft hollow in her throat . . .

If I tried for her—even if I didn't succeed—and Eddie found out about it, he'd have to come after me. Maybe the job would explode along with his temper. Maybe I wouldn't have to deal with Condon and Rico.

"Tony doesn't know how to fight," I said. "That doesn't mean he isn't dangerous."

"Yeah, but you're dangerous, too. And *you* know how to fight."

She was wearing dark blue sweatpants. They were big on her, the crotch loose and yielding. If I let my right hand do what it wanted to do, I'd find the soft flesh between her legs moist and open. I indulged myself in a moment's fantasy, then smiled and said, "Eddie's waitin', Annie."

She turned and walked off toward the back of the apartment. I watched her buttocks rise and fall for a moment, then heard Eddie's voice coming from one of the small bedrooms. He was on the phone, but I couldn't make out the words. He hung up as I walked into the room.

"Is this the principal's office?" I asked, noting the solemn expression on his face. I was going to get chewed out, no question about it.

"Pull up a chair, cuz," Eddie said. He was sitting behind a small metal desk. "You want a cup of coffee or somethin'?"

"Coffee wouldn't hurt. Light and sweet."

"Annie, get the coffee. And bring in some sandwiches."

"Anything particular?"

I looked at her closely, but I couldn't see any sign of resentment.

"Whatever you got," Eddie said, "and close the door on your way out." He waited until she was gone before starting in on me. "You should'na done what you done, cuz." I started to interrupt, but he cut me off with a hard look. "This ain't the time for wise-guy answers. I told you I didn't want no drugs before the job and you show up, on ya first fuckin' day, with a bundle of dope. This ain't the right way. It don't show respect."

"You told me to handle it," I said. "You didn't say how I should do it. What'd you think, I was gonna spend the next two weeks poundin' on his head? He wouldn't be much use to us if I put him in the hospital."

"That ain't the point." He leaned forward, his palms on the top of the desk between us. For a moment I thought he was going to come after me. "The point is that you didn't come to *me* first. And the reason you didn't come to me is that you figured I'd turn ya down. So what you did, cuz, was run a scam. You're runnin' it right now. Pretending that I gave you permission, when ya *know* you shoulda come to me first. What I gotta ask myself is what the fuck you're gonna do next? What's the *next* fuckin' surprise?"

We had one of those long silences while I tried to guess the proper response. The fact that I was in serious danger didn't help me concentrate on the problem. When I spoke, I was careful to show respect but not fear.

"You're right, Eddie. I didn't tell you because I was sure you wouldn't go along. But try putting yourself in my position. If I settled for beating him down, I'd have to be watching my back every minute. Tony would kill me without thinking twice about it. Without worrying about whether Eddie Conte would approve or disapprove."

"He's *still* dangerous. Whatta you wanna bet that a couple of days from now, when he's used to bein' stoned, he starts in again? And if you increase the number of bags, he's gonna be too fucked-up to do the job."

"I was figurin' to cut him off two days before we go. By the time he sees that truck, he'll be crazy enough to scare the devil himself. He'll see that armored car as one big pile of dope."

"Another plan you didn't tell me about? Another fuckin' surprise? What is it, Pete, April Fools Day? Did I forget to check my calendar this morning?"

"Look, Eddie, I get the message. You want me to walk, just say so." Of course he *couldn't* let me out. He had the same problem with me as he did with Morasso. The only way to get rid of us was to kill us, and that option created more problems than it solved.

"What I want is no more surprises, cuz. *None.*" He banged the top of the desk with his fist. "You get a brilliant idea, come to me first. No excuses. No bullshit. No wise-guy answers." He waited for me to get the point, but the message I received, which should have been obvious from the beginning, was if he'd already decided to eliminate Morasso, how did I know he hadn't decided to eliminate me as well? He talked about one big score and out, but a third of $750,000 wouldn't buy him a piece of that fantasy. Half of $750,000 might do it. *All* would do it for sure.

It wasn't going to come to that, but I filed the information away, then flashed him my sweetest smile. "No more problems, Eddie. I'm with you a hundred percent. I should've spoken to you before I brought the dope into your house, but I only thought of it on the way here this morning. That's the truth. I thought of it and I knew it would work. You remember I was on the psychological annex in Cortlandt for a month? I saw drugs like Thorazine and Haldol turn maniacs into puppies."

The conversation might have continued indefinitely if Annie hadn't shown up with the coffee and sandwiches. I was determined not to show fear, and fear was what Eddie wanted to see. When Annie put the food down, Eddie took the opportunity to relax.

"It went all right," he admitted. "Morasso's calm and that's one less thing to worry about." He picked up a sandwich and bit into it, chewing thoughtfully. "I got a few things I want you to do this afternoon. First, I'm giving you a car. A shiny red Ford. It might be that I need you in a hurry and it's a forever trip on that fuckin' subway. The car's rented and the papers are in the glove compartment. This afternoon take the car and go on a little shopping trip. Go to Stern's in Little Neck and look it over. Think of it like you was plannin' the job. Then drive over to where the cop's staked out and do the same thing. Here's another five hundred. Dope is expensive, so you're gonna need it. And here's your i.d. Check it out."

The package included a passport, a social security card, and a driver's license. They looked good to me, but I'm not an expert. "Where'd you get the picture?"

"Ya don't remember how I liked to use my little Polaroid when we was on the courts?" He was grinning now, proud of himself. "I try to think of everything, cuz. Maybe that's why I don't like surprises. That passport will get you through customs. I know, because I already took a little trip to Mexico. Lookin' for a place to relocate."

"You're some piece of work, Eddie. You never stop."

"That's a compliment, right?" He didn't wait for me to respond. "Two other things. From now on, you give the dope to me and I give it to Tony. No arguments. What I'm gonna do is control the situation. Second, three days before the job, you're movin' in with us. Nobody's gonna run you down in three days and besides, when Tony finds out there's no more dope till after the job, he's gonna need supervision. *Intense* supervision, if you catch my drift."

I got up and began to move toward the door. "You sure you don't wanna come along?"

"I got things to do, cuz. Better you should see it fresh. Also, I almost forgot, tomorrow I got a little treat for ya. Big Momma's comin'."

"To see me? She must've liked my smile. Or maybe it's my boyish charm."

"Hey, cuz, she's comin' because I'm payin' her. She's a whore." Eddie grinned maliciously. "An expensive whore, but still a whore."

"She doing the other guys, too?"

"Wear a rubber."

I was on my way out the door when Avi called to me from the top of the stairs. I trotted up and he led me into his room. In the lower apartment, the kitchen and the living room were fully furnished, but the rest of the house was almost barren. Eddie hadn't given himself luxuries he denied the others. The lower apartment was a front; its sole purpose was to impress unexpected visitors. Avi's room was bare except for a bed, a chair, a lamp, and a table. The table was covered with rifle parts.

"Cleaning up?" I asked amiably.

"Over there is AK47 and Galil. All parts mixed up. I am learning to put them together in darkness."

I grunted my appreciation. Avi lived for his weapons like Parker lived for his computer. "Which one are you gonna use on the cop?"

"I would not use such weapon for that job. For sniping I use bolt-action hunting rifle with scope. Large caliber. I have not yet decided which one."

"Ya know, Avi, I've been wanting to ask you something. You're gonna *kill* the cop, right?"

"Yes. I have been to the site and it will be easy. I will not miss."

"I never even considered the possibility that you might miss. That's not what I want to ask you about. See, I wasn't in on the original planning, so there's a lot of details I don't know about. For instance, if the purpose of shooting the cop is to create a diversion, why not put a few rounds into the patrol car instead of the cop? Blow out the windows and tires. The result would be the same, right?"

Instead of answering, he fished out his pipe and filled it with tobacco. Pipes are forbidden in the Institution—it's too easy to turn a pipe into a weapon—but Avi hadn't switched to cigarettes during his years in Cortlandt. He'd done without. It was the soldier's way, the German way. Despite being a Jew from Israel, Avi's blond hair and solid features, his upright posture and ice-blue eyes, proclaimed his family's heritage. He looked Aryan as hell.

"First," he announced, "this question is not for Avi Stern. This question is for Eddie. Eddie is commander for this job. Second, if cop is not dead or wounded, other cops who are responding will fan out to search area. If cops see blood, they will wait to see if wounded cop is dead."

"And it doesn't bother you? Killing this cop?"

He shrugged. "I have killed so many. It is all the same to me. Now you have asked me these questions and I am answering for you, but you are not to be asking me again. Operation is set. I would not like to see changes." He paused, but I didn't respond. "I have called you up for a reason. You remember old girlfriend? Ginny?"

My heart flopped over in my chest, but I kept my face composed. "How could I forget?"

"I have seen her. She is working in real estate office. In Flushing on Union Street. Ling-Teng Realty. Near Northern Boulevard. I watch her go into office and sit behind desk."

"Did she see you?"

"Yes. She gave me greeting, but she was not wanting to be near me. I do not think she likes to remember."

"Did she mention my name?"

His eyes softened for a moment. "It was only very quick I saw her. Just saying hello and going our ways."

TWENTY

Eddie's house in Woodhaven was only a mile and a half from the Long Island Expressway. The L.I.E., if I'd taken it, would have dumped me off within sight of the small shopping center in Douglaston that housed our target, but I chose a longer route. I went north along the Grand Central Parkway, then exited at Northern Boulevard in Flushing. One or another of the city's ten thousand agencies was tearing up the road and I had plenty of time to look around. Flushing had changed during the years I'd been in the Institution. Before, it had been a white working-class neighborhood with a few black enclaves. Now a majority of the shop signs were written in Chinese or Korean with an English translation below.

I didn't take the turn at Union Street, even though I could see the real estate office—Ling-Teng—as I drove past. It'd been ten years and more betrayals than I could count. With no hope of a warm reception, I couldn't see the point of opening those wounds again.

How is it possible to love a woman and exploit her at the same time? I'd treated Ginny like I'd treated Simon Cooper, promising reform while relentlessly pursuing a criminal career. Coming home with pockets full of unexplained cash. Or sick and broke after a week of dedicated drug abuse.

Ginny had taken me back each time, though not always without complaint. This, in itself, isn't surprising. If you're not willing to settle for a woman whose predatory instincts match your own, you have to go with a woman who wants to reform you, who sees something worthwhile in your black soul. The drug-hungry women you find on the street are expensive. You have to feed their habits as well as your own. Women like Ginny have regular jobs, clean apartments, stocked refrigerators.

It's a wonderful life. As long as you don't fall in love.

I'd run directly from Armando Ortiz and the blood in the bodega to Ginny's apartment in Astoria, waking her as I walked through the door. The disappointment in her face was expected, but I was too wild to deal with it. I paced the floor for hours, until the cocaine passed out of my system and exhaustion overcame me. By that time, Ginny had gone off to work and I was able to sleep through the day.

I was still asleep when she came home, still fully dressed. She sat at the edge of the bed and gently shook me awake, suggesting a shower. I looked up into her face, knowing that she loved me and that I loved her and that I couldn't stop what I was doing to her. As I undressed, peeling away my sweaty clothes, I remembered the ring I'd taken from the bodega. I fished it out of my pocket and held it up.

"I bought this for you," I announced grandly.

She was touched, surprised that I'd been thinking of anything besides cocaine in the time I'd been away.

"Is it stolen?"

"I couldn't say for sure. But the broad who sold me the ring took it off her finger, which is at least a good sign."

I wanted to make it up to her. As if loving Ginny and being a good boy would erase what I'd done. I stayed close to the apartment, shopped for food, did the laundry, made love to her every night. I swore—to myself, naturally—that I would never return to a criminal life. If the Lord would only spare me this one last time, I'd put it all behind me. I'd marry Ginny, hold a straight job, have righteous children. I'd be a good boy forever.

The Lord had other ideas. Eight days after the shooting, the cops found my cocaine buddy, Armando Ortiz, at his sister's apartment in the Bronx. Drawing on all of his Latin macho, he held out for two hours before giving me up to the detectives. The detectives went before a judge. They got arrest and search warrants, then arrived, along with ten uniformed cops, at Ginny's apartment.

I was hustled off to the 7th Precinct on the Lower East Side before the search. The detectives put me in a lineup, but the old man who owned the bodega failed to make a firm identification. After a month at Rikers, when the boy came out of the hospital, they took me back to the precinct and put me in a second lineup. The boy, too, failed to pick me out and despite their hustling me back to Rikers, I began to hope that I'd beat it.

Sure, Mando Ortiz would testify against me, but it's hard to convict solely on the testimony of a co-conspirator. Mando's rap sheet was longer than mine. In the eyes of a jury, he would be a lowlife Puerto Rican while I would be a white kid with a million-dollar smile. If I didn't testify, the prosecutor would not be allowed to bring up my past. Maybe the cops would find someone who'd seen us together that night, but there wasn't a single piece of evidence to put me at the scene. The prosecution was without ammunition.

Meanwhile, what the prosecution did was arrest Ginny for the crime of receiving stolen property. They knew she wasn't part of the robbery, but she was wearing the ring that'd been taken from the bodega, and that was enough to keep her at Rikers Island until she was ready to cooperate.

I continued to drive east on Northern Boulevard, passing through one neighborhood after another, until I got to Bell Boulevard, where I took a right and cruised up to Fifty-sixth Avenue. There was a school on the corner of Fifty-sixth and Bell. I made another right and found a blue and white police car two blocks away. A uniformed cop was sitting behind the wheel, smoking a cigarette. He was young, blond, and obviously bored. As I drifted by, he got out of the cruiser and walked up to the house. The door opened and he stepped inside.

I circled the block, hoping that he'd stay there forever, that he simply wouldn't be available when Avi climbed to the roof of the school. But he was back in the car before I came around, his bladder undoubtedly empty. I drove past without taking a second look at his face. Even though it was unlikely that he'd be the one in front of the house when Avi pulled the trigger.

It was only a couple of miles to the small shopping center on Douglaston Parkway where Stern's Department Store shared space with a number of smaller businesses. The center had been cut from the eastern side of a deep ravine. The ravine had in turn been cut by Little

Neck Bay centuries before. The bay had receded, but the steep sides of the ravine remained.

The shopping center was on two levels. The upper came almost to the top of the hill, but the lower was nearly invisible from Douglaston Parkway, the only residential street adjoining the center.

I parked the car and walked to the edge of the ravine. The sides were so steep, the builders had covered the hillside with small stones, then covered the stones with wire mesh. All to keep the hill from sliding down into the receiving area behind Stern's Department Store. A short roof projected out over the loading docks and the rear end of a parked semi-trailer with the Stern's logo on the side. I backed ten feet away from the edge of the ravine and found myself on the sidewalk. All I could see was the top level of the shopping center. The loading docks, where all the action would take place, were completely concealed.

I made a U-turn and drove to the lower-level parking lot, where I found a drugstore, a liquor store, and a huge Waldbaum's Super Market. The entrance to Stern's, hidden beneath the upper-level parking lot, was far back. I drove to the entrance and sat for a few minutes. There wasn't much to see, just three pairs of glass doors and a few customers wandering in and out. A sign on one of the glass doors announced a "Super Sale." It would take place on the weekend of the job.

The back of the store was almost deserted. A few cars, probably belonging to workers, were parked well away from the loading docks. The semi was still in place, its rear doors open. Two workers were unloading pallets of merchandise with small forklifts. As I watched, a middle-aged man wrestled a large box off the edge of the dock and slid it into the back of a station wagon. The wagon had not been visible from the top of the ravine. I continued around the building and found a one-way ramp that led directly to the street. We would be able to get away without having to recross the parking lot in front.

It was perfect. Eddie had covered every detail, and I had to admit it to myself before I could take the next step. I parked the Ford on the upper-level parking lot and went into Stern's in search of a telephone. According to my own script, I was supposed to call Rico and Condon, to admit the bullshit of the night before, to accept the bullshit guaranteed to follow.

I managed to find a pay phone easily enough—there was a bank of them in the credit department—but I couldn't bring myself to make the call. A small voice kept whispering, "Let the pig die, let the pig die, let the pig die."

What difference could it make to me? One dead cop, one big funeral, one more chance for the politicians to demand the death penalty for murder. Society had been playing that game for a long, long time. If I didn't want to be part of it—and I didn't—I could take Eddie's money and put my ass in the wind. I was under no obligation to protect an anonymous cop who undoubtedly hated me and everyone like me. Eddie, Parker, and Avi, on the other hand, had been as close to friends as convicts ever get.

I'd spent ten years in Cortlandt without having a single outside visitor. The C.O.'s had made their attitude clear from the first day. The prison motto may be Don't Trust Anyone, but even convicts need companionship. As I stood next to the phones, a quarter in my hand, I recalled a freezing cold January day. We were up on the courts, gathered around a fifty-gallon drum filled with burning wood. Below us, on the flats, two prison football teams, one mostly white and one mostly black, were pounding each other into the frozen turf.

We were all there, including Tony Morasso, drinking a nauseating mixture of prison hooch and black coffee that assaulted the stomach even as it made us forget the cold. Our team—the white team, naturally—was never behind, and as they piled up the points, we were already collecting our bets. We'd put up twenty cartons of Marlboros and Salems against ten 2-pound steaks one of the black crews had smuggled out of the mess hall.

It was as if Cortlandt had ceased to exist. The walls, the C.O.'s, the anger, the grief, the endless biting fear—all vanished as if a genie had wished them away. You don't get many moments like that in the Institution. They never come when you're alone or in the company of the Squad or sitting with a couple of hundred murderers in the mess hall. They come when you're with your allies. When you feel almost-forgotten emotions pulling you toward the false promise of friendship.

I'd been thinking about this moment all day, the moment when I'd have to do something I couldn't take back. As soon as I dropped that quarter in the slot, I'd be committed. Committed to putting Eddie Conte, John Parker, Avi Stern, and Tony Morasso in jail for the next twenty-five years. Avi was well over forty. He'd be seventy before the gates opened. Seventy or dead.

I looked down at the quarter in my hand, then put it back in my pocket. Ideas flipped in my head like playing cards in the hands of a magician. *Take the car and the five hundred and just start driving. Join the twenty thousand parole and probation violators trying to keep one step ahead of the law. The car isn't rented in your name, and Eddie can't very well go to the police with the plate number.*

They'll find you, of course. Sooner or later, you'll commit a crime and your prints will come up dirty. They'll ship you back to New York, to Rikers Island, to Cortlandt. But that's way in the future. You've got a lotta livin' ahead you, boy. Best get to it.

When my head stopped spinning, I found myself on Northern Boulevard. I was driving into Flushing, and this time I made the turn on Union Street and parked in front of Ling-Teng Realty. There didn't seem to be any clients in the office, just real estate agents sitting at their desks. They were all Chinese, except for a black woman by the window and Ginny way in the back.

Ginny had broken down on the witness stand, refusing to look at me until that moment when the prosecutor demanded that she identify the man who'd given her the ring.

"Do you see that man in the courtroom now?"

"Yes."

"Would you point him out."

Her eyes had swept the courtroom as if she was seeing it for the first time. She'd looked directly at me for a second, then slowly raised her arm, one finger extended.

I'd written a letter to Ginny during my first year at Cortlandt, telling her that she wasn't to blame for what had happened. That, as usual, I'd done it to myself. I had no right to expect a reply, and I hadn't gotten any

As I watched, Ginny left her desk and walked to the front of the office. She was wearing a light gray business suit over a black silk blouse. A small gold pin, a sunburst, glittered above her right breast. I'd given it to her on her twenty-fifth birthday and she hadn't thrown it away.

She sat on the edge of an empty desk and began to go through a stack of paperwork. Her blond hair had faded somewhat over the last ten years, and a few thin lines had formed at the corners of her eyes, but she still held her mouth slightly open when she was concentrating, still laid the tip of her tongue on the edge of her lower lip. I'd imagined her as unchanged, an icon resting in a niche, but I found myself glad to see her as a human being again, as a living, breathing woman.

She dropped the papers on the desk, said something to the Chinese woman sitting at the adjoining desk, then glanced out the window. Her mouth dropped open for a second, then snapped into a thin, hard line.

TWENTY-ONE

Adolescents in the Institution lack the skills to jail properly. There are dozens of small things, physical and psychological, a prisoner can use to make his time go more easily and they have to be learned. The kids make up for their ignorance with their only abundant asset—pure rebel energy.

I spent more than four years of my adolescence in Spofford Youth Center, almost all of it in some kind of trouble with the hacks (they called themselves "counselors") or with my fellow aspiring criminals. In some ways I was just like Tony Morasso. Although I don't think my eyeballs rolled in my head, I was ready to go to war at the drop of a hat.

One day I was coming from the gym to my room. I was seventeen and had managed to bench-press my body weight for the first time. The glory of it raised my macho self-image to new heights. My eyes glowed with insolence and my slow, proud strut warned the prison world to keep away.

At the peak of this prison high, I rounded a corner to find my archenemy, Olivera Santana, standing in the hall with six of his companions. Their eyes lit up when they saw me coming and my attitude peeled away like the skin of a tomato in a pot of boiling water. The only emotion I felt was panic. For a minute, I was paralyzed with fear, then I turned and ran for my literal life.

Ginny was no threat to me physically, but when she put on her coat and pulled the door open, what I felt was pure terror. I didn't speculate on what she might say or do. The intensity of my fear had nothing to do with my mind. I slammed the car into gear and whipped the Ford into traffic.

It was after six when I got back to The Ludlum Foundation. Sing-Sing was behind the security desk, as usual, though he looked a little fresher. I nodded to him, then wandered into the kitchen and got a typical shelter meal—overcooked spaghetti, half-raw meat balls, and a wilted salad.

I forced myself to eat it, then went off to McDonald's office and worked out for more than two hours. At ten-thirty I picked up the phone and dialed the number Condon had given me. He picked up on the third ring.

"Yeah?"

"Condon?"

"Yeah."

"It's Pete Frangello."

"Well, well. Right on time. You must be gettin' the message."

"I got the name of the bank."

"Give it to me."

"The Grant City Savings Bank. On Hylan Boulevard."

"That's it?"

"Right, that's it. The Grant City."

"That ain't what I mean, Frangello."

I was starting to enjoy myself. In my line of work, you don't find many opportunities to bust a cop's balls.

"I don't get it," I said.

"There seem to be a few small gaps here." He got right into the spirit of the exchange. Maybe he was bored. Or maybe the name of the bank was enough to take the edge off his temper. "Like who's the guy ya gonna snatch? Like what's the date when the heist is goin' down? Like what're the names of the rest of the perps? Little gaps, like I said."

"I don't have that yet."

"You tellin' me ya spent the whole day with Eddie Conte and all you got for me is the name of the fuckin' bank?"

"We spent the day in Staten Island, checkin' the location. The thing is, Condon, I'm still playin' it tough. I'm comin' on skeptical. You wanna hear what Eddie's plan for *me* is?"

"You bullshitting me here, Frangello?" Veteran cops are much sharper than criminals like to believe. When they put up that cop radar, they can pick up a scam from a thousand yards out.

"What do you want me to do, Condon? You want me to take a lie detector test?"

"Maybe."

"Then set it up, because I don't have another way to prove myself."

"You have another way, Frangello."

"Like what?"

"Like wear a wire."

"That's fucking suicide. I'd rather go back to jail. Eddie's more paranoid than you. And that's saying something, because you're *completely* paranoid."

I heard him sigh into the phone, trying to decide what to do next. He didn't trust me, but there wasn't a lot he could do about it at the moment. Later, maybe, he'd put me to the test, but for now he'd have to settle for taking notes.

"Where's Conte livin'? What's his address?"

"I'm not gonna tell you that. Not yet."

"You better stop fuckin' with me. I'm gettin' sick of it."

"If I tell you the address, you're gonna set up surveillance, right?"

"How's that *your* problem?"

"If Eddie spots you tomorrow, who's he gonna blame? One day *I* arrive and the next day *you* arrive. Who they gonna find in a Jersey swamp? I'm tryin' to survive here. Now let me tell ya what I'm supposed to do. It's got a nice murder in it, so you oughta be happy. I'm the one who stays with the family while Eddie does the job. After the heist, I get a call, then eliminate the witnesses. Bing, bing, bing. Execution style."

"Conte wants to kill them all? The kids? The women? Everybody?" He seemed impressed, almost respectful.

"But it's not gonna come to that, right? Because, unless I missed something, you and the cavalry are gonna show up before the shit goes down." I didn't wait for a response. "Eddie also swears the bank is getting a shipment of cash from the Federal Reserve the day before the job goes down. He won't tell me how he knows, but he says the bank needs the cash to make up payrolls."

The conversation rolled on with Condon firing questions and me dodging as best I could. I don't know if he was satisfied, but by the time I hung up the phone, I knew he'd wait a few more days before he had his partner work me over.

I went up to my room and showered. For once, my roommates were nowhere to be found. I fell asleep thinking of Ginny, but I dreamed of the jewelry store and the fat proprietor and blood everywhere. As usual, the dream repeated like a stuck record. And, as usual, I woke early, more tired than when I'd gone to sleep. I tried to will myself awake, but I kept drifting back to the day of my release from Cortlandt. My dreams were closer to reality than my fantasies on that day. Death Before Dishonor? Shit Happens? I felt like I was on a mountain, holding a stop sign up to an onrushing avalanche. I could hear the gods laughing.

I jumped into the shower again, washing the sweat away before shutting off the hot water. In the box, in Cortlandt, the showers are timed to give two minutes of hot water. I don't know who dreamed up this particular punishment, but the C.O.'s added their own wrinkle. They started the timer as soon as they opened your cell. The showers were set up on the eastern side of the building, so if your cell was on the west side, you had to run past the other cells, soap yourself, and rinse off before the hot water shut down. Most of the time you didn't make it.

After dressing, I went downstairs. I would have liked to hike around the city, but it was raining pretty hard, so I settled for a conversation with Sing-Sing. We swapped stories about life in the Institution for an hour or so, then the pay phone in the hallway behind us started ringing. It was barely seven o'clock.

"Yeah!" Sing-Sing rubbed his hands together. "I been waitin' on this call. This here is a *money* call."

He answered the phone, muttered a few words, then turned to me in surprise. "It's for you," he said.

"Shit." I went to the phone and announced myself, expecting Eddie or Condon. When I heard Ginny's voice I nearly dropped the phone.

"Pete. Is that you? It's Ginny."

"How'd you find me?" I had to say something and that was the first thing that came into my head.

"I got your number from Simon."

I should have known. The last time I was on the street, Ginny and Simon Cooper had been co-conspirators in my rehabilitation.

"Ginny, I don't know what to say. It's been a long time." My voice was soft and gentle, though I didn't want it to be. Behind me, I heard Sing-Sing snort a line of coke. It was a fitting counterpoint to the conversation.

"I want to see you, Pete. I really need to see you. To explain."

"Explain what? You don't have anything to explain." Was she actually blaming herself? It didn't seem possible. Then again, the simple fact that she'd loved me didn't seem possible, either.

Her voice dropped a notch, became huskier, as it always had when she was being serious. Or when she was turned on. "I know it's been a long time, Pete, and I don't have any right to ask you, but if you can just give me a few minutes, I'd like to explain what happened."

"You think I don't know what they did to you?" Why was I putting her off when I would have given my right arm to be with her? Images rushed into my head. I remembered waking up with her warm body curled into me, soaping her back in the shower, her childish excitement when she won a two-dollar bet at the racetrack.

"Maybe I shouldn't have called, but it's been haunting me for ten years. That I was part of it."

"No, it's all right. You want me to come out there now?"

"Can you?"

"This is America, Ginny. Land of the free and home of the brave. Even ex-cons on parole are allowed to go to Queens."

She managed a small laugh. "I have to be at work by ten."

"It's only seven. I could be out there in forty-five minutes."

"How can you do that so fast? Do you have a car?"

"I'll take a cab."

It was the first lie.

TWENTY-TWO

I stopped long enough to buy a bundle of heroin from a dealer standing in a doorway out of the rain, then drove against the rush hour traffic to Cherry Avenue in Flushing. I was hoping I could handle Ginny, reassure her with a few well-chosen words, then get her out of my life. The last thing I needed was another complication or a replay of yesterday's panic, but when she opened the door and looked into my eyes, my heart dropped and I felt like a ten-year-old boy waiting for a nonexistent mother to rescue him from the orphanage. All through our time together, she'd symbolized the normal life that, consciously or unconsciously, beckoned like a rainbow. I'd never really believed that I could have it (or her), but I never dropped the fantasy, either.

Ginny was wearing a dark blue sweatshirt over faded jeans. Her hair, still wet from the shower, was wrapped in a white towel. Ten years ago, Ginny could have been described as beautiful. Maybe her delicate features and bright blond hair weren't cover girl material, but she'd turned heads wherever we went.

She looked tired now, her gray eyes were duller, her mouth somehow smaller and sad. But her body was just as I'd remembered it from the time when she'd worked out five days a week at a local health club. Her hips pushed against the fabric of her jeans, insistent and demanding.

"Thanks for coming," she said, stepping aside to let me pass. When we'd first met, Ginny had been writing copy for an ad agency in Manhattan. She'd been sharp and ambitious. That job, according to her testimony, had evaporated after her arrest. "Do you want some coffee?"

"Yeah, I do."

We sat at the kitchen table, coffee mugs and buttered corn muffins before us. I didn't know what she wanted to hear, so I kept my big mouth shut and let her do the talking.

"I should have hated you," she began, "but I didn't. It wasn't actually a decision I made—to hate you or not. I just couldn't stand the idea of you going to jail again. The cops said, 'All you have to do is tell us where you got the ring and agree to testify and we'll let you go. We don't want to arrest you. We know you didn't have anything to do with it.'

"I said, 'If you know I'm not guilty of anything, how can you arrest me at all?'

" 'You were in possession of stolen property, miss, and that's a crime.'

" 'I don't mean technically. I mean morally. If you know I'm not guilty, how can you put me in jail?' "

"I bet they turned mean when you said that." I finally interrupted her. "When they realized you weren't gonna give me up voluntarily."

"Yes, that's the way it happened. They booked me. Took photographs and fingerprints, then forced me to strip for a search."

"Did the detectives stay in the room while you were being searched?"

She looked down at the table. "Yes. They made . . . they made comments. Then they put me in a cell in the basement. There was another woman with me. She had a knife and she was as strong as a man. She made me do things to her. I couldn't get away."

"Don't tell me. For god's sake."

"Are you all right? Are you angry?" Puzzled, she reached out to touch the back of my hand.

"I have enough nightmares already. I don't need any more."

Ginny looked at me carefully, then went on with it. "She said I was her property and she was going to rent me out to the other dykes. She said she'd kill me if I didn't obey her and I believed it. The guards came by every couple of hours. They saw what was going on. They wanted it to happen, because they knew I couldn't take it. And they were right, Pete. I wasn't used to that life. I couldn't take it."

I think she wanted to cry, but she didn't. She leaned back and took a deep breath, trapped by her memories in spite of the years. It must have been like having an arm or a leg amputated. Every time you look in the mirror, you're reminded of the simple fact that your leg will never grow back, that you'll never be the same. I'd taken similar blows many times in my life and I'd responded with anger and rage. I'd sworn never to submit, and that decision was enough to hold me up. Ginny had absorbed the pain and it still gnawed at her mind like a psychic tapeworm. I reached out and took her hand, holding it gently until she calmed down.

"The thing is," I said, "that you're right when you say that you should hate me. It would make the whole thing easier for you."

She pulled away, raising her eyes to meet mine. "How did you stand it? All those years in jail. The cops, the guards, the prisoners. How?"

"I started young."

"Don't be a wise guy, Pete. I need to know."

"When you're in the Institution and you know you're going to stay there, your first obligation is to simply survive. There're lots of suicides in the Institution, especially in the kiddie jails, but if you're not going that route, you do what you have to do. Say you're trapped in a cell with a bull dyke. The dyke is much stronger than you and she's got a knife. You can't fight back, so what you do is submit until you get your chance. Until she goes to sleep, for instance. Then you try to kill her. If you succeed, or if you hurt her bad enough, word gets out and the next dyke leaves you alone. The C.O.'s are a different problem. All you can do is hate them, so that's what you do. You bury every human emotion and learn to live for drugs or prison hooch or a contraband roast beef sandwich. Most of all, you live for the day you get out. If you start down that road early enough, you come to believe that there's nothing else out there. That every citizen is just like you, wanting the same things, but afraid to take them."

"I wish I could hate," she said, "but I can't. It's been ten years and I still can't shake it off. A piece of me is missing and it won't grow back and I don't have anything to put in its place."

"You're a victim, Ginny. Can't you understand that? A crime has been committed against you. By me, by the cops, by the Institution. You should talk to someone. You have to get help."

She stood up, took the percolator off the stove, and filled both mugs. "In the beginning, I used to go see Simon. He told me the same things you're saying now. I wanted to write you, to explain why I testified, but he told me not to do it. He said the reason you were so attractive was because of your intelligence. You can see the trap and you can talk about it, but you can't change. He said your line of bullshit is so perfect, you should have been a con artist instead of a . . . a thief."

Good old Simon. I'd spent ten years in Cortlandt without a visitor, without a letter. I felt the anger rising. It was all so fucking predictable.

"What do you want me to do, Ginny? I can't forgive you because I never blamed you in the first place."

"Last night, after I saw you, I realized something that I should have known a long time ago. I can never go back to the life of a good citizen. The smug security, the idiotic belief that the police and the system are out there to protect *me*—that's gone forever. Maybe I won't rob somebody's home or mug somebody on the street, but I'm just as much of an outlaw as you are. What I have to do is learn to accept it. And the loneliness that goes with it." She paused for a moment, sipping at her coffee. "What are you going to do, Pete? Are you going to . . . you know, go straight?"

I grinned and she answered my smile. The question was so naive. "It's not that events work to keep me what I've always been or that I simply can't get my shit together. It's that events work to keep me what I've always been *and* I can't get my shit together. But I'm trying. I feel like a high jumper standing in quicksand, but I'm trying."

That was the second lie.

Ginny stood up suddenly. "I've got to get ready for work," she announced.

"I gotta be places, too."

"Come back tonight. Have dinner with me."

The question hung in the air for a second, then dove for my crotch. In retrospect it seems funny, but the truth is that she already had my heart, so there was no other place for the question to go.

"I'm living at a shelter and I have to sign in by ten o'clock. Simon's orders." The third lie. "I might be able to come over for a couple of hours, but I can't promise."

"You're already involved with something, aren't you?" She waved her hand back and forth as if erasing the question. "Never mind. It doesn't matter. I don't want to reform you. That's gone forever. I just want to be with you. The men I've gone out with don't understand. It's not their fault, but when I'm sitting across the dinner table, I feel like a peeping Tom looking through a keyhole. I want to be with someone who knows what happened to me. And what it means." The tips of her teeth clicked together and she stuck her chin out. It was her determined look. The one she'd always put on when she took a stand.

I got up and crossed the room. "I've got a problem—a *big* problem—and I'm trying to work my way out of it. Right now it doesn't look like there's any escape. What I'm trying to say is don't count on a long-term relationship. Settle for what you can get."

I got to Eddie's about nine-thirty. Annie opened the door and announced that the master wanted me to report immediately.

"He's in the office," she said. "You remember where."

I found him sitting at his desk. He seemed almost jovial as he waved me to a chair.

"Siddown, cuz. You sleep good last night?"

"Like a baby." I assumed he was asking me if my tour of inspection had reassured me, but when I started to get into it, he interrupted me with a wave of his hand.

"You didn't sleep on Cherry Avenue, did ya?"

"What?"

He'd caught me off-guard and he knew it. He grinned like a kid in a pile of chocolate bars. *Stolen* chocolate bars.

"Avi told me what he told you about the old girlfriend. Ginny Michkin. Funny thing about Avi—he never forgets anything. Make a great fuckin' witness. I looked the girlfriend up in the phone book. There was only one Michkin. G. Michkin on Cherry Avenue."

"You disrespected me, Eddie. You shouldn't have done that. It wasn't right."

The tone of my voice brought him up short. He gave me a hard look, realized it was having no effect, and dropped back into his old-buddy stance. All in the space of a few seconds.

"I got a responsibility to the rest of the guys, cuz. How would it be if I let everybody run around on their own? I gotta *control* the situation. And what *you* gotta do is understand."

"That right, Eddie?"

"What else could I do?"

"You could stop disrespecting me."

"Look, cuz . . . "

"Maybe Avi's happy with his guns. And maybe Parker's too stupid to know better. And maybe you don't have a choice with Morasso.

But I'm not your fuckin' dog. I'm not gonna sit up just because you wave a biscuit. I'm not gonna cringe when you raise your voice. And, most of all, I'm not gonna kiss your ass because you happen to think you're fucking Napoleon."

"Cuz . . . "

He leaned forward, trying to pin me with his eyes while his right hand slid toward the desk drawer. I grabbed the edge of the desk, pushed it over on top of him, and followed it with my full weight. The drawer popped out and the expected piece, an S & W .38, rolled onto the carpet. We both went for it, but Eddie was closer, so I evened the contest by kicking him in the gut as hard as I could. He doubled over and the revolver was in my hand and pointed at his head before I even considered what I was going to do with it.

"Don't. Don't." Eddie's eyes were bulging out of his head. He thought I was going to kill him and I'm not sure I wasn't. I kept the gun to his head for a long time. My finger pulled on the trigger hard enough to move the hammer back.

"For god's sake, cuz, it ain't enough to kill about."

He was right. It wasn't enough reason to kill. I eased the hammer down, then stood up over him. "Avi's got guns. You've got guns. Now I have a gun."

I picked the desk up and sat in front, pulling my chair up close enough to conceal my left knee. It was shaking uncontrollably.

"I'm not walkin' away," I said. "You got me in here and I'm goin' through with it."

I watched him pick up his chair and put it behind the desk. As the fear dropped away, he became enraged. It was so predictable. Sooner or later, probably later, he would try to balance the scales. It was the only honorable thing to do.

"Maybe I been too hard," he said after he got control. "Like I known you for a long time and I shoulda figured that you gotta have your head. Sometimes ya get so involved in a situation that ya don't see the obvious."

"You know what's obvious, Eddie? What's obvious is that you planned the best job I've ever seen. I went out there yesterday hoping I'd find something wrong, but I didn't. The fucking thing is perfect."

He looked at me for a long time, obviously surprised by the quick switch. "You seem pretty sure of yourself."

"What I'm thinking is that if you want me off the job, you gotta whack me. There's nothin' else you can do. Leaving me alive is like sleeping with a time bomb under the mattress. So if you wanna get rid of me, you gotta whack me, but that makes even more problems, because I'm not easy to kill and I'm gonna be watching my back. Now look at it from my point of view. If I walk away from this job, you're gonna send Avi to pull my ticket. Avi's a fucking pro. He knows how to use weapons that I never heard of. Sooner or later he'll probably get to me. Face it, Eddie, ain't neither one of us going anywhere. If you respect me, we'll do the job and we'll all be rich. If you don't, everybody loses."

He answered me by grinning and rubbing his stomach. "What'd you do, learn karate after I left? If I start pissin' blood, I ain't gonna be in a good mood tomorrow."

"Guns motivate me." I tossed Morasso's heroin supply on the desk. "Here's Tony's medication."

"Good, the prick's already screamin' for it." He tucked the dope into a shirt pocket. "You ready to go to work?"

TWENTY-THREE

We went back and forth over the details of the job. I kept at it diligently, respecting Eddie's obsessive nature. He'd been the same way up in Cortlandt, worrying details to death. He'd also been very successful, working scheme after scheme without ever, to my knowledge, catching a keeplock or, worse, being sent to the box. This time he was considering ways of disguising the two of us while we were taking control of the loading docks. We couldn't very well come out of the van wearing ski masks, but we didn't need to leave five eyeball witnesses behind, either. If one of the workers picked us out of a mug book, the cops would put our shit together in a hurry.

I played along, but for all my apparent attention, my mind was on other things. I was thinking about Ginny and all the reasons why she didn't want me in her life. Ginny claimed to need a man she could relate to, a fellow "outlaw," but what she really needed was the company of other victims. Some kind of victims' support group would ease her isolation. There's plenty of that kind of thing for criminals, both in and out of the Institution. You sit there and tell the others about all the vicious things you've done to society and somehow you feel better. You don't stop committing crimes, of course, but you definitely feel better.

Ginny would feel better, too. And, like me, she would return to her normal life. All I had to do was put the idea in her head, then remove myself from her company. But I didn't really believe I would (or could) do it. I wanted her so bad, my heart jumped whenever I thought of her. Ginny claimed that her experience on Rikers Island had left an emptiness that she couldn't fill. I also felt that something was missing, but I thought I could fill the empty place with Ginny.

Annie called us in to lunch at twelve o'clock. The boys were already seated when Eddie and I came into the kitchen. Parker looked happy to see me and Morasso was positively ecstatic, but Avi merely grunted and went back to his franks and beans.

After lunch I went up to Parker's den and resumed my conquest of the subterranean depths. Somehow, my skills had eroded over the prior twenty-four hours and I couldn't get past the second level of the game. Parker, on the other hand, slaughtered monsters with all the nonchalance of Fred Astaire putting a move on Ginger Rogers.

"This is a great game," he told me, "because it illustrates human thinking at its most irrational. The Lizard People have their own society. They live underground and they never bother human beings. We're down there trying to steal *their* treasure, yet we think of *them* as evil monsters."

As he spoke, he pounded on the computer keyboard. Each time he pounded, another creature exploded. "If we were even remotely honest, we'd put ourselves in their place. Suppose *they* were coming to steal *our* treasure? How would we feel? The funny thing is that most of these computer games involve heroes who go out in search of adventure. They don't defend against invasion. Just like us, they're looking to take something that doesn't belong to them and they feel perfectly justified in doing it. Crazy, right?"

"Actually, it doesn't pay to think about it too much," I responded. "If you want to be successful in the criminal business, you can't put yourself in the place of the victim."

What I wanted to say was, "If you can understand how a fucking lizard feels about his treasure, how come you can't understand how a cop feels about his *life*?" But we'd been through that already, so I settled for killing lizards.

By two o'clock I'd had enough. I said goodbye to Parker and went in search of Eddie. Morasso was in the living room, watching cartoons as usual. He looked up at me through sleepy eyes. His pupils were tiny, tiny dots.

"Best go easy with that shit," I said, still walking. "You don't wanna o.d. before you get rich."

"Ya can't o.d. when ya snortin' the shit," he announced. "Ya gotta be shootin' up to get an o.d."

"Right, Tony. And you can protect yourself from AIDS by washing your cock with Listerine."

Eddie wasn't in his office, so I knocked on the bedroom door across the hall.

"Come in." It was Annie's voice.

I opened the door a few inches. She was sitting by a small, lighted vanity putting on her makeup. Her hair was still wet from the shower and she was wrapped in a large gold towel.

"Eddie around?" I asked.

"Eddie went out."

"Yeah. Well, I'm takin' off for the day."

"What about Louise?"

"Who?"

"Big Momma. You remember? She's comin' by after dinner."

"I'll take a raincheck. She'll have plenty to do without me."

Annie leaned in toward the mirror. Even though her back was turned to me, I could see the tops of her breasts reflected in the mirror as the towel slid down to her nipples. She lifted herself off the bench slightly, moving her face to within a foot of the glass. The towel barely covered her ass.

"I thought you'd be really horny. Just gettin' out of prison and everything."

I was, but not for a prostitute. Or for Eddie's wife. Annie loved Eddie. She'd waited nearly ten years for him to get out of jail. But that didn't mean she didn't like to sleep around. There are plenty of men who love their wives and still put it to any woman who'll let them.

"You fucking around with Avi?" It couldn't be Morasso. He was too crazy. It couldn't be Parker either. He wasn't violent enough. "Avi and all his guns?"

She turned toward me, startled. "What'd he say about me?" She was trying for indignation, but it came out scared.

"Nothing, Annie. I haven't even spoken to him. And I don't give a shit what you do with Avi, but I want you to stop coming on to *me*. I don't need the aggravation and I don't want the pussy."

She shrugged and went back to her makeup. As I left the room, I heard her laughing to herself.

I went out and started the car, thinking how the whole scene disgusted me. In my own mind, I was through with that life. But it was a closed book that kept opening. The only way to keep it closed was to burn it. Then I remembered the .38 tucked behind my belt. It sat there so naturally that I wasn't even aware of its presence, but if I got frisked by a cop, it would put me back in Cortlandt for the next five to ten years. I didn't stop thinking of Terrentini until the piece was tucked behind the spare tire in the trunk.

I drove over to Queens Boulevard, parked the car, and found a telephone. Condon picked up on the third ring.

"Yeah?"

"It's Pete Frangello."

"You're early." His voice was instantly alert. Like a sleeping dog catching an unfamiliar scent in the air.

"I gotta see you this afternoon. I gotta show you something."

"I'm kinda busy here, Frangello. Can't it wait till tomorrow?"

By tomorrow I might change my mind again. "Well, the thing of it is, Condon, I been lying to you all along. About the bank in Staten Island and the kidnapping. I want you to come out here so I can show you what's actually going down."

I figured that piece of information would get him moving. It would also give him a chance to get used to the idea before he got his hands on me.

"Your games ain't gonna do you no good, Frangello. And your attitude ain't helpin' either. The fact is that I'm just about ready to pull your fuckin' ticket. Where are you?"

The waiting was the worst of it. I didn't want them to know about the car, so I left the door unlocked and the keys under the seat, then stood on a corner for thirty-five minutes while the boys made their way out of Manhattan.

When they finally arrived, they acknowledged my patience by cuffing me and throwing me into the back of the old Plymouth they were driving. Rico got in next to me. I could see the beating coming and I tried to prepare myself to take it without fighting back.

"What's the story?" Condon spoke from behind the wheel. He didn't bother to turn his head.

"I'm not gonna tell you. This time I'm gonna show you."

"You're gonna do whatever we tell ya to do," Rico hissed. He jabbed a finger into my gut. Not hard enough to hurt—it was more like a promise of things to come. I took this as a good sign. They were going to give me chance to tell my story before they broke my ribs.

"If you drive the car, I'll show you where and how it's going down."

"The whole thing? Not some little piece of it, but the whole fucking thing?" Condon sounded bored. Like he'd already made up his mind and he was just looking for the evidence.

"All of it. Names, dates, places. You drive out the Expressway to Francis Lewis Boulevard and I'll tell you about it while we're moving."

He started without any more bullshit and I began to wish I'd asked him to take the cuffs off. Nobody was volunteering. As promised, I gave them the details as we poked along in heavy traffic. First I told them about Parker's background and what he'd done with the computer. By the time I'd finished, they were beginning to believe me. It wasn't something you'd make up on the spur of the moment. Then I told them about Avi and what he could do with a weapon. Then Morasso and his end of it. Then Eddie and the fact that he'd begun his planning and recruiting in Cortlandt. I kept back the car, the .38, the false i.d., and Ginny.

"The piece of shit sounds pretty real, don't he?" Rico finally broke the silence. "Looks like I'll have to kick his ass just for the fun of it."

"Shut up, Rico," Condon said. It was nice to know which one of them was butch. "Why you telling me this, Frangello? Why did you decide to open up? An angel come out of the sky and tell you to do right? Something like that?"

"Yeah—something like that. Take a right here." We were on Fifty-sixth Avenue. The patrol car was parked in the same place, but the cop inside was different. "You see that cop?"

"What about him?"

"He's dead. Avi Stern is gonna get up on top of that school you're driving toward and blow the cop away."

"Why?"

"Because whenever a cop gets shot, 911 puts out a 10-13. You know what that is, right?"

"We know what it is." There was no boredom in Condon's voice. It sounded more like he was frightened.

"When the dispatcher puts out a 10-13, every cop in the area comes running. *Every* cop. The only way this job goes wrong is if we're caught in the act. You can't trace any part of the computer thing back to us. We don't have any connections inside the company. Eddie's got everybody locked up in that house, so your snitches won't be able to help you either."

"Except for you," Rico interrupted, grinning. "We do got one little rat squeakin' in our ears."

"That's right." I ignored the disrespect. "One and only one. You won't get another."

"Uncuff him," Condon said.

"Gimme a break," Rico responded. "I haven't even slapped him yet."

"Just do it. You're not gonna get any more out of him by hurting him."

"But I *wanna* hurt him."

"Jesus Christ." Condon finally turned around. "I'm too old for this shit. Uncuff the motherfucker."

I'd already decided not to rub my wrists, a decision which took all of five seconds to reverse.

"I make them cuffs too tight?" Rico asked. "I'm sorry."

"No tighter than I expected from a tough guy like you."

He wanted to come after me—I could read it in his eyes—but he wasn't running the show and he knew it.

"My time will come," he predicted. "You'll fuck up. You can't help yourself. When ya do, I'll be waitin'. I'm gonna put your mutt ass in the hospital."

I didn't respond. There was no sense to it. We could play Ring-Around-the-Rosie for the next two hours, but I wanted to get to Ginny.

"Why don't we drive over to Douglaston Parkway and take a look at the job?" I suggested.

"Where?"

They were Manhattan cops and didn't know or care about the outer boroughs of New York City. I directed them back to the Expressway and had them standing at the edge of the ravine a few minutes later.

"That's it," I announced. "It's all gonna happen back there. First the Pope comes. Then the cop dies. Then we're all supposed to get rich. Parker'll verify the armored car's route so there's no chance we'll come up with an empty truck. The detectives'll go to the company first, looking for an inside man. The cop is guarding the home of a protected witness, so the detectives investigating *his* death will have to look at the witness's enemies, even if they suspect a tie-in with the robbery. By the time they figure it out—if they ever figure it out—we'll be long gone."

"It works," Condon admitted. "Except for you."

"Except for me," I admitted. "Which leads to a question. When do I get cut loose? I don't wanna get booked. I don't wanna spend ten minutes in jail."

Without warning, without showing a twitch of emotion, Condon slapped me across the face. Rico's .38 was in my ribs before I could respond.

"This is what you get if you're a *good* boy," Condon said matter-of-factly. "You could imagine what you're gonna get if you're bad. You report every night, like you should have been doing. We'll let you know what's going down. If you're a good boy."

"Yeah?" I could taste the blood in my mouth. "You think that slap scares me? Listen, Condon, I'm not goin' into this without protecting myself. My P.O. knows what's happening and he's gonna know more by the end of the next ten days. If I had a lawyer, I could get a guarantee, but I don't. So I'm telling you flat-out—when the bust is over, I'm walkin' away."

Condon responded by walking away himself. He turned on his heel and strolled back to the car. After a second, Rico followed him. They drove off without bothering to say goodbye.

TWENTY-FOUR

It took me over an hour to work myself back to my car. By then it was after three o'clock. I knew I should have been thinking about Condon and Rico and what I'd done, but I couldn't concentrate. The best I could do was realize that I had no guilt for what was going to happen to Eddie and the boys. It was my out, just as taking the armored car was Eddie's out. There was relief, too. Deliberate murder had never been part of the war I'd been fighting with society. My own particular Geneva Convention had forbidden it decades before, even if it had taken all this time for the information to filter down to me. I couldn't possibly face Ginny, couldn't hold her in my arms and make love to her, if I was about to betray her once again. Somebody had to go.

That didn't mean I wasn't a rat. Cooperating with the pigs is the ultimate dishonorable act. In Parker's computer game, the hero fights until he's got the treasure or he's killed. There's no place for betrayal or retreat. Whoever created the game forgot to include the possibility of fear. Maybe that's why the hero gets killed ten thousand times before he reaches the treasure.

But there's a good side to being a rat. Now that I'd become thoroughly dishonorable, I couldn't really go back. If I should happen to violate parole, Eddie and the boys would be waiting for me up in Cortlandt. They'd have to kill me. It would be the only honorable thing to do.

Years ago, while I was doing my first serious bit in the Institution, I took part in a riot. A group of cons seized a cell block, driving the C.O.'s out and barricading the doors. As these things go, it wasn't much of a riot. Without hostages, it only took an hour for the administration to mass enough force to break through our defenses. Just enough time to end the career of a prison snitch named Billy Balsack. They tied him to the bars of his cell, then jabbed broom handles into his ribs, his gut, his balls, and his face until he was dead. The handles hadn't been sharpened and it took him a long time to die. The boys responded to his screams with a chant.

"The rat squeaks. The rat squeaks. The rat squeaks."

Snitches take up the profession for two reasons. Sure, they want to stay out of jail or draw light sentences, but they also want to further their criminal careers. A steady flow of information can keep a snitch on the streets for a long time. Eventually, of course, he does something so awful that even the detectives protecting him won't intervene. Or he runs out of information, which, in the eyes of the cops, amounts to the same thing. That wasn't going to happen to me. For me, ratting was the equivalent of paying dues. It was the price of freedom.

I called Simon Cooper from a pay phone on Queens Boulevard, told him I was still alive, and made an appointment for the next morning. I had every intention of following through on my threat to Condon and Rico. And no illusions about their sense of honor. If they could find a way to convict Eddie and the boys without my testimony, they would throw me to the wolves. I was one of those rats with no more information to give.

A half hour later, I was sitting in front of Teng-Ling Realty, waiting for Ginny to come out. I should have been thinking about practical things like finding a job and getting off parole. But I was the hero who'd conquered the 10th Level and stolen the Saurian treasure. Now I would live happily ever after.

Ginny's face told me otherwise. She looked more tired than ever, as if she hadn't slept for ten minutes the night before. I wasn't the hero come to rescue the fair maiden. I was a last attempt to find a life she could deal with, the ultimate long shot. She got in the car without looking at me.

"You don't have to go through with this," I said. "If you want to forget about it, it's no big deal."

"You just got back. Don't walk out on me before dinner." She managed a quick smile. There were a few small lines at the edges of her mouth. They disappeared into her dimples for a moment, then reassembled themselves.

"Don't worry. I'm not going anywhere." The smile took me back up.

But at least I wasn't trying to do the impossible. I wasn't trying to stop an avalanche. I was going with the flow. I was trying to *surf* the motherfucker.

"Where do you wanna go to eat?" I asked.

"There's a place called Santoli's on the other side of the Expressway. It's right up Main Street."

I'd been hoping we'd have dinner at her apartment, but I kept a straight face as we plodded along behind heavy traffic.

"You wanna hear something funny?" I said.

"Anything." Another quick smile.

"You know Simon's my P.O. again. What are the odds against that? There's maybe five thousand parole officers in New York and I get Simon."

"Be grateful. Simon's on your side."

"I used to think that, but I'm not sure now. He told you not to write me. I didn't get a letter in ten years. He told you that I couldn't help myself, that I'd be a criminal for the rest of my life. I don't wanna start feeling sorry for myself, because I've been down that bullshit road before. But I also don't wanna say that Simon was right. I don't wanna convict myself, because the trial's not over till I'm dead."

"Simon thought he was protecting me, but he didn't really understand what was happening. Back then, I didn't understand it, either. The truth is that I don't care if he was right or wrong. What does it matter?"

I leaned over and kissed her on the cheek. "There's no big mystery here, Ginny. It matters because of the victims. Like you, for instance."

I pulled the car to the curb in front of a small Italian restaurant. There was a cemetery across the street. An elderly woman was sitting on a stool in front of a granite cross. I watched her lips move as she carried on an active conversation with the empty air.

"You take me out of the picture," I continued, "and none of that happens to you." Why was I putting myself down? I wanted her more than ever. I should have been throwing the blame on the cops or my childhood or the foster care system or the Institution. Hell, Ginny, the devil *made* me do it.

"Whatever you did, you didn't do it to *me*." Her voice was strong and intense. "I've had ten years to think this out. If you had just been arrested and sent off to prison, it would have hurt, but I'd have gotten over it. I would have healed. The cops changed all that. No matter how many times you told me different, I really believed that cops draw a line between the innocent and the guilty."

I switched off the motor and leaned back in the seat. "It was routine for them. A bodega robbery, a kid shot—it doesn't amount to anything. If the old man in the bodega hadn't given Armando's name to the cops, most likely the cops wouldn't have bothered to conduct an investigation. It didn't get interesting until Armando fell into their hands and gave me up. I was a career criminal, a diagnosed sociopath, and putting me in jail would be a feather in their caps. Not an eagle feather, mind you. More like a pigeon feather. But a feather is a feather and cops make their reputations with good collars. You were just a means to that end."

"They tortured me."

"I know that. You had two months, between the time they let you go and when you testified, to change your mind. You were so terrified you probably didn't even speak to a lawyer."

"How do you know that?"

"Because a lawyer would have told you their threats were all bullshit. The cops could never have convinced the D.A.'s office to prosecute. The courts were full, the jails were overflowing. It was a bluff and that's all it was, but they got to you because you really *were* innocent. Too innocent and too frightened to know what was happening."

"I hate them."

"Didn't you tell me yesterday that you *couldn't* hate?"

She ignored the comment. "First they took my picture, then my fingerprints. Then the matron ordered me into a private room. When the two detectives—their names were O'Neill and Grimes—followed us inside, I couldn't believe it.

" 'Strip down,' she said. 'Turn your pockets inside out and put your clothes on the table.'

"I looked over at the detectives and they stared back at me. Right into my eyes. 'Better hurry up, miss. We don't got all night.'

"I turned to the matron and she said, 'Strip down, bitch, or I'll get someone else in here and we'll do it for you.'

"Someone began to undo the buttons on my blouse. It wasn't me, because I wasn't there. Even though I was aware of everything going on, I wasn't there."

"Ginny, you don't have to tell me this." I was beginning to sound like a broken record. The truth was I didn't want to hear it. It hurt too much and it made me too angry. It brought back too many memories. What I needed was perspective.

"As I undressed, one of the cops—Grimes, I think—began to chant, 'Take it off; take it off.' When I unhooked my bra, he whistled.

" 'Nice set,' he said.

" 'Too small,' the other one said. 'The nips're too small. I like 'em big and brown. The kind that cover half the fuckin' boob.'

"I started to unbutton my slacks, but the matron screamed that I should turn out my pockets first. I became confused. I couldn't understand what she meant. Then she reached into my pockets and did it herself. I stopped again when I had to take down my . . . my panties. I got my thumbs up to the elastic, but I just couldn't bring myself to pull them down. The matron had to help me again.

"After I was naked, I wanted to cover myself with my hands. I could feel my hands floating in front of me, looking for someplace to go.

" 'Turn around and bend over.' The matron's voice was so matter-of-fact. It was like the cops were *supposed* to be watching. Like it was all routine.

"I said, 'I don't think I can do it with them looking at me. Shouldn't they be somewhere else? Why do I need to do that?'

" 'You'll do it,' the matron said, 'one way or the other.'

" 'What about them?' I pointed at the two cops.

" 'The bitch don't care for our company, Frankie.'

" 'I like a hairy pussy. That pussy ain't hairy enough.'

" 'First the little nips, now the pussy hair. Ain't you ever satisfied?'

" 'Face the wall and bend over.'

"The voices went around and around. I turned without deciding to turn; I bent from the waist without deciding to bend. I felt the matron's finger in my vagina.

" 'Man, that hole is *biiiig.*'

" 'She must be fuckin' with some of your people, Grimes.'

" 'Well, she didn't get that way from no white boy.'

" 'Asshole looks tight enough, though.'

" 'Oh, you finally found somethin' you appreciate.'

" 'I'd like to work on it with a nightstick.'

" 'Now you're gettin' sick, Frankie. A real man don't have to do that shit to get off.'

" 'Yeah? Well, maybe you got a whanger that could fit that pussy, but I gotta put mine where there's a little friction.' "

I expected her to break into tears, but she didn't, though she came close a few times.

"How could they do it?" she asked. "How could they do it to someone who was innocent?"

I didn't answer. Instead, I watched the old lady in the cemetery as she made her way through the gate. She was incredibly dirty, her clothes torn and soiled. Her mouth continued to move, though I couldn't hear what she was saying.

"If people knew what went on, they'd have to do something about it," Ginny said.

"They don't know because they don't want to know. If you're a criminal, you deserve everything you get. Nobody thinks about what you'll do when you get out. The public acts as if every conviction was a final solution."

"But I wasn't a criminal," she insisted.

"You were my old lady and I was a diagnosed sociopath who'd been in and out of jail since he was eleven years old. In the cops' eyes, you were guilty enough to put the squeeze on. If it'll make you feel any better, I don't think they put you in the cell with the dyke on purpose. The first part, yeah. They were probably hoping you'd break on the spot. The dyke was just the luck of the draw."

"What about the knife? She had a knife."

"*Everybody* has a weapon in the Institution. That's how you survive."

"I still hate them. I can't help it."

"Hate is a losing proposition. It doesn't get you anywhere." I sounded like a prison counselor, but there wasn't much else I could say. On one level I was enraged. On another, I was glad. The crimes committed against her had brought her back to me.

"I don't think I can eat now. But I feel a little better. Do you want to go to my apartment?"

"Well, I don't know, Ginny. I was kinda hoping we could spend the night sitting in the car."

She leaned across the seat and kissed me. There was no tenderness. Her kiss was hungry and demanding. Nevertheless . . .

* * *

The sex, when it came, was equally demanding. Ginny kept urging me to thrust harder. Her legs were wrapped tightly around my hips and her pelvis snapped up each I came down into her. I watched her closed eyes and the determined twist of her mouth. The sweat was dripping from the tips of her hair onto her shoulders. I knew she wasn't after orgasm. Despite the sudden twists of her head, despite the moaning, despite the fingernails digging into my arms.

I wanted her to want *me*, but I knew that wasn't happening. Sensible people medicate their depression with drugs, but Ginny hadn't turned to coke or dope or alcohol. *I* was her medication of choice. In some ways I was further away from her than ever.

Not that I didn't enjoy what I was doing. Grimes had been wrong about Ginny. She felt almost virginal, and despite the condom, the heat and the friction forced me to hold myself in check. Ginny needed a long, hard fuck and the only way I could give it to her was to draw away and watch her work. In the end, she pulled me in with her legs and began to grind her pussy against me. Her lips opened into a little sneer and the tips of her front teeth came together. Then I was lost, my own eyes closed, life rushing out of me and into her.

Or it would have run into her if I hadn't been wearing that condom. Rubbers aren't as bad as men say they are, but there *is* a moment when you're on your knees, half-hard, the tip of the rubber full of genetic information, that jars your carefully developed self-image. Instead of pulling your woman into your arms, you have to go to the toilet and flush the thing away.

"I'll be right back," I said. It used to be *her* line.

I took enough time in the bathroom to check myself out in the mirror. (Evaluations come *after* the sex.) What I saw wasn't too bad, though I would never again have the skin-stretched definition of my youth. I was bulkier, now, and fifteen pounds heavier. Most of it was muscle, but I had the distinct feeling that Ginny could do better.

Maybe Ginny was thinking the same way. When I came back into the room, she was sitting up in bed with the sheet pulled over her breasts.

"That's cheating," I said. "You're taking advantage."

"Pardon me?"

"I'm standing out here butt naked and you've got that sheet pulled up to your neck. I feel like a stripper at a men's smoker. Throw a ten-dollar bill on the chair and I'll pick it up with my cheeks."

She grinned, then slowly let the sheet drop until it hung on the tips of her nipples.

"Watch out!" I yelled.

She jumped and the sheet fell into her lap. Her breasts were softer than I remembered. Maybe they hung a little lower, too. Memory is too tricky. It tends to get wrapped up in dreams. Ginny had grown into a woman without showing a trace of middle age. The muscles of her arms and shoulders were smoothly toned, flowing into each other like ocean waves.

"You've been working out." It was a statement, not a question.

"I've been taking ballet lessons."

She raised a leg into the air, letting the sheet slide down even further. The long muscles of her thighs jumped to attention. I let my eyes run along the inside of her leg.

"Looks hairy enough to me," I said.

Her eyes clouded for a moment, then she began to laugh. Genuinely laugh. "I always thought I could handle anything. That was my reputation and I thought I could live up to it. In my junior year at Hunter I caught a bad flu. I was carrying seventeen credits and I missed a month of classes. My student adviser told me I should drop most of my courses and make them up in the summer. Instead, I borrowed other students' notes and finished the semester with a 3.4 grade average. It was expected of me."

"Are you trying to say that your jail experience didn't fit your self-image? It never does, if you're human. Not the first time."

"When I was in the cell with the dyke, I thought about all the things you said. That I should try to hurt her, to gain some kind of respect. But I couldn't bring myself to do it."

"You weren't there long enough."

"That's not it."

"Yes," I insisted, "it is. The Institution is like a war zone. It doesn't matter what a soldier thinks before he goes off to battle. Once you get there, you do what you have to do to survive. After a while, you'd have realized that submission carries a higher price tag than violence. It's not that violence doesn't have its price. It's just that violence is cheaper than submission."

She grinned happily. "You're sure of that, are you?" Her hand closed on my arm and she pulled me down onto the bed. "Sometimes you have to see the other person's point of view. Like, if you submit willingly, I won't have to get too violent."

An hour later, we were in the shower together. Ginny was soaping my back, letting her slippery fingers run over my ass.

"Take it easy," I said. "I have to get back to the shelter."

"We haven't eaten yet."

She was disappointed, thinking, maybe, that I was walking out on her again. I wanted to stay with her, of course, to share her bed, to feel her body next to me if I woke up in the middle of the night. But I couldn't take a chance that Eddie or Condon would decide to call me. I didn't want Eddie to know I was spending my nights with Ginny, and I didn't want Condon to know about Ginny at all.

"Felt like a feast to me. I can still taste it."

"You're a pig. You always were and you always will be."

"Oink, oink."

She spun me around and stared into my eyes. She was still smiling, but the look was very serious. "A lying pig."

"Say that again."

"This morning you told me you were taking a cab out to Queens. This afternoon you showed up in a car."

DTA—Don't Trust Anyone. It's not a joke. The prisons are full of convicts who opened up in a moment of weakness and found their confidant on the witness stand a few months later. The military uses the phrase "need to know." You never tell your allies and subordinates more than they need to know. The rest you keep for yourself.

"It's a long story," I said. "Give me the soap." I spun her around and ran the edge of the bar along her spine.

"You're in some kind of trouble. Already."

"I guess the soap trick isn't going to work."

She turned back to me. This time her eyes ripped into mine. "It's different this time. I don't think about 'forever' anymore. Not even in my fantasies. I don't think about changing you either. You can tell me anything and I won't condemn you. You can trust me."

"Yeah?" My reaction was quick and automatic, pure prison reflex. "And if they put you back in a cell with a bull dyke? What happens then? The truth is real simple—you can't testify about something you don't know."

"I'd die before I'd do that to you again. Do you think I'm the same person I was ten years ago?"

"If you trust me, you must be pretty close to it."

"Trust doesn't have anything to do with it."

But, of course, trust had everything to do with it. I had to trust her or lose her. It was that simple, although I don't think she understood.

"Ginny, did you ever hear the phrase, 'shit happens'?"

"No, I don't think so, but I can guess what it means."

"How about, 'shit happens and you *have* to deal with it'?"

"Tell me what you have to tell me, Pete. You don't have to beat around the bush. And you don't have to lie, either."

So I told her. I began with Terrentini, with the sound his flesh made as it cooked, and took her through my reception at The Ludlum Foundation, my reaction to it, and the unexpected appearance of Condon and Rico. I told her about Eddie and the boys, detailing the heist and Eddie's plan for the cop sitting on Fifty-sixth Avenue.

I was nearly dressed by the time I wrapped it up. "So what I am is a rat," I said. "I'm letting someone else do my time. Take him, not me. I can bullshit myself with excuses like I'm not willing to commit deliberate murder. Or, if I don't bring the cops into it, Eddie is more likely to kill me than not. You're smiling, but it's not a joke. It's like chopping off your arm."

"I'm smiling because it looks like I might get you after all."

TWENTY-FIVE

I dreamed that night. And the night after and the night after that. It wasn't fair. I was walking away from murder. I was walking away from the life. I was sacrificing my honor in order to avoid the very thing the dream threw in my face.

On the fourth night, my psyche showed a little creativity. Instead of the jeweler, I shot Ginny or Simon or Eddie. Even Morasso put his ugly face in front of the .45 I waved so proudly. And now the jewelry was real instead of phony. I was thanking them, even as I killed them.

Every time I woke up, I vowed not to go back to sleep. Sleep wasn't helping me anyway; I started each day more tired than the last. But I fell back, despite my determination, and just before dawn on the fourth day, I slid into an entirely different dream.

I'm walking down a hallway in one of the projects. I know I'm in the projects, because the doors are smaller and the ceiling is much lower than in ordinary apartment buildings. I can touch both walls of the narrow hallway with my elbows as I walk.

At the far end of the hall, fifty feet away, the sun is shining through a filthy window. The dirt diffuses the light as if the window was aglow with the rays of a rectangular sun.

I feel good. No particular anxiety, though I know I'm going to see my mom for the first time. It's taken me years to locate her, but now that I have, I feel confident. All those damned conflicts I've been carrying around are about to be resolved forever.

The door to 5C is exactly the same shade of flaking green as all the others. Somehow I expected it to be different, like the gates of par-

adise, but it's just another door in a long hallway. No angel with
flaming sword. No St. Peter with his long list of questions.

I grind out my cigarette on the gray concrete floor and ring the
bell. It opens immediately and Ginny's face appears.

"You're late," she says.

"Story of my life. We got a problem?"

She steps back to let me in and I see that she's wearing a nurse's
uniform. Then the stink hits me. Piss and antiseptic, sharp and sour
at the same time. Two distinct odors that refuse to blend.

"Where's my mom?"

"The old bitch is in the bedroom. Waiting for her dope."

I'm standing next to a hospital bed. There's no transition. I was
there and now I'm here.

"Is that my mom?"

"Yeah."

"How'd she get like this?"

"She couldn't wait anymore."

This close to the bed, I can smell the musty odor of death. My
mom is rotting away.

"Too bad, cuz."

Eddie is next to the bed, pushing an IV needle into a stick-thin
arm. "This way she gets it steady." He jerks his chin toward the bot-
tle hanging from the IV pole. It's enormous, as big as one of those
blue plastic bottles you find in office water coolers.

I move closer. The print on the label is so small I can barely read it.

WHAT SHE NEEDS, MOTHERFUCKER

"Enough is enough," I shout. "If you don't fix her up, I'm takin'
off."

"What could I say, cuz. Ya gotta do what ya gotta do."

My days began to take on a routine. Eddie in the morning and the
cops at night. Ginny was the fixed point. The days revolved around
her. I told her everything that happened and she took it in without
flinching. We seemed to spend all our time in bed, folded into each
other. I had a key to her apartment and I was usually waiting for her
when she came home from work. I'd have the evening planned, dinner out or a movie, but we always ended up in bed, surrounded by
containers of Chinese takeout.

Somewhere along the line, we began to talk about the future. In a week or so, I'd be out of the jam, but I'd still be on parole. Ginny and I had gone to see Simon together and he'd made his position quite clear. The state was demanding "intense supervision" and that was what the state was going to get.

"The fact is, Pete, that you committed a felony the day after you got out of Cortlandt. The cops may be willing to overlook your indiscretion, but as far as the parole board is concerned, you're still a dangerous, violent, high-risk sociopath. I'm putting it bluntly because I don't want to be misunderstood."

Ginny had taken up my defense. Not that it did any good, but Simon let her talk herself out.

"Words ain't gonna do it, Ginny. Deeds are gonna do it. The only way Pete can prove he's an *ex*-criminal is to stay clean for a long, long time. The next five years, to be exact."

"And if he's violated for some petty bullshit, what do you think will happen to him in jail?"

"The same thing that'll happen if Eddie's people catch him on the street. Look here, Ginny, you knew what Pete's life was like and you had ten years to get it out of your system."

"It was the system that kept him inside me."

Simon hadn't responded because he hadn't understood what she was talking about. As for me, I'd enjoyed the conversation immensely because the dialogue was so familiar. It was like watching one of those crappy sitcoms where you know the punch lines in advance. I'd had a reason for bringing Ginny with me to see Simon and it had nothing to do with begging him for some slack. I wanted Simon to know every detail of my devil's bargain with the good detectives and I wanted a witness to his knowledge.

Simon was a decent guy, even though he was pissed off. If worst came to worst, he'd go to bat for me. But that didn't mean he'd be willing to confront the system head-on. It didn't mean, for instance, that he'd stand up in court and accuse two New York City detectives of perjury. He might or he might not, and I wasn't willing to take the chance. Ginny's presence was an insurance policy.

I'd told her that before we went. I wasn't holding anything back. We were co-conspirators in each other's lives.

"I don't trust the cops. My name won't appear on any of the warrants. The phrase they use is 'confidential informant.' Not that Eddie won't figure it out sooner or later, but we'll have enough time to get our butts out of Flushing before anyone comes looking for us. Only suppose the four of them decide to plead it out. Suppose the prosecution doesn't need my testimony. I can't be sure that Condon and Rico won't take the opportunity to put one more perp where he belongs."

"What about parole?" she asked. "You could be violated if they charge you, even if they don't get a conviction."

I leaned over and kissed the tip of her right breast. She responded by shoving me away.

"I want an answer," she insisted.

"How does the song go? The answer is 'blowing in the wind.' "

"You can forget about 'blowing' until you tell me what's going on."

"Okay. I'm not worried about what Simon will do within the parole system. He can manipulate the board without exposing himself. It's not the same as testifying in open court. Look, Ginny, if I was a Vegas bookie trying to calculate the odds, I'd have to make it ten-to-one against something going wrong. Most likely this whole thing'll come off smoothly. Eddie, Parker, Avi, and Morasso will be arrested and go to jail for the rest of their useful lives. Condon and Rico will cut me loose, just like they promised. Even Simon'll come through. Yeah, he'll play that 'intense supervision' crap just to show me how tough he is, but after a couple of months he'll ease up. He knows I can't go back."

"One more question, all right?"

"Ask away."

"Right now I'm holding you down and threatening to tear your balls off. Is that correct?"

"Yes."

"So how come you have an erection?"

"That's two questions."

"With one answer."

The jokes ended a week before the job was scheduled to go off. All three New York newspapers put the Pope's impending visit on the front page. That's when it became real. In the planning stage, battles are little more than clouds moving across the sky. You have a map and a few models (Parker with his computer; Avi with his guns) which you manipulate this way and that, looking for the most efficient dance. Then something happens, something as real as the beaming face of Pope John Paul, and the abstract suddenly becomes tangible. You can reach out and touch the tension.

I was at Eddie's when I first saw the headline: POPE ARRIVES WEDNESDAY. A formal portrait, head and shoulders, covered the front of the tabloid.

Parker came down the stairs as I turned the pages.

"Every detail's falling into place," he said happily. "Things couldn't be better. Did you see the schedule?"

"The Pope's?"

"Yeah."

"I was just looking it up."

"Don't bother. The big *putz* is doing a mass at Yankee Stadium next Saturday." Parker had been a Presbyterian in his former life and had a longs-tanding dislike for the Catholic Church and its ceremonies. "Every Irish cop in the city'll be there praying. The Puerto Ricans and the guineas, too. It couldn't be better for us. Ya know how he's getting up to the stadium?"

"Gee, John, I don't."

"A motorcade." He paused for effect. "Through fucking Harlem and the South Bronx. They're gonna have to call out the National Guard to protect him."

"It's like he's workin' for *us*, cuz." Eddie strode into the room and put his arm around me. "I mean, did you ever see a better job than this one? Ever in your fuckin' life?"

I shook my head sincerely. "If I was ever involved in a sweeter deal, I don't remember it. It's like they're giving us a gift."

"Wait," Parker said, "it gets even better. I went into the computer today. To get the final schedule. Listen to this. Chapman Security has six new vehicles on order, all GMCs. That is, the chassis are manufactured by General Motors. The bodies are custom made by an independent outfit named Secure Coachworks. Secure was supposed to deliver the new vehicles on Tuesday, but they're behind schedule. Meanwhile, Chapman has six trucks that are barely running, two of which are coming out of service whether the new vehicles arrive or not. *Their* schedules are being distributed among the rest of the fleet. For instance, truck 345, our target, is making three extra pickups in Fresh Meadows, a big drugstore on 188th Street, and two movie complexes on the Long Island Expressway service road. The complexes have a total of twelve theaters between them."

"You got all this out of the computer?"

He looked at me with disdain. "It's not like it was written down the way I told it. I put it together piece by piece. Like, when I saw that three pickups had been added to 345's schedule, I started looking for a reason. I went to the overall schedule and found two fewer trucks than usual. So I went to Maintenance and—"

"Enough," I said. "I get it. People don't leave paper trails anymore. The trails are electronic."

"Big trails you don't need an Indian to follow. When companies start using computers, they tend to put *everything* in the memory. I went into the cargo file and found records of prior pickups for every company on 345's schedule. It's really nice the way they broke it down into cash, coins, and checks. If we get any kind of break, we're looking at well over a million dollars."

Eddie took me into the office just before lunch. He locked the door and took a small 9mm automatic out of the desk drawer, a Walther PPK.

"I changed my mind about Morasso, cuz," he announced. "I want you to bang him out after all." He waved a hand in my face. "Don't interrupt me. The first thing is that I'm gonna be drivin', so somebody's gotta be ready in case Morasso gets outta hand. Also, Avi's gonna get to the Bronx before us. He'll be waitin' when we pull up. I ain't gonna say I don't trust Avi, but life is full of traps. The reason they call 'em traps is because they're designed so you don't see them coming. Me, I like to keep my eyes open all the time. What I want is to know that after we finish the job, Morasso's gonna be covered every minute. He's got a double hard-on, one for you because of what you did to him and one for me because I brought you here."

"I get the point, Eddie. And I don't really have a problem with it." What problem could I have? We were never going to get that far, anyway. As long as Eddie didn't try to take the gun out of my hand, I was ready to go along with anything. "But what I wanna know is why I can't use the piece I already have."

He took a short, narrow cylinder out of the desk, a silencer, and screwed it into the barrel of the automatic. "We don't need to be makin' a lotta noise just when we're about to enjoy the fruits of our fuckin' labor." He pointed the 9mm at the back of a couch and pulled the trigger. The sound was a good deal louder than the "poof" you hear in the movies, but it was nothing like the roar of a .38 going off in an enclosed space. The bullet, on the other hand, went right through the back of the couch and embedded itself in the wall.

We made the exchange and went into lunch a few minutes later. As if on cue, Morasso decided to act out. He'd been a good boy all week, snorting his dope and switching back and forth between *Teenage Mutant Ninja Turtles* and *Popeye*, but halfway through the soup he lost his cool.

"Tell him to stop slurpin'."

"You talkin' to me?" Eddie asked. There was no give in his voice.

"Tell the little faggot to stop slurpin'. I can't eat when he's slurpin' the fuckin' soup. It's disgusting." He jabbed his spoon at Parker. "We don't need this fucker now. What're ya keepin' him around for?"

"We didn't need *you* from the beginning," I said quietly.

He looked up at me in surprise. Maybe he'd forgotten I was there. It's hard to know what goes on inside a psychotic's mind. One thing was certain, though. Morasso was feeling the tension. By the day of the job, he'd be seething.

I picked up the bowl of soup in front of me and sucked down several mouthfuls. Slurrrrrrrrrrrrrrppppp.

"Ahhhhh, that was good." I put the bowl on the table and stared over at Tony. He thought about it for a moment (I could tell he was thinking because his eyes went blank), then returned to his food.

TWENTY-SIX

Toward the end of that first week, I began meeting Condon and Rico in a small coffee shop on Second Avenue in the Twenties. It was usually the last stop on what was getting to be a series of very long days. I'd start at six in the morning with a drive to Ginny's place in Flushing. She'd still be in bed when I arrived, her body warm and flushed with sleep. I'd begin tossing my clothes as soon as I closed the door, then slide under the covers. Her landlord wasn't sending up heat, now that it was officially spring, but we made plenty of our own.

By nine-thirty, Ginny would be in her office and I'd be walking into Eddie's Woodhaven apartment. The days were full of the usual bullshit. Avi was still trying to decide what rifle to use on the cop and Eddie was pushing him to make an immediate decision.

"No last-minute problems, cuz," he'd lecture. "Ya gotta make a choice and live with it."

"The rifle must be right for job. It is not for me to work in half-assed manner." Avi's voice would be calm, almost placid. He was the only one of us who seemed immune to the spreading tension.

After dinner I'd make an exit and drive to my nine o'clock meeting with Condon and Rico. I kept expecting them to provide me with details and they kept asking more questions. As my answers were always the same, it got to be pretty boring. By Monday, five days before the job, I began to lose my cool.

"I been watching for signs of a stakeout at Eddie's place, but I don't see anything. You going into this blind?"

"You don't ask questions, you answer them." Condon was still playing it tough.

"You expect me to just walk through it without knowing when you're coming in?"

"I expect you to do what you gotta do to stay out of jail. That's why you're here. That's why you're rattin' out your buddies."

"Bullshit. There's at least a good chance that Eddie and the boys won't go down without a fight. Especially if you fuck it up on your end. You know what I'm gonna do when the bullets start to fly? You know what I'm gonna *have* to do? I'm gonna have to start shooting, too. How can I get out of it? Now suppose one of your people gets hit. Or even killed. And there I am, firing away. What you said about staying out of prison is right on the mark. For me, those're plans A, B, C, and D. I wanna know when and where, so if shit happens I can remove myself from the scene. Does that make sense to you?"

"Why don't you stop playin' the tough guy?" Rico asked. "It's gettin' a little tired."

"You keep me in the dark, I'm gonna fly."

"Say that again?" Condon's face was even redder than usual. I'd finally caught his attention.

"If you don't let me know what's going on, I'm gonna take what money I have in my pocket and get in the wind. Like a magician—one minute I'm here and the next I'm gone. Suicide is not part of my career path."

They gave each other one of those significant cop looks, then turned back to me. Rico was really hot—if we weren't sitting in a public place, I think he would have come after me—but Condon was calm enough.

"We're gonna take 'em in the act," he said. "If we do it before, the only charges we got are conspiracy and weapons possession. And the only proof we got is your testimony."

"That's right," Rico echoed. "All we got is the testimony of a piece of shit co-conspirator. Juries don't like pieces of shit."

"Every time I turn around," Condon said, his finger jabbing out at me, "you threaten me with some kinda bullshit. One minute you're gonna walk away. The next minute you're gonna talk to your P.O. The minute after that you're gonna punch me out. Somehow that don't sound reliable to me. It don't sound like your heart's really in it. We're gonna nail these motherfuckers in the fuckin' act and you're gonna be right there. That way, if you should happen to have an attack of conscience on the witness stand, the whole thing'll fall on your deserving head. You understand what I'm tellin' you?"

"What I think," I said, sipping at the inevitable cup of coffee, "is that you should save your motivations for your psychiatrist. I'm not asking you why; I'm asking you what, when, and where."

"We didn't set up surveillance because there's no safe way to do it," Condon said. "*You're* our surveillance."

"That's smart." Truth be told, I was relieved. I hadn't been kidding about Eddie's potential reaction to the sudden appearance of the cops. If he had any chance at all, he'd most likely fight. "What about the rest of it?"

"Lemme think about it."

"What does that mean?"

"Lemme think about it and we'll talk tomorrow."

They bullshitted me again on Tuesday, taking me through all the details without giving me any hint of what they planned to do. Instead, they cross-examined me like I was a suspect in a precinct interrogation room. What was our escape route? Where was the garage in the Bronx? How would Avi get from the school to the Bronx? What would he be driving? Would he be taking the same route as the rest of us?

"In the first place," I told them, "there aren't that many ways to get to the Bronx from Douglaston. In the second place, it's not going to get that far unless you let us go through with the job, which is clearly impossible. What's the point of it?"

"The point," Rico explained, "is to make sure the rat squeaks the same story every time he tells it."

"The point," Condon explained, "is that why should we trust you more than you trust us? You went to your parole officer and told him about us so you could cover your back. Why should we trust someone who don't trust anyone else?"

He had a point, actually. Trust wasn't really part of our deal. So I told them about truck 345, listing each pickup and Parker's estimate of the cash 345 would be carrying by the time it got to Stern's, in Douglaston. "Now, what you can do is go back to Chapman Security and check their schedule. See if it matches what I'm telling you. You could also ask them, if you haven't done it already, to look for an executive with full access who doesn't exist anywhere else but in the soul of the fucking computer. That'll be Parker. You should be able to find out exactly when he was in the computer and exactly what he looked at. But don't take a lot of time with it, because tomorrow at noon that executive will cease to exist. Gone. No trace except for a few outgoing phone calls to a number that belongs to an unmarried postal worker in Queens."

I ground to a stop, but nobody jumped in to pick up the slack. Instead, they exchanged meaningful looks.

"He rats good," Rico said. "I gotta admit that he rats good."

"Rico's a rat connoisseur," Condon announced.

"That's right. A good cop's gotta know his rats. Who's got time for clues? Who's got time for canvassing neighborhoods? What ya gotta do is go down to the garbage dump and shake the rats until one of them tell you what you need to know. That's what we done with *you*."

They went on and on, taking every opportunity to rub it in my face. They didn't even have the *possibility* of professionalism. Their egos were bound up in everything they did. Of course, my ego was right there, too. I felt it every time the blood rose in my neck and ears. My instincts told me I could take Rico out with one hand. He was nothing, an asshole trying to throw his weight around. I knew a lot of hacks like that. They shoved us around to show how tough they were. Smart cons tried not to attract their attention. If we shoved back, we were headed for a beating and the box. If we didn't shove back, we lost face.

I controlled myself by thinking of Ginny. I was still haunted by dreams, but I didn't carry them into the daylight. The stakes were too high. Later, maybe, I'd have to pay a price. I'd look in the mirror and know myself for a coward. A man without the courage to give up all hope for an ordinary life with the woman he loved. To give it up and go back to the tender bosom of a New York State Max A Institution.

"Look, boys," I said, "you're only gonna get one more chance to play it straight. After tomorrow, you're not gonna see me again."

"What's that supposed to mean?" Rico demanded. He was sniffing the air like a dog.

"Eddie's rule. I told you about it last week. Everybody comes indoors three days before the job. Ya know, I can't tell you how much I'm gonna miss these conversations." I was lying. Eddie, after a great deal of persuasion (when women do it, it's called nagging) had agreed to give me another night of freedom. I was going to spend it with

Ginny, and the fact that Eddie's place wasn't being watched didn't make it any harder.

"This is bullshit. You never told us nothin'." Rico was livid.

"Yeah, he did." Condon looked disgusted. "He told us on Friday. I got it in my notes."

"Now listen carefully," I said. "After tomorrow, you're not gonna get another chance to make this thing right. If you fuck it up tomorrow, you lose everything. I wanna know what's going on. And I especially wanna know exactly when my part is over and I can walk away."

The message must have gotten through, because the next night Condon finally gave me the details. The cops would be waiting inside the loading area behind Stern's. They'd disarm me and Eddie, then surround the van. Morasso could come out or not, as he chose. Parker's fate would rest in his hands. As for Avi, he'd be taken when he stepped out of his car behind the schoolhouse. The rifle, broken-down, would be in a small suitcase. Eddie had insisted that Avi not carry a pistol on the street; he'd called it "unacceptable risk."

After the arrests, we—those of us who were left—would be taken directly to Central Booking. We'd be fingerprinted, photographed and searched, then separated, which is routine in a big case. I'd give a statement directly to Condon and Rico, then walk out the front door.

"I don't think you'll have to testify," Condon explained. "Eddie and them'll plead. We're takin' them in the act, for Christ's sake. But they're gonna know who ratted them out. When you don't turn up at Rikers or the Men's House in Queens, they'll know it was you. We got a place for you to stay up in the Bronx. Until after they plead."

"I'll get a place of my own."

Ginny was already working on it. She'd promised a rent-stabilized apartment in the Sheepshead Bay section of Brooklyn by Saturday. Real estate was her field and she'd done enough favors over the years to make the whole thing routine.

"Yeah?" Condon shrugged, then gave Rico another meaningful look. "It's your life, Frangello. Just make sure you're available. You're gonna have to give a sworn deposition to the prosecutor."

"I'm still on parole."

"This I already know."

TWENTY-SEVEN

It was almost nine-thirty when I got to Ginny's. I opened the door to find the apartment completely dark. My hand went to my belt, looking for the gun I'd left in the car. Then the lights flashed on and I was staring at a mass of balloons and hanging crepe paper. The table was set in the dining room, complete with pointy hats and noisemakers.

"Surprise!"

"Goddamn it, Ginny, you scared the hell out of me. It's not my birthday."

"It's your *re*-birthday we're celebrating." Ginny held up a bottle of champagne. As the days went by, she was looking more and more tired. Without having gone through it, there was no way she could understand how important it is to pace yourself, to save your energy for when it's needed. Though she never complained, I had the feeling that her low would be just as sharp as the high that had followed my sudden reappearance in her life.

But her smile was as bright as ever. It was full of hope, an emotion almost unknown to me. Standing in the doorway, my heart still pounding away, I had a quick flash of myself returning after the arrests. Of Ginny waiting in the hall as I came out of the elevator, her eyes filled with tears of joy. Or glowing with pride. Or bright with desire.

"Ya know, I haven't done much drinking since I got out. Be warned. When I get drunk, I'm liable to do *anything*."

"Promises, promises. That's all I ever get."

We drank most of the champagne over dinner. Ashamed as I am to admit it, I have to report that I got drunk and let her take advantage of me. We were on the couch before we cleared the table. If Ginny had been hungry before, she was ravenous now. There was no foreplay. She pushed my cock inside her, jammed her knees against my thighs, grabbed the balls of my ass, and we were off to the races. I did the gentlemanly thing and rode her until she was exhausted.

Somehow we ended up in the bathtub. It was a narrow fit, but I'm not sure that was a disadvantage. Once again I played the part of the gentleman and took the end with the faucets. Ginny was lying back, a towel behind her head, while I sat up straight, trying to avoid the cold metal. Her legs, however, did come up along my shoulders and I was able to run a soapy washcloth down her calf, her knee, her thigh . . .

"What happened with Condon and Rico?" she asked.

So much for romance. I gave her the essentials of the meeting, hoping to return to her leg as soon as possible. We'd taken the champagne into the bathroom with us and I was too far gone to see the effect my story had on her. She pulled away as soon as I touched her.

"I don't understand what Condon meant when he said Morasso could come out of the van or not come out. How can he be arrested if he doesn't come out?"

Ginny had been drinking, too. Just enough to avoid the obvious, to make me spell it out for her.

"Morasso's an M.O. It's hard to predict exactly what he'll do."

"What's an M.O.?"

"It stands for 'mental observation' and it means a prisoner is crazy enough for the hacks to notice, but not crazy enough to be separated from the rest of the convicts. The cons mostly use the word 'bug' to describe the same situation. Morasso's a bug."

"That means he might decide to fight it out. Go down in a blaze of glory."

"I couldn't have said it better myself."

"But what about Parker? He'll be in the van with Tony."

"That's also true."

"So what you're saying is that if Morasso decides to fight, John Parker will be killed."

"Ginny, if Morasso and Parker don't come out of that van, the pigs'll put so many holes in it, you won't need the air conditioner in August. What'd you think, it was gonna be free? I'd whisper a few words into Condon's ear and all my problems would blow away? Somebody has to pay, Ginny, and what I'm doing is trading their payment for mine. 'Okay, Officer Condon, here's the deal. I'll give you a hundred years of other people's time if you'll give me five years of my time.' "

She got out of the tub and began to dry herself. You don't often get to see a woman both naked and unaware of her nakedness, but Ginny was so wrapped up in her thoughts, I might as well have been on Mars. She'd dried herself completely before she got it straight.

"I'm part of it, too," she said, turning to face me. "I listen to everything you say. I encourage you, help you plan for the unexpected. If Parker gets killed, then I'm also responsible."

"Spoken like a true Christian."

Her face reddened with anger. "You keep hiding behind that attitude. Why don't you tell me what you really think."

I pulled myself out of the water and reached for a towel. "You want me to say it's okay?"

"I don't know what I want. I'm new at this, remember?"

"Yeah, well this world isn't about right and wrong. There are no good guys here. Everybody's got their own brand of bullshit. This is about survival. I'm a wise guy because it helps me not to feel sorry for myself."

"What about Simon? He wants to help you."

"Simon's a decent guy. He'd *like* to do the right thing, but he can't. He's trapped by the system. For instance, I came out of jail and Simon shipped me out to a battle zone. He said, 'This is your new home, Pete. Try to be a good boy.' If I'd bothered to say, 'Simon, how do you expect me to follow the guidelines for parole if I have to live in a battle zone?' Simon would have responded with his own helplessness. The politicians have sold him out. There's no money for programs or decent housing or job training. What can he do?

"It's no different with the cops. They know Calvin got what he deserved. Just like they knew you didn't rip off that bodega. But the end justifies the means. Criminals must be stopped. Arrests must be made. Careers must be furthered.

"Eddie's got his own brand of bullshit. 'Guys like us, cuz, we never had a chance.' Parker? Avi? It's the same with both of them. Ask them and they'll catalogue all the evil society's done to them. Well, I don't want that, Ginny. It doesn't work for me. I can't go back to jail and I'm doing what I have to do."

I was lying, of course. I'd left out the bit about Ginny and the straw and the camel. She was part and parcel of my long rat tail, my shiny rat whiskers.

"What about me?" she asked quietly. "What's my bullshit?"

"That's not for me to say."

"I don't owe Eddie Conte a damn thing. I don't care what happens to him."

"Spoken like a true Christian."

Her face reddened again, this time from embarrassment. She started to speak, stopped, then started again. "I need you and I'm willing to sacrifice people I don't even know to keep you. The rest of it— the arrest, the strip-search, the dyke—is pure fantasy."

"Actually, *you* haven't sacrificed *anyone*. If you recall, I jumped off this particular cliff without consulting you."

I put my arms around her and pulled her close to me. She resisted for a moment, then laid her head on my shoulder.

"I'm tired," she admitted. "I've been tired for a long time."

"Ya know something, I don't sleep too well, either."

I told her about the dreams and what had happened to me in the Cortlandt psych unit. When I'd finished, it was her turn to play the parent. Her arms encircled my neck and she gently kissed my mouth.

"It'll be over soon, and when it's over, you'll come to stay with me. No more shelters. We'll live happily ever after."

"*Happier* ever after is more like it. Ya know, we forgot the dessert."

"Right. I have a key lime ice cream pie from Baskin Robbins in the freezer. And I think I have some brandy in the cabinet."

She got me drunk. Again. With the same result. When I woke up (at six o'clock, as usual), my head was pounding and my bowels felt like they were ready to explode. I stumbled into the bathroom and somehow managed to put my butt on the seat and my head in the sink at the same time, a strategy that gave me just enough strength to get into the shower. The shower gave me the strength to gargle, brush my teeth, and shave. By the time I finished, I felt as close to being human as I ever got.

Ginny was sitting up in bed when I came out of the bathroom. I don't know if it was the alcohol or the situation—it might have been both—but she looked almost haggard.

"You hung over?"

She shook her head. "I keep thinking about all the things that can go wrong."

"In a couple of hours I'll be gone."

"What?"

"It's time to suck it up. There's no going back, anyway. I'll get breakfast ready while you're in the shower."

Once I got a cup of coffee down, I began to feel good. Maybe a soldier is only happy when he's going into combat. True, there was an element of fear, but there was excitement, too. Like sitting in the front car of one of those loop-the-loop roller coasters while the other riders are being loaded. Ginny picked up on my attitude the minute she entered the room.

"You're different this morning."

"Yeah. I feel good. The bullshit is finally over and I can go to work."

"Is that the way you see it? As work?"

"It's not like I made a decision, Ginny." She stared at me blankly. "Let's face it, this is what I do best. Dreams give me problems, but I can handle the reality. Practice makes perfect and all that crap."

"I haven't had that much practice."

"Ginny, it's Friday morning. By Saturday night it'll be over. And don't worry about Parker and Morasso. I'd bet my right arm there'll be more than a hundred cops in that shopping center—cops don't care for even-money situations—and they aren't going to start shooting without giving Parker and Morasso a chance to come out. Too many witnesses. Condon and Rico are probably rehearsing their press interviews even as we speak.

"And there's something else I forgot to mention. For a while I was thinking about going through with the job. I was gonna invent a bullshit story for Condon and Rico, rip off the armored car, and run as far and as fast as I could. If I'd gone that route, it's even money that Eddie would have tried to kill me. I disrespected him. I took *his* gun and put it in *my* pocket. You already know about his plans for Morasso. Why should it be different for me? Because we're old prison buddies? Eddie wants the money. Eddie's slick and devious. Eddie needs revenge."

"And you're just getting him before he gets you? You told me you didn't need excuses."

"I don't. *You* do. What do you want for breakfast?"

We ate in silence. It was so wrong, it felt right. It felt like all the upside-down schemes I'd been pursuing all my life. The funny part was that I knew it wouldn't make any difference. If Ginny was having second thoughts—if she told me it would never work out between us—I'd still keep my end of the bargain.

"You sorry, Ginny?"

"Sorry about what?"

"That I jumped back into your life."

Instead of tossing out the first line that came into her head, she thought about it for moment. Then she looked up at me. "I want you in the worst way. Fuck Eddie and Morasso. Fuck Parker and Avi. Fuck all of them. I want you and this is the only way I can get you. It's wrong and I know it, but that's the way I feel." It was exactly what she'd said the night before, though I doubt she was aware of it.

I started to say something, but she silenced me with a wave of her hand. "Just be careful. There's a lot of things that can go wrong. Don't turn your back on Tony Morasso for one second. He's going to be coming off the drugs and—"

"Ginny?"

"Yes?"

"I love you. You love me. And we all know the gods look out for lovers. You want more toast?"

TWENTY-EIGHT

It's tempting—especially for people whose lives are filled with awful deeds, both given and taken—to see all human beings as equally corrupt. The sadistic C.O. who routinely brutalizes inmates becomes every C.O. in the Institution. The career bureaucrat who views clients as pieces of paper to be shuffled onto someone else's desk becomes every parole officer in the system. I'd included Simon Cooper in my cynical little speech to Ginny and it wasn't fair. Simon had gone the extra yard for me on more than one occasion. He'd stepped outside the system far enough to cause serious trouble for himself if his deeds came to light. What he was doing for me now—acting as a guarantee for my eventual freedom—was in no way part of his job description. I was wrong and I knew it.

So what I did by way of atonement was call him one last time with my bullshit. I found a pay phone in a drugstore on Queens Boulevard and got him on the second ring. Lucky Simon.

"It's Pete."

"Pete? You got a problem?" His voice was filled with concern. It made me feel much better.

"No problems. I just wanna let you know that I'm on my way to Eddie's. I'll be out of touch until it's over."

"What about Condon and Rico? They ease up any?"

"They've been keeping their hands to themselves, but they can't control their mouths. I expect they'll hold up their end. There's not much else they can do."

"There's still a hundred ways things could go wrong."

"This is true."

"You call me Saturday night after it's over. If I don't hear from you, I'm gonna turn up some rocks. See what's hiding in the dark. Hell, I'd be *there*, if I could. Right when the bust goes down. I asked Condon for permission to attend."

"What'd he say?"

"He laughed. Told me it was none of my business."

"No surprise. If somebody starts shooting, the cops don't want any witnesses."

"But I *am* an officer of law enforcement. I carry a gun and I arrest parole violators routinely. It's not like I'm a civilian."

"Simon, you worry too much. I'll call you on Saturday night."

"Be careful, Pete. Watch out for Avi Stern. If Eddie decides to move on you before tomorrow night, he'll use Avi. And, Pete . . . "

Great. Now I had a mommy *and* a daddy. Maybe I'd be adopted, after all.

The kennel in Woodhaven was seething when I arrived at ten-thirty. Eddie started barking the minute I came through the door.

"You're late, cuz. You asked for an extra day and I was nice enough to let ya have it. You at least coulda got here on time."

Annie was standing next to him. She was wearing a pair of green gym shorts and a red halter. No bra and, as far as I could tell, no panties, either. As the job drew closer, she was becoming more and more aroused. It added a nice flavor to the tension.

"Don't be too hard, Eddie," she said. "You know how it is with young lovers. Peter prob'ly had to get one last piece before—"

"Shut the fuck up," Eddie snarled. "I don't wanna hear that cunt bullshit anymore."

I thought he was going to hit her, but he settled for ordering her into the kitchen, then turned back to me.

"We're gonna meet in my office in an hour to go through it again. Be there."

"You got it, Eddie."

The last thing I needed was a confrontation with Eddie Conte. The whole deal would be over in thirty-six hours and I'd already decided not to rock the boat. If Eddie needed to see me crawl, I'd crawl. I'd do anything short of giving up the 9mm tucked behind my belt.

I strolled into the kitchen, looking for a cup of coffee. Annie was bent over the sink, washing dishes. The view from that angle was spectacular. She *wasn't* wearing panties and the seam of her gym shorts cut a deep line from her crotch to the top of her ass. Parker and Morasso were sitting at the kitchen table. Morasso was drooling. Parker was oblivious.

"Whatta ya say, John," I called out. "You fit and ready?"

"I'm in mourning," he announced.

"For who?"

"For me. We tossed the computer last night. Just took it and threw it in a dumpster. It was horrible."

As far as I could make out, he was serious.

"Well, what'd you expect to do, carry it along on the job?"

"Yeah," Morasso snorted. "If shit happens, he was gonna ask the fuckin' computer what to do."

Actually, Parker wasn't going to get out of the van at all. His job was to jam any attempt by the guard inside the truck to broadcast an alarm.

"I understand what you're saying, Pete." He ignored Morasso. "But why couldn't we leave it where someone could take it? Even if the serial number was traced, it couldn't come back on us."

"Ain't that sweet," Morasso persisted. "The asshole wants to find a nice home for his baby computer."

"What is problem here?" Avi came into the room. His voice was rock hard. Even Morasso jumped.

"No problem, Avi," I said. "Tony is just being his usual cooperative self." I noted the the huge revolver Avi carried in a shoulder rig. It was either a .44 or a .357. I couldn't tell which and didn't care. With its eight-inch barrel, it looked more like a cannon, anyway.

Avi sat down at the table. The tension had finally gotten to him. "This job we are doing tomorrow is perfect. We are only ones who can fuck it up. This will not happen."

He gave me a significant look. It told me that we were in this together. Eddie was too distracted, Parker too obsessed, and Morasso too crazy. He and I would hold it together.

At least that's what I thought he meant. It's easy to make mistakes when you try to read people's minds. I nodded my acceptance, hoping for the best.

"You pick out a gun yet?" I asked.

"Is not called 'gun.' " He shook his head in disgust. "Is called rifle. Is called weapon. Is not 'gun.' "

"Excuse me, Mr. Stern. Have you chosen a rifle? Or a weapon?"

"I have."

"It's about fuckin' time," Morasso growled. Eddie had cut out the dope and Tony had gone right back to being a complete asshole.

"Ya wanna eat, you better get your orders in. You got a meeting in an hour." Annie had managed to turn around. She was leaning back against the counter, probably pissed that we weren't paying any attention to her.

I looked closely at Avi while he and the others mulled over the possibilities: eggs and bacon, eggs and sausages, onion omelets. Avi looked directly at Annie without showing a hint that anything besides food was on his mind. I decided that I couldn't trust a man I couldn't read. Then remembered that I'd just made a pact with him. Then decided I'd have to watch him all the time. Then remembered that he was going to be arrested before he ever got to the roof of that school.

"I don't want a fuckin' omelet," Morasso shouted. "Omelets are fa fags. Whatta you say, Pete? You want a fuckin' omelet?"

"I ate before I got here. I'm not hungry."

"So it's onion omelets?" Annie asked.

"Two against one," Parker announced. "Democracy in action."

"I ain't eatin' no fuckin' omelet. That's fuckin' Jew food."

I came across the table, putting everything I had into my right hand. Morasso froze and I caught him flush on the mouth. He went head over heels, taking the chair with him. The back of his skull smashed into the linoleum with a satisfying thud.

When he came up, shaking his head to clear the dizziness, the top of his shirt collar was already soaked with blood.

"I'm gonna kill you," he hissed through broken teeth.

Death threats are never tolerated in the Institution. That's because the convict making the threat *has* to follow through. To do less would be dishonorable. My hand dropped to the little 9mm, but the weapon never cleared my belt. Avi had dragged the cannon out of his pocket and trained it on the center of Morasso's forehead.

It was funny, in a way. I hit Morasso because I was afraid that Avi would kill him. Avi once told me that a Jew is a Jew forever. Despite the fact that an Israeli court had sent him to prison for doing what the army had trained him to do. Despite the fact that he'd been hounded out of the country after his release. Avi had been the only Jew in Cortlandt, and as far as I know he'd never taken a backward step.

Now Avi was out there trying to stop *me* from killing Morasso. At least I hoped he was. He was giving a very convincing performance. Especially when he drew back the hammer.

"Why are we needing this man?" he asked. "I cannot understand why we cannot do this without him."

Morasso's eyes widened, then he said the magic words: "Please, don't kill me, please."

"Don't do it, Avi," I said, playing my part. "Let it go. Tony's gonna be good. Right, Tony?"

He nodded, his eyes glued to the barrel of the gun.

"Let the hammer down, Avi." I glanced at Parker and Annie. Parker was watching with interest, Annie with anticipation. Nobody in the room saw Tony Morasso as a human being about to have his heart blown through his rib cage. He was an expendable detail or a pain in the ass or a problem to be solved. Anything, but human. "C'mon, Avi. Think about how you'll feel if you blow the job over a piece of shit like Tony Morasso."

Avi tilted the barrel of the gun up toward the ceiling and let the hammer down. "You are right. Even if we are not really needing this man, Eddie is thinking that we do."

I went over to the refrigerator and filled a towel with ice. I'd played my part to the hilt, but now that our little domestic drama was over, I felt the weariness fill my body. I wanted to go into a bedroom and lie down, to face the wall and ignore the bullshit, to sleep without dreaming.

But of course I didn't do anything like that. My life was on the line, too. I turned back to the table and handed Morasso the towel. "Put this on your mouth," I said. "You wanna look nice for tomorrow."

A half hour later we were in Eddie's office, running through the details. It was maybe the tenth time we'd done it in the last three days, and halfway through, I realized this was Eddie's way of dealing with the tension. The meeting didn't last very long, because we all knew our lines.

Eddie asked me to stay after the others left. He asked me what had happened to Morasso's mouth and I explained it. Then we spent an hour trying on blond wigs, dark glasses, and false beards. Eddie had researched the matter himself and knew, in theory at least, how to apply the phony hair. Still, no matter how we arranged our disguises, we looked like refugees from a bad movie.

"Perfect," Eddie announced.

"Perfect? You gotta be kidding me."

"All right, cuz, so it's not *perfect*. But it'll get us up on the platform and it'll keep us from bein' identified later on."

"What about Tony?"

"What about him?"

"No disguise?"

"Tony's gotta look ugly, cuz. That's the whole fuckin' point. I don't see how it's gonna matter. Where he's goin', he don't have to worry about witnesses. What you and Avi did before was good. Now he knows that you got a gun and I got a gun and Avi got a gun, but *he* only got his dick to shoot with. Even a fuckin' bug like Morasso could figure it out from there."

Eddie dismissed me a few minutes later and I wandered through the upstairs apartment looking for something to do. Avi was busy cleaning his weapon of choice, a .30-06 Winchester Model 70. Parker was in the garage, fitting out the van with a two-way radio. Morasso was in his room, nursing his wounds and his grievances. I decided to go to my own room and get comfortable.

Annie was making up my bed when I walked into the room. She turned to me and smiled.

"You really put it to Tony," she said. "What a shot. He's lucky he's got his head."

"Yeah? I guess somebody up there likes him."

She sat on the bed and patted the mattress. "Nice and firm," she announced, emphasizing the last word.

"Ya know, Annie, one day Eddie's gonna figure it out. He's gonna figure it out and he's gonna kill you."

"Never." She shook her head firmly. "Eddie loves me. Besides, he already knows. I tell him about it in bed. It gets him hot." She leaned back against the wall, put her heels on the edge of the mattress, and let her knees fall apart. "Speakin' of hot . . ."

"Forget it, Annie. I'm not interested."

"That girlfriend must be something else. Looks like she got it *all*. Too bad. By the way, if you and her should ever feel like doin' a three-some, make sure to let me know."

I took her by the arm and led her to the door. I was tempted to swat her on the ass, but I was afraid my hand would get stuck. As I closed the door, I heard her laugh. Somehow it didn't bother me. There was a small bureau against the wall. I dragged it in front of the door, put the 9mm under the pillow, and fell asleep.

TWENTY-NINE

I'm in charge of erecting a massive structure. Not a single building or even a complex of buildings, but an entire city. The city is composed of transparent boxes, twelve fluorescent white lines against an inky-black sky.

Nothing goes right. I jump from one crisis to another, repairing and rearranging. Doing whatever's necessary to keep the project going.

There are no other workers to be seen, but still the structure grows. I know I should be anxious, because the city will crumble if I make a mistake, but I feel calm, almost peaceful.

Suddenly I realize that I'm falling behind. The structure is too elaborate and I can't cover the whole project by myself. I lose a wing, then a tower, then entire neighborhoods.

These disasters fuel my determination. I introduce new designs, reinforce foundations, convinced there's some way to get it right; some arrangement that will support the weight of the project.

Though I don't slacken my efforts for a minute, a depressing thought enters my consciousness. I don't know what I'm making. I can't summon up an image of the finished structure. There's no way I can be the master builder. I'm an ordinary worker, maybe even a slave.

Nevertheless, I continue to work at top speed. I never stop to consider the possibility of another approach. I don't have time for that. If I slow down, disaster is sure to follow.

I woke to a knock on the door. Parker's voice followed, announcing that dinner was almost ready. I looked over at the clock. It was six-thirty.

"All right, John. I'll be out in a few minutes."

"I'd like to talk to you."

I glanced down at my crotch. I had a firm erection, one of those nocturnal jobs that won't go down. "Let me get my pants on." The request must have seemed odd, considering that we'd come from a world without privacy. Where, as often as not, the most intimate acts—dressing, showering, shitting—were performed in the company of others.

Whatever Parker thought, he waited patiently while I dressed. I tried to move the bureau away from door as quietly as possible, but it scraped and squeaked despite its being empty and made of glued sawdust.

"Did I wake you up?" Parker asked as he stepped into the room.

I took a quick look down the hall. It was empty and the other doors were shut. "It doesn't matter." I closed the door. "Actually, I feel pretty good. If I had a cup of coffee, I'd feel even better."

Parker's face lit up. "I'll get it. Give you a chance to wash your face."

I closed the door behind him, then took the 9mm from under the pillow, and shoved it behind my belt. I hadn't been lying to Parker. Despite the dream, I felt refreshed and alert. I went into the bathroom, took a leak, then washed my face, combed my hair, and brushed my teeth. Halfway through the last operation, I heard the bedroom door open. The piece was in my hand before I made a decision to pull it.

"It's only me," Parker called.

I didn't bother to tell him how close he'd come to being shot. Instead, I resolved, awake or asleep, to keep the door blocked.

"You oughta knock, John," I announced, coming into the living room.

"Sorry, Pete. I didn't think."

I took the coffee and drained half of it. "It don't pay to be an absentminded professor if you're in the crime business." I must have expected some sort of an answer, because I took the time to finish the mug. "What's up, John? Whatta you need?"

He pointed at the gun at my waist. I wasn't making any attempt to hide it.

"That's a weapon."

"Damn, you scientists don't miss a thing."

He blushed, then grinned. Parker was very easygoing. Add that to the fact that he had no conscience and you come up with a very rare combination—the amiable psychopath.

"All right, wise guy, here's what's bothering me. You, Eddie, and Avi are all armed. We're not going to do the job for another twenty-four hours. Is there something I don't know?"

"There's lots of things you don't know. But they have nothing to do with this specific situation. You're very intelligent, John, and you've got balls, too. What you *don't* have is experience. When you're confined to a house with four violent criminals, anything can happen. Why do you think they call us criminals? Because we're good at social cooperation? There's a lot of strain here. It pays to watch your back."

He grimaced. "I see your point and I'd agree with you except for one thing. Eddie told us no guns. I remember feeling relieved because of Tony Morasso. I also remember assuming that Eddie's gun rule was to last until we were actually doing the job. Now, all of a sudden, I find that I'm the only one *without* a gun."

"You and Tony."

"Tony doesn't count."

I waved him into a chair. "I have a gun because I took one and put it in my pocket. You wanna know about Eddie and Avi, ask *them*. But I have a question for you: if you did have a piece, what would you do with it? You already told me you never handled a gun in your life."

"That's another reason why I was happy with the no-gun rule."

"Your problem is that you started too high up. You should've done a few burglaries first, maybe a couple of gas stations. You need to get a feel for treachery. Now you're in the shit and you don't have a shovel."

But Parker did know something about *prison*. What we were doing was negotiating. He needed protection and I was the one most likely to supply it. Not that he could come right out and ask me to do it as a favor. You don't ask for favors in prison. You don't accept them, even if they're offered, because if you do, you become obligated to the giver. Sooner or later the favor must be returned and there's no way of knowing exactly what repayment will entail.

"You think shit'll happen," he asked quietly.

"Shit *always* happens, but if someone has plans for you, I haven't heard 'em."

He hesitated, shifting in his chair. I could see the words forming in his mind.

"Why don't you just come out with it, John? Say what you gotta say."

"I need someone to watch my back."

Protection, the most common of prison rackets. The going rate varies with the resources of the particular inmate seeking the service, but a carton of cigarettes a week is usually enough to keep even the richest convict safe from attack.

"What's in it for me?"

"Five percent of my take."

I have to give Parker credit. He didn't waste his time trying to bind me with emotional ties. Of course, the irony of his coming for protection to the very man who intended to betray him wasn't lost on me either.

"The price is right, John, only you should understand what I can and can't do for you. First, you've got nothing to worry about until after the job is done—Eddie needs you to jam the radio—but even if he has something else in mind, I'll be up on the platform and that doesn't do you much good. So what we're looking at is the period between the end of the job and the final split in the Bronx. You wanna pay five percent for that? We could be talkin' about ten grand."

"Yeah, that's exactly what I want." His voice was steady, as hard, in its own way, as Avi's. "If Eddie wants my end for himself, he'll take me out in the Bronx. You keep my ass in one piece until I get to the airport and I won't have any problem parting with five percent. No matter how much it comes to."

Our high finance brought to a satisfactory conclusion, we got up and headed for the dinner table. Annie had fried up a dozen tough, greasy pork chops, but nobody complained about the meat or the burned string beans. We were still chewing on the first mouthfuls when Eddie dragged a sawed-off, double barreled, 12 gauge shotgun out of a box and laid it on the table next to Morasso. Even lying on its side, it was vicious enough to command our total attention.

"You like that, Tony?" Eddie asked. "That's yours."

The shotgun was so old it was impossible to tell the make. Morasso picked it up and began to fondle the dual triggers. His eyes were glowing.

"Man, you could do some shit with this," he hissed. His fingers found the release and he broke it open. It was unloaded.

"You get two shells when we're at the site," Eddie said matter-of-factly. Morasso started to protest, but Eddie slammed his fist on the table. "Don't say a fuckin' word. I had enough bullshit from you already. You do the job the way I tell ya."

"All right, Eddie. Whatever ya want." Morasso was cradling the shotgun in his arms.

"That ain't a fuckin' baby." Eddie shook his head in disgust. "It's not gonna suck ya tit. Why don't you tell us what you're supposed to do with it."

Morasso grinned like a proud schoolboy. He'd been taking a lot of abuse for the last two weeks, but tomorrow he'd be the star of the show. "Okay, here goes: the two security guards come outta the cab of the truck and walk up to the platform. You and Pete step out in front of them and I come outta the van behind 'em. We take their pieces, then I drag one of them back to the truck."

"Which one?"

"Yeah, I almost fuckin' forgot. First I take a look at the guard who's still locked in the back of the truck. If he's a nigger, I pick another nigger. If he's white, I pick a white guy. If there's no match, I pick one at random. *Then* I drag his ass to the truck and put him up against the window in the back. I make sure the one inside can see my face and the shotgun. Then I tell the one inside to open the fuckin' door or I'll blow his buddy's brains all over the parking lot."

"What happens if he doesn't open the door?"

"I whack the first guard and grab the next one."

"How long do you wait?"

"I wait until you tell me to shoot."

"If you gotta whack the first guard, what do ya have to be careful *not* to do?"

"I don't get it."

"You gotta be careful not to pull both triggers at the same time. The shotgun only holds two shells, right? If you pull both triggers, ya got nothin' left. See how the trigger on the right is in front of the one on the left?"

"Of course, whatta ya think, I'm stupid?"

"Yeah."

"C'mon, Eddie."

"If you pull the first one just right, you can fire one barrel without firing the other. I want ya to practice. Tomorra morning you could show us all how good you are."

We spent the next few minutes trying to make slices of pork small enough to swallow. All of us except for Tony. He kept dry-firing the shotgun, pulling one trigger, then the other. I'd never seen him happier.

THIRTY

Eddie made us go through every detail, outlasting even the pork chops in his zeal. I didn't mind reciting dutifully when my turn came. It figured to be a long night, anyway. Avi delivered his lessons with military precision. Parker rambled on enthusiastically, describing the devilish concoction he'd created for Chapman Security's central dispatcher.

"What I did," he explained, "was record ten minutes of computer transmission, a message I sent out and had the Chapman computer send back. The message is, 'We're robbing your truck!' Of course it doesn't sound like that when the computer receives it. The computer hears a series of high-pitched squeals and squeaks, like a power saw going through plywood. I'm gonna broadcast it at four times normal power and keep it coming until the job is done and we're ready to take off."

It was ten o'clock when Eddie dismissed us. Avi followed me back to my room, but he didn't step inside without asking permission. This was my space and he couldn't disrespect it without insulting me. I don't think he would have bothered with the formalities if he'd come to visit John or Tony.

"You have perhaps a moment?" he asked.

"There's gonna be a lotta moments tonight. I'm not expecting to sleep." I nodded him into a chair and closed the door behind him. "What's up, Avi?"

He crossed his legs and took a second to think about it. "This job, you are liking it?"

I shrugged. "Whatta you mean by 'like'?"

"It seem to you good? Acceptable?" He was struggling to find the right words.

"You asking me if I think we can pull it off?"

"Yes."

"I think we already talked about this."

"Still, please, tell me your feelings at present time."

"What can I say, Avi? It's as good as a job can get, but that doesn't mean it's guaranteed. You want a guarantee in life, check out a casket."

He shook his head. "I am sorry to be disagreeing with you, but job could be better. Problem is Tony Morasso. This man is crazy. There is no knowing what crazy man will do. I am thinking about time in Israeli army. We are doing patrols into Syria. Sweeps to find terrorists before they cross border into Israel. If I am given such man as Tony Morasso in my squad, I would refuse orders. Missions are dangerous and I must know how all others will act in dangerous situation."

"So what do you wanna do, Avi? Resign your commission? Eddie's made up his mind and that's that."

"I want to go right now and kill him."

"Who? Eddie?"

"Please to stop busting balls." Avi managed a grin. It had all the warmth of skull in a bag of maggots. "I am saying to go this minute and kill Tony Morasso."

"Just like that?"

He looked at me strangely, as if an invitation to murder carried no more weight than a stroll to the supermarket. I wondered how many he'd killed in his life. Ten? Twenty? A hundred? Avi had told me about the treachery of politicians and superior officers, but he'd never told me exactly what he'd done to capture the attention of those who'd rather not know.

"This is what must be done. Why is to argue? World does not need Tony Morasso."

"Avi, this is bullshit. If you kill Tony, Eddie's just gonna call the job off. You're a military man, right? Then you should know that you waited too long. Parker dumped the computer yesterday. We'd have to start all over again."

"This is true. If *I* kill Tony, Eddie will not go ahead. But if *we* kill Tony, he will think differently."

It was disgusting, really. I thought of Ginny. A single bad experience had convinced her that she understood what it meant to be "outside the law," but she had no idea what it was really like. What it was like, for instance, to solve your personnel problems with a bullet.

"Enough, Avi. You're disrespecting me here."

"How so?"

"You're disrespecting me because it's my job to control Tony and you're saying I can't do it."

"I did not know this." He looked surprised, then contrite. "You must be careful with this man. You cannot know in advance what he will do."

"Well, I'll try to stay behind him. If it's any consolation, by the way, I think Eddie knows he made a mistake. He's just too stubborn to admit it. Or do anything about it."

"This is Eddie's problem. He is stubborn. Like army officer. He cannot be wrong."

"Yeah? Maybe we should kill Eddie? Eddie, Annie, and Morasso. Forget the cop. You, me, and Parker could do the job ourselves. Make for a nice split."

He thought about it for a minute, then shook his head. "You are joking with me."

"Am I?" I took the 9mm and put it on the table. "We could take care of them, force Parker to hold up his end, then take care of him, too. Probably end up with half a million each."

I lit a cigarette while he thought about it. Wondering what I'd say if he accepted.

"I *am* joking with you, Avi. You gotta forgive me. What I really need is some sleep. How 'bout we do the lines the way they're written? Morasso'll hold up his end. I guarantee it."

He looked relieved. "Yes, this must be the way. Morasso would be easy to kill, but I think Eddie will be prepared."

"Right. He'll probably have Annie come all over us."

Avi left a few minutes later. I watched him go down the hall, noting that every door was shut and the lights were off downstairs. It was almost eleven, but I wasn't close to sleep. What I'd told Avi was true enough. I needed rest, but that didn't mean I'd get it.

I dutifully pulled the bureau across the door, then began to work out. I didn't want to think about Ginny, about Condon and Rico, about Eddie's reaction when he figured out who set him up. I didn't want to think about how ugly it was or that there were no good guys and no honorable course of action for anyone.

One more day. That's what I thought about. One more day and I'd be out of this jam. I'd move in with Ginny, into a world where "shit happens" means the car won't start on a rainy morning. Or somebody left the coffeemaker on. Or the nine o'clock showing of this week's hot movie is sold out.

I worked myself as close to exhaustion as I was likely to get, then lay down on the bed. I dozed off around one o'clock, but couldn't even get deep enough to dream. The job kept running through my mind. I tried to imagine the look on Eddie's face when the cops made their move. Sometimes the shock froze him as stiff as a block of ice. Sometimes his face contorted with rage and he grabbed for the pistol under his jacket. As I saw it, my one and only job was to prevent him from carrying out the latter course of action. If the cops opened fire, we'd both go down.

The problem was simple enough, but I couldn't see any clear solution. If I jumped on Eddie's back or pinned his arms or knocked him down or made any sudden move of any kind, the cops were liable to misunderstand my motives and put two or three thousand shotgun pellets in my chest. That's *if* they even bothered to analyze the situation. Condon and Rico could be hoping for a slaughter. They could be looking for any excuse to start shooting. God knows, I'd given them enough reason to hate my guts.

I might have drifted in this paranoia until breakfast if I hadn't suddenly experienced a more basic urge. I dragged the bureau away from the door and made my way to the bathroom, the 9mm tucked safely behind my belt. As I came close, the door opened and Annie appeared wearing a blue terry robe. She gave a little squeal of surprise, then grinned happily.

"Who's the lucky guy?" I asked.

Her hand went to the robe's belt. "It could be you if you weren't so uptight."

I started to say, "Don't bother," but she pulled the robe open before I got the words out. "Annie," I said (after taking a good look), "I don't need this. It's all very nice. Nice pussy. Nice tits. But I don't want another man's woman. Even if I have his permission."

She slowly retied the robe. "You're all so fuckin' high and mighty. You go to jail and fuck boys in the ass. Or if ya too good fa that, you pull your fuckin' dick. How many years? Six? Eight? Ten? You want us to sit at home like we're nuns or some shit. That's why there's nobody waitin' when ya come out. That's why all your fuckin' wives file for divorce. We're human, too. We got urges, just like men. Eddie wasn't stupid. He tole me, 'I love ya, Annie, and you love me. Do what you gotta do and I won't hold it against you.' "

"How could he hold it against you when most likely someone's already holding it against you?"

She tried to slap me. Her hand shot out, her weight behind it, but I managed to pull back far enough to let the shot pass in front of me.

"Bastard," she shouted.

My hand went down to my waist. I wasn't about to shoot Annie, but her voice was still echoing in the hallway. I pulled her into the bathroom and closed the door.

"Take it easy, Annie. I'm sorry. What I said before was wrong."

"You know what it is? Ya look so pretty. Ya look like a fuckin' altar boy, but inside you don't give a shit about anybody. Two days after you showed up, I tole Eddie, 'Let's get ridda him. He's no fuckin' good.' Eddie says, 'I known him for a long time. He's a scumbag, but he'll do the job. Besides, I'll make sure to keep an eye on him.' Some fuckin' eye. Next thing I know, you're comin' and goin' like the Queen of fuckin' England. A guy who talks as good as you is liable to be talkin' to anyone."

It was hard for me to work up the expected degree of righteous indignation. I'd already betrayed every one of them. So, instead of proclaiming my loyalty, I slid my arm beneath the robe and pulled her in close to me.

"Look, Annie, it's not that I don't want to fuck you." I gave her ass a little squeeze and she pressed against my hip. "You're a good-looking woman. I see you in the hallway and I start thinking how I'm crazy not to take advantage. But me and Ginny have something going. I never asked her to wait for me—never expected that she would—but here she is and, stupid or not, I gotta respect it. You and Eddie have your own arrangement. That's great. Only the thing is, we don't wanna fuck up the job. We're real close to a big payoff and everybody's tense. One spark and there's no job and most likely somebody's dead. Right now, all I wanna do is take a leak and go back to my room, so—"

"Could I hold it?"

"For Christ sake, Annie . . . "

"Awright, awright." She stepped back and rearranged the robe. "I gotta go downstairs anyway. If I keep Eddie waitin' too long, he'll probly jerk off before I get there."

THIRTY-ONE

In my second year at Cortlandt, I got adopted by a young inmate named Zebediah Peters. Most of the prisoners at Cortlandt hail from the Rotten Apple, but Zebediah came from Colden, New York, a small town near the Canadian border. Being inexperienced, he made a big mistake by accepting a pack of cigarettes from an inmate named Burt White. All three of us, Zeb, Burt, and myself, were working in the tailor shop at the time.

Zebediah Peters didn't have much money, but he was young and handsome, a perfect target for an aggressive homosexual like Burt White. Burt started in about Zeb returning the pack of cigarettes, the *same* cigarettes Zeb had been given and which he'd already smoked. Zeb offered to replace the cigarettes with another pack, but, of course, that wasn't good enough.

For some reason, boredom, perhaps, I stepped in. I took out a pack of cigarettes and handed it to Burt and said, "You're even."

Burt didn't argue. Most likely, he figured I was already putting it to young Zebediah. Zeb, on the other hand, attached himself to me like a puppy at the end of a leash. He told me he was the son of a Pentecostal preacher and he believed in justice. Burt White had retreated, but that wasn't good enough. He had to pay a price.

I tried to chill Zeb out by explaining that the only way to punish Burt White was to kill him. Anything less would open Zeb up to the threat of retaliation. Retaliation which might or might not come directly from Burt White.

"Okay," he responded, "then I'll kill him."

Cortlandt is an enormous place. There are thirteen major cell blocks and more than two thousand prisoners. You often go for weeks without meeting a specific individual. If you have a network of allies, you can usually arrange an ambush. If you're Zebediah Peters, on the other hand, you have to hold a grudge for a long time before you find an opportunity to act on it.

It took Peters six months to get it together and he confided in me every step of the way. The first thing he did was settle on the tailor shop as the place. Then he went out to look for a weapon. Not just any weapon, because the tailor shop had a metal detector at the entrance. Of course, we all had scissors, but they were so small they couldn't be used as killing weapons. Zeb would have to stab Burt fifty times and the hacks never took their eyes off us.

Zeb found a con who worked in a maintenance shop where they cut Plexiglas sheets to replace cracked Plexiglas around the Institution. The procedure for turning plastic into a killing weapon is simple enough. All it requires is patience. The con in the maintenance shop waited until the C.O. in charge was busy elsewhere, then snatched a small piece of Plexiglas off the scrap pile and stashed it. The next day, after alerting Zeb, he tossed it out the window. Zeb retrieved it when he came out on the yard and took it to another con, a gardener, who had access to a grinder which was used to sharpen sickles and hedge shears. The convict-gardener put a handle on one end of the Plexiglas and a six-inch, razor-sharp blade on the other. Total cost for both operations: three cartons of Salems.

Just before the big day, Burt White got himself caught with a shank in the yard. The C.O.'s gave him the obligatory beating and tossed him in the box. Zeb took the opportunity to smuggle the Plexiglas shank into the tailor shop. Now it was just a matter of waiting.

I remember trying to call Zeb off. "It's one thing," I said, "to whack someone out in a private place. Even if the C.O.'s get your name from a snitch, the most they can do is kick your ass and throw you in the box. There are no private places in the tailor shop. You gotta kill him right in front of the hacks. You're already doing twelve to life. Is the satisfaction of killing Burt White for something everybody's already forgotten worth an extra twenty-five years in the Institution?"

I might as well have been talking to the moon. Zeb began every workday by searching for Burt White's face. There were six of us who knew what was going to happen and we shared the tension among us. A man was going to die. It wasn't going to be a sudden, unexpected explosion. We wouldn't see a flurry of activity in the yard, then hear the details later on. The drama was going to be acted out before our eyes.

Despite our professed indifference to violence and death, the tension grew sharper and sharper as the days passed. By the time Burt White made his appearance, it had come to dominate our lives. I was sure that Burt would notice the sidelong looks we gave him or smell the crackle of anticipation, but Burt was still in a daze from his three weeks in the box. He'd been beaten pretty badly and seemed twenty pounds thinner. When Zeb came up behind him, Burt didn't bother to look around. When the shank slammed between his ribs, his eyes widened, but the rest of his face remained calm. His fingers continued to work the sewing machine and the fabric he was stitching for a moment, then he fell gently forward.

The tension on that Saturday morning in Eddie's Woodhaven apartment was as thick as it had been in the tailor shop on the day Burt White came out of the box. Eddie sat with us at breakfast, but for once he didn't make us recite our lessons. Morasso didn't complain about the food, either, and Parker seemed to have forgotten his lost computer. Even Annie was quiet. She cooked breakfast, moving from one frying pan to another without saying a word.

After breakfast we went into the living room. Avi suggested a card game, but after half an hour we gave it up. Nobody seemed able to concentrate on the hands. Finally, Avi announced that he was going upstairs to clean the Winchester. Morasso left, too, probably to watch cartoons while he stroked the shotgun. That left me, Eddie, and Parker. Annie was still in the kitchen with the dishes.

"How you feelin', cuz?" Eddie asked Parker. "You up for this?"

"Why don't you ask *him*?" Parker indicated me with a flip of his hand.

"Don't take it the wrong way, cuz. Ya know how it is with a virgin. You never know for sure if you're gonna get in or not."

Parker managed a faint grin. "It's harder than I thought, but I'll be all right. I mean it's not that I'm having second thoughts or anything. It's just hard."

"You're probly worried about gettin' caught. That's natural. We get popped, cuz, we ain't gonna see the outside for a long time. Maybe forever. This job is as good as a job can get, but that don't mean nothin' can go wrong. If shit happens, you know what you gotta do. You're gonna be the only one in the van."

One of Eddie's contingency plans involved Parker driving if things got too hot and we had to get out in a hurry.

"I know what I have to do," Parker said firmly.

"Don't get excited, cuz. What *I'm* tryin' to do is make it easier. Here." He handed Parker a revolver, an S & W .38, the same one I'd exchanged for the 9mm. "All you gotta do is point it and pull the trigger. You might not be able to hit nothin', but we're the only ones who know that and we won't tell."

Parker took the gun and put it in the pocket of his jacket. He grinned over at me, reminding me of the deal we'd made. Maybe he was regretting the offer. Maybe he figured it wasn't likely that Eddie would give him a piece if Eddie was planning a doublecross. Maybe he didn't understand that, for Eddie, giving a revolver to a man who didn't know what to do with it besides point and shoot might be just another brushstroke in the art of betrayal. Or it might be just what it seemed—a good officer reassuring a rookie before his first battle. If there's no way to be sure, it pays to prepare for the worst-case scenario. I don't think Parker understood that, either.

Annie served lunch a little after noon. Avi ate with the nonchalance of a veteran warrior, but the rest of us only picked at our food. Eddie kept looking at us. I couldn't tell if he was happy with what he saw, but somewhere between the soup we didn't drink and the tuna fish we didn't eat, he walked over to the refrigerator, took out a bottle of champagne, and opened it.

"The bunch of yiz look like you're goin' to a funeral. Lighten up, for shit sake. Today God is gonna give us a fuckin' gift. We should have proper gratitude." He filled five paper cups with champagne and handed them out. "Drink up. Then I got a treat for ya."

The treat turned out to be a porno film. Two hours of watching half-hard cocks pound into sweating, pink vaginas. There was nothing sexual about it that I could see, but it passed the time. We sat straight in our chairs, each of us wrapped in our own thoughts, while the women moaned and the men sweated. After the final scene, an orgy involving eight people, Eddie snapped off the VCR.

"Awright, boys, it's game time. Parker, get your ass down to the van. Make sure the radios are workin' right, especially Avi's portable. Tune in to the Chapman dispatcher and find out where 345 is. We'll be down in twenty minutes." He waited for Parker to get out the door, then turned back to Avi. "Avi, you're gonna be on your own. I don't want no improvisin'. You don't move till we signal you on the radio that 345 is leavin' its next-to-last stop. You don't get a signal, you don't do nothin'. You come back to the apartment and wait for us."

Avi started to voice his contempt, but Eddie waved him off. "Don't say a fuckin' word, cuz. You ain't gonna hear my shit after this minute, so you could put up with the paranoia. When the time comes, you're gonna get five beeps. No voice, because sure as shit, if we go vocal, some asshole with a ham radio's gonna pick up the transmission. Now suppose good old 345 should burn up an engine and the dispatcher sends a substitute truck I don't know nothin' about. If shit like that should happen and I gotta call the job off, I don't want you to go shootin' no cop." He tossed Avi a set of keys. "Take the fuckin' gun, pick up ya portable from Parker, and get in the wind. No bullshit."

Eddie spun on his heels to face Morasso. "Tony," he snarled, "if you ever in your whole fuckin' life bother to do somethin' with your head instead of ya fuckin' fists, this is the time to do it. We're talkin' about a million dollars here. And if that ain't enough, I'm tellin' you personal that if you fuck up, I'm gonna kill ya. You got a shotgun that'll put a man's head in fuckin' orbit. You pull the trigger without me givin' the word, *your* head's gonna follow."

Now it was my turn. Eddie looked at me, started to say something, then stopped, then started again. "You done good, cuz. You got us here, which in some ways is more than I expected. But you're too independent. You don't know how to follow orders. From here on, it's by the numbers. Understand what I'm sayin'?"

"No problem, Eddie."

"Glad to hear it, cuz. Now, I'm gonna go and say goodbye to Annie. You and Tony should try to keep each other from gettin' lost."

I was as wired as if we were actually going to do the job. That strange mixture of fear and exhilaration, of smug satisfaction in being the outlaw and greed in anticipation of the reward to follow jumped back and forth between me and Tony like lightning flashing from one cloud to another. We stood there in the middle of the living room, not even bothering to sit down on chairs two feet away, and waited for Eddie. The wait was interminable.

"What the fuck is he *doin'* in there?" Tony finally asked.

"Tell you the truth, Tony, I'm afraid to think about it."

"And how come he's always jumpin' on me?"

"He thinks you're gonna shoot someone."

"Ain't that what I'm here for?"

He still hadn't gotten it right. After all this time.

"Just the opposite, Tony. You shoot somebody and most likely the guard inside the truck will decide you're gonna shoot him, too. Think about it. If you were locked inside that truck and you just saw your buddy's head go flyin' across the parking lot, would you open the door?"

His mouth was swollen and discolored, his eyes round and hard as marbles, his breathing fast and shallow. If it was me in the truck, I wouldn't open the door whether he killed my buddy or said, "Pretty please." But then again I'm a criminal.

"What you gotta do," I explained, "is *look* scary, but not actually do anything."

He thought about it for minute, then stared up at me with a mixture of hate and triumph. "Then how come Eddie's givin' me shells to go wit' the shotgun? If I ain't supposed ta do nobody, wha'da I need with a loaded shotgun? I could do it unloaded."

Which is exactly the way I'd have him do it, if it was my job. I shrugged my shoulders. "Have it your own way." Actually, Eddie had anticipated the possibility that the guard inside might decide to abandon his buddies. If we couldn't get the door opened then and there, I was going to drive the truck up to the Bronx and park it in the garage. Given enough time, we'd be able to cut our way in with a torch.

Eddie came out a few minutes later, Annie in tow. She raised a glass of soda and said, "Until we meet again on a beach in Rio. Good luck, boys."

Parker was waiting in the van. He had the radio humming.

"What's the story?" Eddie asked as soon as the door closed. He and I were sitting up front, him driving. Parker and Tony were crouched on the floor in the back.

"Three forty-five just left Alexander's on Queens Boulevard. They've got two supermarkets before they get to the movie theaters in Fresh Meadows. I figure about two hours until they show up in Douglaston."

Eddie checked his watch. "That's almost an hour early."

"Maybe they'll go for coffee," I suggested. "Anyway, the sooner the better."

"Yeah, cuz, you got *that* right. Let's move."

We drove out to Parsons Boulevard in Flushing, to a large parking lot surrounding a Waldbaum's supermarket, then parked the van fifty yards from the rear loading docks. An armored car bearing the name Chapman Security and the number 345 was standing in the loading area, its motor running. As Eddie and I watched, two men, both white, came out of the supermarket. One of them, the taller of the two, was dragging a large canvas bag. Both had their weapons out, barrels pointed toward the ground. When they got to the back of the truck, the rear door opened and the bag was tossed inside.

> *Three forty-five to base, K.*
> *Three, four, five?*
> *We're 10-16 on Parsons Boulevard. Proceeding to account number . . . let's see, account number S8776 on Union Turnpike.*
> *Roger, three, four, five. Tell George to phone Evelyn. She's drivin' the operators crazy.*
> *Will do. 10-4.*
> *10-4.*

Eddie took off before the truck left the parking lot. He drove to an A & P on Union Turnpike, but instead of turning into the parking lot, he pulled the van to the curb across the street. The armored car lumbered into the parking lot ten minutes later.

When the the two guards climbed out of the truck, the only thing they carried was a clipboard and some papers. Both men kept their weapons securely holstered. They disappeared into the supermarket, reappearing twenty minutes later with the expected canvas bag. Their weapons were in their hands.

"Did I tell ya, cuz?" Eddie said. "Did I tell ya? It's a fuckin' gift. They been draggin' them bags out all day."

> *Three forty-five, K.*
> *Three, four, five?*
> *We are 10-16 on Union Turnpike. Proceeding to account number T1161 on Horace Harding Boulevard. 10-4.*

Negative, three forty-five. You are ahead of schedule. Pickups are not ready. Repeat. Not ready. Take a 10-20 and tell George to call Evelyn.
10-4.
10-4.

We followed the armored car from stop to stop. It was stupid, really, because there was always the remote possibility that we'd be spotted. I think Eddie wanted to see the money as it was being loaded, the way kids like to go into toy stores before Christmas. Or like a man watching a porno movie before going home to screw his wife.

Somewhere on our travels we passed a Catholic church bearing a large white banner over the front doors: ST. IGNATIUS LOYOLA WELCOMES JOHN PAUL II.

Eddie blessed himself as we passed, his hand moving from his forehead, to his belly button, to his left shoulder, to his right shoulder.

"Whadda ya doin?" Morasso demanded. There were no windows in the back of the van. As paranoid as he was, Tony probably thought Eddie was passing a signal to aliens from outer space.

"I'm countin' my blessings," Eddie responded.

"What's that mean?"

"It means shut the fuck up."

"When am I gettin' my shells?"

"When I give 'em to ya."

"When is that?"

"You believe this?" Eddie said to me. "Punch him out, cuz. Stop that diarrhea comin' outta his mouth."

Three forty-five, K.

The radio had been chattering continuously, the dispatcher receiving and giving information to various trucks in the Chapman fleet. It meant no more to us than background music in an elevator, but the minute we heard the words "three forty-five," the question of Tony's discipline became meaningless.

Three, four, five?
We are 10-6 on that 20. Proceeding to Horace Harding Boulevard.

Roger, three, four, five. Did George call Evelyn, K?
Affirmative, base.
Praise the Lord. 10-4.
10-4.

We watched 345 go through its paces one last time, then drove out to Stern's in Douglaston. Three forty-five had another stop to make before joining us and the plan called for us to be in place and ready when it left.

Once in the lower parking lot, Eddie and I squeezed into the back of the van next to Parker and Morasso. From outside, the van was just another empty vehicle in a crowded parking lot. Nobody said a word. We listened intently to the crackle of the radio, the crisp voice of the dispatcher as she moved the fleet along. Maybe it'd been elevator music half an hour ago, but now it was all jazz, sharp and insistent. I felt my diaphragm tighten as the adrenaline rushed through my arms and legs. My mind was absolutely clear, as though I was in a movie theater a million miles away. It was demanding and important, but it didn't have anything to do with me. Not for the moment, anyway.

I could hear the others breathing. I could hear myself breathing. Each time the dispatcher signed off, we expected to hear the next voice say, "Three forty-five." We stared at the radio with its glowing amber diodes as if the urgency of our desire could draw up the words like a magician pulling silver dollars from the empty air. Come to Papa, honey. Come on, sweet mamma. Come on home.

"Here," Eddie said, "put on the wig."

Three forty-five, K.
Three, four, five?"
We are 10-16 on Utopia Parkway. Proceeding to account
number D8967 on Marathon Parkway.
That's a roger.
10-4.
Three, four, five?
Three forty-five.
Did George say he called Evelyn?
This is George and that's affirmative, base.

She just phoned the base again.
I don't want to violate radio etiquette, base, but if you want
her psychiatrist's phone number, I'll be glad to give it to you.
Otherwise shoot the bitch. 10-4.
    10-4.

Eddie took his place behind the wheel. I got in next to him, trying
not to think about what was going to happen next. Then the van began to move and I felt the weight of what I'd done fall on me like a
brick tossed from the top of a Lower East Side tenement. Rats are the
lowest form of life in the Institution. Baby rapers do easier time than
rats. M.O.'s who kill their grandmothers do easier time than rats. All
my life, I'd fought to maintain the image of a warrior. The image was
my armor and now I was naked.

I might have chickened out, but there was no way to stop it. Condon and Rico would be waiting on the platform. Avi was already in
custody. It was a done deal.

"You ready, cuz?"

"Let's do it."

Eddie pulled up behind Stern's like any other customer about to re-
trieve a large purchase. The area seemed deserted, no cars, trucks, or
workers in sight.

"Could it be better, cuz? Huh? Could it be better?" Eddie's voice
was joyous.

"I don't see how."

"Morasso, take these." He casually tossed a pair of 12-gauge shotgun shells into the back of the van. "Pete, let's go."

I tried to stay a half step behind him as we climbed the four steps to
the floor of the loading dock. Condon had told me that the platform
would be clear. He wanted us to walk through the open doorway into
the back. That way Morasso wouldn't be able to see us when we were
taken, which lessened the risk of a shoot-out.

"Anybody here?" Eddie called. He actually managed to sound
friendly. "Yoo-hoo."

We stepped through the doorway, from daylight into shadow. It
took a few seconds before my eyes adjusted. It would have been a perfect time for Condon and Rico to strike, but all I saw was a young
black man sporting a t-shirt imprinted with the map of Africa.

"Yo," he said, "you got your sales slip?"

"Sure," Eddie said, "right here." He hauled out his automatic and put it under the man's chin. "You wanna live?"

"Don't kill me, man. Please, don't kill me."

"How many other workers you got on the platform?"

"One."

"Get him out here. Anything goes wrong, you're dead."

"Sure, man, whatever you say. Just don't kill me. *Elroy, come on out here.*"

I was in a state of shock. Eddie had his piece in his hand. If Condon and Rico showed up now, there'd be blood on the concrete. My blood, most likely. I remembered the 9mm and drew it out.

"Wha'chu want, Sam? Ah'm takin' a goddamn shit."

Sam looked up at Eddie. He shrugged his shoulders helplessly. "What you want me to do?"

Eddie responded by walking over to a door. "This the crapper?" he asked.

"Yeah."

"Good."

Eddie kicked out and the door flew open. The boy sitting on the toilet was reading a newspaper. He hadn't even bothered to take his pants down.

"Oh, that's bad," Eddie said. "You're fuckin' off. You could lose ya job for that. Right, nigger?"

Elroy was a little slow on the uptake. "Who the fuck are you?" he asked.

Eddie answered by ramming the gun barrel into the Elroy's face. It missed Elroy's mouth, catching him on the cheekbone just below the left eye. The blood began to flow before Eddie pulled the gun back.

I kept my own piece trained on Sam, but my eyes were wandering through the work area, searching for the cops. I kept running over answers to the obvious question. Maybe Condon and Rico would be in the armored car when it pulled up. Maybe they'd be wearing the guards' uniforms. Maybe they'd decided to take us in the Bronx when we made the split. None of the answers made sense, and I might have gone on trying to find a reasonable explanation if Eddie hadn't yanked me back to reality.

"Get the other nigger in here, cuz. Let's go."

I put my hand on Elroy's back and pushed him into the tiny room.

Whatever game Condon and Rico were playing, I couldn't afford to waste my energy thinking about it. Sam was moaning and cursing; Elroy was shaking and crying. Eddie shoved them both onto the floor and cuffed their hands around a water pipe running from the floor to the sink.

"Now look here, little monkeys. Listen real fuckin' close. You don't wanna try to get outta here and you don't wanna make a sound. 'Cause if this door should happen to open before we're finished, I'm gonna kill the both of you. I won't give a shit about who done what. I'll kill the both of you. Understand what I'm sayin'?"

He didn't wait for an answer. He backed out of the room, motioned for me to follow, then closed the door. We took up posts just inside the doorway leading to the outside platform. Lost in the shadows, we'd be invisible until the Chapman guards were right on top of us.

"How ya feeling', cuz?" Eddie was grinning like a circus clown.

"Feelin' strong, Eddie." What I was actually feeling was disoriented. And what I needed to do was ground myself in the present. There was no point in trying to analyze the situation. Condon and Rico weren't here, and "here" is where the action was. The man standing across from me was carrying a short-barreled Colt .45, an automatic with a special twelve-round clip. He wouldn't hesitate to use it on me or anybody else who got between him and the sacks of money locked inside Chapman Security truck number 345. Plus, the Chapman guards, when they arrived, would be armed, including the one locked in the back of the truck and, worst of all, Tony Morasso had already loaded a sawed-off 12 gauge shotgun.

I squeezed myself down, narrowing my focus until the universe shrunk to the size of a sun-drenched parking lot.

We might have been standing there for two minutes or two hours. I had no sense of time. But the waiting didn't bother me. I'd been there before and I knew what to expect. The Chapman truck, when it finally lumbered around the corner of the building, seemed as big as a battleship. I searched out the faces of the men in the cab, looking for Condon and Rico. They weren't there. The truck was being operated by the same two men we'd been following all afternoon.

The truck parked with the rear doors facing the platform. The guards stepped out, their weapons holstered, and strolled across the parking lot, chatting back and forth. We waited until they were on the stairs leading up to the dock before we stepped out into the light.

They froze for a moment, then let their hands drop slightly. It was a reflex action, but Eddie took it badly.

"Your hands touch them guns, you're a couple of dead motherfuckers."

Eddie was in a semi-crouch, two hands supporting the Colt. The barrel was less than five feet from the closer of the two men. The guards hesitated, looked at each other, then gave it up. They went through the transitions so smoothly, I was sure that surrender had been part of their training.

"Ya do this right, nobody gotta get hurt. You fuck it up, you'll never see ya kids again. Put your hands on top of your head and turn the fuck around."

They complied without hesitation. Until Tony Morasso and the shotgun came into view. When they saw his swollen face, they stopped, realizing, maybe, that they'd made a mistake.

"Keep movin'."

It was too late for them, too late to fix it up. With us behind and Tony in front and their hands on top of their heads, they had all the control of a pair of gnats in a hurricane. Both men were shaking.

I disarmed the two of them, praying that Tony Morasso wouldn't decide to pick this particular moment to lose control. I was right in the line of fire, as was Eddie. If Morasso let loose with that 12-gauge, he'd most likely kill everybody on the platform.

Morasso advanced until he was right on top of the taller of the two guards. He yanked the man off the steps, kicked him as he went down, then kicked him again.

Shepherding Tony through the job was my responsibility. I left Eddie with the second guard and jumped down off the platform. "Let him up. What the fuck is the matter with you?"

I pulled the guard to his feet and shoved him toward the truck. Morasso accepted my direction, urging the guard forward by jabbing the shotgun into his back. When they were right up against the truck, he laid both barrels against the side of the guard's head and pushed the man's face against the bulletproof window.

"Uhhhhhhhh," he said. "Uhhhhhhhhhh." It was as close as Tony could come to intelligible speech.

I looked into the back of the truck. The guard inside was pressed against the rear wall, a shotgun in his hands. "Open the door and nobody gets hurt," I shouted. He shook his head slowly. I could smell his fear through two inches of steel armor. "You don't open it, your buddy's gonna lose his fuckin' head. Throw down the shotgun and open the door."

Tony continued to grunt. Sooner or later he was going to pull those triggers, and the only thing I could do about it was get that door opened in a hurry.

"You, inside the truck," I screamed, "you're not gonna get another chance. You wanna let your buddy die to protect Chapman Security's money? What does Chapman Security mean to you, anyway? A paycheck? A pension? Open the door and nobody gets hurt."

Eddie came up behind me. Without speaking, he pushed the second guard's head against the glass.

"Think about it," I continued. "These guys are your pals. You're together five days a week. You know the names of their children, their wives. Can you let them die and live with it? Open the door and we'll be out of here in five minutes. Don't be a fool."

I saw him hesitate, his eyes flicking from Tony's face to the faces of his co-workers. There was no way he could look at Tony and still think we might be bluffing. On the other hand, he could easily believe that opening the door would result in a bloodbath.

"You're not gonna get hurt. Just open it. All we want is the money. If you don't open, we'll burn this fucking truck with *you* inside it. Open the fucking door."

Something clicked. Maybe he finally realized that opening the door was his *only* chance to survive. Maybe he was acting out of loyalty, putting himself at risk to protect his buddies. Whatever the reason, he dropped his weapon, walked to the front of the truck, unlocked the door, and pushed it open. Tony Morasso rewarded him by jamming the shotgun into his belly and pulling both triggers.

THIRTY-TWO

The guard's body jackknifed as he flew into the back of the van. One of his companions, the one Tony was holding, shouted, "Chuck, Chuck, Chuck." The last guard turned and started to run. I grabbed him by the shoulder and threw him down on the asphalt.

"Just stay there, motherfucker. If you wanna live, stay on the ground." I wasn't worried about Tony. With no more shells for the shotgun, he was just another defanged snake. Eddie, on the other hand, would have killed the man before he got fifteen feet.

"Get in the truck, Tony," Eddie said. His voice was calm and steady. "Toss out the bags."

If Eddie had ever meant to carry out his threat to kill Morasso on the spot, the sight of those canvas bags washed his resolution away. I stood over the two guards, keeping them quiet, while Morasso threw bags of money to Eddie, who threw them to Parker in the back of the van. Several of the canvas bags were covered with blood.

Five minutes later, Eddie slammed the van into gear and we tore up the ramp. He slowed it down once we were on the street, following the light traffic over the Expressway and onto the Cross Island Parkway. Nobody said a word until he passed through the toll on the Bronx end of the Throgs Neck Bridge.

"I fucked it up, didn't I?" Morasso said.

"It don't matter," Eddie declared. "One more body ain't gonna mean shit. We're in the clear. There ain't no way they can find us now."

"But I fucked it up."

I think Tony finally realized that he was the only one in the van without a weapon. Not that I gave a shit. I was thinking about the guard in the back of the truck, of the astonishing quantity of blood pumping from his gut, of the two cops who were supposed to prevent his death.

"Well, John," Eddie said, "whatta ya think? Did we do it or what?"

Parker was sitting on top of a small mountain of canvas bags. He looked stunned, like a high-diver coming down on an empty swimming pool. "Why did Tony shoot that man? What was point of that?"

"Bad things happen to good people, cuz." Eddie grinned. "I want you and Tony to combine those bags. Break the contents down, toss out the checks. And don't get any blood on ya clothes if ya can help it."

Tony lifted up his hands. They were covered with rapidly drying blood. "I already got it on me," he said.

"C'mon, Pete," Eddie said, "give us a smile. Ya gonna be a rich man."

I managed a weak grimace. Despite the fact that I knew Condon and Rico were going to be waiting in the garage. They'd arrested Avi, then decided to take us when we made the split. There was no other explanation, outside of two unexpected heart attacks, that made any sense. I didn't know why they'd decided to wait or how they'd explain it to their superiors. I just knew they'd be waiting.

I said a quick prayer of thanks for Simon Cooper. There was an awful lot of blood in the back of that armored car. The media would cover it, even on an afternoon when the Pope was in town. Condon and Rico would be tempted to invent a scenario which included no prior knowledge of the crime. Maybe they'd resurrect the proverbial "anonymous informant."

Acting on information received from an anonymous source, Detectives Rico and Condon proceeded to a schoolyard in Bayside where they apprehended one Avraham Stern. After waiving his rights, Avraham Stern led Detectives Rico and Condon to a garage in the Throgs Neck Section of the Bronx where four other suspects were placed under arrest.

They couldn't very well play that game now. Not without my cooperation. The only question for me was how I was going to react when they made their appearance. The garage had a small room in the back. I suppose it'd once been used as a work space, but now it was empty except for a kitchen table. The plan called for us to divide the money on the table where everyone could see what was happening. Except for Tony, of course. I was supposed to kill him as soon as we got inside the garage.

I screwed the silencer into the 9mm while Parker and Tony were busy with the money. Eddie gave me a slight nod of encouragement.

"How's it look back there?" he asked. "We rich, or what?"

"Some of this money has blood on it," Parker replied.

"We'll wash it, cuz. We got plenty of time."

He turned the van into a short driveway and stopped in front of the garage. I got out, opened the garage door for the van, followed it inside, then closed the door. When I turned around, Avi was standing at the far end of the room.

I wasn't surprised to see him there. I wasn't surprised when Condon and Rico stepped out of the back room, either. What shocked me were the stockings the two cops had pulled down over their faces. And the military-style weapons they carried. I'd missed the street upscale from Saturday night specials to 9mm automatics and assault rifles. I didn't know what Condon and Rico were pointing at us—Uzis, M16s, AK47s—but the long banana clips just in front of the trigger guards told the whole story.

"Who are you?" Parker asked.

"You sure you wanna know?" Condon asked. His lips curled into a grin beneath the sheer fabric of the stocking. Lacking a Tony Morasso, he was doing his best to fill the part. "Nobody has to get hurt. But that don't mean nobody *will* get hurt. If we have to kill one of you, we might as well kill all of you. Now, I want you to drop them weapons. One at a time. You first, Eddie."

Eddie's head jerked when he heard Condon use his name, but he wasn't stupid enough to try anything. He took the automatic out of his belt, handling it with two fingers, and dropped it on the concrete floor.

"Awright, you next, Tony."

"I don't got nothin'," Tony said. "The shotgun ain't loaded. I left it in the truck."

"Pete, go pat him down. Then take all the weapons and put them in the trunk."

Eddie's eyes snapped over to meet mine. Avi's followed an instant later. Now it made sense to everybody. Condon and Rico had been after the money from the beginning. They used me to set up the job and now they were setting me up to take the fall. Eddie and the boys would come after me, but they wouldn't find me unless they happened to look in the East River. With me out of the picture, there'd be no way for Eddie to link Condon and Rico to the rip-off. They could look forever, grab and kill every ex-con I'd run with in Cortlandt, but they'd never find the two cops.

I suppose I should have felt something, anger or betrayal or fear, but I was functioning on a different level. The only emotion still operating was the will to survive. Simon Cooper's face swam into what was left of my mind. Condon and Rico must have found a way to eliminate him as a factor in the equation. I didn't know how and I didn't care. That was for later, that was for after I survived.

Morasso began to shake as I approached him and my boyish smile only added to his agitation.

"What's the matter, Tony. You cold or somethin'?"

I came up behind him and ran my hands over his ribs, then let them slide forward to gently pinch his nipples. "I ever tell you that you're my kinda guy?" I let my hand slide down his belly to cup his balls. "Yeah, you are, Tony. You're my kinda guy. That's why I'm *fucking* you."

"Cut the bullshit, Pete," Condon ordered.

If it hadn't been for the fact that he was staring into the barrel of Condon's rifle, I think Tony would have gone off on the spot. Of course, I was staring into the barrel of the same rifle, so what I did was obey. I gathered Parker and Eddie's weapons, carefully added my own, then dumped them in the rear of a 1991 Ford Crown Victoria. It was supposed to have been Eddie's getaway car. The other cars were parked in the street.

"Real good, Pete. Now empty the van."

I dragged the two full bags out of the van and heaved them into the Ford's trunk. On the way, I grinned at Morasso. "Easy come, easy go. Right, cutie?"

"That's it? That's all you got?" Rico sounded like he was going to cry.

"Don't worry, Rico, we combined the bags as we drove up here. There's enough in there to keep you in pig feed for the rest of your life."

Rico's head jerked when I said his name. The barrel of his rifle swung around until it was pointed at my chest.

"Don't do it," Condon ordered. "And you, Pete, don't fuck up again. Now let's get out of here."

"Take the keys first," I said. "They've got four cars parked outside. Take the keys."

Condon looked at me for a minute. He couldn't have cared less about Eddie's cars. They wouldn't be pursuing him, because they had no idea who he was. They'd be coming after me. And they'd begin their search at my last known address: Ginny's apartment on Cherry Avenue.

"Cough 'em up," he ordered. "Throw 'em over to Pete."

As I picked the keys off the floor, Condon and Rico walked over to the Ford, drew automatic pistols, then calmly tossed the rifles into the trunk.

"Whatta ya say we get the show on the road, Pete?" Rico opened the rear door and waved me inside.

I was close enough to see his features through the stocking as I stepped past him. He was so nervous, his eyeballs were shaking.

"You really oughta let the safety off," I said. "If you plan to use that piece."

His eyes snapped down involuntarily, then snapped back up to meet mine. If I'd had any doubt about his intentions, which I didn't, that look would have erased them.

"Still the tough guy," he muttered, jamming the gun barrel into my ribs.

"What could I say, Rico? I guess I'm just the kinda guy who likes his work."

He wanted to kill me in the worst way, but didn't. Lacking Tony Morasso's spontaneous charm, he would follow through on whatever plan he and Condon had concocted. I suppose that his control gave him confidence, but it didn't change the fact that he was a rank amateur at the art of kidnapping and murder. A pro would have killed the four of us as soon as the garage door was closed.

Rico pushed me across the backseat, then got in after me. That was his first mistake. He should have gotten in from the other side, where he could keep an eye on Eddie and the boys, especially Tony Morasso. I leaned forward, pressing my back against the front seat and waved at Tony. He was right on the edge.

Condon opened the garage door, then got into the Ford and put it in gear. I took the opportunity to blow Tony a kiss. Maybe that's what set him off. Or maybe it was the thought of all that money rolling out the door. I'll never know, because what Tony did was scream and charge the car. Rico turned at the sound and discovered Tony almost at the window. I would have loved to see Rico's face at that moment, but I had to content myself with the back of his head. Rico fired three times and Tony Morasso flew backward, imitating the security guard he'd blown apart half an hour before.

Condon had no choice except to drive out of the garage. Despite the fact that I was on top of Rico. Despite the fact that I held Rico's gun with my left hand while I smashed my right fist into his face. Again and again and again. I didn't expect Rico to offer much resistance and he didn't. He made a feeble attempt to grab me with his free hand, but my body was above his and I was forcing him against the door while keeping my own back wedged against the front seat.

When Condon finally slammed on the brakes, I didn't miss a beat. I continued to pound Rico's face until his eyes closed and his fingers relaxed on the gun. Condon was struggling to pull his own piece, but his fat gut was pressed against the steering wheel and he couldn't manage to free the automatic and turn to face me at the same time.

"If you're still holding that weapon two seconds from now, what I'm gonna do is surrender to my base instincts. You won't like my base instincts." I pressed the gun barrel into his temple.

"Whatta ya doin', Pete? It's yours, too. You're in on it." He dropped the pistol on the floor.

"You were planning to put a third in my coffin? How sweet."

I wasn't thinking about the money. I was thinking about Ginny and how fast I could get her out of her apartment. "Listen close," I said, "because I only wanna say it once. First you're gonna take off the mask. Then you're gonna get out of the car, open the back door, and take Rico out. If you should see a cop, you're not gonna wave hello or make any noise at all. Remember the money in the trunk. Remember the piece in my hand. You don't wanna fuck up here. Not even a little bit."

THIRTY-THREE

I left Condon and Rico in the middle of East Tremont Avenue and drove away. Traffic was heavy, as usual, with cars and trucks double-parked on both sides of the street. I wanted to fly to Ginny's, to shoot across the East River on a rocket, but I knew I was going to crawl. I was afraid for the first time, afraid that Eddie would somehow beat me to Ginny's apartment, that even if I got there first, she'd be out, that she'd eventually walk into a trap.

Eddie wouldn't expect to find her. He'd have to figure that I'd already taken care of that angle, but he'd go there anyway. There was no other place for him to begin. If he got his hands on her, death would be the least of Ginny's problems.

By the time I got the big Ford through the toll gate on the Whitestone Bridge, I was half crazy. I careened through the traffic at eighty miles an hour, snapping the Ford from lane to lane as if it was a Porsche. The last thing I needed was an accident or a ticket, but I couldn't stop myself. I jumped off the highway at Linden Place and forced my way through downtown Flushing, running lights and stop signs. The horns went crazy, but nobody tried to stop me. I pulled the car next to a fire hydrant on Cherry Avenue, shoved the cops' automatics under the seat, grabbed one of the canvas bags out of the trunk, and ran up the stairs to Ginny's apartment.

When I heard Ginny's voice and saw her face, I began to calm down. I shut the door and threw both locks.

"What happened?" It was Ginny's turn to panic. I was too early, much too early, for things to have gone smoothly.

"You have to get out of here. Right now. I don't have time to explain it. Grab your money and your credit cards and get out."

I expected her to stall, to ask me about the canvas bag, to demand that I tell her what happened, to refuse to leave without an explanation. I got none of that. Ginny took a small gray bag out of the bedroom closet and began to throw underwear into it. She added a pair of jeans, a blouse, and a dress.

"I just have to get my purse," she said, looking up at me. "Then I'll go."

She was crying and I wanted to take her in my arms, to protect her with the full force of my criminal macho bullshit, but all I could do was whisper.

"Do you want to tell me where you're going? If you don't want to, I understand."

She answered by walking into the front room. "You think you'll get out of this?"

"Maybe. Tony's dead, one of the guards, too. The cops turned up in stocking masks instead of blue uniforms." I took the canvas bag and emptied it onto the rug. "Eddie's blaming me. That's why you have to run."

She was standing at the door, one hand already working the dead bolt, staring at the pile of cash. "What's that for?"

"Tribute, motivation, a bribe. It doesn't matter. You have to go."

"Why don't you come with me? How would Eddie find us?"

"Eddie wouldn't; the cops would. They have the resources. But the cops don't know you exist. The only way they could find out about you is if we go together."

"I'm going to my sister's," Ginny said. "She lives in Tennessee. Can you remember the phone number?"

I walked to the window and looked out onto the street. A gang of kids were playing stoopball in front of the building. White, yellow, Spanish, black—a regular United Nations. They should have been on a poster. "You better write it down. My brain is doing cartwheels at the moment."

She took a second to scribble a number on the back of a business card, then opened the door. "Call me," she said.

I walked across the room and took the card. "I'll try, Ginny."

Her eyes narrowed. For a minute I thought she was going to hit me.

"If I don't get a phone call within a few days, I'm coming back to look for you."

"It won't help to come back. I'll get to you if I can." I tried to keep my voice calm, but she wasn't buying it.

"I can't stand not knowing. I *have* to know, one way or the other." She stood there for a few seconds, looking up at me. "What I'll do is call Simon."

"You can try, but I don't think it'll help. They must have found a way of neutralizing Simon Cooper."

"How? Simon would never betray you."

"And cops don't wear stocking masks. Let's get going, Ginny. I'll walk out with you."

Elevators are traps. I took her down the stairs and out the side door. The kids on the street were arguing, something about a fair or foul ball. Ginny took my hand as we threaded our way between the two teams. We didn't have time to say what was really on our minds and I didn't have the heart for bullshit reassurances.

When we reached her car, I took her in my arms and kissed her. I wanted to memorize her, the smell of her hair, the feel of her skin, the taste of her lips. Something to take with me if I ended up doing twenty-five to life in Cortlandt.

"Try Simon," she said.

"I plan to try everything."

I watched her car turn the corner, then went back to my own car and drove down Parsons Boulevard to a bank at the intersection of Parsons and Roosevelt. I pulled the Ford into the parking lot, backed it into a slot in the rear, and shut the engine down.

I didn't have long to wait. Half an hour later, a red Dodge Dynasty drove past. Eddie was behind the wheel, Parker alongside him, but Avi was nowhere to be found. I wondered what John and Eddie would think when they found Ginny's door open, when they they saw that pile of money on the rug. I wasn't worried about what they'd do. There was only one thing they *could* do—take the money and run. Later on, when things settled down, Eddie would call his mob buddies and put out a contract on me. He wouldn't have any choice. In his world, treachery can never be ignored. In my world, too, come to think of it.

That canvas bag had left a two-foot-tall mountain on the rug. The second bag, as it turned out, contained $480,000 dollars. I'd have to guess the first had about the same. You can go a long way on half a million dollars and a good set of bogus i.d. Maybe Annie would get to sample a few Rio beach boys in spite of everything.

Avi's absence meant problems of a different kind. I'd hoped to pursue Condon and Rico on my own, but now I'd have to worry about Avi, who was undoubtedly in pursuit of *me*. Of course there was always the possibility that Eddie had killed Avi, that they'd had a thieves' falling out. My only problem was that I couldn't quite bring myself to believe that Eddie would survive a disagreement of that kind. Not that I spent a lot of time considering the question.

I gave Eddie a few seconds to disappear, then drove the Ford out of the lot and back to the Bronx. On the way, I switched my little 9mm for one of the automatics under the seat. I wanted a big gun, a gun to scare people enough so I wouldn't have to shoot anyone. Condon's .45 would do nicely. It felt like it weighed ten pounds and threatened to drag my pants down to my knees.

The Ford had to go, because at the very least Condon and Rico would be looking for it. I had three sets of car keys in my pocket. The cars they fit (two of them, anyway) were still parked on Quincy Avenue in the Bronx. I suppose I could have gone to Hertz and used the phony credit card Eddie'd given me, but I didn't know how long I'd be in New York and I didn't want to start a paper trail. If I got lucky, I'd end up with an untraceable car.

As I came up East Tremont Avenue, I kept looking for cops. If Morasso's shooting had been reported, there would have been half a dozen cruisers in front of the garage. There weren't. The garage door was down and padlocked. The street was quiet.

I parked close to the garage and looked around. There were people on the block, sitting on the stoops. Predation is a fact of life in poor neighborhoods and I didn't intend to be the prey. I retrieved the 9mm, shoved it inside my belt, and got out of the car with my jacket unzipped. Two-Gun Pete Frangello. Walkin' tall in the Wild Wild Bronx.

I unlocked the garage door, backed the Ford inside, then relocked the door. Morasso was lying on the concrete. The pool of blood surrounding his body had dried to a deep reddish-brown. It looked like a bull's-eye. I felt something rise within me. Anger, disgust, fear . . . whatever it was, I didn't have time for analysis. I took the canvas bag out of the trunk and looked down at the two assault rifles.

They promised enormous firepower, but I didn't have the faintest idea of how they worked. Or how to break them down so I could carry them without looking like a demented sniper.

I closed the trunk and wiped the Ford down. I'd only been to the garage once before and Eddie had insisted that I wear surgical gloves. For once his paranoia was paying off. There were five suitcases in the backroom. That's where the money was going. The canvas bag was too conspicuous.

It took me five minutes to fill two suitcases. I added the 9mm before I closed the last one and headed for the street, stepping over Tony on the way. As I bent over to raise the door, I felt a sudden rush of fear. Somebody was on the other side. Eddie, Avi, the cops . . . it didn't really matter. With one hand on the door and the other trying to manipulate a couple of heavy suitcases, I'd be a dead pigeon no matter who it was.

I let the suitcases go, pulled the .45, and drew back the hammer. Then I got as far to the side as I could and shoved the door up. There was a man standing right in front of me. His clothes were ragged, his face and neck a patchwork of dirt and open sores, his trousers down by his ankles. He was holding his dick in his right hand, taking a long leisurely leak.

I jumped back, but I wasn't quite fast enough. My cuffs and shoes got splattered. I raised the .45, more as a reflex than anything else, but the man went right on pissing. He wasn't blind, just insane. Another homeless wreck in need of the Institution.

THIRTY-FOUR

So much for Two-Gun Pete. I dumped the suitcases in the back of the Buick Regal Eddie'd been using and headed north, up toward Westchester County. I planned to drive into Mt. Vernon to find a telephone book, but I didn't have to go that far. There's a Store & Lock just over the city line. You can see it from I-95. I got off the highway, rented one of the small garages, dumped the suitcases (after filling my pockets), and drove into the gathering darkness. It was seven-thirty. The whole deal, from the arrival of the armored car in the shopping center parking lot until the present, had gone down in two and a half hours.

I needed time to think and now I had it. Everything I'd done up to that point had been absolutely necessary. Getting Ginny out of danger and Eddie off my back, ditching the Ford and stashing the money—a robot could have performed those tasks. They were like the compulsory exercises in a figure-skating contest.

I'd gone through it on automatic pilot, trying not to think or feel, but now I'd come to the point where I didn't know what to do next. I'd arrived at the "wall" long distance runners talk about.

I drove north, toward Connecticut, and found a shopping mall in the town of Rye near the New York border. I picked up a small suitcase, a change of clothing, and a shaving kit, just enough to pass for a traveler in the eyes of the clerk at the Blue Point Motor Inn, a nondescript motel on Route 1 near the town of Port Chester.

"This here is a proper place," the clerk muttered into a copy of *Time*. "That means no parties. You bring in a woman or a bottle, keep it quiet. Checkout is ten o'clock. On the dot."

I opened the door to my room, expecting the worst, but the space was clean and the furniture had been purchased within living memory. A bed, a chair, and a table, a bureau with a portable television bolted on top—it wasn't much, but it would do. I was tempted to throw myself on the bed, to shut the whole thing out for a few hours, but I knew I couldn't. At the very least, I had to put together the pieces I understood, to stitch them in a line the way I'd stitched seams in the tailor shop at Cortlandt.

Instead of sleeping, I shoved the .45 into my new shaving kit and went out to get something to eat. I opened the Buick's trunk before I took off and slid the kit behind the spare tire. There was a diner about a quarter of a mile down the road. It was a warm evening and I was tempted to walk it, but I couldn't take a chance that a passing cruiser would stop me for a spot check. Not with the 9mm tucked behind my belt. I drove down and parked the Buick in the lot.

I took a booth and ordered coffee. The waitress started to tell me something about a minimum in the booths, but I assured her that I'd be ordering dinner in a few minutes. I just had to make a call first. When she returned, I took the cup off the saucer and carried it to a pay phone by the rest rooms. She didn't like that, either.

The call was going out to Simon Cooper. This puzzle had a lot of pieces missing. If I could put one back, I'd consider it a major victory. I dialed Simon's home number.

"Hello?" It was a man's voice, not Simon's.

"Is Simon there? Simon Cooper?"

"Who's this?"

"John Gotti." I shouldn't have said it, but I did.

"You a wise guy?"

"Simon's my parole officer. I'm a client." "Client" was the word Simon used to describe his customers. I suppose it sounded better than "parolee" or "ex-con."

"This is Simon's home you're callin', not his office."

"In that case why don't you stop acting like his secretary and go find him? I didn't get his number out of the phone book. He gave it to me."

"Yeah? Well, I can't go out and find Simon because Simon's dead. Some piece of shit just like you shot him down in a tenement on West 48th Street. Those sounds you hear in the background are his wife and kids crying."

I hung up. Partly because there was nothing else to say and partly out of fear that he might be a cop. My waitress, order book in hand, was waiting for me when I got back to the table.

"Ready to order?" She was skinny and middle-aged, with a smile that carried as much warmth as the grimace of a street prostitute with menstrual cramps.

I ordered a steak and watched her walk away. Simon Cooper's face drifted through my mind. I heard his voice warning me to be careful, to beware the treachery of Eddie Conte and Avi Stern. He hadn't mentioned the cops. Most likely, in his own mind, they were above suspicion, the one sure element in a volatile equation. He'd been stupid just like me.

Did they try to deal with him? Did they approach him in some crumbling hallway and offer him a piece if he'd just forget he'd ever spoken to me? Probably not. Most likely they'd come up to him with smiles on their faces. "Hey, Simon, what're you doin' here?"

I was angry, but I couldn't feel the anger. I once spent a twenty-four-hour keeplock with a con who'd just come back from three years in the box. His name was Paulie Sheehan and he'd tried to shank a C.O. Paulie told me the hacks hadn't stopped beating him for a month.

"Every day?" I asked him.

"No, every shift. After a while I didn't feel it anymore. I could hear the sound of it. Hell, I could hear myself screaming. But I couldn't feel it."

What I felt was weary. I waited for the waitress to refill my cup, then drank it down in a gulp.

"Do it again, dear."

This time she didn't bother to fake a smile. I watched her walk away, then forced myself to think. The only important question was whether Condon and Rico would find a way to send the rest of the NYPD after me. I had no illusions. If the cops want to find you and you stay in New York, you're found. But I couldn't think of a way Condon could involve his fellow officers without incriminating himself. How, for instance, would Rico explain his battered face?

Most likely they were sitting in some empty apartment, pissing their pants. I was a loose cannon. If I was arrested and spilled my guts, they'd go down for Simon's murder. The prosecutor might not want to believe me. He might, for instance, put me on a polygraph machine, but in the end he'd *have* to prosecute. Second-degree murder in New York State carries a mandatory sentence of twenty-five to life.

Cops don't do well in jail. If I was after revenge, I'd have to go a long way to make it worse than twenty-five to life in a Max A prison. I didn't have to wait to be arrested. All I had to do was find a lawyer and make a phone call. The lawyer would listen to my story and arrange a meeting with the District Attorney's office. I'd have to testify, but I was already a snitch. Informing on Condon and Rico wouldn't make my rat whiskers any longer than they already were.

I think I would have taken that option if I hadn't given half the money to Eddie and the boys. The cops would never believe that I'd casually tossed away half a million dollars, not if I took a *thousand* lie detector tests. Maybe they send the three of us—me, Condon, and Rico—to the same prison, give us adjoining cells. We could hang out with Terrentini's ghost.

The waitress brought my steak, setting it down along with a plate of greasy french fries and a wilted salad. In the Institution, you always eat. No matter how bad the food is. The chow becomes one more reason for hating the society that put you in prison. If Condon and Rico had kept their end of the bargain, I'd be having dinner with Ginny. I'd be celebrating, looking forward to a life in the world instead of in the Institution.

I finished every crumb, wiping the last of the grease with a piece of mushy white bread. My waitress appeared before I could swallow it.

"Everything okay?"

"Scrumptious."

"You want dessert?" If she was aware of my sarcasm, she didn't show it. She didn't wait for me respond, either. The check floated down onto the table and she was gone.

I drove north from the diner, up into Connecticut, to a rest stop on I-95. There was someone I needed to speak to, and I didn't want to use a phone within twenty miles of where I was staying. At some time during my last bit, the cops had installed a system that traces the caller's phone number before the phone is even answered. There was a lot of talk about it among the professors in the crime university known as the Cortlandt Correctional Facility.

Condon had given me a business card with two numbers on it. The first went directly to his desk at the precinct. I didn't know where the second went, but I assumed it was to a place where Condon could talk to his snitches without being overheard by other cops.

I dialed the precinct number first and was told that he was off-duty. No surprise. I dialed the second number and Condon picked up on the first ring.

"Yeah?"

"It's Pete Frangello."

"What happened to you, Frangello? You go crazy or what?" The words came without hesitation. I could imagine him rehearsing his approach just in case I didn't get out of town.

"You and Rico took me by surprise. What could I do except react?" I kept my own voice apologetic. "How's Rico doin'?"

"He'll live. Where are you? We have to get together."

"I can't do that."

"Why not, Pete?"

"Because if I do you're gonna kill me."

He hesitated a moment, trying to decide if bullshitting me was worth the effort. I felt like I was inside his mind.

"I can understand why you might think that," he said, "but we have to work this out. If we don't, we're *all* gonna go down."

"Great, let's work it out." I gave him almost a minute to come up with a *way* to work it out, but he obviously couldn't. "That's what I thought. That's *exactly* what I thought. Look, Condon, the way I see it, between you and Eddie I'm gonna be lookin' over my shoulder for a long time. I don't see any way out of it unless I get *somebody* off my back. What I'm thinking is that my best move is to contact a lawyer and lay out the whole thing. I'm thinking that if I give the money back and testify, they'll put me in the witness protection program."

I hung up and drove back to the motel. On the way, I stopped at a mall, found a Newmark & Lewis, and bought a minirecorder and a package of cassettes. What I was looking for was a way out. Something besides killing two cops and running for the rest of my life.

THIRTY-FIVE

I was tired and I wanted to go to sleep, but there was one more thing to be learned that night. I flipped on the TV and tuned in Channel 5 for the local news. The anchorman led off with the Pope, detailing his triumphal procession through the slums of Harlem and the Bronx, then switched over to the armored car heist. The footage included a black body bag sliding into a medical examiner's van and a statement by a Chapman Security spokesman who estimated the loss at three million dollars, roughly three times the actual take.

I expected all that, including Chapman's insurance scam. What I was looking for and what I didn't find was any mention of a dead cop. Condon and Rico had taken Avi before he'd pulled off the assassination, which was good news for me as well as them. The NYPD would assign five or six detectives and a dozen patrolman to investigate the Chapman ripoff. If a cop had been killed, the task force would be ten times as big.

I shut off the TV and went into the tiny bathroom to wash my face and brush my teeth. Looking in the mirror, my mouth filled with white foam, I wondered why Condon hadn't let Avi go through with it before they'd taken him. Maybe they had scruples when it came to killing cops. A security guard? Fine. A piece of criminal shit? Great. A parole officer? No problem. But a cop could never kill another cop. That would be dishonorable.

I slept so soundly that I couldn't pull myself out of my dreams.

We're in the parking lot behind Stern's. All of us—Condon and Rico as well as Eddie, Avi, Tony, John, and myself. When the guard in-

side the truck finally opens the door, I see that it's Ginny and that, all along, she's been keeping me from the treasure.

"Shoot the bitch," I order.

The shotgun roars and then I'm running. I'm on a street in Manhattan, cutting through tenement backyards, running without fatigue and without result. I can't shake my pursuers. Even though I never see them, I know they're closing in on me.

Eddie's face appears next to mine. "Ya fucked it up, cuz. Ya always gotta do shit ya own way. You could never follow nobody's orders. Now whatta we gonna do?" He's gone before I can answer.

I'm in a room with Armando Ortiz, snorting line after line of cocaine. My heart is beating a thousand times a minute.

"Let's do it," I say. "Let's just go and do it."

"One more line, man. Do another line an' we'll be ready for tha' shit."

"Now, motherfucker," I shout. "Let's cut this crap and do what we gotta do."

I'm sitting behind a long oak table in a Manhattan courtroom, my lawyer beside me.

"Here comes the bullshit," he whispers.

The door opens and Ginny comes through. She's sitting in a wheelchair. A fringed cotton throw covers her lap. She appears grim but determined.

"This ain't gonna be good for us," I tell my lawyer.

He chuckles. "Next time try takin' better aim."

The prosecutor rises slowly, then approaches the witness.

"Ms. Michkin . . ."

"Please call me Ginny." She looks down at her hands, then smiles bravely. "I'm very nervous," she says.

"Perfectly normal, Ginny." The prosecutor turns away from her to face the jury. "Now, Ginny, do you see the man who shot you in this courtroom?"

"Yes, I do."

"Would you point that man out?"

I left the motel at nine o'clock in the morning, drove down to the Store & Lock, and retrieved one of the suitcases. An hour later I was in Manhattan. Stuck in heavy traffic on FDR Drive, my mind began to drift.

I recalled a conversation with Eddie. Years ago, up on the courts. We'd come to trust each other and he was telling me about a job he'd pulled off in the Flatlands section of Brooklyn, near the airport. He'd stopped a truck carrying a load of Japanese electronics out of one of the cargo hangars. It'd all been carefully planned (at the time, Eddie'd been doing three trucks a month for almost a year) until the driver suddenly turned and started to run. Eddie had shot him in the back.

"Ya know me, cuz," Eddie had said. "Ya know me good enough ta know that I ain't no hard guy. I don't wanna hurt nobody, right? Like I didn't slap this guy around or nothin'. I took him outta the truck and told the asshole, 'Don't worry about nothin'. Just stand here and ya gonna be fine.'

"First time I look away for a second, he takes off. I'm tellin' ya, Pete, the guy was screamin' at the top of his fuckin' lungs. He *made* me kill him."

I'd been feeling pretty good at the time. A pint of prison hooch will do that to you. It'll give you a loose mouth.

"What you could've done," I'd said, "was not rob trucks."

He'd looked at me like I was crazy, then launched into his "guys like us" speech.

"Guys like us don't have no choice. We are what we are 'cause that's the way the world made us. You should know who you are, cuz. I mean, take a look around. Look at the fuckin' walls, the C.O.'s. Ya think ya gonna come outta here and be a doctor? A lawyer? I ain't about ta push no fuckin' broom. Not fa nobody."

At the time, I'd put his little lecture down to prison bravado. "Sorry" is a word you save for the parole board; sorrow is dishonorable in a world ruled by defiance. But, sitting there in heavy traffic, craning my neck for some sign of an accident or a road repair crew up ahead, I began to understand that Eddie really *didn't* give a shit. He didn't see a dead truck driver, couldn't imagine the man's wife or his children. He'd shot a problem, not a human.

I could forgive Morasso. Morasso was crazy, pure and simple. Not only was he blind to anyone else's point of view, he was blind to his own point of view. Tony was a mass of nerves, reacting without thought. I might want to keep him locked away in some dungeon, but it was hard to hate him. Of course, now that he was dead, it really didn't matter.

I wondered about Condon and Rico. Did they go to mass every

Sunday? Maybe they belonged to the Holy Name Society in the NYPD. Maybe they attended Novenas, made the nine First Fridays, spent their summer vacations at Franciscan retreats in the Adirondack Mountains. I'd never know for sure, but I would have bet my left hand against a C.O.'s dirty underwear that they had some way of bull-shitting themselves.

Be grateful for your dreams.

The thought floated up out of nowhere. It was an interesting idea, like being grateful for leprosy.

The traffic crawled through a mile of torturous construction. First the left lane closed, then the right, then the center. The roadbed was badly chewed up and the cars were coming to a full stop at the lip of some of the deeper craters. I flipped on the Buick's radio and caught one of the twenty-four-hour news stations. The Pope was still in town, still railing about the evil things men do to each other. I wondered if he knew that pressure from one of his cardinals had prevented the De-partment of Corrections from passing out condoms to homosexual prisoners.

The traffic broke up just above 34th Street and I pushed the Buick up to forty-five miles an hour, bouncing over the potholes like a two-ton Slinky. Five minutes later, I pulled off onto Grand Street and drove the few blocks to Broome and Pitt.

I was assuming that nobody was looking for me *except* Condon and Rico. It would be months before the cops investigating the Chapman robbery connected me to the crime, if they ever did. I had no fear of them.

I had no fear of the parole board, either. Simon's caseload would be parceled out to other parole officers. Each client would have to be given a new reporting time and notified. That would take a week, even if they did it by telephone. Most likely they'd wait for the parolees to report on their own, then refer them to their new P.O.'s. Since I did-n't have to report at all, my case would take even longer to draw at-tention.

Still, I couldn't go after Condon and Rico. The only thing I knew about them was that they were working out of the Midtown South Precinct. A precinct house isn't the best place to stalk a cop. I did have a brief fantasy in which I spotted them from a nearby rooftop, then tailed them to a more favorable location. But I didn't know a damn thing about surveillance, and if they left in a car I'd be fucked altogether. Midtown South is located in the heart of Manhattan. Unless you're a cop, you can't park on the street anywhere near it.

Much better to let them come to me, even though they'd encounter the same problems finding me as I would finding them. Worse, they wouldn't even have a starting point. Unless I gave it to them.

THIRTY-SIX

I parked the car in a fenced lot, got out, and found myself looking at a peaceful spring day. The sky was clear and the air warm enough to hint of the summer to come. Sunlight poured down on the tenements, encouraging the few blades of grass pushing up through cracks in the sidewalk. I walked north along Pitt Street, under the Williamsburg Bridge, then past the Gompers housing project.

When I'd begun serving my sentence, the blocks between Delancey and Houston streets were as bad as any in Manhattan. The west side of the street was lined with crumbling and, for the most part, abandoned tenements. That was where the dealers hung out. The twenty-story brick buildings of the Samuel Gompers Houses, on the east, not only provided the dealers' clientele base, but also a labor pool for the replacement of busted (or murdered) dealers.

There were lots of people on the east side of the street, near the projects. Women were out with their children, heading for the laundromat or the supermarket or the playground. Knots of men, older mostly, stood around bullshitting while they sipped at cans of beer wrapped in small paper bags. The older kids were still in school. Later, when they got home, the ghetto blasters and boom boxes would echo between the buildings. The girls, Latina mainly, would sway to the music while their boyfriends' eyes spit fire at would-be rivals.

The west side of Pitt Street was a different proposition altogether. The men huddled in doorways weren't elderly Latinos looking for a game of dominoes. They were dealers. Their eyes swept the street like radar dishes in search of enemy aircraft. Everything about them was hard and mean. They worked the shittiest end of the drug business, making the least money, constantly subject to violent rip-offs, the first to be arrested when the NYPD decided for the ten thousandth time to sweep the streets free of drugs.

I felt completely comfortable on the west side of Pitt Street. It was like coming home after a long vacation. I joined the coke junkies with their bulging eyes, emaciated bodies, and tightly locked jaws as they trudged from dealer to dealer. The dope junkies were there, too. Many of them had open sores on their necks and faces. All of them looked sick.

Pitt Street was everything I'd wanted to avoid when I was released from Cortlandt. How long ago was that? Three weeks, a month, a year, a decade? If you think about all the plans you've made in your life that went wrong, you'd never do anything. Better to look at the few times you were right and pretend that you're running the show. Better, still, to bury yourself in the details and save the rest for your memoirs.

I was looking for someone—anyone—that I knew. I wanted the word to get out that Pete Frangello was back in action, that he was working and that he was hot. Strung-out junkies, on heroin or cocaine, will give up anyone, sister, brother, wife, or child, before facing withdrawal in the holding pens beneath Central Booking. Braced by a desperate Detective Condon, they wouldn't hesitate to point the way to little Pete Frangello.

"Pete. Yo, Pete. C'mon over here, boy. Check it out."

The voice was coming from inside a red Lincoln parked at the curb. It belonged to a tall Dominican named Oono. That was his street name and the only name I knew him by. He'd gotten it a few weeks after losing his right eye in a street fight. We'd spent some time together, partying mostly, before I went into the Institution. Our play had included a memorable brawl, complete with knives and clubs, in a shooting gallery on Stanton Street.

I strolled over to the car, careful to keep my face hard. As I walked, I noted the eyes of the dealers, taking it all in, making me for a player.

"What's happenin', Oono?"

"Nothin' to it, Pete. When you come out?"

"Last week. Been puttin' myself together. Gatherin' a little bank."

"Check it out." He nodded toward the backseat. "I wanna rap to you a minute."

I got into the only unoccupied seat in the car. Oono's two Latino buddies eyed me coldly, waiting for some definitive sign from Oono. They wanted to impress me with their macho cool in case I turned out to be another dealer.

"Put out your hand, bro."

I knew what he wanted and did what he said. There was no way to get out of it. I stretched my hand, palm down, over the seat rest. A grinning Oono poured a thick line of glistening cocaine across my knuckles.

"You know how long I been looking forward to this?" I asked, pulling half the line up into my right nostril. "Ten fuckin' years, Oono. Ten fuckin' years." I took the rest of it into my left nostril. It was the ritual "one and one."

"Check it out, bro," Oono said. "You ain' gonna tell me they don't have no powder upstate."

"They got it, but when your world is concrete and steel, it ain't the same. You wanna do dope or juice."

The cold hands of the white lady reached out to me like the ghost that lived in my five-year-old closet, the one I *knew* was just waiting for me to get out of bed, to put my feet on the floor. The one that whispered, "Come to me, little Pete, I'm your sweet, lost mama. I want to take you home where it's safe."

You never feel better than you do when your body is vibrating with cocaine. And you never feel worse than you do when you have to come down. The high is purely physical—an orgasm wrapped in a dream and prepared to go on forever. Then you run out of coke or money and the penalty phase begins.

I'd learned my coke lessons ten years ago, had stayed far away from it in Cortlandt. The most strung-out heroin addict still gets four to six hours of peace between fixes. Coke junkies are lucky to get four or five minutes.

"So, Pete, you back in action?"

"Same shit, Oono, between the Institution and the street. You gotta hustle to survive. I ain't the type to push a broom."

"Check it out, bro." He stuck his pinky nail into the bag of coke and took a nonchalant sniff. "If you're like lookin' for a job or some-thin', I could use a bro with a brain." He shook his head, then threw his two boys a contemptuous glance. Their faces remained cold and impassive. Apparently they were used to it.

"Gotta pass, Oono. I work alone. The last time I went partners with someone, I ended up doin' ten years."

He laughed appreciatively, then looked down at a huge Rolex. "Time to go back to work. If you're on the block around midnight, we'll go up to a club I know in the Bronx."

I continued my stroll along Pitt Street. The dealers, having observed my conversation with Oono, besieged me as I passed them. I made sure each one looked in my face as I explained that I was looking for a gram or two, but I wasn't interested in greasy lumps of street cocaine. I wanted something special I could flash around as I made my way through what the Puerto Ricans call *Loisaida*.

I found what I wanted between Rivington and Houston streets. One of the dealers took me to an empty apartment, explaining that he was Oono's biggest dealer and he had a special cut for special customers. The only problem was that he couldn't sell less than an eight ball—three and a half grams—because it'd been prepackaged and he didn't have a scale. On the other hand, the eighth had been cut from a single rock and then ground into a fine powder. It was ready for use and came in a small glass vial instead of wrapped in paper. Also, the price was right, especially for a friend of Oono's. Two hundred and fifty dollars: his cost exactly. Just try this sample line. See for yourself.

In another life, he would have been working on Madison Avenue. It's funny how fast hard-eyed dealers loosen up if they know and trust you. It's tempting to believe that dealers have no side except the one they display on the street, but many of them have families and, one and all, they want to get off the street.

I did the line, paid the man, and left. Now that I'd secured my little package of hospitality, I had a lot more freedom to roam. I crossed Houston Street and strolled up Avenue C. I was amazed by the number of newly rehabilitated tenements. And the number of well-dressed whites on the street. The bars were different, too. They weren't bars anymore; they were taverns, complete with neon artwork and Continental menus.

But the Yuppies hadn't driven out the junkies or the players. As I walked my way through the afternoon, I kept running into people I knew well enough to spend a minute bullshitting with.

"Hey, Pete, where you been? On vacation?"

"Yeah, baby, I won me an all-expense paid, deluxe, five-star vacation in beautiful upstate New York."

Some I knew well enough to offer a line of coke, but none of them was exactly right for what I had in mind. Still, I tested them, hinting that I was hot, that the man was looking for me. I wanted them to pry, to push me for details, but I didn't get my wish. They weren't rats looking for a salable piece of information.

I was having a beer at the Life Cafe, across from Tompkins Square Park, when I got my first break. It came in the form of a high-pitched greeting.

"Petey-Sweetie!"

If the voice was vaguely familiar, the face was instantly recognizable. Choo-Choo Ramirez had come to the Institution cursed with the triple whammy of being Dominican, gay, and the size of an undernourished jockey. His only hope of survival was to latch on to some stud and (for reasons beyond my understanding) he initially chose me. I had less than no interest in the homosexual scene at Cortlandt and I discouraged him, gently at first, then with curses and the back of my hand. Eventually he got the point and turned to one of the wolves who prey on feminine homosexuals, but his affection for me remained undiminished. Whenever we ran across each other, he tossed me sorrowful looks that drove his lover crazy.

"Petey-Sweetie, wha'chu doon in my world?"

Choo-Choo wasn't in full drag, but he wasn't exactly subdued, either. He was wearing a flaming red silk shirt and pair of incredibly tight, blood-red trousers. My first instinct was to tell him to fuck off, but something about the phrase "my world" caught my attention.

"You want a beer, Choo-Choo?"

"A beer? Do I look like a construction worker?" He patted his hair, then turned an exasperated face to the waiter. "A Chardonnay, Roger. When you got a moment to spare." He took the chair across from me. "Is so nice to see you, Petey."

"Look, Choo-Choo, you wanna sit, it's all right. You wanna play this 'Petey-Sweetie,' you're gonna find my foot in your ass."

"Promises, promises. Tha's all I get."

The rules thus established, we set out to do the town. Or at least the small part of it called the Lower East Side. Choo-Choo knew everybody and, fueled by cocaine, insisted on introducing me. Wherever we went, I let the same story out. I was just out of the joint, back in business, and looking for a place to lay low for a few days. My problem wasn't serious. Two detectives, working out of Midtown South, had a hard-on for me. If they caught up with me before their attention turned to more pressing matters, they'd violate me and I'd have to spend thirty days in Rikers waiting for a parole board hearing.

Choo-Choo, as soon as he heard my sad story, offered me his own place.

"Is only one room, but we be comfy-comfy."

I politely declined and he didn't pursue it. Nobody else went for the bait. Not until we got to a small bar on Avenue B and 6th Street called Downtown Sarajevo. It was a trendy bar, in its own way. The walls, of splintered plywood, were painted a dead, flat black and decorated with instruments of torture—yokes, whips, thumbscrews, electric wires, and batteries. The centerpiece was a rack, complete with block and tackle.

Most of the patrons were leather-jacketed punks, but a few bone-thin anarchists seasoned the stew. They were very impressed with my being an actual real-life ex-convict. I suppose they wanted to be tough, but they seemed more like a gang of middle-class kids at a costume party. Still, they had enough street smarts not to offer me a place to lay up. They nodded sympathetically, drank a beer, did a line, then moved on.

I was about to give up on Downtown Sarajevo when a tall, fat kid entered the bar and came directly to our table. He was wearing the proper uniform—black leather jacket, stiff crew cut, studded bracelet, and motorcycle boots—but he lacked the youthful innocence of the other patrons.

"What's happenin', Choo-Choo?" he asked before turning directly to me. "My name's Jocko."

"Wha' you wan' here, Jocko? This ain' no place for you." Choo-Choo tossed me a warning with his eyes.

Jocko shook his head, jerking his thumb in Choo-Choo's direction. "Ever since I told her that she couldn't suck my cock, she's got a fuckin' attitude."

"Pete," Choo-Choo cried, "don' let him talk to me like tha'."

"You wanna sit at this table," I said evenly, "you respect everyone else sitting here. This is not a difficult concept, even for a slimeball like you."

If he was legit, he would either have walked away or gotten in my face. But, of course, if he was legit, he wouldn't have insulted Choo-Choo in the first place.

"Hey, take it easy, man," he said, rubbing his wrist across his mouth. "I'm just havin' a little fun." He had large, fleshy lips, a short snout of a nose, and piggy black eyes. If I'd been a casting director making a movie, I would have chosen him to play the role of informant without hesitation. "Anyways, I heard about how you got a problem and I think I could help."

I leaned forward, thankful that at least I didn't *look* like a rat. "Keep talkin'."

"He said you were feelin' some heat. And, like, you needed a place to chill out."

"Who?"

"A street kid. Name of Marty. Said he ran into you and Choo-Choo in the Cafe. I figured I could help."

I was tempted to keep pushing his buttons, to see just how much abuse he'd take before he reacted, but I couldn't afford to indulge my curiosity. "Let's go outside. Too many ears in here. Choo-Choo, it's been great."

It was almost ten o'clock and much cooler. My jacket had been driving me crazy all day. I couldn't take it off, despite the heat, because I had the PPK tucked into my belt. Now I was grateful for it.

I took young Jocko into a doorway and put several lines up his nose by way of getting started.

"What'd your friend tell you about me?" I tried to put a little desperation into my voice. Just enough to let him know that I needed him, despite the fact that I didn't like or trust him.

"He said you had a beef with some cops. You're lookin' for a place to stay."

I took my time answering. "You ever do time, Jocko?"

He grinned, driving his fat upper lip into his nose. His front teeth were yellow. "Not *hard* time. No. I spent a few nights at Rikers on a piece of shit reefer bust, but I never been upstate."

"What happened with the bust? You beat it?"

"I got probation."

I knew that he expected me to question him about what he'd *done* to get probation, but I turned the conversation in a different direction, offering him the exalted status of comrade when he expected to be called a rat.

"Then you could understand my problem," I declared. "I'm on parole, so even if I'm popped for bullshit, I'm gonna have to spend a month in Rikers before I get a hearing with the board. Meanwhile, I got these two pigs from Midtown South climbing up my ass, the same two pigs who got me sent away. I need a place to lay quiet for a couple of days. I'm tryin' to make contact with a friend of mine on the coast. As soon as that comes through, my ass is in the wind."

"Why don't you got to a hotel?"

"I thought you knew what was happening?" I eyed him suspiciously. "I don't have no luggage. I'm wearing blue jeans and a cheap jacket. Where am I gonna go, the fuckin' Plaza? And forget about a flophouse. There's more snitches in those shitty hotels than there are whores. Hey, I hope I'm not wasting my time here."

"No, man, it's cool. I just, like, spoke out without thinking. Whatever reasons you got are your own." He dropped his eyes. "But I, uhhhh . . . I gotta get somethin' for it."

"How much?"

"Two bills."

"No problem, Jocko. If it's *right*." He started to describe the wonders of my new home, but I cut him short. "Just tell me where it is."

"A couple of blocks from here. On 6th Street."

"Let's go."

The building he took me to was sealed up. Sheet metal covered the doors and the lower windows. I'd known a lot of places like this and they were always filled with drugs, with shooting galleries and crack dens, junkies and dealers.

"This is bullshit," I said. "I need someplace quiet and you're takin' me to dope fuckin' heaven."

"No, it's not like that." He looked at me closely. "You must've been away for a long time. What you're lookin' at here ain't a dope house. It's a squat."

THIRTY-SEVEN

"A squat is what you do when you gotta take a shit in the woods." Between the coke and the general situation, I'd reached a point where I no longer cared for (or was able to deal with) bullshit. "If you dragged me over here for nothing . . . "

"Take it easy, man." He wasn't so blind as to misinterpret the look in my eye. "Squats are, like, for squatters. They're condemned buildings. Nobody's supposed to live here."

"Except for dopers and coke junkies," I insisted. "*If* you wanna call what they do living."

"No, it's not like that, man. I mean, yeah, *sometimes* it's like that. But sometimes people move into these buildings just because they need a place to live. They fix 'em up, then try to get the city to turn the property over."

I thought about it for a minute. I *had* been away for a long time. "Does it work? Does the city just give the property away?"

"Sometimes yes and sometimes no. It depends on the real estate developers. If they want the building, the city kicks the squatters out. Man, there were riots over this shit last year. You didn't hear about it?"

"I must've been preoccupied. Let's go inside and take a look."

He led me down a narrow alleyway to the rear of the building. The door was a hole in the back wall. I took one look and drew my piece.

"You first, pal."

"Wait a—"

"Forget about it. You're not backin' out." I'd like to say that I was giving him another excuse to hate my guts, to rat on me without feeling guilty, but the truth was that walking into a dark, abandoned building on the Lower East Side of Manhattan scared the crap out of me. For all I knew, this asshole was setting me up to get ripped off. He had enough reason. I'd been flashing money and coke all night long.

His whole face began to quiver. I thought he was going to cry. "Please, Pete, I'm playin' straight with you. I'm tryin' to help you out."

"Then you won't have any problem. Let's go."

I was expecting a typical abandoned building—busted-up furniture, ripped-out plumbing, fallen plaster covering the floor—but the building was clean. Pieces of the ceiling *had* fallen down. Parts of the floor had been torn up, too. But someone had carted the rubble away and swept the floors. There were lights in the hallway, though I hadn't been able to see them from outside, twenty-five-watt bulbs that cast just enough light to reveal patches of newly applied plaster.

I followed Jocko up to the top floor, noting that half the doors we passed had people living behind them and that everything seemed to be exactly as he'd described it, although the building became more and more decrepit as we climbed the stairs.

"I got the whole floor," Jocko announced, "but, like, it ain't real fixed up yet. I'm just gettin' started."

He surprised me by pulling out a set of keys and unlocking the door. I'd never been in an abandoned building with a working lock. I let him walk in ahead of me, then followed, trying to penetrate the deep shadows.

"I'm still working on the electricity." He thumbed a cigarette lighter and began to light candles. "I'll have it going in a couple of weeks."

The room had been swept, I'll give it that, but it was a long way from looking like home. A few pieces of ancient, dusty furniture, a mattress on the floor, an electric coffeemaker, and that was it. The bare windows were a uniform dirty brown and parts of the ceiling seemed about to fall away at any moment. It was perfect.

"Lemme show ya this." He crossed the room and pulled a sagging armchair away from the wall to reveal a small hole. "You can use this to get out in a hurry." He tossed me a wink.

The hole was maybe three foot square and I had to kneel to get through. I was much closer to trusting Jocko, but I kept him in sight as I crawled into the adjoining apartment. When I got up, my knees and elbows were covered with dust.

"I haven't started in here yet." He swept his hand across the room, then wiped his mouth with his sleeve. "But take a look at this. You can get to the roof *and* the fire escape from here. If, like, someone you don't wanna meet up with is comin' through the front door." He managed a weak smile. "So whatta ya think? Is it all right?"

"It'll be okay for a couple of days, which is all I need."

I took him back into the first apartment, laid out several thick lines of cocaine, watched while he snorted them up, then poured out several more. When I had his head where I wanted it, I started to talk. I told him about getting out of prison and how these two cops, Condon and Rico, met me as I got off the bus. How they told me they were going to have me violated, get me sent back to Cortlandt for another five years. How they were preventing me from doing what I had to do.

"It's bad luck, ya know? I was away for a long time. They should've retired or been transferred to another precinct, but there they were, waiting for me when I got off the fuckin' bus. Where's the justice in that?"

Actually, I had several plans in mind. Or, more exactly, one plan with several methods of execution. The easiest, by far, involved my good pal Jocko making a phone call to Midtown South, locating Condon and Rico, then selling my ass for whatever he could get.

But there was always the possibility that Jocko would be satisfied with the two hundred, so I intended to phone Condon and make sure he knew where to start looking. I wanted him to come down to the Lower East Side armed with a mug shot, ferret out his own snitches, beg for the use of his brother officers' snitches, canvass the area for however long it took to find me. When I was finished, he'd have no choice in the matter. But there was still a chance that Jocko wouldn't make the call *and* Condon wouldn't be able to pick up the well-marked trail I'd left for him. In that case, I was going to put the barrel of my 9mm against Jocko's head and guarantee that Condon got the message from the horse's mouth.

Jocko listened to every word I said. Stoned as he was, he would have listened to a Haitian translate a Japanese phone book into Creole. When I told him we were finished and that he should take off, he seemed positively crushed.

"I don't have any other place to stay."

"Try the subway. And give me the keys. I'll leave the door open when I split."

One more reason for him to hate me. One more excuse to sell me out. Just in case he needed an excuse.

After he left, I waited fifteen minutes, then went down the fire escape. I found a bodega and bought ten cans of tuna fish, a can opener, a dozen small candles, and four liters of Diet Coke. With no way to know how long this thing would drag out, I'd need some kind of nourishment and plenty of caffeine. Then I walked up the street to a pay phone and picked up the receiver.

Somewhere in the midst of my wanderings I'd remembered that the system I'd been warned about in Cortlandt was named Caller I.D. Condon would have the number of the pay phone before he took the call. The cops have a book that let's them go from a phone number to a name and address. In this case the name would be New York Telephone and the address would be the northeast corner of 7th Street and Avenue D, a block from where I was holed up.

I listened for the dial tone, dropped in my quarter, punched in Condon's precinct number, and was rewarded with a second dial tone. I did it three times before I gave up and walked to the next pay phone, a block away. This time I didn't have to bother with the details because the phone had been torn off its support.

My brain formed the constructive phrase "dick, shit, fuck, piss." I took it as evidence of a growing maturity and walked back the other way, to Avenue D and 5th Street. The phone on that corner was intact, a good sign, no doubt. I punched in Condon's precinct number and heard it ring on the other end.

"Brelinski."

"Who?"

"Brelinski."

"I'm callin' Officer Condon."

"*Detective* Condon."

"Yeah, Detective Condon."

"He's in the toilet."

"You know when he's coming back?"

"What am I, the towel boy?"

"What you are is the odds-on favorite for the cops' ballbuster of the year award."

He laughed appreciatively. "Hold ya water, mutt, he'll be here in a minute."

"Whatta ya mean by 'mutt.' You got radar?"

"You're callin on the mutt phone. We got one phone for humans and one for mutts. You're on the mutt phone."

I should have known. "I'll try to catch him later."

"Who should I say called?"

"Tell him Old Yeller."

"Wait a second, he's comin'." He let the phone crash down onto the desk.

"Condon."

"It's Pete."

He took a deep breath. "Jesus, Pete, where ya been? We nearly gave up on ya."

"Where I've been is none of your business."

He took another deep breath. "All right, I'm not gonna argue about it. So where do we go from here."

I wanted to say, "Upward and onward," but I didn't. "I'm trying to figure a way out of this."

"Why don't you stop being such a hardhead and let us help you? We can handle Eddie and others. You can't, Pete. You can't do shit to stop them. How long are ya gonna hide? A week? A month? Sooner or later you're gonna have to run and then *everybody's* gonna be after you. Eddie, the parole board, me, everybody. What's the point?"

"I don't trust you. If you get the chance, you're gonna blow me away."

"Pete, you *gotta* trust me. You don't have any other choice."

"I have a choice, Condon. I definitely have a choice."

He took a third deep breath. This was exactly what he *didn't* want to hear.

"And I don't see any reason why I shouldn't take advantage of it," I continued. "You set me up. You told me you were going to prevent a murder and now I'm a co-conspirator in *two* murders. Correction, *three* murders. I forgot about Simon."

"Who's gonna believe you? You got no proof. Most likely *you're* the one who'll get arrested."

"We could go on like this forever. You want me to trust you, you gotta prove yourself."

"And how am I supposed to do that? You want me to take a lie detector test?"

"I want you to kill Eddie. And I'm giving you forty-eight hours to do it. If you don't get it done, I'm gonna take the money and my story and walk into the D.A.'s office."

"I need more time, Pete. Two days ain't enough."

"Bullshit. We're talkin' about four people on the run, three ex-cons and a woman. They don't have any money and they can't *all* be staying with relatives. One or two of them gotta be on the streets somewhere. You find that one or two and convince them to take you to Eddie."

"Pete, don't hang up. Don't—"

On the way back to my hole, I tossed the rest of the cocaine into a storm sewer. At the time, I considered it the noble thing to do. Maybe it was, but half an hour later, I wanted that coke almost as much as I wanted to lock the sights of my 9mm on Condon's head.

I knew from past experience that if I held on for another couple of hours, the urge would disappear. I understood that my desire was chemical, even though it felt like my very soul was crying out for co-caine. Somewhere along the way, I began to tell myself not to be a fool. Cocaine would give me the energy to stay awake until Condon showed up, even if it took a few days. What was the point of playing the reformed convict? All I had to do was climb down the fire escape. They were selling coke two blocks away.

I ignored it all, but in the end I had to pay another penalty. After the cocaine pushed through my system, I flipped from energetic and alert to exhausted and nearly unconscious. I crawled through the hole into the adjoining apartment. There was an ancient sofa near the wall furthest from the window that led to the fire escape. I wedged myself behind it and fell asleep.

I woke to the sound of sirens. A dozen voices screamed in my head. The cops were coming, hundreds of them. Condon had found a way out of it, a way to keep himself clear. I was going away forever, away from Ginny and back to the hell of the Cortlandt Correctional Facility.

Mmmmmrrrrowwwwrrrrrr.

My head was up and the gun was out before I could form anything like a coherent plan. What were the sirens doing in the room? How did they get sirens in the goddamned room?

Mmmmmmrrrrrrowwwwrrrrrr.

What I saw, when I was able to focus my eyes, was a large gray tom-cat sitting on the windowsill. The son of a bitch had a meow that spread itself across three octaves.

"Jesus, cat, you have any idea how close you came? Maybe you *do* have nine lives, but you oughta consider that what I'm gonna shoot you with is called a *nine* millimeter."

He stared at me with calm cat eyes, then jumped down into the room. I opened one of the Diet Cokes and drank directly from the bottle. There's enough caffeine in regular Coke to raise the dead. If you take away the sugar, you get the full effect. I won't say the taste of warm chemicals was pleasant, but a few minutes later, I was close to being awake.

Mrrrowww.

Now that he had my attention, he was shortening his act.

"C'mere." I opened a can of tuna fish and put it by my feet. The cat paid no attention until the smell hit his nose. Then his whole body stiffened and his eyes locked on mine.

I gouged out a chunk of tuna and ate it. "You better get in on this before it's too late."

There's no way to know what a cat's thinking by looking into its eyes. I knew there was something behind that stare, but I couldn't guess what it was.

"Last chance, brother."

The cat must have read my mind. He came across the room slowly, his body in a crouch, every muscle alert. I pushed the tuna away from me with my foot and he jumped back ten feet.

"You wanna—"

I heard a crash down in the yard behind the building and a dog began to bark. My heart froze for a moment, then I crossed to the window and looked out, careful to conceal my body and as much of my head as possible. I found an elderly man picking through the rubble and a Latina woman shouting at him in Spanish from a window.

I turned away, sighing, resolving to get my fear under control. I couldn't afford to react this way if I meant to be in command of the situation when Condon finally showed up. I needed to be more like the cat. He'd taken advantage of my panic to enjoy a free meal.

I watched him pick at the food. A hungry dog would have eaten the whole thing, can and all, by this time, but the cat only nibbled at the tuna, its ears and whiskers pulled back, its eyes narrowed to yellow slits.

"Chew your food. You wanna make yourself—"

The *dog*. An idea formed in my brain like it'd been shot from a cannon. When the commotion started, a dog had barked. It was the same dog that'd barked from inside the second-floor apartment as I made my way up and down the fire escape last night.

I gave the dog a name on the spot. Radar. Which is exactly what he'd be. For the first time I began to think I might actually do what I had to do and still get away to Ginny. Good ol' Radar was a big break for me, a personal Distant Early Warning Line.

Something touched my arm and I felt my skin curl. The damn cat had finished the tuna. Now he wanted love and understanding. I ran my hand over his skinny body. The poor bastard had scars everywhere. One of his ears looked like it'd been put through a paper shredder.

Cats born on the streets never come close to people. Once upon a time, this cat had had a home. Then his trusted humans had tossed him out into the street like so much garbage. I wondered what he'd done? Had he missed the litter box once too often? Or scratched one of the children?

Maybe they just got tired of feeding him. Maybe they just opened the door and dumped him in the hall. He'd hung out for a while until hunger overcame whatever need he had for humans. Then he'd gone out onto the streets where he'd been (and was) subject to vicious children, careening vehicles and, most of all, other street cats. Now his life was nothing more than an expression of the will to survive and to reproduce.

"You keep this up," I told myself, "you're not gonna be able to see Condon through the tears. Stop feelin' sorry for yourself. You know you don't give a shit about the cat."

I opened up another can of tuna and found the cat's face in it before I could grab a chunk for myself. I pushed him away and tossed him a piece.

"Look here, cat, this ain't the supermarket. You gotta pace yourself."

Good advice for the both of us. I finished the tuna, took a healthy pull on the soda, then went back to the window and looked outside. I wanted to get an idea of the layout before it got dark again. It'd been near dawn when I fell asleep and, without a watch, I had no idea of the current time.

Peering through the open window didn't help much—the sky was carpeted with heavy, dark clouds—but I could see well enough to know there was only one way out, the alley between my building and one to the east. The small yards separating the buildings on the north and south were fenced. In the dark, I'd be a blind man running an obstacle course. Much better to kick out the front door if I had to leave before Condon showed up. That alley was ambush heaven.

The rain began an hour or so later. Accompanied by distant thunder and an occasional flash of lightning, it came straight down, exploding against the concrete, brick, and stone of the city. I had no particular problem with April showers (or May flowers either), but the noise of the rain, echoing in the courtyards, would provide cover for Condon and Rico if they came before it ended.

Well, those are the breaks—a dog for me, the rain for them. I got up and went back into the front apartment, lit several new candles, and found a sharp knife. Then I cut a hole through the back of the couch, just big enough to see the window and the far wall, and settled down to wait.

The cat curled up on my lap and fell asleep with its motor running. I ran a finger along a particularly gruesome scar that ran from the base of his tail to his shoulder blades. He responded by arching his back and turning his purr up a notch.

"You're stupid, cat. You're rubbing up against me like I was your momma. Only problem is I'll be gone in a couple of days and you'll have to go back to eating maggots out of garbage cans."

Rrrrrrrrrrrrrrrrr.

I think he was asking for a lawyer.

It was well after dark when Condon finally showed up. I could make out a lighted window across the yard, but just barely. If it wasn't for the glow of the candles in the next room, I wouldn't have been able to see anything *but* the window. As it was, the few pieces of ragged furniture were merely shadows against the darker flat shadow of the far wall. The only real light came from the hole between the two apartments. It was a beacon, a guide, and I was pretty sure Condon would go toward it.

I don't know anything about the size of the dog in the lower apartment, but I guarantee he was loud enough to be a lion. I lifted the cat off my lap, put him on the floor, and drew my weapon. A minute later the fire escape began to rattle and Condon's bulk appeared in the window. I'd been up and down fire escapes many times in the course of a long career. You need a very light touch to keep all that metal from vibrating. Condon didn't have it.

He stayed out on the fire escape for a long time. I could hear him panting, despite the rain. And I could see the small revolver he held in his hand. He must have been desperate to come at me like this. To come head-on into the distinct possibility of a setup.

I was tempted to take him as he came through the window but I couldn't be sure he was alone. There was no hurry, either. Condon was already trapped by his own mistakes. He should have shot me down in that garage. Now, with no access to the might of the thirty-five-thousand-man New York Police Department, he was just another assassin, an amateur taking a professional's risks.

An *obese* assassin, at that. He could barely squeeze his fat butt through the open window, and when he dropped to the floor, he grunted like a pig. I kept one eye on the window, looking for a silhouette, but the window remained empty.

Maybe I'd hurt Rico more than I thought. I suppose there was always the possibility that he was waiting in the alley or in front of the building, but it didn't seem likely that Condon would have come up the fire escape if Rico, fifty pounds lighter, could have done it.

Condon began to inch his way across the room. He went straight for the light, stopping just short of the rectangular glow cast by the candles. I came up over the top of the couch and put the PPK's sights on his head. It was time to shit or get off the pot, but I continued to wait. I waited until his head and shoulders disappeared into the next room, until he was thoroughly stuck.

"You don't wanna move, Detective," I said quietly. "You don't wanna move at all."

He took the hint, freezing in his tracks. "Jeez, Pete—"

"Forget 'Jeez, Pete.' Forget any excuse of any kind. What you're gonna do is back into the room. And when your hands appear, they better be empty."

Stuck in that hole, he couldn't very well spin and fire the way he'd been taught at the police academy. Condon was trapped and he knew it. He slowly inched his way back into the room, then turned to face me.

"Don't kill me, Pete."

"Stand up and do exactly what I say. I wanna warn you that I'm very nervous here and if you make any quick moves, I'm not gonna wait around to see what happens next. I'm gonna blow your fucking head off."

"All right, all right. Please, don't get crazy. We can work this out."

"Take off your coat. Do it with one hand and do it slowly." I waited until he finished, then ordered him to do the same thing with his jacket, then his shirt, then his pants. Sure enough, he had a small revolver neatly tucked into an ankle holster.

"Kneel down with your back to me. Draw the piece with two fingers. Slide it across the floor."

The tension was so heavy the room appeared to be vibrating. Condon must have been sensitive enough to understand my feelings, because he pulled the piece as if he was handling a bottle of liquid plutonium. When he finished, I had him kick his clothes out of reach, then turn to face me.

"Why'd you do it?" I asked, finally drawing a deep breath. "Why?" The answer, money, was too obvious to say out loud. Condon simply stared at me, his fat jowls, for once, motionless.

"Well," I finally said, "enough chitchat. I have some good news for you. Some good news and some bad news. The good news is that I'm not gonna kill you. The bad news is that you're gonna make a full confession."

I took the minirecorder out of my pocket and laid it on the floor between us. "Start with Eddie Conte. What you knew about him and how you began your investigation. Don't leave anything out. Do it as if your life depended on it. Which, of course—"

"Pete, I'm cold. I'm freezing my ass off."

"Now, ya see, Condon, that's exactly what I was talking about. If you said that *after* we started taping, it'd look like I was torturing you in order to make you confess falsely. If I can't get a *convincing* statement out of you, then I have no reason to leave you alive. Are you beginning to catch my drift?"

Condon, now that he was sure I wasn't going to shoot him on the spot, appeared to accept his helplessness. As for me, I had a job to do and a guy named Avi Stern to worry about. I wanted to finish with Condon, then get the hell out of the Lower East Side.

"What are you gonna do with it, Pete?" Condon's voice was reasonably firm, which was all to the good.

"With what?" I said innocently.

"The tape. Are you gonna hand it over to the press?"

"The *press*?" It was funny. He was more worried about publicity than his own life. "I have a lot of things on my mind, Condon. I have Eddie Conte and Avi Stern and thirty-five thousand cops to worry about. Eddie and Avi? They're *my* problem. The cops? Well, if *I* go down, you and your buddy, Rico, are goin' down with me. Now let's do it."

I picked up the minirecorder and fingered the button. "I want you to start with Eddie Conte. Tell me exactly how you found out about him. And don't worry about protecting your informants. Worry about protecting your life."

My finger tightened on the trigger as I pictured Simon Cooper baby-sitting his kids. Worried about popcorn spilling on the rug, about vacuum cleaners and orange juice. The reaction was completely spontaneous. It surprised me as much as it surprised Condon.

"Pete, please. Please don't—" His eyes were wide with terror. He knew just how close he was.

I flicked the switch on the minirecorder and set it down. Condon began without prompting, and to give the bastard credit, he went through it without leaving anything out. At first, all he and Rico had wanted was a prestigious collar, but after I detailed the size of the robbery, they'd gotten greedy. Simon Cooper had been their biggest problem. They'd made an attempt to bring him into their scam, but he'd refused outright. Rico had murdered him with a throwaway piece they'd taken off a street junkie.

It took Condon about fifteen minutes to run through the whole thing. When he was finished, I shut off the tape recorder and slipped it into my pocket.

"One more question, Condon," I said. "Why didn't you kill me when you had the chance? Hell, why didn't you kill *all* of us?"

Condon sighed and looked over at his shirt and pants. "Pete, it's really cold in here. I'm freezing."

"It's a lot colder in the grave. Which is where Simon Cooper is. You make one move toward your clothes and you're gonna join him. Answer the question."

"We talked about it for a long time. At one point, we made up our minds to do it, but then we couldn't get our hands on a silencer. Not without attracting attention. I mean, how could we be sure the mutt who sold us the silencer wouldn't turn out to be some other cop's snitch? We were carrying AK47s, Pete. There were people out on the street. Citizens. If they heard the shooting (and they'd *have* to hear it), maybe they'd come to investigate. Or maybe somebody would get a plate number. Or dial 911. Rico said we should force everybody into the back room, then do it like a mob hit, but I didn't think—" He stopped for a moment, then bit the bullet. "I didn't think four prison-hard criminals would allow themselves to be executed. I told Rico that we had to control the scene. We couldn't even be sure that one or two of you didn't have a backup piece. Things could get out of hand in a hurry, especially if Tony Morasso went crazy. Which he finally did."

"So you decided to settle for killing *me*?"

He looked down at the floor. "Yeah," he admitted. "That was the deal. You were the only link. Without you, there'd be no way for Eddie to find us. It wasn't something we wanted to do, but we didn't have any choice. I swear it, Pete."

"Is that the way it was with Simon? Did you say, 'Sure, he's got a wife and two kids, but we gotta do what we gotta do?' Are you saying the same thing about the security guard Tony Morasso killed?"

Condon raised his head and took a deep breath. He was just about to speak when his head exploded. I saw it clearly. Saw a thick mixture of pink and gray tissue stream across the room, then heard what I took to be the crack of a lightning bolt. Instinctively, I turned toward the sound. It was pouring rain and at first I couldn't see anything. Then lightning flashed in the distance, silhouetting a man bent over a small suitcase. The man held the barrel of a rifle in one hand, the stock in the other.

It was Avi Stern come to get his revenge, and if I'd been the one sitting near the window, he would have succeeded. The room was barely lit, a few candles providing the only illumination. Avi, seventy or eighty feet away, had fired at a shadow.

I continued to stare at the window, catching Avi's silhouette in half a dozen flashes. I couldn't tear my eyes away, couldn't make my brain work. It wasn't until he closed the suitcase and stood up that I began to think.

What I wanted was for Avi to pack his bags and leave, but I knew that wouldn't happen. He was convinced that he'd killed me. If he wasn't, he would never have broken down the rifle. Unfortunately, there was still the money. Avi, the sound of his assassination covered by the storm, wouldn't abandon ship until he'd made an attempt to find the loot. Maybe the money wouldn't be in the room, but it was certainly possible that he'd find a receipt or a key that'd lead to the three million dollars claimed by Chapman Security.

I pulled a chair across the room and left it between the window leading to the fire escape and Condon's body, then crawled back behind the couch. I hoped the chair would block Avi's view long enough to get him into the room. Seconds after I settled down, I heard Radar go off a few floors below. The dog went berserk, growling and barking furiously. A moment later, Avi's head appeared in the window.

He bore no resemblance to the fat detective who'd gone before him. Avi moved with the silent grace of a snake after a mouse. He slid into the room, an automatic in his right hand, his eyes darting around the room. I knew I wasn't supposed to warn him. I was supposed to lay the sights of my 9mm on his skull and give him what he'd given Condon.

But I didn't do it. I wasn't a killer and I didn't want to be a killer. There are any number of pure assassins in the Institution. Men who'll commit murder for a few cigarettes or simply to build their own reputations. The simple truth was that I wasn't one of them. Despite the macho. Despite the tattoo. Despite the need to survive.

That *didn't* mean that I was about to unload the gun and beg for mercy. No. I sighted down on the broadest part of Avi's back, ready and willing to pull the trigger in self-defense. "Please, Avi," I said as calmly as I could. "Please don't make me kill you."

His head turned toward me, but the hand holding the automatic remained motionless.

"Please, Avi," I repeated. "Drop the gun and kick it away."

It was very dark in the room. And I was very scared. I couldn't make out Avi's features, but I could sense the wheels turning in his head. I drew back the hammer of my weapon. Just to give him one more thing to consider.

"Not to shoot," he said, dropping the automatic. He kicked it across the room, then turned to face me.

"Wrong way, Avi. I want to see your back."

I waited until he complied, then came up behind him and smashed the 9mm into the back of his skull. He dropped like a rock, completely unconscious. I went through his pockets, found no other weapons, then dug out Condon's handcuffs and cuffed Avi's left wrist to a floor-to-ceiling pipe.

A few minutes later Avi awakened. He moaned several times, then sat up and looked around.

"You should have joined police," he said. "Handcuffs are very tight."

"Where's the briefcase, Avi? The one with the rifle in it."

"Why should I say this to you?"

I leveled the gun, but the threat only made him laugh.

"One thing I now know. You are not killer. You cannot kill."

"Maybe you're right," I admitted. "But the fact that I won't kill doesn't mean I won't hurt. It doesn't mean, for instance, that I won't hurt *you*. I'm not real interested in hanging around here any longer than necessary. If you don't tell me where the briefcase is, I'll dig up a knife and cut your fucking toes off."

He took a moment to think about it, then shrugged. "Briefcase is on fire escape."

I retrieved the case, carefully wrapping my hand in an old rag before touching it, and set it down a good distance away from Avi.

"This man is who?" Avi asked, pointing at Condon.

"He's the man you killed, Avi. Just another notch on the gun, right?" I waited for a reply, but he merely snorted his contempt. "That lump of meat used to be a cop," I continued. "His name was Condon."

"A cop?" Avi's voice registered his surprise. It didn't make any more sense to him than it had to me.

"What difference does it make? I don't wanna bother explaining, because Condon isn't my problem anymore. My problem is *you*. I've taken care of Eddie and Parker. Morasso is dead. You're the only one left and I can't live with the idea that you'll be trailing me for the rest of my life."

"Then you must to kill me."

"It's a funny thing, Avi, but I don't see it that way. What I see is a dead cop and a trapped murderer. I see a murder weapon with your fingerprints all over it. I see a sentence of fifty years to life."

"This is against everything you are believing," he replied. "I would prefer you show courage and kill me now."

I stood up and walked over to the fire escape. On the way, my leg brushed something warm and moving. I nearly pissed my pants before I realized it was the goddamned cat.

Mrowwwwwwr.

"He likes winners," I said to Avi as I stepped through the open window. "Live long and prosper."

THIRTY-EIGHT

I'm sitting on a beach in a South American country finishing up these last few pages. Ginny is standing at the edge of the surf, looking out to sea. She bought a new bikini the other day. It has a single strip of fabric that disappears altogether as it runs between her cheeks. Joan Rivers claims these bathing suits make a woman look like she's flossing her ass. If that's the case, may I die and be reborn as a mass-market aid to proper dental hygiene.

I suppose the top comes next. Then Ginny can brag that she's truly gone native, that there's so many jiggling breasts and buttocks on the beach, she blends right in. Which, I have to admit, is all to our advantage, considering the fact that we're fugitives and likely to remain fugitives for the rest of our lives. Or until we get caught.

When Ginny first got the suit—when she held up its several square inches for my inspection—I confess to having felt a twinge of jealousy. Those were *my* buttocks, *my* breasts. I didn't want anyone else caressing them, not even with their eyes. But, as it turns out, I can sit here and watch her stroll across the sand without wanting to wrap her in a blanket.

I understand that Ginny, like many women, needs to be sexually admired by men, even if she herself has no sexual interest in them. But the real point is that I'm not afraid of losing her. The two of us are welded together like the steel plates of a ship. The only flame hot enough to cut that bond issues from the acetylene torch of the American criminal justice system.

As I watch, Ginny turns and comes back to the blanket. She kneels and gives the cat a quick rub. The cat, curled up in the shade of a beach umbrella, arches its back and lifts its tail. I think I said the cat's former life was an expression of the will to live and to reproduce. Now it consists of little more than the will to sleep and to eat. The damn thing looks like a furry balloon.

"How you doing?" Ginny asks.

"I'm writing it down and feeling stupid. As usual."

Telling the story was Ginny's idea. She's convinced that its publication, along with Condon's confession, will galvanize political opinion. That the American criminal justice system will be forced to set me free. I have my doubts.

In the first place I'm still a parole violator. I may never be charged with any of the crimes related to the Chapman robbery, but I still owe New York State five years. In the second place, even if I convince the American public that I came out of the Institution with every intention of keeping my nose clean, the system isn't based on fairness or justice. It's based on politics and the ordinary citizen's need for revenge. In the third place, instead of going directly to the District Attorney, I was party to the killing of a cop.

"Writing this last part is the hardest," I continue. "I'm supposed to explain everything, but I don't know what to say. I don't know what it means or why I did what I did."

"You didn't have any choice, Pete. I don't know why you torture yourself with it." She leans forward, letting the bikini top slip down. It hadn't been covering much to begin with. "I'm going back to the room, take a shower, then get into bed. I'm gonna try to think of a way to take your mind off your troubles. Maybe several ways."

I reach out to stroke her arm. Despite what I said about the two of us being welded together, I'm always touching her, always making sure she's still there.

"I'll be along in half an hour. Meantime I'll work myself into an aroused state by observing the fashion habits of South American females."

She walks away and I achieve the desired state of arousal by watching *her*. The cat groans and stretches. He sticks his head out into the sunlight, then blinks and pulls back. His name, by the way, is Lazarus. I wanted to call him Lucky, but Ginny thought Lucky was too much of an understatement. And maybe Lazarus wasn't so lucky, either. When he first came to us, he announced his approval of the accommodations by spraying every inch of Ginny's sister's living room.

Now he has another scar where a vet in Chattanooga made an incision before removing his testicles.

My basic problem is that I don't know who's after me. If the parole board is my biggest (or only) problem, I can probably slide through with my false identification. I've crossed enough borders in the last few years to have complete confidence in my passport.

But suppose a trapped Avi Stern decided to get revenge by claiming the man (namely myself) who handcuffed him to that pipe was actually a co-conspirator? I don't think Avi would rat me out, but I can't be sure. Or suppose the detectives investigating the Chapman robbery or Simon's murder were sharp enough to nail Rico. There was an awful lot of evidence floating around, including Morasso's body, the blood-soaked money bags in the van, and whatever entries Simon made in my file. Recording the fact that I no longer had to report every week and the reason I'd been relieved of that obligation would have been standard operating procedure.

If the cops had Rico, they'd have me, too. Rico would give me up in a second, for revenge if for no other reason. Of course, even if the NYPD has the name "Pete Frangello," that doesn't mean they'll find the person I am now. Not if I don't come within a thousand miles of the United States. But suppose the cops also have Eddie Conte's name.

If Rico started naming names, would he stop with me? Not likely. And it's also not likely that Eddie Conte is as cautious as I am. I'll bet my left arm against a nickel that he and Annie pissed away every penny a long time ago, that he went back to the United States, that he's in custody right now. If the cops have Eddie, then the cops have the name I'm currently using.

But even if the cops don't have my new identity, Eddie does and Eddie, if he's free, will seek revenge. I don't know exactly how he'll find me, but I do know that Eddie's mob-connected and that I've left a paper trail a mile wide. I've been trying to get another passport for the last six months, but so far without success. I can't devise a way to approach a professional forger without revealing that I'm a fugitive. What's the motto, boys and girls? Can you recite your lessons?

D.T.A. Don't Trust Anyone.

I sit for a moment, watching the edge of the surf break the sun into a million tiny fragments. A child, maybe five years old, stands at the edge of the water, chasing the waves back into the sea, then fleeing before the next onslaught. Her sunburned parents hover in the background.

I've been possessed by jealousy for as long as I can remember. I saw myself as pieces of a human being and I thought that ordinary family life was the only glue that could hold me together. Why should everybody else have it and not me? Why should that kid walking down the street, holding his mama's hand, feel safe and protected while I had to fight every single day in order to survive?

Now I know that we're all in the same boat. We've all died so many times that nothing can make us whole. No matter how many times we go to church on Sunday. Or war on Monday.

Still, I continue to hope for it, to believe the answer is right around some unturned corner, to get up each morning and plan my life.

"What are you going to do today, dear?"

Oh, I don't know. Maybe I'll drop by the bank and take out a thirty-year mortgage. Or maybe I'll jump off a cliff. I can't seem to make up my mind."

I'm tempted to describe myself as a reformed addict taking it one day at a time, but I feel more like a man recovering from a bad heart attack. I want breakfasts to last forever, walks along the beach to end in China, orgasms to go on for thirty seconds.

I said earlier that Ginny was demanding in bed, that she wanted to pull my whole body inside her. Now it's the other way around. She's become inventive and playful, while I can't seem to go deep enough. Our sex, when I get my way, is slow and grinding. I wrap her in my arms, press my chest and belly against hers, drag it out until the sheets are soaked with sweat. It takes a long time, but Ginny, ever understanding, refuses to complain.

I don't want to give the impression that I live my life surrounded by doom and gloom. I've been to places far outside the fantasies of Institutional children. And my dreams are no longer painful, either. The only time I wake in the night is when Ginny pounds my back to stop my snoring. I have occasional nightmares, like everyone else, but they don't involve me. Terrentini is the superstar of my nightmares. Terrentini on fire. Terrentini crashing from wall to wall. Terrentini screaming as the C.O. sprays him with foam.

I don't expect the money to last more than six months. The fugitive life is filled with bills, just as it is with apprehension. In fact, I have a sense that as long as I manage to pay the bills, I'll remain free. Like going to church once a month to light a candle.

I don't work, of course. I can't. I enter each nation as a tourist. If I should apply for a work visa, I'll be asked for a social security number. I have no idea if the number on the card in my wallet belongs to anyone, but, either way, whether it comes into the IRS as a duplicate or an unissued number, its use is bound to attract attention.

Ginny sometimes talks about finding a job. She's virtually mastered Spanish, picking up new words with every breath, while I struggle along with a few *Loisaida* phrases. *Chinga tu madre, maricón.* But Ginny's talent for languages doesn't translate into a thorough knowledge of South American real estate, the only field in which she has any serious training.

I suppose she could find some bullshit p.r. job in one of the big hotels, but I don't see how her salary could pay the bills. We're not talking about a cottage, a television set, and a Toyota. We're talking about hotel suites, room service breakfasts, and airline tickets. *Lots* of airline tickets.

So the problem remains. How will I pay for a new passport when my own has been stamped so many times that even the dullest customs officer becomes suspicious? How will I pay for a private plane or a fast boat on that inevitable day when I have to get out of town in a hurry? How will I bribe the *policía* when they finally drag me into an interrogation room?

I suppose I could always steal.

Death Before Dishonor.